THE
STARLIT
SHADOW

CIDNEY MAYES

CRANTHORPE
—MILLNER—
PUBLISHERS

Copyright © Cidney Mayes (2025)

The right of Cidney Mayes to be identified as author of this work has been asserted by them in accordance with section 77 and 78 of the Copyright, Designs and Patents Act 1988.

All rights reserved. No part of this publication may be reproduced, stored in a retrieval system, or transmitted in any form or by any means, electronic, mechanical, photocopying, recording, or otherwise, without the prior permission of the publishers.

Any person who commits any unauthorised act in relation to this publication may be liable to criminal prosecution and civil claims for damages.

This book is a work of fiction. Names, characters, places and incidents are either products of the author's imagination or are used fictitiously. Any resemblance to actual events or locales or persons, living or dead, is entirely coincidental.

First published by Cranthorpe Millner Publishers (2025)

ISBN 978-1-80378-313-0 (Paperback)

www.cranthorpemillner.com

Cranthorpe Millner Publishers

Printed and bound by CPI Group (UK) Ltd
Croydon, CR0 4YY

For Adam

I WRITE TRUE LOVE BECAUSE WE LIVE IT EVERY DAY

Chapter One

Corvus

A tang hit the back of my throat as I passed into the courtyard of the House of Night. Tonight was only the second time I had ever made the journey up the long drive to the pleasure house, but the burly fae at the front gate, who acted as a façade of security, waved me through without ceremony. The real protection lay in the magic wards that surrounded the manor, though how the madam maintained them was anyone's guess.

The illegally imported bottled magic that the house was known for was decidedly less potent than whatever guarded her domain. Perhaps, as ruler of one of the Great Fae Houses, she still clung to the innate magic in her blood that had not yet been snuffed out. The rest of Tenebris's fae couldn't say the same. Most of them lived like common mortals, their magic withered since humans conquered the land two centuries ago.

The bitter taste faded as I sauntered over to the black marble fountain set in the middle of the courtyard. A naiad sat in the wide basin, greeting patrons, and handing out masks. She looked human, except for her flowing seaweed hair and the delicate little fins at her elbows. I accepted a smooth black mask from her with a wink and slipped it on.

Once inside, I walked through the black-and-white tiled foyer into a parlor that was set off from the main hall. A tall window had been opened to let the warm summer air waft through the room. I approached an attractive curly-haired fae in a dark mask that shimmered with deep blue undertones. His skin glittered with icy blue and silver powder. "Good evening."

The courtesan's eyes widened for a moment as he took in my wings. He recomposed himself quickly. "Hello, handsome. Care to join me in a game?" He touched my upper arm, stroking it lightly.

I sighed. "If only I could. I'm here on a much less entertaining errand. Where can I find your madam?"

The courtesan sucked in his lower lip. "You're here to see Madam Andromeda on business?"

"I am."

"Your name, sir?"

"Corvus Stormfall."

His shoulders tensed as my name registered. It seemed my reputation preceded me. "Follow me."

He led the way upstairs, past a long hallway of closed doors to his employer's office. He knocked, and a curt voice sounded from inside.

"Enter."

He held the door for me. "Lord Corvus Stormfall to see you, ma'am."

The madam sat behind her desk, her mask of silver glinting like moonbeams in the dim light. She swept her skirts behind her and stood. "Leave us."

The courtesan departed quickly.

"To what do I owe this unexpected visit?"

I gave her my best charming, crooked grin. She knew why I had come. The black-market fees I had collected from her last time had been short. But if she wanted to dance around the issue, so be it.

"I have a request," I said.

Her eyebrows shot up. "I see," she crooned. "Can I offer you some refreshment? Perhaps a drink?"

"A drink would be welcome." I smoothed the front of my

jacket as she swept over to her liquor cabinet.

She handed me a crystal glass and gestured to a pair of plush burgundy chairs. Once seated, she sipped daintily. I took a hearty swallow and set my fingers on the rim of the glass, swirling the contents. It was good liquor, though I expected nothing less.

"We cater to many requests, Lord Stormfall, and handle each with utmost discretion."

I took another sip, letting the burn trail down my throat. "I fear you might dislike this request, Madam."

She waved a dismissive hand. "It is not my business to judge. Where would I be today if I did? Of course, there are some rules. We are a reputable establishment, sir. A house of quality. Tell me what you desire, and I shall see what we can do for you."

There were many things I wanted, but I highly doubted Madam Andromeda could give them to me. I set my glass on a low side table and leaned toward her.

"What I desire is for you to pay the remaining two thousand dinar owed to House Stormfall."

Andromeda set down her own glass with a *thunk* and crossed her arms. "What you're asking for is, frankly, insulting. We have already paid our dues. It's ridiculous for the Forum to impose more taxes."

I arched a brow. To speak publicly against the Forum was bold. "Madam, you know I am simply the messenger here. Two thousand are owed, two thousand must be paid. Surely a mere trifle to your illustrious house."

"It matters not how much it will dent my coffers. It is the *principle* of it all."

"Listen." I crossed an ankle over my knee, making myself fully comfortable.

Andromeda shifted in her wing-backed chair. Candlelight

glinted off her mask.

"You can give me the fee, and I will leave. The Forum, which convenes this week, will never know of this accidental oversight."

"They did not inform me of a meeting." The mask hid her face, but the tightness in her voice betrayed her surprise.

I tapped a finger on my knee. Interesting. All eight houses were usually present at Forum assemblies, even the minor ones of Day and Night. Her ignorance of the meeting did not sit well.

I shrugged. "Or I can inform them of your refusal to pay your dues, and your alarming sentiments of rebellion."

Her face paled. "I said no such thing."

"You certainly implied it."

She was silent for a moment, weighing the seriousness of my threat. Her office was eerily silent, blocking out the chatter of activity downstairs.

I uncrossed my legs, planting my feet firmly into a rug the color of spilled blood.

Andromeda made her offer. "Perhaps we can come to some alternative arrangement? Half of the fee, and you're welcome to stay for the evening. Free of charge."

"One thousand five hundred." I had five hundred dinar with me, which I had intended to spend on my way home. Regret twinged in my stomach at the loss of it.

She nodded curtly. "Done. Please wait downstairs while we retrieve the funds. The Emerald Parlor, second door on the right of the main receiving room. One of my girls will be there shortly. You will not be disturbed."

"Thank you for your hospitality." I gave a curt bow and left.

I had other business to attend to this evening, and I hoped she would not keep me waiting too long. I smoothed the front of my jacket, letting my wings relax as I walked down the darkened corridor.

Chapter Two
Sorsha

I adopted a pose of ease in the Black Parlor as patrons clad in dark domino masks trickled into the House of Night, seeking their favorite courtesans and ready to partake in the many delights we offered. Outfitted in a black mask, corset gown, and dusted with the ridiculous shimmering powder that everyone seemed to love, I lounged on a velvet settee. Potion bottles on a nearby table trailed dusky purple and midnight-blue smoke into the air. Each tiny bottle was worth more than some folk made in a year. More than I could ever afford.

The smell of the distant ocean and sweet peonies hung in the air as folk weaved around hushed conversations and couples settling in for the night. I kept my gaze lowered, not wanting to draw too much attention. I hoped to appear as part of the furniture this evening, a thing to be looked at, nothing more.

After my mother abandoned me here as a child, I had only worked the front, carrying refreshments and magical enhancements to the private chambers where courtesans pleasured their customers. But when I turned eighteen, my madam had given me a choice: become a courtesan or be thrown into the street. Naturally, I chose the former, even though the thought of seducing strangers made my pulse beat frantically and my palms grow slick with sweat. Thankfully, few requested my presence, and if they did, I could ply them with enough potion to keep them at bay. I'd only slept with a handful of customers. The experience was much more pleasurable for them than for me.

A whisper in my ear jolted me from mortifying thoughts

of my first few encounters. "Sorsha. The madam wants to see you." Our new serving girl, a timid woodland fae with pointed ears and pale tree-bark skin, carried a heavy tea tray.

What could I have possibly done to warrant a summons? My stomach twisted into a knot as the serving girl scurried away. I slid silently through the parlors, careful not to disturb anyone as I made my way to the foyer.

My shoes clicked on the checkered marble floor of the entrance chamber, polished to mirror-like perfection. I caught sight of myself in one of the large, gilded mirrors. Loose strands of pale blonde hair hung around my face, framing my black mask. My dress, a high-necked gown with sheer sleeves, was unadorned. Simple, compared to the glittering gowns other courtesans wore, but it did the job of concealing the scars on my back. Smoothing my hair into place, I hurried to the grand staircase, making my way to the east wing.

At my madam's office door, I took a deep breath to calm my racing heart. Audiences with her never got any easier. She was impossible to read, and I never knew from one day to the next if she was pleased with me, or annoyed that I dared to even breathe the same air as her. Since my pulse refused to slow, I knocked twice.

"Come in."

I gripped the handle with clammy hands, then shut the door softly behind me before approaching her desk.

Madam Andromeda radiated brutal fae elegance. A single piece of parchment and an envelope lay before her, alongside her mask. Her silver hair was piled high on her head in delicate curls. She wore the customary black, and her cheekbones were sharp enough to cut glass.

"There is a patron waiting for you in the Emerald Parlor. You are to deliver this to him," she ordered, voice crisp and businesslike. She slid the unsealed black envelope across the desk.

I took it, resisting the urge to peek inside.

Andromeda rubbed one of her temples.

My stomach flipped as I wondered who awaited me downstairs. Was he the source of her agitation? "Is that all?" I asked, hoping my voice didn't betray my unease.

Andromeda dropped her hand quickly and scooped up the parchment on her desk. "Entertain him before he goes."

My heart thudded painfully in my chest. I fought the urge to clench my hands around the envelope, settling instead on gripping the back of the chair. As Andromeda had asked me specifically to entertain, I doubted my usual tricks for avoiding physical encounters would work. "Can't one of the others do it?"

Andromeda's eyes flashed. I should have known better than to argue. She leaned back in her chair, keeping her icy stare on me. "Most would sell their soul for the position I have given you."

It was no easy feat to become a House of Night courtesan. Andromeda collected them like pretty jewels, seeking them out from other brothels in the city.

"Of course."

"Go on, then."

My knees shook as I crossed the room. I had one hand on the door before she stopped me.

"And you're welcome," she snapped.

"Th-thank you," I stuttered and bolted, clutching the envelope to my chest.

In the darkened hall, I fought to calm my breathing. My hands trembled as they bore the weight of the envelope. A faint spark of curiosity burned beneath my agitation. I wondered what was inside. Perhaps a contract for a new courtesan, or an invitation? But the envelope was too thick. I pried open the flap. A staggering amount of money lay inside. More dinar than I had ever seen in my life. Good gods, why had Andromeda trusted me with this?

I forced myself back downstairs, my feet heavy as lead, and tucked the envelope into the pocket of my skirt. In the back right corner of the house, the Emerald Parlor waited for its patrons. I'd have to walk through the Black Parlor again to get to it.

Keeping my eyes lowered, I wove through the parlor rooms on silent steps, well-trained from my years of carrying serving trays and blending into the background.

Fae and humans alike sprawled on velvet chaise lounges and settees of silk, feeling the effects of the magic they had imbibed. The potions and sensual enhancements our customers paid for were scarce, and heavily taxed by the fae nobility who regulated the black market. Though magic was outlawed by the mortals who ruled, those with means still found ways to access and exploit the feeble bottled magics smuggled from the north. The range of potions on the black market were plentiful, but illusions potions — where the drinker found themselves in a world of their deepest desires — became our specialty.

My stomach clenched as I crept by the last settee where Viviana, a courtesan with a sweet face and venomous temper, entertained two clients. I was almost past them when I pitched forward.

I hit the floor, biting back a cry of pain. My mask dug into my cheek as I smacked against the polished black hardwood, and a crash ripped through the soft chatter of the parlor. I lifted my head, blinking back tears, and spied Viviana's foot casually sliding back toward her. A tray lay upturned, its contents spilled. Spiced tea, thankfully mundane, leaked across the floor. No one moved to help me. The silence was deafening. Mortifying. My fingers flew to my mask, making sure it still covered my face.

My cheeks burned. I wished the floorboards would swallow me up, too. I pushed myself with one hand to my knees.

Viviana clicked her tongue against her teeth. Her own mask, black and glittering, could not conceal her triumphant delight. "Careful, Sorsha. You are so prone to these little *accidents*."

I bit back a retort, knowing she'd use whatever I said to get me into trouble. If I could have avoided her, I would have, but I had no way to get to the Emerald Parlor without passing through. I fumed, trying to quell the burning anger throbbing through my core as I reluctantly gathered the contents of the upended tray.

I reached for a sugar bowl that had rolled away. Viviana slid her hands under the jaws of her customers, turning their attention back to her.

"If you'd prefer to stare at the trash, then I shall take my leave," she cooed.

A fae with long pointed ears, a lace mask, and a mop of golden hair murmured his protests.

The other, a green-skinned male with a mask of leaves, clasped a hand around the back of Viviana's neck. "But we have waited over a month for your company, my dear."

Her lips curved in a wicked smile as she placed both of her hands on his chest. The other, not wanting to be ignored, trailed kisses down her neck. Viviana let out a satisfied hum of pleasure and closed her eyes.

Still on my knees in front of her, I glared at the tiny teaspoon in my trembling hand and thought about how satisfying it would be to slam the spoon into Viviana's slippered foot. I couldn't do anything while we had customers, but that didn't stop me from basking in sweet fantasies of revenge.

A pair of sturdy legs wearing black knee-length boots crossed into my view. I bent my head and focused on collecting the rest of the tray's scattered contents.

"I do enjoy when females kneel before me," said a voice as warm as honey.

My hands continued to tremble as I placed the spoon back on the tray. I dared a look at him, peering up through my lashes, but I could only see the vague outline of a tall figure dressed in dark clothing.

He knelt beside me. The scent of rain on a hot summer's night, full of promise and yearning, and the crackling of lightning, flooded over me. My heart thundered in my chest.

"Though, I don't mind getting down on my knees for them, either," he said.

My skin flashed hot and began to prickle. I wasn't used to being spoken to that way. Especially not when Viviana, crown jewel of the House of Night, sat mere feet from me. I kept my head down as my heart continued to stutter in my chest.

His long amber fingers curled around the lid of the sugar bowl, sliding it into place.

I had to get out of here. I grabbed the edges of the tray but froze as he trailed his fingertips along the back of my hand. Gooseflesh skittered over my arms and neck.

"You're sure you're alright?"

"Yes," I replied, hating the quaver in my voice. "I'm sorry, I have to go. Please excuse me." I stood and set the tray on a side table. I turned toward the door, but the stranger blocked my path.

My breath caught in my throat. He towered over me, dark hair framing his thundercloud gray eyes. And he had *wings*. I'd never seen a fae with wings before. The charcoal feathers shone in the low candlelight. He kept them tucked tight into his body.

"Allow me to accompany you." He offered his arm to me.

"Okay," I said, even though part of me screamed for me to refuse. My head spun. I wondered if I'd hit my head a little too hard. "It's just through here."

We walked through the rest of the parlor, arm in arm. I had never seen this male before. We had our regular customers, but new faces were rare. Only those who had been extended a personal invitation could enter our gates. He must be someone important to have been allowed inside.

Only after we had taken a few steps did I realize the entire room remained silent. They watched us as we moved, their gazes sharp as knives. My face still felt hot under my mask. I couldn't wait to hide behind the doors of the Emerald Parlor, safe from their scrutiny.

The winged fae walking by my side was unbothered by their gazes, moving with an ease I envied. I rested my hand as lightly as I could against the crook of his elbow, my fingers sliding against the fabric of his fine jacket.

After what felt like several long minutes, we finally reached the door. "Thank you," I said, extricating myself from his arm. "I'm meeting someone inside." I hoped he'd take his leave without me having to rudely ask him to go.

"Fancy that," he said. "I was told to meet someone here, too. That must be you. I tried to let myself in, but the door is locked. It seemed rude to break it down." He smiled, one corner of his mouth lifting higher than the other.

I fought to keep my mouth from dropping open. He was the patron I would entertain tonight?

I cleared my throat, gripped the cool, polished handle, and unlocked the door. As it swished open, I took a deep breath, steeling myself for what was to come.

Chapter Three

Corvus

Andromeda must have given this girl some magic to wield against me, to make me so enticed by her. I don't know what possessed me to help her, other than an impulsive desire to be near her. All thoughts vanished, leaving only one behind. Talk to her. I blinked, trying to steady myself, but my own name was slipping from my memory. Magic had to be the only explanation for this sudden madness.

I stepped into the parlor, decorated with lush green furniture. Tall windows offered a pleasant view of the lemon grove outside. Muffled, indistinct sounds of pleasure seeped through the walls of the otherwise quiet room. A twilight summer breeze ruffled the curtains, washing the room with the scent of fresh flowers and the tang of citrus trees.

The latch clicked, and I turned to find the girl clutching a black envelope.

There was something intriguing about her, almost familiar. She threw her shoulders back as she approached, tossing her pale-gold hair behind her.

"This is for you."

"You have my thanks." I slipped it into the inner pocket of my jacket.

"And," she said, chin quivering a fraction. She placed a hand on my arm. The heat of her palm traveled through my jacket and shirt, searing my skin. "Madam Andromeda says I am to entertain you before you go."

My eyebrows shot up. "That will not be necessary. Good

evening." Her magic would not take me in so easily. I moved to step around her, but she grabbed my arm. Her strength surprised me.

"Wait."

Her cheeks flushed, and her eyes glistened. She leaned a fraction closer, and her scent wafted over me. Astounding. Like the morning mist of early dawn. Bergamot and rose. I wanted to bottle it up and take it with me. It was... intoxicating.

Gods, what's wrong with me?

She swallowed, her throat bobbing with the motion. Her pulse fluttered at her neck. I placed the tips of my fingers there, unable to stop myself. "Yes?"

She inhaled sharply. I had the overwhelming urge to make her do that again.

"Madam Andromeda insisted I show our appreciation."

I trailed my forefinger along her jaw, to her chin. I applied just enough pressure to tilt her face up. Her gold-flecked eyes shone beneath her mask.

I cocked my head. "Again, that won't be necessary. I don't dally with serving girls." I stepped away, breaking the magnetic pull between us.

"How do you know I'm not a courtesan?" she asked, voice strained.

"You were just on your knees cleaning up a frightful mess and debating whether to kill that girl with a teaspoon."

She flushed an even deeper shade of pink and crossed her arms. "I was *not*."

I couldn't stop the corner of my mouth from quirking upward. "I've seen enough folk kill to know when there is murder in the air, darling."

Her mouth fell open, and she made that delicious gasping sound again. My wings flexed with satisfaction. Gods, this was some powerful magic. "Goodnight."

I marched to the door, anxious to leave before I did something stupid.

"She'll punish me, you know."

Now that the room separated us, I could take stock of her more critically. She stood with her hands clenched into fists at her sides, jaw set in a hard line. I took in the set of her shoulders and the wide stance of her feet. Though her voice betrayed her desperation, she looked hell-bent on getting what she wanted.

The madness took hold of me once more. Words flew out of my mouth before my mind could rationalize them. "Bring me your mistress."

Her face paled. "What?"

"Bring your madam to me."

The girl's eyes narrowed beneath her mask. She studied me a moment longer, then nodded, sweeping past me in a cloud of morning dew and bergamot.

Five minutes later, Madam Andromeda stood before me and the girl. "What's this about?" she demanded.

"Madam Andromeda, you are too generous. I accept your offer of gratitude, but on a few conditions."

She didn't bother to conceal her surprise.

"I want her exclusively. No one else touches her. Understood?"

Andromeda's eyes narrowed, and I knew sums were flying through her mind. Her eyes flicked from me to the golden-haired girl. She flashed her pointy canines at me.

The girl was not so pleased. Confusion, then fury, crossed her face.

I forged ahead, my mouth spilling words without my consent. "I'll be back in two days. We'll settle payment then, shall we?" I slid the black envelope out from my pocket and extended it to the mistress of the house. "Until then, why don't you hang on to this?"

Both women gaped at me, but I didn't care. "Pleasure doing business with you." I turned on my heel and left the parlor. "See you soon, darling," I called over my shoulder.

I shoved my hands into my pockets and strolled out of the dimly lit foyer, tall shadows flitting up the walls against the glowing candlelight. Back out in the courtyard, I gulped fresh air and marched through the wrought iron gates.

The magic of the place had gone straight to my head. In the night air, tinged with sea breeze, I waited for my mind to clear. All I could think of were the color of her lips, the flecks of gold in her eyes, and the utterly addicting scent of her.

Gods, I needed another drink. I turned toward the Golden Lyre, my favorite tavern.

As the House of Night disappeared into the darkness behind me, a terrible realization hit, chasing away any lingering pleasant thoughts.

Father was going to kill me.

Chapter Four
Sorsha

Andromeda hauled me to her office as soon as the arrogant winged fae left the premises. My chest burned as I marched up the stairs behind her. Who did he think he was? What gave him the right to hand over a stack of money and presume he could claim me? Courtesans did not entertain exclusive clients, though I know Viviana had her mind set on attaining such an arrangement for herself. I couldn't begin to imagine why. I was too furious.

Upstairs, Andromeda pointed to the seat in front of her desk, sweeping the door closed behind her. Two visits in one night were too much. My stomach twisted into a knot, settling alongside my anger.

"Sit."

Reluctantly, I sank into the soft chair.

Andromeda remained at the door. She removed a tiny bottle from her pocket. It held a dark blue, viscous liquid that swirled and eddied with each of her steps. She uncorked the potion and trickled it along the bottom of the doorframe. It was a concoction we used when our clients did not want their voices to carry past a room's threshold, but the cloying tang in the air told me this draft was more potent than the others.

A thread of curiosity tugged somewhere beneath my anxiety. If we needed an extra layer of protection from listening ears, I feared what our conversation would bring.

Andromeda returned to her seat. I sat across from her, my back ramrod straight, ignoring the pull of skin as the scars on my back stretched.

"Lord Stormfall appeared quite smitten with you."

I clenched my fists in my lap. I didn't know how to answer her. If by "smitten" she meant patronizing, then yes. But I couldn't talk back to her, so I bit my tongue and nodded.

"You will honor his request and entertain him when he returns."

I fidgeted with my skirt. Spending that much quality time with the conceited fae lord would require employing all my skills as a courtesan, not the potion-tricks I normally used.

"You find yourself in a unique, and very advantageous, position."

I stared blankly at her, unsure of how she wanted me to react to her proclamation. My stomach lurched.

"What I am about to discuss with you cannot, under any circumstances, leave this room."

I shifted in my seat. "Alright." My mind tumbled wildly over possibilities. The House of Night was closing. I was being demoted to a serving girl once more. We were all being kicked out into the street.

"I mean it, Miss Sventura. The retribution will be swift should you break your silence."

I shoved my guesses away, chilled by her threat. "I don't believe I know any information that would be of any interest to you. Or anyone else."

"No, but you will."

My brow furrowed.

"If you swear to secrecy and help me with a delicate matter, you may find that many doors suddenly open to you." Andromeda withdrew another vial, this one silver and as cold as starlight. She placed a dagger, its hilt inlaid with white gold, next to it. The blade caught the light from the vial, refracting it ten thousandfold into a brilliant constellation that bounced off the ceiling.

Something about the blade made my stomach turn rock hard. Foreboding pricked the hairs on the back of my neck.

"What is that?"

"Tools. For a blood pact. I need to be certain you will tell no one what we discuss here."

A blood pact was serious. It was an old magic, one rarely used even when spells and enchantments were easy to come by. When I was younger, the fae who ran the kitchen told me stories about mortals who made foolish pacts with fae to get their heart's desires. Blood pacts were for the desperate, for those with secrets to hide and everything to lose. I would not enter such a bargain lightly.

Failure to fulfill a blood pact means pain. Gradual, at first, then more severe as time goes on and the oath remains unfulfilled. Eventually, death will find the one who fails to uphold their bargain.

I placed my hands on the arms of the chair, the polished wood slick beneath my sweating palms. "I don't have any interest in what you are offering." My voice quavered.

She smirked. "I have a letter from your mother. I meant to give it to you, but it must have slipped my mind."

Andromeda had not made the House of Night successful by accepting refusal. She always had another card to play.

I shouldn't care so much. Shouldn't want, desperately, with every beat of my lonely heart, to read the words my mother had written to me. She had abandoned me, left me here to carve out my existence without her in a place that prioritized profit over everything else. What kind of mother would do that to her child? I wanted answers. I wanted to know why she had left me, even though I'd convinced myself it didn't matter long ago.

"Show me."

Andromeda withdrew a letter, sealed with wax, from her desk. The seal bore a strange triangle and half-circle. It looked vaguely familiar, but I couldn't place where I had seen it before.

"See? You can have it once you've completed your task."

I stood, my hands aching from how tightly I'd been gripping the chair. "No. Give it to me once the pact is made, or there is no deal."

Andromeda tucked the letter back into its resting place. It took every ounce of self-control not to leap across the desk and take it from her by force.

"The terms are these: you will make a pact with me. I will tell you what I need you to do. After you have completed the task I set before you, to my satisfaction, I will give you this letter."

I swallowed hard. "What is it you want me to do?" It had to be something I could plausibly accomplish, or else why would she have asked me here over all the other courtesans? She had many strings to pull, and plenty of people to manipulate to do her bidding. So why me?

She smiled coyly. "Information gathering."

"So, a spy? What am I gathering information about? And from who?"

"Ah ah," she said, waggling a finger in my face. "Pact first. Then I shall tell you exactly what the job entails."

Andromeda had her own network of spies. Fae and humans alike brought her bits of information she used to her advantage. It made little sense why she didn't use one of them.

I could say no to the blood pact. I could leave. But if I displeased Andromeda, she would make my life miserable as punishment for denying her. Viviana and her jealousy would be the least of my concerns. She could lock me in the cellar, make me entertain our worst clients, the drunk and lecherous who came night after night, drowning their miserable lives in magic and pleasure, addicted to what we offered.

"What does to your satisfaction mean, exactly?" Her terms were dangerously vague. I could find myself bound to her for eternity if I wasn't careful.

Andromeda pursed her lips. "When you have given me sufficient information. I'll know when I see it."

I needed that letter. But my mind screamed caution.

"And if I refuse?"

"You can pack your things tonight. You will leave, and you will not return."

An ember of fury burned in my chest. Andromeda had kept my mother's letter from me, and now she threatened to throw me out. The letter was mine by right, and I hated how much I wanted answers. The ember ignited into flame, fueled not only by my desire to know my mother's reasons for leaving me here, but by a dark curiosity. What information did Andromeda want so badly that she would use her greatest bargaining chips on me?

I bit my lip, weighing my options. She wanted me to spy for her. Spies need to go out into the world and gather intelligence. Perhaps this path would grant me freedom and security.

Either way, I needed that letter.

"Six months," I offered, my throat swelling shut. "I will agree to spy for you for six months."

"One year."

"Done." I'd bargained low purposefully, but my chest still tightened. I prayed I was making the right decision.

"Excellent. Give me your hand."

I extended my palm toward her. Something in me screamed not to do this, begged me to run away, but I shut out the voice.

Andromeda picked up the dagger. "Do you, Sorsha Sventura,

willingly enter into this blood pact and agree to the terms I have laid before you? That I shall give you a task which you shall complete to my satisfaction, in return for the letter your mother left for you?"

"And my freedom, after my service of one year," I added.

"And your freedom after service of one year," she agreed.

I ignored my thundering pulse. "I do."

She sliced through the pad of my finger. I hissed as the blade cut through my skin and blood welled to the surface. Without releasing me, Andromeda put the knife down and picked up the silver vial. She squeezed, letting the blood trickle into the vessel, and I winced again at the pressure. She did not let go until my blood filled the vial.

Andromeda pricked her own finger with the knife, letting only three drops fall into the silver bottle. She stoppered it, whispered something I couldn't make out, and set it between us on the desk.

Though the vial looked the same, the coppery tang of magic hit the back of my throat as the magic locked into place, solidifying our bargain. Andromeda breathed heavily through her nose, her face a shade paler than it had been before the pact. I didn't know how she had managed such magic on her own, without the aid of tinctures or potions, but it had taken a significant amount of effort. She smoothed her hair, taming the flyaways, and leaned back into her chair.

"What do you want me to do?" The reality of what I had just done sank into me, heavy as a boulder. I clasped my hands together, ignoring the sting of the cut.

Andromeda ran her tongue over her pointed teeth. The gesture made me shudder.

"What magic is left is leaving Tenebris. Even the goods we import are losing their potency much quicker than before.

We've managed to get by for years, but it's no longer enough. The houses are plotting to do something about it. I want you to figure out what that is.

"Any information you can gather will be conveyed directly to me, face to face, and with utmost secrecy. If you have any information to share, you will use a predetermined signal and wait until I send you a confirmation before approaching my office to discuss it."

I frowned. I could have done this at any time. I had no problem melting into the background, and customers often developed loose lips, especially when they got into pissing contests with each other, desperate to impress. If Andromeda had waited until now to give me this assignment, it could only mean she wanted information from one source.

"You want me to spy on him. Lord Stormfall." My mouth tingled with the vibration of his name.

"Correct."

"And if he tires of me?"

"He won't." She said it with such confidence, she almost had me convinced.

"What makes you so sure he'll have the information you need? How am I supposed to get him to tell me anything?"

Andromeda stroked the silver bottle with a long finger. The possessiveness in the gesture made my blood run cold, and I realized how bound I was to her. My stomach turned to lead once more.

"I don't think it will require much effort on your part. Give him what he wants, tease him if you like, but I expect he will be rather forthcoming with you. You'll figure it out." She let her finger fall and gave me a hard look. "I do have one piece of advice for you, Miss Sventura. Do not let your heart become involved. It will complicate an already delicate situation. Besides, this is a job. He is paying for a service, which you are providing."

I swallowed, fighting the rising lump in my throat. *Service* was a nice way of putting it. He was paying for *me*. I was a commodity. Nothing more.

"Of course."

Andromeda, satisfied with my response, withdrew a pin from her hair. One shining black jewel set amidst a tangle of vines and leaves.

"Take this. When you have information to share, place it over an open flame, and I shall receive notice. When I need you, or when I am ready to see you, the pin will hum. I expect you to wear it at all times."

I examined the ornament. It looked entirely ordinary, something I could wear any time of day without raising suspicion. No one would ever know it was spelled with a communication charm. I twisted my hair around it, pinning my locks into a loose bun. It held fast.

I curled my hand, letting my nails bite into my palm as my pulse beat loudly in my ears.

"You may go. I look forward to your first report," she crooned, giving me a wicked smile, flashing her pointed teeth.

Chapter Five

Corvus

Cool gray mist clung to the wrought iron fences and outer walls of Stormfall Manor as the shrouded sun peeked over the horizon. I led my horse through the front courtyard, his hooves echoing solemnly against the stone. Once, laughter and the clashing sounds of early morning combat training reverberated in the yard.

Now, there was only stillness.

Shaking away the ghosts of those memories, I roused the sleeping stable boy, who kept his head down as he took the reins, careful not to meet my gaze.

I rubbed my eyes as I made my way inside. The night had been long, though not without pleasure. I wanted nothing more than to bathe, fall into bed, and dream of the beautiful girl I'd met tonight. But I knew Father would want his money first.

He sat at the long oak dining table, surrounded by plates of sausages, eggs, muffins, and fruit. The chamber was dim; the stone walls and floor leeched a chill into the air. Weak sunlight filtered in from windows set high into the arched ceiling.

I removed the heavy bags of gold and a black envelope from my pockets and tossed them down unceremoniously in front of him.

His hands darted eagerly for the satchels, and he began counting the coin, not even bothering to bid me good morning.

I took the seat across from him and waited for him to finish, ignoring the food. I wasn't hungry.

"This gold is two thousand less than what was promised," he

said. His displeasure carved deep lines into his face.

"She didn't agree to the fee." I shrugged, even though I knew my flippancy would annoy him. I would *not* be telling him that I'd returned Madam Andromeda's money to her. It was easier to place blame on her, who had indeed first refused to pay.

"When I send you to collect, it is my expectation you retrieve all that is due through *any* means necessary." His face reddened, as I knew it would. "There is no bargaining involved."

I leaned back in my chair, feigning nonchalance even though the gesture cramped my wings. "It was only six months ago that the houses raised the fees. Folk are angry they've increased again." I picked up a butter knife and twirled it idly between my fingers.

He inhaled sharply through his nose.

"We are merely responding to the king's restrictions. Prices go up when the royals crack down."

"I understand how it works. I just think—"

"Corvus," he snapped.

I knew better than to keep talking. His jowls were turning purple, so I shut my mouth and put down the knife.

A muscle in his jaw twitched. "This was a reward for your success these past few months. Despite your whoring, your associations with the brothels are valuable to us. I had assumed, perhaps incorrectly, that you could handle this task."

I crossed my arms. My "success" involved shaking down and threatening some of the more resistant sellers of black-market materials. The daggers at my chest could be quite... convincing. Especially when they were coated with blood. "Are you suggesting I maim a leader of a noble house? The House of Night is no mere brothel," I argued. The madam was a member of the peerage, even though her house was a lesser one. As one of the primary dealers of black-market magics in Tenebris, the money she paid my father, and the Fae Forum, was significant. Two thousand dinar didn't seem like much when she already paid eight thousand gold a month to keep her very lucrative business running.

"Which is why I assumed you'd be keen to visit," my father snapped, spearing a sausage with his fork. "My mistake."

I curled my hand into a fist as my shoulders tensed.

"You will go back tonight and retrieve the rest. I don't care how you do it."

I opened my mouth to argue, but I knew it was futile. Instead of my well-rehearsed reasonings, the words that left me were, "Yes, Father." The coppery tang of self-loathing coated my throat.

My father plunked the gold coins back into their bags and tied the purse strings. "Mercelles would have completed this task easily. Perhaps if you were more dedicated to ensuring the future of this house, instead of spending all your time indulging in unsavory nighttime activities, we would not need to keep having this conversation."

I reached for my mental switch, the one I flipped when my errands called for bloodletting. Detaching from myself was the easiest way to carry out my father's wishes. But exhaustion made my eyes itch, and my gut twisted at my brother's name. I fought to keep my face an impassive mask as I fumbled to shut off the flood of sudden emotion.

Mercelles Maximus Stormfall was the perfect first-born son. He had the stomach for dealing with vain and greedy lords and could sway others with only a few words, including our father. He'd known how to be the son of Lord Stormfall, unyielding and fierce. Max had been everything my father wanted in a son.

I was the exact opposite.

Though I was used to these comparisons, their frequent

utterances did not dull their sting. They always slipped through my defenses like a blade between my ribs. I pressed my mouth into a hard, thin line.

Father sighed. "The Forum meets in two days. They expect the fees to be procured by then. You will not fail me in this."

I forced the corner of my mouth to turn upward. "If you insist, I shall be more than happy to oblige. The House of Night employs such pretty things." In truth, I was eager to return.

"Go." His lip curled in disgust.

I shoved my chair back, sending it skidding across the hard stone floor. I fought the impulse to march out of the room and instead sauntered leisurely toward my bathing chamber, cooling my temper with thoughts of the pale-haired courtesan from the House of Night.

I sat in the bathwater of the copper tub as it cooled around me, my skin scraped raw. No amount of scrubbing ever erased the images burned in my mind, especially on nights when I had to do my father's bidding. My black feathered wings draped over the sides of the cast iron tub onto the floor. I was one of the few fae in Tenebris who had them. Father thought they were a curse, and I had to agree. What good were wings if you couldn't fly?

A terrible ache settled in my chest. I'd promised Max I would take care of Father and uphold the honor of our house. Even if each day I did so tarnished my soul and added fuel to the fires of my self-loathing.

When the water grew icy cold, I got out of the bath and dressed. I crossed the straps of my bandoliers across my chest and belted them before sliding twin daggers into their places. One inlaid with the brightest blue sea stone, the other with night-black onyx. Two daggers for two brothers. Now, I was keeper of them both.

My stomach growled. I shoved a hand through my hair, too caught up in my own thoughts to care. Closing the door to the ornately carved wardrobe, I wondered what Max would have done.

I knew Father thought me the worst sort of rake. While my unsavory reputation provided the perfect excuse to be out at all hours of the night, to see to my father's affairs and my own, I had avoided the House of Night entirely until now. Apparently, I had proven my capabilities in wrangling money from the vendors in the Shale, the waterfront district where most black-market magic dealings were conducted. Father assumed he was giving me an honor by entrusting me with the collection of the House of Night's gold. I should be pleased to be given more responsibility. Max would have been proud, but it made me nauseous.

I sank into the downy mattress of my four-poster bed, swathed in deep ocean blue blankets. As I tugged on my boots, my thoughts flew back to the girl I'd met. I smiled, remembering the fierce way she'd gripped that little spoon. Her eyes had flashed dark before I interrupted whatever violent thought she'd been weighing. I ached to return tonight, but there were more pressing matters that needed seeing to. Besides, Father could wait before I delivered his precious gold.

Training and food. That would do for today. And hiding in the library for a few hours before I conducted my errands in the Shale. The promise of solitude was enough to put me at ease, and I fell asleep, fully clothed, as the sun burned through the morning fog.

Chapter Six

Sorsha

I rose well before the rest of the courtesans the following afternoon. The blood pact weighed heavily on my mind, as did thoughts of my impending meeting with the arrogant Lord Stormfall. As the sun made its descent, I dragged myself out of bed to find breakfast.

I took my food up to my usual spot, one of the mid-sized parlors where we had our meals and sank into the cushioned seat in the bay window. It overlooked the grove of lemon trees, and I could barely make out the corner of the kitchen garden. My bed of herbs and medicinal plants was overdue for a good weeding session.

I started the little patch as a serving girl and had been allowed to maintain it after I moved upstairs. Tending to the kitchen garden was my favorite chore, and Ivy, our formidable cook, had let me plant whatever herbs I wanted. I turned the plants into salves and tinctures for the courtesans. Since the black-market magic we had was purely for pleasure and paying customers, we had no fancy medicines or remedies.

Dry toast and grapefruit sat untouched on my plate as my thoughts turned back to the lord who'd laid claim to me. He'd helped me when I'd fallen, and I had been bewitched by his scent, a dizzying combination of warm summer storms and lightning. His shoulders were broad, and his charcoal wings were dangerously captivating. And I suppose his thundercloud gray eyes were rather attractive.

And that is where any positive thought ended. His kindness

was wholly at odds with the conceited way he'd demanded that no one else should touch me. Once he'd shown his true character, I no longer thought him charming. I crumbled a piece of toast bitterly. Who did he think he was? He hadn't even asked me my name. Prick. And to call me "darling".

My cheeks flushed.

The sound of footsteps on the main stairs jolted me from my musings. The door swung open, and Ferdie tumbled into the room.

Ferdie, my one friend in the house, had a hungry look about him. I stifled a groan. Normally, his passion for gossip was an amusing source of entertainment, but I could tell from the way he marched toward me that I was to be the subject of the latest news.

"Sorsha. I heard a *delicious* rumor about you and that dreamy Lord Stormfall. Tell me everything." His rich brown curls bounced with his excitement.

I set my plate aside, stalling for time. He sat next to me and waited like a greedy seagull as my mouth grew dry. "It's nothing."

Ferdie leaned toward me. "None of your shyness. Give me details, or I shall be forced to make them up."

I rubbed my hands together. Everyone would find out sooner or later, anyway. "He wants me to entertain him exclusively. I am to see no one else."

"Are you serious?" His wide eyes raked me from head to toe. It made me feel hyper-aware of my every flaw. My figure was not lithe and thin like other courtesans. I had muscle from years of carrying trays up and down stairs, and I enjoyed eating as much as I liked, when I liked. The mask I wore concealed my objectively pleasant, though by no means beautiful, face.

I twirled a loose strand of my hair, trying to smooth it out.

"That's what he said."

"Oh, my gods. Viviana is going to be so pissed," Ferdie said gleefully.

"Why?" I picked up my glass of orange juice, trying to hide the sudden surge of anxiety her name caused.

"Not even the rich Thornspring who dotes on her so much is a *lord*. Stormfall is the heir to a Great House. No one close to his rank has come here in ages."

Shit. I did not need another reason for Viviana to despise me.

Ferdie didn't pick up on my unease. He was too busy reveling in this latest juicy gossip. "Oh, this is too good. I had no idea you were so talented in the bedroom, honey."

I choked on a sip of juice. "What?"

"Is that how you convinced him to come back to spend time with you? You're going to have to give me some pointers."

My cheeks burned. "No, nothing like that happened."

Ferdie cocked his head. "What *did* you do?"

I gave him a short summary of what had transpired the night before, claiming I had tripped on my own. I didn't want it to get back to Viviana that I was running my mouth about her.

When I finished, Ferdie took both of my hands in his, eyes shining. "You have bewitched him. Love at first sight. Do you know how amazing this is?"

I fought the urge to roll my eyes. "That is *not* what it is." I didn't want to crush Ferdie's ridiculous dreams, but the idea was laughable. "What was Andromeda giving him money for, anyway?"

"The Stormfalls act like taxmen. He was collecting hush money for the magic we use."

My face pinched. He profited from the fact that magic was illegal. He really was a greedy, arrogant asshole.

The clock on the wall chimed half past seven. More courtesans started to trickle into the room, rubbing sleep from their eyes.

"Maybe this is a good thing?" Ferdie asked hopefully. "Stormfall can whisk you away and keep you like a fine lady in his big mansion."

I took a steadying breath. "I highly doubt that." I wouldn't be going anywhere now I had a blood pact to fulfill. And I certainly didn't want to go anywhere with *him.*

"We'll see," he sang. "Now, chin up. Let's go get dressed."

He swiped a grapefruit from the table on the way out and skipped up the stairs to his room, leaving me to follow behind with heavy footsteps.

An hour later, I left the quiet of my room behind. While no one could touch me tonight, Andromeda had made it clear that I was still expected to be downstairs. Gods forbid she ever give one of us a night off.

Halfway down the hall, the crash of glass, followed by a screech, halted my footsteps.

"Tilly!"

My mind commanded that I continue forward, lest Viviana open the door and choose me as the next target for her wrath, but my feet refused to budge. Years of serving her had given me a thorough education of just how cutting her remarks could be.

Before I could convince myself to move, the door opened. Any chance of escaping vanished, and now I ran the risk of running late. Viviana stood at the threshold. Her eyes widened; then she grinned like a cat who'd spotted a mouse. Her fingers curled around the collar of her blue silk dressing gown.

Raven-black hair curled perfectly around her pointed ears and shimmered with glittering crystals. The mask she wore could not conceal the malice in her eyes.

"Sorsha. I heard someone has demanded your exclusivity. Do they know you're nothing but half-fae trash?"

I stood my ground but said nothing, even as my throat tightened painfully. If she grew bored, she'd let me leave. Viviana raked her gaze up and down me. Under her scrutiny, my body felt too big, my hair too unkempt. I hated it. I hated that she made me feel this way. My face flushed.

I couldn't help my parentage. The House of Night catered to both fae and humans alike and employed both. But outside these walls, half-fae were rare and looked down upon. The fae who once ruled Tenebris still bore grudges against their mortal conquerors, and humans didn't often procreate with fae. Half-fae were like puzzle pieces who did not fit into the larger picture.

I didn't have time for this. I was going to be late, and I didn't need Andromeda hearing of any tardiness.

"Are we done here?" I asked, unable to keep the bite out of my tone.

Viviana frowned and slithered closer toward me. She ignored the sounds of scuffling in her room. I caught a flash of Tilly, the new maid with lichen-mottled skin, cleaning up by the vanity.

"You won't last a week. Entertaining someone exclusively requires more than just spreading your legs. You have to make them *want* you. You have to be everything they desire. What even their innermost selves dare not speak aloud."

The house was not some common brothel. Wasn't the magic the primary reason folks came? Surely Lord Stormfall would be more interested in the potions we had to offer than my company.

As if reading my thoughts, Viviana gripped me by the chin. Her nails dug into my cheeks, and I tried my best not to flinch.

Her eyes burned with righteous fury. "Magic didn't make me the best in Tenebris. *I* did through my own hard work. And no one can take that away from me."

She released me so suddenly I almost lost my balance.

Viviana's nostrils flared. "Get out of here, Sorsha. You'll ruin my complexion." She turned back to her room and waltzed over to her vanity, ignoring me.

Tilly squeezed around Viviana and softly closed the door behind her. She walked in front of me with her head bent low, eyes trained on the ground.

The marks on my face were already fading. I rubbed my cheek, dispelling the lingering sting. I quickened my pace so I could walk beside her. "Why do you stay here? Surely there are other houses who would treat you better?"

Tilly tentatively raised her gaze to mine. "No, miss. This is the best place to work. There is a difference between the House of Night and other houses of pleasure in the city. Here it's all spectacle. Here you have magic." Her eyes shone with unshed tears. "That's why I took the job."

Her chin quivered, and a sinking feeling hit my chest. "Were you a courtesan at another brothel before this?"

Tilly nodded, a single tear slipping down her cheek. "It was not as nice as here."

"I'm sorry. You don't have to talk about it."

She wiped her face and blinked hard. "It is safer here." We walked a few paces in silence before she added, "You know, you could be as powerful as her someday."

"As Andromeda?" I scoffed. Andromeda was a cunning, ruthless fae. Power came naturally to her.

Tilly shook her head. "No, as Miss Viviana. She makes demands of Madam Andromeda. She always gets what she wants. You could, too."

Viviana's screech rang down the hall. "*Tilly!*"

Tilly's eyes widened. She ran back to her shrieking mistress, leaving me to contemplate what she'd said. I rested my hand lightly on the polished banister of the grand stairs as I descended into the foyer. It was true that Viviana held some sway over Andromeda. She was a bully and a brat, and usually got what she wanted. But Viviana was not the one who held my blood in a vial.

I adjusted my mask as my feet hit the checkered, polished marble, and I tried not to dwell on the roiling in my stomach or my oath of servitude.

Chapter Seven

Sorsha

The next evening as the clock struck nine, I paced in the Emerald Parlor, waiting for Lord Stormfall to arrive. My pulse pounded in my ears as I walked. I had to be perfect, or else risk the consequences of failing to uphold my end of the blood pact.

I doubted I would get much information from him this evening. It was our first night together, after all. Customers came back when they felt welcomed and bonded to a courtesan. All my focus would be on establishing a positive relationship with him, ensuring his return. Once we formed a connection, or he believed we had, then I would start to tease information out of him.

My stomach flipped. I wasn't skilled at entertaining clients, but I thought my plan was sound. I only hoped I could pull it off. Otherwise, my future would consist of nothing but pain, then death.

I wiped my damp palms on the skirts of my dress. It was black, of course, but the skirts were light and airy. The bodice helped give my waist an hourglass shape while enhancing my cleavage. Despite my nerves, I liked how I looked. I tried to hang on to that self-assurance. I had to get a hold of myself.

I jumped at the sound of the latch on the door and tried to still my pounding heart.

Ferdie stuck his head in and winked. "Hey! Just wanted to say good luck."

A tingling sensation jolted through my body. "Thanks," I squeaked.

The door opened wider, letting in more candlelight from the hall. "Relax. Sit down or something before you wear a hole in the floor. You're going to do great."

"Yes. Right." I sat on a dark green settee, my back ramrod straight.

Ferdie chuckled and shook his head. "I guess that's better." A soft voice dragged his attention down the hall. "Time to go. Remember to relax!"

He shut the door. Right. Relax. He thought my nerves were directed solely at the charming lord who had claimed me. If only that were true. I curled my hands as a wave of guilt washed through me. We told each other everything, but this was one thing I could never share with anyone.

The clock ticked loudly in the corner, echoing in the silence.

I rolled my shoulders and dug my fingers into the knot in my neck, trying to release it. My scars did not extend too far up my back, but the creeping muscle tension stretched to my neck. The tightness in my muscles heightened my nervousness and irritation. If I weren't determined to extract some information from Lord Stormfall, I would much rather give this entitled prick a piece of my mind than entertain him for the night.

"Maybe I can be of some assistance, my lady?" asked a deep voice.

I dropped my hands and shot to my feet. I hadn't heard the door open, or Lord Stormfall enter the room. He held a small bouquet of white roses.

"Seven hells, you scared me," I said, placing a hand over my pounding heart.

He grinned roguishly. "Sorry, my lady."

My heart slowed, but only a fraction. "You don't need to call me that. I am no lady."

"My apologies. What shall I call you?"

"Sorsha."

He cocked his head. "Well, Sorsha. These are for you." He extended the flowers toward me.

A sharp jolt whipped through me at the sound of my name on his lips. I crossed the distance between us on wobbling legs and gently took the blooms in both hands, stroking the velvety softness of the petals. For an entitled prick, it was a thoughtful gesture. Probably meant to throw me off my guard. It wouldn't work. "Thank you, Lord Stormfall."

"Corvus."

I looked up into his face. His eyes were unexpectedly soft.

"Corvus," I said. His name felt pleasant as I spoke it. Despite my resolution to find him detestable, his eyes captivated me. His dark hair looked as soft as silk. Heat bloomed on my cheeks.

I tore my gaze away, cradled the roses to my chest, and gestured to the settee. "Would you like something to drink?"

"That would be welcome."

I sat the bouquet gently on the low table, careful not to crush the blooms, and poured wine for both of us. The knot in my shoulder pulled as I replaced the bottle. I tried not to grimace. I hadn't been stretching as I ought to.

Corvus accepted his wine and took a delicate sip. His eyes darted to my shoulder.

I wanted to down my whole glass but took only a mouthful.

"Are you injured?"

I tried to relax. "No. I'm fine."

I took another sip of wine. I could do this. "So, what would you like?" My voice sounded foreign. I immediately regretted my choice of words, my fake sultry tone, and fought the urge to slap my hands over my face. I bit my lip instead.

He seemed unfazed by my bluntness and took a lazy sip of wine. "Do you play cards?"

"I haven't played in a long time," I admitted, clearing my throat. Playing games was one of the skills Andromeda liked her courtesans to have. But I typically distracted my clients with magic drafts and empty promises.

"Would you like a refresher course? I am a very skilled teacher."

His voice hummed pleasantly in my chest, traveling through the cushions to reverberate through my body. "Sure. But I can't promise I'll be any good at it."

"You never know until you try." He withdrew a small deck of cards from his pocket. The edges were gilded with gold. "Though I do like to make my games more interesting."

"How so?" My voice shook. I took another sip from my glass. Of course he meant to make this sexual.

"Each time you draw a card, your opponent may ask one question. You must answer honestly."

I cocked an eyebrow. "I have a feeling this will be a very one-sided interview."

"We'll see," he said as he shuffled the cards, a light smile on his lips.

He dealt seven cards into my hand, then placed four cards face up on the table in a cross shape, leaving the deck in the middle, face down.

"Cards go in descending order and must alternate between red and black. We take turns placing cards. If you cannot make a play, you draw from the deck."

He explained a few more of the rules. I started to recall how to play the game. Maybe I could win. Or, at least, keep up. "Got it," I said, once he had finished his explanation.

"You may have the first play."

I placed one of the cards in my hand onto an available crown card. We played in relative silence for the first few turns;

I observed him over the tops of my cards. The golden chandelier cast him in a warm glow. His long fingers gripped the stem of his crystal glass delicately, and he wore a dark blue jacket, the color of midnight ocean. I continued my study, watching how he held his cards, until I had to draw from the middle pile.

I steeled myself, wondering what kind of question he would ask.

"What is your favorite season?"

My brow wrinkled. I'd expected a much more salacious query. "Summer."

He nodded and played another card. Two turns later, he drew from the deck.

One question burned in my mind, but I couldn't bring myself to ask it. Not yet. So, I copied him. "What's *your* favorite season?"

"Winter."

The questions remained innocent for the next half hour. His favorite color was black. Roasted potatoes were his favorite food. I tentatively asked his age, as you could never be too sure. He was shockingly young, only twenty-eight. Five years older than me.

Despite myself, I began to relax and enjoy the game. As we played, I grew increasingly warm and tingly. I'd had almost two glasses of wine.

It made me bold, so I asked the question I most wanted answered. "Why did you want me exclusively?"

His lips quirked upward. "I wondered when we'd get to that."

I held silent, waiting for him to answer.

"I don't know." He lowered his cards and stared at me, as if trying to puzzle it out.

I dipped my chin as my insides twisted. Maybe this was all

a lark to him. A rich lord with nothing to do, bored enough to see how much power he could wield over others. I clutched my cards tightly.

"Perhaps," he mused, "because I simply want to know you better. Any lady who could wield a teaspoon with such ferocity is certainly worth knowing."

I narrowed my eyes. "You mock me."

"I'm serious." He cleared his throat. "Although, I must apologize. I sense you are irritated with me."

I bit the inside of my cheek.

"Are you angry with me?" He cocked his head.

"That's two questions," I said, trying to make light of my obvious annoyance. "Your play."

The candles on the table dripped with wax, and the scent of lemon wafted through the airy room. I fumed as we played the next few hands until I was required to draw once more.

"So, are you angry with me?" he asked again.

"Annoyed would be a better word for it. Who does a thing like that, laying claim to someone you just met?"

"I am sorry, truly. I must have come off as rather conceited."

I averted my eyes and played what cards I could from my hand. At least he was sorry for acting like an arrogant asshole. It still didn't excuse his behavior, though.

On his turn, he couldn't play his last card to any of the piles. There was only one card left in the deck, and I still held three cards in my hand. He would need to draw, but I could still win.

I glared at him over my hand. "What do you want with me?"

"I have already answered that question," he said calmly, fingers hovering over the last card.

"You want to get to know me? That's all?"

"Yes."

"You don't want to have sex with me?"

He barked a laugh. "I never said I *don't* want to have sex with you. I find you highly attractive." His eyes flashed darkly as he leaned forward in his seat. "And *very* tempting."

"Oh," I said. My chest tightened, and my head swam.

"I answered two questions," he noted.

"Ask me one, then."

"When did you have your first kiss?"

My face flushed as my head continued to spin. "Eighteen. But it doesn't count."

"Why not?"

"Because someone paid me to kiss them." What part of my work did he not understand? I hoped he realized that anything that happened between us, no matter how platonic, was only because he was a client.

"I see." A shadow flitted across his face. "Then, how old were you when you had a first kiss that mattered?"

"Never." I clutched my cards, but the game lay forgotten. I could not tear my eyes away from his lips.

"Never?" He closed the distance between us before I could blink. He cupped one hand to my cheek.

My breathing grew shallow.

He drew closer until our noses touched. I licked my tingling lips, awaiting the feel of his mouth on mine. A humming like lightning whipped through me.

"Would you like me to remedy that?" he asked in a low voice that sent pleasant tremors through me once more.

I swallowed the rising lump in my throat. I told myself the kiss wouldn't matter. But he didn't need to know that. "I suppose now is as good a time as any." I closed my eyes as anticipation throbbed through every inch of me.

"Well, *that* won't do." He pulled away.

My eyes snapped open. My cheek grew cold where his hand

had rested. He flipped over the remaining card, placing it on the awaiting crown suit, winning the game.

Before I could protest, he scooped up the cards, shuffled them once, and placed them back in his pocket. "It has been a pleasure, darling."

I gaped at him. "You're leaving?"

He was such a... *tease*. My chest heaved. A strange fire burned in my stomach, smoldering as he collected himself. I couldn't believe I had almost forgiven him for being such a prick.

He leaned forward and said in a low voice, "When I kiss you, I want you to want it just as much as I do."

A shiver raced down my spine, even as my lips pressed tightly together.

Corvus stood. "I will see you in a few days, if you'd like to play again?"

I huffed through my nose and crossed my arms. "I'll be sure to beat you next time."

He bowed. "I look forward to it."

I sat on the settee, unable to move. I should get up, see him to the door at least, but I didn't feel so gracious.

"Until next time, Sorsha." He strode out of the room, leaving me alone in the parlor.

Unbelievable.

I pressed a hand to my forehead as a sudden lightness washed over me. I'd made it through the night without having to do any of the ridiculous flirting or touching that I had been dreading. I dropped my hand and stood, swaying a little from the wine and the realization that if Corvus *had* wanted to spend an evening with a courtesan, indulging in magic and sex, he could have chosen anyone here.

But he'd chosen to spend the evening with me.

Despite his uncanny ability to annoy me, I'd enjoyed playing cards with him. And he wanted to come back, which must mean I had done enough to please him.

Emboldened by my success, I replayed our interaction in my mind, searching for how I would make my next move.

I brushed my fingertips to my lips, wondering what he would have tasted like.

Chapter Eight
Corvus

I took a moment to lean one hand on the wall at the end of the dim corridor. Seven hells, I wanted to kiss her so badly. I didn't understand it. Under normal circumstances, this unexpected desire would bother me, but somehow it felt... right. Had she bewitched me, or was it something else?

There was something comforting and familiar about her that I could not place. She was a puzzle that needed solving. Surely it explained why I was so drawn to her.

I suppose now is as good a time as any.

I huffed a laugh and straightened. No, that would not do at all. I wanted her to beg for it. I wanted her to feel the same infatuation I did. The back of my neck prickled as I thought about how divine her lips would taste; how lovely it would be to cover her gasps with my mouth.

"Excuse me, Lord Stormfall?" A courtesan in a silk dressing gown stood at my elbow.

Shoving off the wall, I straightened my jacket. "Yes?"

"Madam Andromeda will see you in her office before you go," she purred.

"Thank you. I'll make my way there now."

She nodded and waltzed back down the hall, swaying her hips.

I ran a hand through my hair, wondering how much my time with Sorsha would cost me. Upstairs, I knocked on the door, thinking about how to best approach the conversation.

"Enter."

Madam Andromeda removed a pair of small spectacles and placed them on her desk. "Lord Stormfall. A pleasure to see you."

I bowed. My boots sank into the plush burgundy rug, spattered with silver stars. "You're looking radiant this evening, Madam."

She quirked her lips. "Your flattery is no good here, you know."

"Straight to business, then. I believe I owe you for my time with the lovely girl downstairs." I sat in a chair and placed a forearm on the polished wood of her desk. It shone so brightly I could see my reflection as clearly as if I looked into a mirror.

"Ah, yes. I think five thousand dinar a month is a fitting sum for a woman of her charms."

A cold sweat trickled down my spine at the sum. Seven hells.

I could pay. Father would be furious, which might be an unforeseen benefit of the whole arrangement, but I knew that money could be better spent.

"No courtesan in all of Tenebris is worth five thousand dinar."

"Worth is subjective," she said blithely. "At this point, I am curious if you would pay ten thousand for her."

"Not even your prized jewel is worth so much," I countered, tapping her desk with a finger. "Two thousand five hundred."

She frowned. "I run a business. Not a charity. Four thousand."

"Three."

"Three and a half."

"Three," I said, with steel in my voice. It was the most I could do and still be able to see to my own business in the Shale.

Madam Andromeda stuck out her hand. "Three thousand dinar each month for exclusive access to Sorsha Sventura."

Sventura.

A surname given to all orphans and bastards in Tenebris. It meant *misfortunate one*. It clanged around in my head like a piece of iron.

I clasped Andromeda's outstretched hand, perhaps a tad too firmly, sealing our bargain. My palm tingled against hers. I dropped three bags of gold on her desk and stood.

"A pleasure as always, Madam," I said through bared teeth. I did not wait for her reply but saw myself out and tried not to think of how much of a fool I had been.

Candles still flickered in the study when I returned home. Though it was only half past eleven, Father was not one for burning the midnight oil. I longed to retire, but I knew my own hand would be no substitute for the lovely girl I had left. Instead of turning to my chambers, I indulged my curiosity and knocked on the study door. Besides, I needed access to our coffers, and the ledger where my father meticulously tracked our finances.

Horatio, Father's greasy-haired advisor, opened it a crack. His beady eyes scanned me from head to toe in a revolting manner.

"Yes?" he wheezed.

"Who is it?" my father barked.

"Your son, my lord." Horatio opened the door wide enough for me to glance inside.

Father leaned over a table, resting his fist on a map. He looked more like a war general than a tax collector. "Let him in."

Horatio glared at me but allowed me to pass through.

I clenched my jaw and stepped inside, ignoring his disrespect. "Is everything alright?" I asked.

Father let out a snort as he threw himself into a chair. The door clicked shut behind me. Horatio swept over to the table and began to roll up the map.

Father threw out a hand. "Leave it. Let's see what my son has to say about this."

I frowned and stepped unwillingly to the table. I don't know what I was expecting, but it hadn't been another one of Father's little tests. I usually failed them.

I studied the map of Tenebris. The harbor lay to the west, nestled against a large crescent-shaped coast. Mountains, the dominion of the Dawnstones, lay to the north, serving as the natural border between Tenebris and Grauradur, the empire where imported magic came from. Dense Frostgrove forests covered the northeast, where they trailed into Thornspring lakes and streams. House Uriel's lands occupied the southern peninsula, and the Sunbarrow plains spanned most of the heart of our land. Against the crescent-shaped harbor sat the Blackwood palace.

I ran my eyes over the map, noting the addition of little black wooden ships scattered throughout the harbor and soldier pieces placed in the lands above the Dawnstone mountains. I trailed a finger through the open space of ocean waters, thinking. No fae possessed a navy, only the mortal royals who had conquered this land with their armadas. Father had placed them in a specific formation, their bowsprits facing the land.

"The Blackwoods have assumed an offensive position," I said finally.

Father grunted. "Well, thank the gods you're not stupid. Of course they're on the offensive."

I tapped the map, unable to shake the feeling that I was

missing something. "The Blackwoods would not dare attack their own people," I said. They might confiscate or destroy magical contraband, but fae were not the only residents of Tenebris anymore. Their mortal kinsman lived alongside us, ever loyal to their king and queen.

Father leaned forward in his chair, face reddening. "No, they would not attack *their people,* but they sure as hells would attack *us.*"

I swallowed, a knot of unease tightening my stomach. The Blackwoods had left most magic wielders to rot. It wasn't so ludicrous to think they would seek to eliminate all traces of magic with force, especially with the power the Fae Forum still held. Perhaps they grew impatient, waiting for us to tear each other apart first.

The Fae Forum, which was comprised of the Great Fae Houses of Tenebris, still met regularly in an attempt to govern the fae who lived in Tenebris. The Forum negotiated with the mortals and advocated for fae folk, while advancing their own agendas and desire for political power. The Blackwoods, the family that had conquered Tenebris two hundred years ago, ruled through their monarchy.

The rift between humans and fae grew larger with each passing day as, without their magic, the fae fell further into chaos and ruin. Only in rare cases did humans and fae mingle. The House of Night was one of those places. Magic, money, and the desire for status had a way of bringing folk together.

Father groaned and heaved himself out of the chair. "Enough. The Forum convenes tomorrow. Your presence is not required."

"I have nothing better to do," I said, feigning nonchalance. "I might as well come along."

Horatio bristled. Father stared hard at me, calculating. It took more courage than I cared to admit to hold his gaze, but

Madam Andromeda's lack of an invitation to the meeting had piqued my interest.

"Fine."

I gave a curt nod, and Horatio and my father left the room. My shoulders sagged once the door shut behind them.

Max would have known what to do in the face of this threat. I rubbed my eyes with the heels of my hands. Before proceeding to my own chambers, I glanced down at the map again. I picked up one of the wooden ships, studying it. I placed it back on the map, pointing it away from Tenebris and toward the open ocean.

The Blackwoods could be planning an attack on Tenebris's people. Or they could be preparing to defend it. Only time would reveal which one it was.

Chapter Nine

Corvus

Whoever's idea it was to hold these meetings in a marble pit underground was either extremely paranoid or had an allergy to comfort. A large, open-aired temple sat directly above us with plenty of room to seat every member of the Forum. Instead, they chose a sunken amphitheater underground, devoid of sunlight. Little fae lanterns in white and blue, another illegal import from Grauradur, illuminated the space. The marble seats were cold, and my wings tensed as the chill seeped into my bones.

Father sat beside me, unbothered by the temperature. His eyes darted about the chamber, noting the faces of those in attendance and every interaction between houses. Horatio sat on his right, whispering in his ear.

I'd had the good sense to dip into our family coffers last night and retrieve the two thousand dinar, otherwise I might not be here. A quick correction to the ledger in the study ensured my theft would go unnoticed.

We waited a quarter hour for the rest of the Forum to arrive. I tried to keep my thoughts focused on the upcoming meeting, but they kept drifting back to Sorsha.

A pointed cough dragged me from my thoughts of kissing and doing other delicious things with her. I glanced at my father, whose lip was curled into a sneer, eyes trained across the room. Instantly, thoughts of pretty girls left my head as brittle hatred took over.

Lord Dawnstone entered the chamber, trailed by a personal guard, his nephew, and his advisor. They wore gold armor, their breastplates bearing the emblem of their house: a sun rising over a mountain peak. The guards and the nephew, Aurum, wore long swords at the hip. It was all a bit much, in typical Dawnstone fashion. Ostentatious and despicable.

I brushed my fingers over the onyx dagger at my chest as Lord Dawnstone took his seat. Aurum stood dutifully behind him, one hand on his sword. He scanned the room, his gaze lingering on us a fraction too long. I stared back at him. He smirked and continued his perfunctory sweep of the chamber.

Rage, hot and blinding, threatened to black out everything around me. I forced myself to breathe, to bury the impulse to throw my dagger at his exposed neck. It would be so easy. All that armor couldn't stop a dagger to the jugular. The scene played out in my mind. Ruby blood splattering against the marble, his golden armor clanging to the floor...

"Corvus."

I felt a hand on my knee, jolting me back to the present. Father had sensed my rage. He squeezed briefly, then let go. I took another deep breath and tore my eyes away from them.

It was the one thing that kept him from disowning me – I think. My anger and hatred of the Dawnstones, for it rivaled his own loathing of them.

If we could get through this meeting without coming to blows, I'd count it as a wild success. As much as I hated to be here, and as much as I disagreed with Father about practically everything, I wouldn't want to leave him alone in a room with them.

"Control yourself," Father warned.

I nodded and trained my gaze on the center of the room as anger continued to simmer beneath my skin.

They were the ones who had murdered Max three years ago. Any trace that Aurum had ordered the murder was erased, but

I knew he carried the blood on his hands. Justice was never served, and Father forbade me from retaliating, lest our violence decrease our favor with the illustrious House Uriel, the most prestigious house in Tenebris.

There were quiet murmurings as Lucius Uriel himself entered the chamber. His golden feathered wings fanned elegantly behind him. He wore clothes specially designed to put them on display. As the most powerful soul in Tenebris, save for the king, he had no qualms about flaunting the obvious tie to the magic in his blood.

My gut twisted.

Lucius took the floor in the middle of the chamber as silence fell. He began his address, the deep tenor of his voice echoing in the chamber. "My trusted friends. Tonight, we gather to discuss the latest affront to our liberty."

As he spoke, he looked everyone in the eyes. His brow pinched, but the set of his jaw revealed his determination.

"King Blackwood has seized a shipment of magical remedies, destined for the poorest citizens of Tenebris. The cargo was burned."

Cries of shock and outrage filled the chamber, bouncing off one another, amplifying the indignation. My face paled. The Blackwoods had crossed a line.

Lucius gestured for silence, and the Forum stilled.

"It is a dark day when we can no longer trust those who are meant to protect us. That is why I come to you, my brethren, to decide what must be done in light of this latest offense."

The air grew thick with tension. Lucius waited calmly in the center of the room, hands clasped behind his back. A twinge of unease raced through me. This was serious. So why weren't all the houses who comprised the Forum here?

Lord Dawnstone stood, and my father tensed beside me.

"We have tried to negotiate with the Blackwoods in the past, but they continue to turn a blind eye to our plight. They refuse to hear us or see reason. They are sworn to protect their kingdom, their citizens, but our realm falls into decay with each passing day. Our people are dying. Who will save them, if not us?"

"Hear! Hear!" boomed the lord sitting next to him – Lord Sunbarrow.

Father got to his feet and addressed Lucius directly. "I will be the one to say it. We must depose the Blackwoods. We must end their reign."

A stunned, contemplative silence filled the chamber.

"And who will take their place?" Lord Sunbarrow asked, breaking the stillness. "You, Magnus?"

Father shook his head. "No. The Forum will rule as one, as we have these many years."

Quiet murmurings filled the chamber again, weighing the notion.

My heart thrummed loudly in my ears. What they, my father, suggested was treason. And the Blackwoods had been known to snuff out any hint of rebellion with swift vengeance.

Lord Dawnstone broke through the conversation. "It may behoove us to enact a Proclamation of Supremacy to help us navigate these murky waters."

I felt the weight of the room's vacant seats. Anyone who might have disagreed with this move, or sympathized with the Blackwoods, was missing.

"All in favor?" Lord Sunbarrow asked.

Hands rose around me on all sides.

Lord Dawnstone wasn't finished. "The mortal king already lends a favorable ear to Lord Uriel. Until now, we have been successful in our efforts to redistribute magic to the folk of Tenebris. Now that the king is no longer satisfied with turning a blind eye to our imports from the north, we must negotiate with him. I know of no other more equipped to advocate for us than Lord Uriel."

He paused and turned to address Lucius directly. "Lucius. You're the only one who can do this." There was a tense pause before Lord Dawnstone continued. "I motion to proclaim Lord Lucius Uriel as Primus."

Murmurs broke out amidst the assembled, but a voice on my right cut through all the rest.

"I second the motion."

Of course, Father would be the one to second. I was surprised he hadn't thought to start the motion himself.

"All in favor?" asked Lord Sunbarrow.

Again, all hands went up.

Lucius placed a hand on his heart and gave a quick bow, wings shimmering in the gloom. "You honor me, friends. Your trust is well-placed. I pledge to see this tyranny ended, and to restore our honor. Let us dwell no more in darkness. Let magic flourish once more."

My breath caught in my chest as everyone in the room placed a fist over their chest, saluting the new Primus. Could one person convince King Blackwood to lift the ban on magic, one that had been upheld for two hundred years?

The members of the Forum exited the sunken chamber one by one. I fingered my dagger as the Dawnstones swept from the room, trailing behind Lucius.

I followed Father and Horatio, the sound of my steps in the marble chamber echoing one thought. I wasn't so naive to think this was the only motive for the houses in attendance today. What would Father gain from these negotiations? He made all our money collecting black-market fees. It didn't make sense. The tightness in my stomach lingered. Even though the Forum sought to make magic free again, I couldn't help but feel uneasy. Surely, everyone in Tenebris would benefit once the Blackwoods agreed to lift the ban.

We emerged from the sunken chamber into pale twilight. Lavender and pink clouds streaked through the sky, and a cool breeze tinged with salty sea air blew through the open columns of the temple. Melancholy pulled at my heart. Max would know what to make of all this. Hells, Father probably would have confided all his plans with him already. As for me, I was lucky to be invited along.

I took a deep breath, letting the warm air fill my lungs. It would be dark soon. My grief dulled as anticipation swelled in its place. Tomorrow I would return to the House of Night. I climbed into our carriage, unbothered by Horatio's sneer and my father's pointed disregard for my company as I turned my thoughts away from rebellion toward much sweeter fare.

Chapter Ten

Sorsha

"You conniving bitch!" Viviana shrieked as she threw open the back door.

I stood and brushed the soil from my hands. I had been enjoying a quiet afternoon in the kitchen garden. Thoughts of Lord Stormfall – Corvus – had kept me awake for most of the night. No amount of tossing and turning, covering my eyes to block out the midday sun, or stretching had calmed my racing mind. He had been so close to kissing me. I played the words over and over as a strange heat bloomed from my chest into my stomach.

When I kiss you, I want you to want it just as much as I do.

I couldn't believe how conceited he was.

The sound of Viviana's shriek, and the loud bang of the door as it crashed against the wall, turned my thoughts cold.

She stood before me, breathing heavily as she squeezed her hands into fists. Pink splotches bloomed on her cheeks. "*Three thousand dinar?*"

"What are you talking about?" My voice came out small and weak. I hated it.

"Lord Stormfall is paying three thousand dinar for you? A *month?* What are you trying to do to me?"

Seven hells. I licked my bottom lip and bent down to collect my pruning shears and basket of herbs. My pulse quickened. I wouldn't let Viviana see me rattled, though. "Is that a lot?" Playing dumb sometimes freed me from her torment.

"Is that a lot?" she mimicked. "You sniveling whore, you

know it's a lot of money."

"The only whore here is you," I snapped. I immediately regretted it, but I was so fed up with her talking down to me at every chance she got. And now, it seemed, I had some power to wield. She wouldn't have come barging into the garden if she didn't feel threatened.

Viviana's mouth fell open, though her eyes narrowed in suspicion. Her fingers twitched. "How *dare* you? What the hell did you even do last night?"

I stood and clutched the basket, letting the wicker dig into my palms. "I don't think that's any of your business."

"I don't know what you think you're doing," she hissed through clenched teeth. "But you'll never be better than me. You're *nobody*."

When I didn't offer a retort, she turned on her heel and stormed back into the house, shrieking for Tilly. I heard another distant bang, and then quiet.

The anger in my chest remained, but a smug sort of satisfaction accompanied it.

"Sorsha?" Ivy stood in the doorway, her apron coated in flour. The little white flowers and dark green leaves that grew from her skin swayed in the gentle afternoon breeze. "Andromeda wants to see you. Her Royal Highness was supposed to tell you, but I gather it slipped her mind."

I gave Ivy a weak smile. She had no love for Viviana, either.

"Okay." Apprehension clawed through my giddiness, sinking like a rock in my stomach. Blood rushed in my ears as I collected the rest of my things and went inside to wash up.

Upstairs, voices seeped through the closed office door. A male's, deep and agitated, and Andromeda's placating tones. I paused, my hand poised to knock. Instead of announcing my presence, I leaned my ear to the door.

I closed my eyes and concentrated, trying my best to make out what the muffled voices said.

"Again, you have my most sincere apologies," crooned Andromeda.

Another unhappy customer, then. She'd been getting more complaints than usual the past few months.

I pressed my ear to the door a little harder.

"I have never had an unpleasant experience here before, Madam. I trust it will not happen again," he snapped.

"We are working on a solution. You know the challenges better than most. For your trouble, your next visit will be free of charge."

My mouth dropped. Andromeda gave nothing away for free. Chairs scraped against the floor, accompanied by the rustling of fabric. I pushed myself back from the door. For good measure, I tiptoed back down the hall a few paces, then breezed toward the door again like I had just arrived.

I knocked smartly and waited.

The door opened, revealing a tall fae with pointed teeth. He wore a fine velvet doublet and carried a polished walking stick with a handle that glinted with inlaid gems. I stepped aside and kept my gaze trained on the floor as he passed, thankful I had put on my mask before coming upstairs. Clients were never supposed to see our faces. It was all part of the allure and drama of the house. Once, Andromeda had taken a switch to the back of my legs for coming downstairs without one.

The patron swept past without a second glance, and marched down the hall, his walking stick thumping on the plush carpet as he went.

"Come in, Sorsha."

Andromeda seemed as cool and unbothered as ever. Her usual pens and ledgers were stowed away, her desk pristinely clean. "Shut the door."

I obeyed.

"From your eavesdropping, I assume you heard our latest complaint?"

I nodded. I should have known she'd catch me listening. Although, given our current arrangement, I should have known that she'd wanted me to hear.

"The information you seek is critical. Things cannot stay the way they are."

My head began to throb. A slight ache beneath my temple. I sighed.

Andromeda's eyebrows raised.

I reined in my weariness and dipped my chin submissively. "My goal is to establish good rapport with Lord Stormfall. I will ask him questions as he grows more comfortable with me. He assured me he would return within a few days."

Madam Andromeda flicked an invisible speck of dust from her desk. "Males are so predictable," she muttered to herself. She met my gaze. "Very well. Use your time to prepare for Lord Stormfall's visit tomorrow. Entice him. Build this *rapport* and get me some answers."

"Tomorrow?"

She reached into her dress pocket and handed me a dark blue envelope.

I broke the seal and read the short missive.

Darling Sorsha,

I should very much like to see you again tomorrow evening. Nine o'clock. Perhaps this time you'll beat me at cards, though I doubt it.

Yours,
Corvus

Insufferable. I was more determined than ever to beat him now. I snapped my head up and crushed the note to my chest, wondering how she'd known what it said.

CHAPTER ELEVEN

CORVUS

The carriage bounced and swayed as we made our way to the city's southernmost border under the bright mid-morning sun. Horatio shot another irritated glance my way as I shifted in my seat. He probably hoped I wouldn't rouse myself in time to join them. But my behavior at the Forum yesterday had proved satisfactory, and Father had agreed to let me tag along to his next meeting at the Sunbarrow estate.

It took an hour by carriage to reach the Sunbarrow's manor here in the city. Each house kept a residence in the capital, eliminating the tedious travel when the Forum was in session during the summer and winter. Were we to trek to the Sunbarrow plains, it would take two days.

Stormfalls had always lived in the city. Tenebris and its crystal blue coves and rocky shores were our territory. Before magic had gone and the Blackwoods had established their reign, this had all been ours. Trade flowed in and out of our harbors, and we gained the wealth that went with it. But our house was a shadow of its former self, stained like my wings.

The carriage jerked to a stop outside the warm brown terracotta walls of House Sunbarrow, nestled inside golden gates bearing a blazing sun motif. Lush gardens filled with every bloom imaginable framed the front walk. I trailed behind Horatio and my father as they marched up the sandy path to the front doors.

A footman with hair of stalks of golden barley, bade us welcome and escorted us to a private study on the second floor.

Stained glass windows depicting fields of wheat and brilliant blue skies let in filtered light. The room smelled of dark amber liquor and beer. The Sunbarrows were well known for their brews and supplied nearly all the taverns in the city with their drink.

Elias Sunbarrow and Lucius Uriel sat around a long oak table, with the newly appointed Primus at the head. His golden wings fanned out behind him, catching the light. Lucius's eyes flicked to mine for a moment, a tiny frown of displeasure creasing his chiseled features before he adopted an amiable smile, flashing too-white teeth at my father.

Elias was not so tactful. "You brought the boy? I thought we agreed this would be a closed meeting."

A tiny glimmer of hope, a wish from my childhood, flickered, even as I bristled at being called "boy."

Please let him stand up for me. Claim me. Be proud of me.

Hard as I tried to eliminate those foolish wishes, they had a nasty habit of creeping back when I least wanted them. I kept my features cool and disinterested as I waited for my father to reply, snuffing out those hopes before they had a chance to ignite.

"For all his many faults, he is still the Stormfall heir. If he becomes a problem, I will deal with him. Harshly." He pulled a chair back from the table and took a seat on Lucius's left side.

I strolled to the end of the table and flopped down in the seat across from Lucius as my stomach pitched. I contemplated cleaning my nails but thought that might be pushing it a bit too far. Instead, I flashed a lazy smile at the men assembled, crossing an ankle over my knee.

Elias Sunbarrow's brown skin flushed in irritation while Lucius narrowed his eyes, as if he did not quite buy the act.

"So, what are we drinking?" I asked.

The hardness left his gaze. It took so little to play into their expectations. So very little.

Father's shoulders tensed, but he ignored the comment. "To business," he said, tapping the table.

"I admit, I was surprised to receive your request to meet," Lucius said smoothly. "It must be of significant importance if the matter could not be sent by missive."

Elias regained control of his temper, letting his breath go in a *whoosh*. "Not all correspondence is secure. We are concerned about Malachite."

"And before you ask," Father added, "this is not some resurgence of past grudges between House Stormfall and Dawnstone. We would not waste your time with such trivial matters."

"Certainly." Lucius nodded his head gravely.

Elias continued. "Reports have reached us that Malachite has been meeting with Tyrin Blackwood. We are concerned he will jeopardize our attempts to negotiate with the royals."

I kept a look of boredom on my face. It was easy to read my father's and Lord Sunbarrow's play here. Malachite Dawnstone was competition. Lucius favored him over our house, but it was exceptionally bold for them to whisper secrets of betrayal and sow discontent between them. Lucius would see straight through their viper's tricks. Unless they had a very convincing argument, or proof, they stood to risk all favor they had. Unease curled around my stomach.

Father gestured to Horatio, who reached into his dark blue jacket and withdrew a piece of parchment. He handed the letter to Lucius, who accepted it with a furrowed brow. "We intercepted this last week," Father explained.

Lucius scanned the letter. "I see."

I itched to read it myself, but I had purposefully seated

myself as far away from them as possible. I shifted, placing both feet squarely on the ground.

"The Blackwoods cannot remain in power," Father said, the steel of self-righteousness coating his words. "They are choking the life out of Tenebris. If we want any chance to regain what they took from us, to reclaim what is ours, they must be deposed. No bargaining. No concessions. That's what got us into this mess to begin with."

"It is time for the fae to reclaim our rule," Elias added.

"With you as Primus, there will be no limit to what we might achieve. The Blackwood ships in the harbor bode ill, as do the gathering of Grauradurian forces to the north. We need a strong leader to see us through this conflict. Not someone who negotiates with the enemy in secret."

Lucius set the letter on the table in front of him and steepled his fingers. His wings flexed. "I understand your concerns. Truly, I do. I ask that you trust in my judgment in how I approach this matter, and who I employ to convey messages to the king. Change can be disquieting, even if we know the change will be for the better. It is how we weather the seas of uncertainty together, as a united front, that will determine how successful we are in our endeavors." Lucius flicked his gaze to mine once more. I held his stare with disinterest, even as my pulse quickened.

Elias smiled blandly, placated. "Of course. You know best, Primus."

Was I the only one who had recognized the pretty speech as thinly veiled chastisement? Father was on shaky ground, too blinded by his desperation for power and approval that he could not see it. Not that he would ever listen to me if I told him.

Lucius stood, scraping the legs of his chair against the stone floor. "My lords. If that is all, I have another appointment across the city."

We followed suit. Lucius clasped Lord Sunbarrow and my father on the shoulder. "Trust me, my lords. All I need is your trust."

Father nodded, bringing a fist to his chest.

Everyone copied the gesture. I did so too late and halfheartedly. Lucius frowned but left without another word.

We stayed for another quarter hour. I listened to talk about the harvest and a pestilent rot that ravaged the Sunbarrow wheat and barley. I'd hoped they'd speak more of the ships in the harbor, or the mysterious legion to the north. But no, their businesses were more important. I had to swallow down the bile that rose in my throat as I listened to Father suggest ways to increase profits by cutting the wages of laborers, increasing taxes on family land, and hiring children to pick through the threshed wheat. Cold, heartless bastard. It was moments like these where I missed Max's easy way of redirecting Father's miserly machinations with a jovial tone and jest at his own expense.

I made a show of admiring the stained-glass windows while they spoke, Horatio agreeing with everything my father said. I walked around the polished wood table, keeping them in my line of vision. Only when they thought I had grown tired of their talk did they speak of treason.

"A coup is the only answer," said Father.

"Malachite certainly made it seem like it was a possibility." Elias gestured to the note between them.

I found it odd that Lucius hadn't taken it with him. If he wanted to quell their questioning, he should have removed the source of their speculation.

"The king's ridiculous masquerade is next month. If Malachite is planning on striking then, there could be trouble," grumbled my father.

"We'll be ready."

One of my wings brushed against an ornate vase, tipping it. I lunged and caught it before it could fall from its pedestal, but the sudden movement sent a soft gust of wind throughout the chamber.

Those at the table, reminded I was here, lowered their voices to a whisper.

The tips of my ears grew hot. I righted the vase and continued to study the windows as my throat grew tight.

A coup against the royals could be very dangerous, especially if Lucius did not approve of it. He could deliver a fiercer punishment than any mortal king ever could, especially now he was Primus. He could strip titles, banish usurpers from the Fae Forum, exile them.

Father snapped in my direction, signaling our time to depart.

Elias led the way to the door, followed by my father and Horatio. They'd carelessly left Malachite Dawnstone's note on the table. I took the edge of the damning letter with a practiced swipe and tucked it into my jacket pocket.

Back inside the carriage, neither my father nor Horatio uttered a word. Horatio busied himself with scribbling notes. The scratch of his pen, a black-market self-inking indulgence, echoed in the thick silence. Father stared out the window, brows drawn low and eyes as hard as winter storm clouds.

The letter burned in my pocket, begging to be read. I withdrew my dagger and a cloth, desperate for something to do, and set to work polishing my onyx blade.

Once we rattled into the cobblestone courtyard of home, I practically threw myself out of the carriage, ready to lock myself in my quarters and read the letter I'd nicked. Then I'd find Dio at the Golden Lyre and have a mug of ale, or three, as a consolation prize for making myself go to the meeting.

I made it halfway across the courtyard before my father called me back.

"Corvus." My father stood, hands fisted at his sides and a muscle feathering in his jaw. I knew that look. I gritted my teeth and approached, knowing if I delayed, it would only be worse. With a lump in my throat, I stood before my father.

I saw stars before I registered the impact of his fist against my face.

He was fast and strong for his age, despite his generous middle and habit of groaning whenever he rose from a seat.

I breathed heavily through my nose, clenching my teeth against the pain. But I would not show weakness. Not while Horatio watched a half-step behind my father, eyes glittering with sick delight.

I spat into the dust, noting the crimson stain of blood, then straightened to look my father in the eye.

"Embarrass me like that again in front of Lord Uriel, and it will be the last thing you ever do."

He brushed past me, Horatio trailing behind him like the faithful dog he was, leaving me alone in the courtyard.

A detached numbness spread from my chest through my limbs. Father had made good on his promise to Elias and Lucius. Perhaps he wanted the mark visible, a brand of shame on his own son, to show his loyalty.

Once inside my own chambers, I withdrew the note I had stuffed into my pocket.

I have communicated the latest to the king. The pieces are set. The masque will provide an excellent stage.

I folded the letter into a tidy square. My heart sank. I thought there would be more to this note. But it didn't concern me. Father was grasping at straws, trying in vain to climb above the

Dawnstones, as usual. But if Malachite did plan to overthrow the king at his own ball, there could be trouble.

In my bathing chambers, I wet a cloth and held it over my swelling cheekbone as I continued to think, careful to avoid my own reflection in the gilded mirror.

Would it be so bad to overthrow the mortals? They had done nothing to help us. Their stubborn banishment of magic made things worse and worse. I'd seen the effects of magic's absence in the city, especially those in the Shale. Things were growing dire. I shuddered, remembering gaunt and haunted faces.

I tossed the cloth into the basin and grabbed a change of clothes. This was a bigger problem than I needed to worry about. The likelihood of a coup taking place at the biggest party in Tenebris seemed ridiculous, though not impossible. I would attend, and make sure Father didn't get into trouble or do anything foolish. The best-case scenario was that I had a pleasant evening with a certain House of Night courtesan.

The thought of her made my pulse quicken, and I wondered if there was a spell to make time move faster.

Chapter Twelve

Sorsha

I fluffed my silky skirts as a bubble of anticipation swelled in my chest. I studied my reflection, feeling rather pretty. The black dress had a bustle of gathered fabric which spilled into a small train. Satin cap sleeves helped cover the scars that crept up my back. The corset hugged me tightly, thrusting my breasts upward.

I was eager to make progress with Lord Stormfall this evening. For the thousandth time I wondered what my mother had written to me in her letter. Whenever I started to doubt my decision of agreeing to the blood pact, I reminded myself of my prize. Her words and my freedom.

Maybe she would finally tell me who my father was. Whenever I tried to call up some memory of him, of my childhood, I hit a black wall. The accident, whatever had given me these scars, had taken that away, too.

I couldn't remember where the scars had come from. My mother had never let me see them. I'd only ever been able to glimpse the shiny red and white skin. The splotches at the tops of my shoulder blades were easiest to see if I twisted the right way.

Even now, when I had access to a full-length mirror and could look if I wished, something kept me from facing the damage. I didn't want to know how ugly the scars made me. Not when I needed to feel my best.

I turned to my night table and tried to focus on getting dressed while ignoring my thundering heart. I had enjoyed spending time with Lord Stormfall, but Andromeda was right. There was no use for butterflies. He was paying for a service. This was a business arrangement, nothing more.

I tied a black velvet ribbon around my throat and a mask around my eyes. Delicate leaves and blooms were cut out from the stiff fabric, showing more of my face through the gaps than most masks, but still concealing. A small smile tugged at the corners of my mouth. Part of me hated to admit it, especially after years of scoffing at the long hours other courtesans spent primping in mirrors, but I was developing quite a liking for these nice clothes.

I tried to hang on to the feeling as I left my bedroom to wait in the Emerald Parlor for Lord Stormfall to arrive.

As promised, he arrived at precisely nine o'clock. Candlelight cast a warm glow across his features. The soft rustle of his wings sent a shiver down my spine, and my stomach flipped as he shut the polished black door behind him. He crossed the room silently, the lush emerald carpet softening his steps. He placed a light kiss on my hand.

"Darling Sorsha. How lovely to see you again."

"Hello, Lord Stormfall."

His brow pinched. "Listen, when it's just the two of us, I really would prefer if you called me Corvus."

"Very well."

His expression relaxed. I wanted him to trust me, well enough that he wouldn't think twice about sharing sensitive information. But I had to play this just right. I placed my hands on his arm and led him to the green velvet settee. "Well, Corvus, are you ready for me to beat you at cards?"

"I am exceptionally good at this game, you know," he said, settling into the seat, draping his wings over the arm. "It will take more than luck to beat me."

I rolled my eyes. "So confident. I think it's high time someone knocked you off your pedestal." I reached for the bottle of wine and poured two glasses, handing one to him.

He took a hearty swallow. I could see more of his face now that we sat closer to the large candelabras on the table. A dark shadow crept from under the edge of his mask. A bruise.

"Are you alright?" I asked, leaning forward. A crushing wave of embarrassment made my face hot. "I'm sorry," I stammered, as Corvus raised one eyebrow. "I shouldn't pry."

"Actually" – he set down his glass – "do you mind if I take this off?" He tapped the edge of his plain black mask. "It's making it worse, I'm afraid."

My eyes flicked to the door. Everyone knew better than to bother us. I had an aching curiosity to see his face. There was no harm in him removing his mask, as long as I kept mine on. Rules were rules, after all.

"Of course."

With one hand, he pulled the mask free and set it to the side. I swallowed. Concern swept through me like a wave crashing on a rock. A fist-sized bruise, new and blue-black, bloomed on his cheekbone.

He took another swallow of wine, and I did the same, wondering what to say. I finally settled on: "That looks painful."

"I've had worse."

I set my wineglass down on the table. "I have something that will help, if it does pain you."

One side of his mouth quirked up. "Some magical salve, I presume?"

"Just simple herbs. Andromeda makes us pay for any magic we use personally, so we prefer a more mundane approach to scrapes and bruises."

Corvus's face turned serious, his voice steely. "Are scrapes and bruises something that must be treated regularly here?"

I knew what he was asking. There were other establishments in Tenebris that did not treat their staff as well as they should or prevent their customers from becoming too rough with them. On very rare occasions, a client would think himself above the rules, but Andromeda did not tolerate violence. Who would need it when we had a slew of magical delights to indulge in? Offenders were banned from ever returning to the House of Night.

"No, not in that way," I said gently.

His shoulders visibly relaxed.

"Let me take care of it. Please." I did want to help if he'd let me. He had shown me some kindness, and even though I knew he was a paying customer, there was something about him that differed from all the other folk who dropped their gold into Andromeda's coffers. He was conceited and egotistical, to be sure, but there was no real cruelty there.

"Very well. If it will make you feel better. Though I was planning on using it to my advantage," he said, gesturing at the mark, his easy manner of speaking returned. "When your opponent feels sorry for you, they'll let you win. Even if it's subconsciously done."

"And now you've told me your strategy. That's a shame. There goes any morsel of hope you had for winning tonight."

"It depends how you define *winning*," he said, a genuine smile lighting up his handsome face. His voice vibrated pleasantly in my chest, all along my ribs. If he weren't so damned arrogant, it might be attractive. An image of our bodies tangled together, lips meeting and hands frantically pulling at each other's clothes flashed quickly before I snuffed it out.

I laughed, banishing the thought. "Let me get you some salve." I went to the door, feeling the warmth from the wine already hitting my cheeks. I flicked the tiny black bell that hung discreetly next to the doorframe, signaling for service. Tilly knocked four times a moment later. I opened the door a crack, blocking her view of the interior. Her cat-like yellow eyes glowed in the low light.

"Could you fetch some healing salve from Ivy, please? And some shortbread."

Tilly blinked her assent and left to fetch what I had requested. I closed the door, turned back to Corvus, and found him watching me. Without the mask to conceal his face, the intensity of his gaze was startling. His scrutiny made me feel suddenly self-conscious.

I pressed my palms into the soft fabric of my skirt. "What is it?"

"That dress is splendid on you. You look beautiful."

Crossing my arms, I was suddenly very aware of how much of my breasts were visible, aided by the corset. "I suppose I tidy up nicely." It was an odd feeling, being complimented on my appearance while a mask concealed my face.

Corvus leaned forward, his wings adjusting to his new position. "I mean it. You are lovely, Sorsha. And not just because that dress does wonders for your figure. I thought you were stunning the first night I saw you."

A faint blush swept up my neck. Four knocks at the door saved me from replying. I took the gold tray from Tilly, careful to block her view once more, and carried it back to the settee. Sitting next to Corvus, I dipped my fingers into the pot of salve, releasing the sweet scent of lavender and calendula. "Here," I said, leaning forward.

The heady scent of summer rain mixed with the salve, flooding my senses. Gods, he did smell divine. I half expected him to look down the front of my dress as I gently swept my fingers across his cheekbone. But when I slid my gaze toward his, I found his eyes firmly locked on mine. There was some quiet sadness there beneath the thunderous intensity. My breath caught, and my fingers stilled. Sparks jumped through me at our proximity.

I blinked, breaking the moment, and air filled my lungs once more. I was here to do a job. Feelings of physical attraction could not cloud my judgment, or my decisions. I busied myself with wiping the residue from my fingers on a small linen towel. "That will speed up the healing. It won't be gone overnight, but it should feel better tomorrow."

"Thank you."

I offered up the plate of shortbread, determined not to fall back into the trap of his eyes. "Would you like one?"

He grabbed a square, and his lashes fluttered as he took a bite. My chest swelled.

"These are *divine*," he said through a mouthful.

I snapped a piece off a biscuit and placed it on my tongue. Tart lemon burst along it, followed by the savory taste of salted butter and notes of lavender. I couldn't help but smile. They *were* good. "Thanks. I made them."

"You *made* these?" He grabbed another biscuit from the gold platter and popped it into his mouth.

"Mm-hmm. And the salve, too, though that doesn't taste half as nice."

He made a little moaning noise as he swallowed, and a flush of heat spread through my core at the sound.

"When do you have the time?"

"We work at night. The day is our own. I'm allowed in the kitchen if I leave everything where I found it and stay out of the way."

"And when do you sleep?" The corners of his mouth pulled

down. Soft light from the lit candelabras on the table danced shadows across his face.

"I don't sleep much." I brushed my hands of crumbs, painfully aware of the silence that descended. "Shall I beat you at cards now?"

Corvus withdrew the gilded deck of cards from his pocket, and shuffled them between his long, deft fingers, settling back into the plush settee. "Since I've already given away my strategy, I hope you're prepared for my backup plan."

I cocked an eyebrow. "Which is?"

He shook a finger in my direction. "Nice try." He finished shuffling and laid out the cards between us.

"Same rules as last time? A question for a question?"

"No, I think we're ready to up the stakes. The winner of this game may demand a favor." He studied me as mischief danced in his eyes.

I took a deep breath. Whatever it was, I had to be prepared to give it to him. But if I won, I might get the information I wanted.

"For a favor, then." I examined the field of play and my hand, and I felt a glow of triumph. It looked like I would be the first to make demands. I played my card, and Corvus drew from the deck.

"I'm surprised you came back," I said. A little vulnerability could go a long way. If I shared a fraction of my mind with him, he might do the same for me.

He cocked his head as he studied his cards. "You think me as fickle as that?" He placed an eight of cups on the pile closest to him.

I shrugged. "We met only a few nights ago. I don't know you at all."

"You know my favorite color, season, food, how I spend my

leisure time," he countered.

"I don't think you mentioned that last one."

"Reading. Training. Sharing drinks with a friend if I'm feeling social."

"It's a start," I conceded, and placed a red seven of scepters atop his card. Then, I placed another card on the opposite corner pile. "I thought that maybe once you spent time with me, you'd find me boring. Or take issue with the fact that I'm half-fae." My stomach squeezed, bracing for his reaction.

"Why should that matter?"

I arched an eyebrow. "It matters to some. Enough that they should demand their money back when they find out."

He shook his head. "That is, frankly, disgusting."

The painful memories that threatened to surface were quieted by his words. It was a relief to know my lineage did not bother him.

"And to your other point, you do not bore me," he continued.

I rolled my eyes. "I'm sure you say that to all the girls."

The corner of his mouth quirked upward as he placed another card down. "I don't waste my time with folk who don't amuse me, female or male."

My cheeks turned hot. "Sorry, I shouldn't have assumed."

"Don't worry about it."

I drew a card, and silence bloomed between us. He didn't seem upset, but I hoped I hadn't offended him.

"And you? You're particular to the company of men?" he asked.

I'd started this conversation intending to be honest, but this was quickly getting into highly vulnerable territory. Shockingly, I didn't seem to mind. It was foolish, trusting him so much, but I couldn't help it.

"I've never had much time to think about it." I would not

admit that I'd once had a horrible crush on Ferdie when I first started working here, but it quickly dissolved once I realized he only enjoyed relationships with males. And there was something rather magnetic about the sounds the girls made behind closed doors, but I'd never given my preferences any serious thought. My job was to pleasure others, after all. My own satisfaction mattered little. The heat from my cheeks moved down my neck as I drew another card.

"Well, perhaps you can explore what you like."

I made a noncommittal noise in my throat. That was plenty of honesty on my part for one night. Andromeda would expect some sort of information by the end of the evening, and I don't think she had any interest in a history of Corvus's lovers, or my uncertain sexual preferences.

"Tell me what you think of this place. Truly," I said, anxious to move the conversation away from intimate conquests.

Corvus studied the cards in his hand. "I think it is a terrible waste of resources, and all too gratifying for the esteemed citizens of Tenebris who ought to be spending their time in other ways." He placed his card.

I bit my bottom lip. *He* was a lord of Tenebris who spent an incredible amount of money to be in my company. If he didn't care for the House of Night, then why was he here? I could not beat his card in play, so I drew from the deck. A breeze wafted through the open windows, making the gauzy curtains dance.

"Oh? And what ways would those be? Restoring magic?"

His eyes flicked up for a moment, and I saw the briefest shadow pass across his face.

"Among other things, yes."

"And yet, you are here."

He leaned forward as his eyes darkened. "I find myself unable to stay away, and my defenses are weakening by the minute."

My heart pounded in my chest and my lips tingled.

He reached his long fingers toward the table and plucked up another piece of shortbread. He popped it into his mouth and hummed in satisfaction. "For instance, I won't be able to stop dreaming of these shortbreads. They are divine. Start expecting me nightly, Miss Sorsha, so I may get my fill of them."

I laughed, and we played a few more turns as my heart continued to thump in my chest. After a few minutes, I had three cards remaining, but Corvus dashed my hopes of winning.

"My lady, I believe I've won." He played his winning hand.

I scowled, wishing I could wipe the stupid smile off his face. Tossing my cards down, I admitted defeat. "What is it you want?"

He laughed and scooped up the cards. "You're quite a sore loser. I want you to come sit over here."

We'd sat on opposite ends of the settee to make room for our game. Now the cards were gone, a significant expanse lay between us.

He removed his evening jacket, unbuttoning clever panels that made it easy for him to wear it around his wings, and rolled up his sleeves. I jerked back. He wore a belt strapped across his chest, which held two sheaths. I glimpsed the handles of two daggers. The pommels were inlaid with two stones, one a deep shining blue edged with dark veins, the other wholly black. It was against the rules to bring weapons into the parlors.

He saw me recoil at the sight of them and immediately turned sheepish. "Sorry. I keep them with me wherever I go." Corvus unbuckled the bandolier and set it on the table. "Better?" he asked and rested his back against the arm of the settee, turning his body toward me. One wing draped over the back of the low couch, the other cascaded to the floor, perfectly relaxed.

I nodded and scooted closer, sitting in the center of the

couch.

"I promise I won't ravish you, darling. Come, sit next to me."

I cocked an eyebrow. "This is the favor you demand?"

He splayed his hands defensively. "It was that or demand a lifetime supply of shortbread. I thought you might appreciate this more."

I slid the rest of the way across the seat, brushing my knee against his as I settled into the cushion. "Better?"

"Much."

He peered at my face, searching for something.

I rubbed my hands together, uncomfortable at the intensity.

"Have we met before?" he asked.

"I'm fairly certain I would remember you," I said. Who could forget his arrogant smile or his imposing feathered wings?

"You're right. But I can't help feel as if I have known you a long time. There is something about you that is so… familiar. I'm not sure how to describe it." He laughed to himself. "That probably sounds absurd."

"No," I said. "Not absurd. A bit fantastical, maybe, but not absurd."

I refreshed our wine glasses. My hand brushed his belt of weapons on the table, recapturing my attention.

"May I see one of those?"

He withdrew the black stone dagger and flipped it, catching the point. He handed it to me with gentle reverence.

"Do you have any occasion to use such a thing?" I asked, running my hands over the handle. It was heavier than I expected. The black stone at the hilt was darker than a pool of ink, reminding me of my new hairpin from Andromeda. Only this gem seemed to be made of something darker than night, as no light reflected off its surface.

Looking into it made something deep within me stir with unease, like the latch on a box long kept shut had been unlocked, ready to be pried open. The longer I held the dagger, the stranger I felt. My fingers prickled against the cold metal handle. It didn't hurt, but it felt like bees were crawling over my hands, burrowing into my skin, vibrating between my bones and flesh and some dark, secret well within me.

Corvus wrapped his hands around mine, gently taking the weapon from me. "Only as a last resort."

The humming feeling stopped as soon as the dagger left my hands. Was it magic? Spelled somehow? Corvus held the blade nonchalantly. If he felt the strange vibrations from the weapon, he did not let on. "You don't like me touching your things?" I teased.

A wry smile danced on his lips. "Perhaps you have already forgotten the first night we met. I thought you were going to drive that spoon through that poor girl's eye. I'd hate to see what you would do with this." His smile fell slightly, and the light in his eyes dimmed a fraction. "This one is part of a pair. The other belonged to my brother."

He sheathed the dagger back into his belt, resting it alongside its twin, the one inlaid with a glimmering blue stone.

Belonged.

The sudden sadness that washed over Corvus was palpable.

I changed the subject, unsure of what to say in the face of such grief. "I would like to learn how to use a dagger. Andromeda expects us to always be sweet, to distract and delay when confronted with unpleasantness. But it would be nice to know how to defend myself if the occasion ever called for it."

"Perhaps I can teach you," he said, his tone lightening once more.

"I'd like that." I smiled up at him. My eyes flicked to his

mouth, and the sudden memory of the other night made my stomach pool with warmth.

When I kiss you, I want you to want it just as much as I do.

He brushed an escaped curl away from my face, his fingers barely grazing my cheek.

My heart thudded almost painfully, its pace increasing with the contact. I forced myself to sit back, breaking the tension between us. I would not be so easily taken in by his tricks.

You have a job to do, I reminded myself.

"Well, it is getting rather late," I said, setting down my wineglass with a soft *clink*. It was barely midnight. But I had learned a few things over the years. One of them was to keep clients wanting more, to ensure they came back.

His eyes crinkled at the corners, and his chest jerked as if suppressing a laugh. "You're right. May I kiss you goodnight?" He bent toward me until our noses almost touched.

He could most definitely hear my heartbeat. "Yes," I whispered.

Corvus took my hand. The touch of his skin felt like sparkling sunlight, soft and warm. He brought my hand to his mouth and brushed his lips softly against the backs of my fingers. That soft feeling turned into the sharp crackle of lightning, and a warm rush filled my stomach and chest.

"Goodnight," he said, then stood, reaching for his jacket.

Oh, no. He would not repeat the same trick as last time.

It was a good thing my body reacted so strongly to his. It made what I had to do much easier, even if he was an entitled, arrogant prick.

I got to my feet and gazed up at him, not bothering to hide my attraction. "Corvus?"

He froze. The teasing smile vanished as mild incredulity wrinkled his brow.

I took the jacket from his hands and let the fine material slide through my fingers. Something crinkled in one of the pockets. I dropped the jacket back onto the couch. Taking a step, I narrowed the space between us. "I want you to kiss me." I placed a hand on his chest, letting the heat of him sear through to my palm. "Please."

He trailed his fingers lightly along my jaw, stopping at my chin. He tilted my face up slightly and brought his mouth down to mine.

I closed my eyes, anticipation thrumming through my entire body, threatening to sway me from my true intentions.

"Not yet, darling," he whispered. The soft puff of air against my mouth only made the craving for his touch worsen.

My eyes flew open, shocked he would refuse.

He brushed the backs of his fingers along my cheek, stopping at the bottom of my mask before withdrawing and leaving me speechless.

It was downright maddening.

"Goodnight, Sorsha," he said. He kissed the back of my hand once more, then stepped away.

He reached for his belt and strapped it on.

I picked up his jacket and wordlessly held it out for him. He slipped into it, then turned to face me.

"I'll be back tomorrow night."

I felt like a spring, too tightly wound. "So soon? You weren't jesting. I'll have to make a double batch of shortbread," I said with a levity that did not betray the tension coiled within me.

"How else will I be satisfied? I'll surely dream of the taste of them tonight."

I knew he wasn't talking about baked goods. I rolled my eyes, despite the fluttering in my stomach.

"I'll see you soon, then."

"Yes. And do wear pants," he said, striding to the door.

"Whatever for?" I called after him.

"I don't doubt you could learn to wield daggers in that splendid dress of yours, but pants will make it much easier."

He shut the door, leaving me alone in the parlor once more. It wasn't until he'd gone that I realized my cheeks were aching from smiling.

Seven hells.

Andromeda had warned me not to get my heart involved, but she'd said nothing about satisfying my own physical desires. There was no way I could fall for such an egotistical jerk, anyway. I had nothing to worry about. But I absolutely wanted to kiss him. And maybe more.

After such a pleasant evening, it wasn't without some guilt that I examined the note I'd stolen out of his jacket pocket.

I have communicated the latest to the king. The pieces are set. The masque will provide an excellent stage.

I refolded the missive, tucking it safely into my bodice, and gathered up our empty glasses. My thoughts rushed over the words like a stream over river stones.

I should be elated I'd found such information so quickly. I was one step closer to earning my way to freedom, and my mother's letter.

So why did my chest feel so heavy?

Chapter Thirteen

Corvus

Back home, my best friend waited for me in the study. The candlelight glinted off his silver hair, almost spectral in its glow. His ice-chip blue eyes danced with mirth and a hunger for trouble. He sat in my favorite reading chair, one leg thrown over the arm, a half-empty glass dangling from his fingers. "Corv," he cried. "Where have you been?"

My lips quirked in a half smile. Dio had no trouble making himself at home and helping himself to my liquor.

"Sorry," I said. I crossed the room and poured myself a drink. I took a hearty swallow, hoping the burn would chase away my smoldering desire. "I was occupied this evening."

"I mean, where have you been all *week*? I've hardly seen you," he pouted.

"At the House of Night."

"You've been at that witch's brothel *every night*?"

"She's not a witch."

"She might as well be. She's the only one with all that magic," he said with a hint of bitterness. "Anyway, you're deflecting. Why have you been spending time there when you could have been with me? Or Mira?"

I took another gulp of liquor, and my mind turned easily to Sorsha. "I met someone."

"What?"

"Her name's Sorsha."

"Shit, she must be great in bed if you've been there every night."

"We haven't slept together."

Dio swung his legs around, sitting upright. "You haven't even had sex with her?"

I shook my head.

"Holy fucking seven hells. Are you in *love* with her? A girl I haven't even *met* yet?"

I drained the rest of my glass. My heart pounded in my chest. Thinking of her, of her tantalizing scent, her smile, made me want to go back to the house and ravish her immediately. I wanted her. But that didn't mean I loved her.

Dio plowed through my silence. "Mira is going to be furious."

I ran a hand through my hair and grimaced. I hadn't even thought of Mira, the girl I had been casually seeing for half a year. "Yeah, well, it happens. I'll break it to her gently. It's not like we were serious."

"No, but she *seriously* has a thing for you."

"Next time I see her, I'll tell her we're done."

"Please make sure I am there to witness it. In fact, why don't we head there now?" He gripped one arm of the chair, ready to bolt for the door at the slightest possible hint of my agreement.

It would be the right thing to do. I rubbed my eyes, dreading the thought of hurting her feelings.

Dio rested his forearms on his knees. "Come on, Corv, a night out will do you good. No offense, but you look like you need it. Especially if you haven't even slept with your new paramour."

"Do I look that bad?" I winced. The last few days had taken their toll. Between the gathering of the Forum, the meeting at the Sunbarrow's, my time with Sorsha, and impending visits to the Shale to collect more money for my father, I'd gotten little rest.

Dio leaned in closer. "You know I'd oblige myself, but since you've apparently fallen in love…" He brushed his fingertips lightly against my jaw. It'd been a long time since we'd shared a bed, but Dio was the sort to be affectionate, even after breaking it off. "Please?" he begged.

I groaned but gave in. "*One* drink, I break up with Mira, then I am coming back home, you hear? No putting slugs in anyone's ale tonight."

Dio released the arms of my chair and grinned, his slightly pointed canines flashing. "Oh, please. Slugs are so juvenile. I was thinking more like stealing another's conquest right from under his nose. Maybe having a little fun with her on the bar for everyone to see."

"If you're planning to do that, then I am *definitely* not coming out tonight. I don't feel like rescuing your sorry ass when someone's chasing after you with a blade."

Dio waved a dismissive hand. "Fine, I'll fuck her in a closet. Nice and dark and secret. Deal?"

"I mean it. I'm not getting in any fights tonight. Even though you're the one who starts them all."

"On my honor as your friend, I will use all the discretion I can muster."

It wasn't an ironclad promise, but it was the best I could expect. I pushed myself out of my chair and grabbed my bandolier.

Dio clapped me on the shoulder and steered me out the door.

The Golden Lyre buzzed with activity. The establishment was anything but golden and beautiful, as the name suggested, but the ale was cheap. Dio kicked two of his upstart relatives out of our usual table while I went to fetch our drinks. Drunken fae and mortals alike talked loudly over the fiddlers and drummers who played a cheery tune. The music filled the room, bouncing off the ceiling's exposed wooden beams. I drank the foam from the top of both pewter mugs before making my way across the creaking wooden floor to Dio. Most folk sidestepped out of my way, clearing a wide path for me. Those who were not so quick were yanked out of the way. No one wanted to associate with the fae with charcoal wings.

Dio's kin gathered around him, asking what he had planned for the evening. For one who got into as much trouble as he did, no one held it against him for too long, especially not other Frostgroves. They cleared out quickly as I set our mugs on the table, leaving us be.

He grabbed the ale and gulped it down. He needed very little liquid encouragement, and his eyes already danced with cool fire, looking for his fun. Meanwhile, I sipped from my own tankard and scanned the room, keeping an eye out for a different sort of trouble.

My hand clenched around the handle of my drink as I spotted the distinct golden hair of a Dawnstone fae, but I couldn't see his face. His companions jostled him around, revealing the crest emblazoned on the back of his leather vest. It was insufferably pompous the way they branded nearly every article of clothing they wore with their house symbol.

I lifted a finger, about to point him out to Dio, when I felt a hand stroke my right wing, sending a rush of warmth through me. Only one person would dare touch me like that.

"Hello, Mira," I said, my voice low and gravelly.

She sat down next to me and placed a finger under my chin, tilting my face toward hers. Her green eyes flashed, and her dark red hair spilled down her shoulders. "Corvus. Where have you been? You know I miss you when you've been gone too long."

"My apologies." I drained my ale in four gulps and wiped my mouth. "I'm here now. Shall we?"

She grabbed my hand and pulled me along behind her toward the stairs. I pointed a finger at Dio as I let her drag me away. "Behave yourself."

He only waved, a sly smile showing his pointed teeth.

I hadn't had the chance to warn him about the Dawnstones. Hopefully, he'd steer well clear of them tonight.

Mira's suite was small, yet comfortable. Gauzy curtains danced in the breeze from her open window, and candelabras cast long shadows up the walls. She reached for me, ready to pull me on top of her like usual, but I stepped back.

"What's the matter?"

"Mira..." I cleared my throat, unsure of how to proceed.

She folded her arms and frowned. "Save it. I know that look."

I opened my mouth, ready to placate her, but she cut me off. "And, yes, I know it's not me. It's you." She marched to the door and held it open.

I made no move to leave. "I don't think it would be fair to stop seeing you without saying anything about it. You'd hate me if I cut off all contact. Or if you saw me downstairs, and I'd never broken it off officially."

She sighed, weariness creasing her brow. "You're right. I appreciate you telling me in person." Her eyes flicked to the bed, and one corner of her mouth twitched up in a bittersweet smile. "We had fun together."

"We did."

Her smile faded. "Goodbye, Corvus." She leaned against the doorframe, waiting for me to leave.

"Goodbye."

Without a backward glance, I closed her door and headed down the hall. The tightness in my chest eased now that the unpleasant task was behind me. Our relationship, if you could call it that, had been casual. I knew she saw others, and I hadn't minded. I didn't feel a true connection with her. And from the way she'd just dismissed me, I wondered if Dio had been exaggerating her wanting to see me again.

As I descended the stairs, my thoughts were interrupted by the telltale sounds of scuffling. Chairs scraped against the floor, the music petered out, and voices were loud. It wasn't yet a full-out brawl, but folk were clearing out, not wanting to be caught up in whatever violence was about to ensue.

I found Dio chest to chest with the Dawnstone prick. My fists clenched as I approached; my wings flexed impulsively. The remaining spectators pressed up against the walls and bar, clearing the way. My fury threatened to cloud my vision, but I tapped into the clarity that years of training had taught me, ready to defend or attack.

Overwhelming fear twisted my stomach into knots. Flashes of the night everything went horribly wrong shot through me, but I couldn't think about that now. Dio was in over his head. The Dawnstones were a bloodthirsty, ruthless lot. I didn't recognize this one. He hadn't been there that night two years ago. But it didn't mean his hands were clean. All of them were guilty. Every single one of them.

"The lady made her choice, sir. It's not my fault you can't keep her satisfied," said Dio. He smirked, cool fire dancing in his eyes.

"I ought to slit your throat for your insults," the Dawnstone said.

My first instinct was to draw my dagger and plunge it into

his back, but I knew that would only cause another surge of violence between our houses. Instead, I grabbed Dio by the shoulder and pushed him back a few inches. I reached into my pocket for another small bag of gold. "Sorry for the trouble," I said through clenched teeth. I thrust the bag into his chest.

The Dawnstone tossed the bag of coins on the ground and spat on it. "I don't need your filthy Stormfall gold."

I itched to bend down and pick up the money. There were better uses for it than bribing a Dawnstone. But that would be stupid. The most important thing was to get out of here in one piece. "Dio, we're going."

"Aw, but I was just getting started." He laughed, almost maniacally, drunk on his own daring and thirst for danger. His gaze fixed on the source of the feud, a woman who looked like she wanted nothing more than to disappear.

I gripped the back of his neck, shaking him, forcing him to look at me. Something in my expression jolted him from his mania. His pupils shrank back to a reasonable size as he blinked a few times. "We're going," I said again.

"Fine, fine. Didn't know it was so close to your bedtime. He gets so unreasonably cranky," he said over my shoulder.

A sudden rush of movement behind me made instinct take over. I tucked my useless wings in close and whirled, withdrawing my dagger in one fluid motion.

A sickening crack of flesh and bone rent the air. Blood poured out of Dio's now crooked nose. The golden-haired fae shook out his hand. "That'll teach you. Get out of here before I break more than your face."

Dio stumbled, one hand covering his gushing nose. I caught him, helping him stay on his feet. "Leave it," I said in his ear, even though every muscle, every fiber, screamed at me to plunge my dagger into the soft flesh of the male behind me. I had every right to kill him. Blood had been spilled, and my mind screamed for vengeance. I clutched the hilt of my weapon, trying to shake my bloodlust.

A clatter of steel and shouting near the entrance snapped my attention away from the Dawnstone. Soldiers in purple and black, armed to the teeth, swarmed into the tavern. The air crackled with tension. There was no love here for the Blackwood soldiers.

"Nobody leaves until we've conducted our search!" shouted the guard in front, a portly man with a black mustache. He gave orders to his men as panicked patrons pushed toward the side door, desperate to escape the raid.

I clenched my jaw. Fucking royals. This was the third raid this month. Father was right, they were cracking down, desperate to root out any illegal magic. I tucked my wings tightly to my sides and grabbed Dio's shoulder as we were swept out the door with the crowd.

We stumbled out of the Golden Lyre into the warm summer evening. Folk ran in all directions, skirting around the tavern. There was no magic here, but no one wanted to be hauled away for further questioning. We didn't speak as we joined them, hurtling into darkened alleyways. Blood continued to gush from Dio's face, leaving a trail on the cobblestones. I didn't sheath my dagger until we reached home.

"Sorry, Corv," Dio said, his voice thick as we approached the tall iron gates.

I let us in the back, not bothering to take a taper to light our way. We shuffled to my rooms in the dark. Only once the door to my chambers was closed did I dare speak, keeping my voice low. "You can sleep here tonight. I don't have anything for the break, though."

Dio let himself into my bathing chamber. It wasn't the first time he'd cleaned himself up after a night out, nor would it be the last. I rubbed my eyes with the heels of my hands, exhausted. I took off my boots and flopped down onto my bed. Dio tossed something onto my chest. The bag of gold I'd tried to pay off the Dawnstone with.

"Wouldn't want that to go to waste," Dio said as he took the low sofa in the corner.

I picked up the bag of gold, now splotched with blood, and tossed it onto my side table. I dropped into sleep, where my dreams turned to nightmares of blood-soaked hands and white wings stained crimson.

Chapter Fourteen

Corvus

The pants were going to be my undoing.

Sorsha had followed my instructions and worn tight-fitting pants, a loose shirt with billowing sleeves, and some half-belt, half-corset contraption that made her look godsdamned gorgeous. The pants hugged the generous curve of her ass, accentuating her very tempting figure, as she led the way through the garden gate.

A half-moon hung in the dark blue summer sky, illuminating the gravel path. We walked toward the glen I had selected for our training grounds, not too far off the road but surrounded by thick enough tree cover to give us some privacy.

It took a small amount of convincing to get her to agree to leave the bounds of the house. When I explained we couldn't throw daggers inside the very fine parlors, she'd bitten her lip and rubbed her thumb and forefinger together. I didn't want to push her to do anything she didn't feel comfortable with, but when I suggested we play cards instead, she snapped her chin up.

"Better to ask forgiveness than permission, I suppose." Her eyes lit with a fiery determination I found extremely attractive.

"If your madam has any objections, I'll take full responsibility."

"Good," she huffed, and swept out of the room, leaving me to follow behind her.

Once we emerged onto the sandy gravel path, I took the lead. We walked in silence for a few minutes, and I could sense her apprehension. She kept rubbing her fingers together, fidgeting as we walked. I longed to reach out and take her hand in mine, but found I was not brave enough. Her anxiety was making *me* nervous, and I didn't know what to say to comfort her.

When we reached the clearing, my shoulders relaxed. Enveloped by the sweet scent of the forest and shrouded in darkness, I immediately felt more at ease. The gentle *shh* of leaves as the wind blew always calmed me.

I removed my mask and turned to Sorsha, ready to begin our training. "Here we are. Ready for your lesson?"

"It's so dark. How am I supposed to see anything?" she asked, crossing her arms.

"You are a House of Night courtesan. I'd think learning to wield these weapons in darkness would be much more beneficial to you than doing so in the afternoon sun. Though, I still hope you never have cause to use them."

"Neither do I." She shrugged. "But it would be nice to know I could, if the occasion ever called for it."

"We'll make a warrior out of you in no time. I'll be right back." I walked to the edge of the glen where I'd hung a few fae lanterns that afternoon. The soft blue glow provided us with more than enough light to see by. I draped my jacket over a tree branch and withdrew a few training daggers from my bandolier. I let my wings flex to their full length, glad to be out of the constricting evening wear.

Sorsha stared at me, her lips parted ever so slightly. Seven hells. My desire to kiss her pulsed strongly as I rejoined her in the center of the clearing. If it went well, maybe I would. I nearly had last night. But there was something so delicious about teasing her, in stoking her budding desire. For now, I cleared the thought from my mind.

I placed one knife in my palm, showing it to her.

"That looks nothing like a dagger," she said.

She was right. There was no fancy pommel on these blades. They weren't even sharp. But they did come to a point, which is all we needed for tonight. "We'll get there, I promise. These are training knives."

I passed it to her and grabbed a second one. I took a step closer, letting my shoulder brush hers. The contact sent a shiver through me. I pressed on, ignoring it for now.

"Put your thumb on the top of the blade. Keep your grip firm, but not too tight. You want control, but not so much tension that it will interfere with the rotation."

I grabbed her wrist, testing her grip.

"Loosen a little."

She obeyed. "Alright. That's not too hard."

I smiled. "Good. It shouldn't feel forced." I grabbed her shoulders and spun her to face a nearby oak tree, its broad trunk framed by fae lanterns. "There's your target."

Releasing her shoulders, I coached her through her form. "Point your forward foot toward your target and give the knife a firm throw. The goal is to slow the rotation down, not to make it spin fast. You'll have much more success in getting it to land."

I cocked a knife back, the motion ingrained within me from years of training. I suppressed the sudden twinge of sorrow at the memory of sparring with my brother, letting the memories go as I released the knife. It landed with a soft *thunk* into the tree.

"Now, you try."

Sorsha pivoted her foot, directing it to her target. She squared her shoulders and brought the knife back, then threw it hard.

It whistled into the darkness, not even coming close to her target.

"I'm sorry," she said, clamping a hand over her mouth. "I

have no idea how we're going to get that back."

"I brought more than enough. They're training weapons, not valuable. It's okay if they all end up in the forest tonight. I'll retrieve them once it's light out."

"Still, I don't want you to go to too much trouble."

"Then don't miss again."

Her eyes hardened, and she opened her mouth before quickly snapping it shut.

I smiled, amused at the quick shift in her emotions. She wordlessly held out her hand for another knife.

I placed it gently in her palm and watched her take her stance. She cocked the knife back at her shoulder, ready to let it fly.

"Wait." I came up behind her and placed my hand over hers. "Not too tight, remember?"

She relaxed her grip beneath my fingers. The moon shone in her golden hair, utterly enchanting. I could feel her pulse quicken as I slid one hand to her hip, adjusting her stance ever so slightly, squaring her to the target.

"Better?" she asked, her voice strained.

"Much," I breathed into her ear. I let go, stepping away so she had enough space to throw.

This time, she released the knife with much more fluidity, and the point stuck into the tree, just shy of the edge. She whirled to face me with a grin of triumph.

"I didn't miss," she said, beaming.

"Good girl."

She quickly averted her gaze. Even though she wore her mask, I could still see her cheeks turn a shade darker.

"Do it again," I said, handing her another blade.

She accepted it, and this time got the knife to stick closer to the center.

We practiced for another half hour until the fae lights dimmed so much that we could barely make out the target. To my surprise, she didn't miss the tree again.

"I hope I never end up on the wrong side of your dagger, darling," I said, removing the knives from the trunk. I sheathed them back into my belt, shrugged on my jacket, and lifted a lantern from a branch, bringing it close so I could see her face.

"Speaking of, when will you teach me to use them against someone up close?" she asked, bouncing slightly on her feet. Her face flushed with exertion and pride. Standing this close to her again made those devilish thoughts resurface. It was hard to focus on anything but her mouth.

"Next time. We need much more light for that, and blades that don't have any sharp edges."

"That makes sense, I suppose. I'd hate to stab you."

I pressed a hand to my chest. "I'm relieved to hear it."

She swatted my arm playfully. "Or maybe I *will*, you arrogant prick."

A hint of conviction lay under her jest, enough to give me pause. "You really think me so conceited?"

"Corvus, the only reason we're spending time together right now is because you demanded exclusive access to me. You are paying for the privilege of my company." Though her tone was light, I could see her true feelings in the pinch of her face. She pressed her lips together, as if regretting the words.

It shouldn't have bothered me so much, but I found it hard to bear the thought that she had a low opinion of me. From her point of view, she had every right to feel this way. I didn't know how to explain my actions. I still wasn't sure why I had said those things to her madam, or what drew me to her in the first place. All I knew was that I craved her beyond all reason.

"I'm sorry, Sorsha. It must have felt terrible, me claiming

you like I did."

Her brows rose slightly. "It's alright. I shouldn't have said anything."

"No, it's not alright. No one should make you feel like a commodity."

She smiled sadly. "And yet, you are paying a large sum of money to spend time with me."

She had a point. Gods, I *was* an arrogant prick. "I could release you from the agreement if you'd like. Stop paying for the pleasure of seeing you."

She rocked back on her heels and wrung her hands together. "I don't think Madam Andromeda would find that as agreeable."

"This isn't about her. It's about you," I said firmly.

Her mouth twisted into a frown.

"I am sorry, Sorsha. I'll speak with her when we get back and remedy the situation."

She balked. "You don't have to."

"If it would make you feel more comfortable, then of course I will."

Sorsha rubbed her thumb and forefinger together. "And you... you would still want to spend time with me?"

I swallowed, my mouth suddenly dry. "I am incredibly attracted to you. You must know that." My chest squeezed, and I braced myself for the aftermath of my confession.

"Thank you," she breathed, and I felt the tension leave me. "Can I think about it? About you canceling the contract?"

"Of course. I am yours to command." I bowed, trying to hide my unbridled elation. She didn't return the confession, but she didn't storm off either.

"You're still a little conceited," she said.

"I prefer to think of it as excessively charming." I extended an arm to her. "Shall we head back?"

She looped her hand through my elbow, and we set off into the trees.

"I hear the king is having a ball," she said, stepping over a large rock.

"Yes, one of those masked affairs."

"Andromeda said that a few of the courtesans will be selected to attend." She kept her gaze on the ground, watching her footing.

"And are you hoping you will be one of the few?" I asked with as much nonchalance as I could muster.

"I've never been to the palace before, or a ball. But I don't think I'll be attending," she said quickly. "Andromeda will ask Viviana, and then she'll probably demand that all her friends go with her."

"Well, you could always stab her in the foot. She'd have a difficult time dancing if she's been mutilated with the tea service."

"You're never going to let me forget that, are you?" she asked, exasperated.

I laughed. "Never."

A tendril of doubt curled around my pleasant thoughts. If there was going to be trouble at the masquerade, I didn't want to place Sorsha in danger. Should I invite her to come with me? Would she be crushed if I didn't?

The fae lantern had almost gone out entirely, leaving us cloaked in darkness. Moonlight filtered through the tops of the trees, which thinned as we neared the road.

Sorsha slipped her hand from my elbow and threaded her fingers through mine, casting a furtive glance my way.

I stopped, my feet growing rooted to the soft, fragrant forest floor. The air pressed closer around us, and the hair on the back of my neck stood in anticipation.

The simmering desire I'd felt all evening ignited into a roaring flame. Heat coursed through me, pushing out all rational thoughts.

"Do you want to kiss me, Corvus?" she asked, leaning in toward me, eyes sparkling.

"That depends, darling." Gods, I could barely breathe. The heady scent of her washed over me, making me want her even more than I had all night.

"On what?" she asked, voice low.

Hadn't I already said? It seemed she needed reminding. "On if you want it as much as I do."

She placed a hand on my chest, and I could feel the heat of her skin through my shirt. "And how badly do you want to kiss me?"

"I have been thinking of very little else," I confessed.

Her breathing hitched, and she leaned back.

Perhaps she didn't realize this was not simple flirting. That she was all I could think about, day and night, ever since I'd first met her. I had stopped trying to make sense of it, stopped wondering if she'd used magic to bewitch me. Besides, we'd been outside the bounds of the house all evening, and I was more drawn to her than ever.

If being with her meant I would lose all reason, then I would fall into madness willingly.

I brushed a thumb against her cheek, caressing the edge of her black lace mask, smoothing her soft skin.

"We should go," she said softly.

I nodded, unable to speak. I grabbed her hand and pulled her behind me. We made it three steps before I could no longer restrain myself.

I whirled, pulling her to my chest, and I dropped the lantern to the ground. She gasped in surprise, the sound sending a thrill through me. I covered her mouth with mine, chasing her indrawn breath, and every inch of me hummed in satisfaction as our lips finally met. I grasped the back of her neck, letting my mouth brush softly over hers, moving with tenderness, savoring the moment. The taste of her was intoxicating. I slid my other hand around her waist, pulling her closer. She let out a low moan of satisfaction, and I deepened the kiss.

She parted her lips for me willingly, eagerly, as if she had been starving for me just as I had been for her. Sorsha gripped my shoulders, sending another rush of heat through me. I clenched my fingers in her hair, unable to stop myself from pressing my hips into hers. I darted my tongue between her lips, letting passion and days of slow, torturous teasing ignite.

It was better than I had dreamed. Better than any kiss I had shared with anyone. I traced her jaw with my fingertips, felt the delicate flutter of her pulse throbbing beneath my touch. She inhaled sharply through her nose as I reached the spot between her neck and shoulder, and ground against me. Gods, this was perfect. She was perfect.

A hoarse shout rent the stillness of the night. "Over here, Captain! Some of those magic lights in the trees."

I froze and cursed the interruption, my chest heaving as I fought to regain control.

"Search the area. Whoever lit them might still be here," responded another voice, lower than the first. Footsteps crashed in the brush to our left near the road.

Blackwood guards. What the fuck were they doing up here? They knew better than to come this close to the House of Night. They were growing bolder, tiring of tavern raids where there was nothing to find.

An icy chill of foreboding made the hair on the back of my neck stand, dousing thoughts of lust and retribution. I knelt and flipped the switch on the fae light, plunging us into darkness.

Wordlessly, I moved to cover Sorsha. I placed one hand on her shoulder, guiding her until her back was flush with the nearest tree.

She let out a soft gasp as she hit the tree. The sound sent another thrill through me. I didn't need to, but I pressed my body against hers, savoring the feel of her softness. She let out another low moan from the back of her throat at the contact of our bodies. My wings flared, encircling her.

I bent close and whispered in her ear, my heart still pounding with desire and the threat of danger. "Royal guards. We need to leave."

My eyes adjusted to the darkness, taking in Sorsha's face, bathed in pale moonlight. Her amber eyes were wide, face solemn, though her cheeks were still flushed and her lips were swollen from kissing. One of her curls had escaped her pins. It trailed along her neck, inviting me to brush it back and press my lips there.

The sound of footsteps and clanking armor grew closer. I groaned inwardly, irritated that our evening had to end like this.

"This way," I said, grabbing her hand. We stepped lightly over roots and moss. I tucked my wings close to my body as we walked, putting a good amount of distance between us and the mortal men stumbling around in the woods. I took slow, measured breaths, trying to calm the rushing heat in my blood. Every instinct had me screaming to bring her to the forest floor and taste every inch of her.

The guards were gaining. They were either picking up our trail, or they were smart enough to head to the House of Night. I shoved my lustful thoughts away and gave Sorsha's hand a reassuring squeeze as we strode over roots and stone.

Soon, the trees thinned, and I could see the pale sandy path that led to the House of Night. I was loath for the evening to end and slowed my steps, even though we weren't out of danger yet.

Sorsha squeezed my hand, a wordless question: are we safe?

We had a large expanse of terrain to cross before we reached the gates. "We need to get inside the grounds. Shall we run?" I whispered, hoping she would say no. I still wanted that kiss, after all. And so much more.

"Yes, let's," she replied, pulling me along behind her, hand still clasped around mine.

We raced to the house. The stars shone brilliantly above us, illuminating our path, and I swear in that moment I'd never felt so free.

The metallic tang of magic settled in my nose as we crossed the threshold. I followed Sorsha through the grove of fragrant trees until we reached the small kitchen garden. She finally released my hand to undo the latch.

"Good night, Sorsha," I said, still a little dizzy with desire and adrenaline. The world spun unsteadily around me as her eyes met mine.

"Good night. When will I see you again?"

"Tomorrow."

She nodded and swung the little wooden door open.

"You definitely need to wear those pants more often," I blurted.

"Good *night*, Corvus," she laughed, and shut the garden gate. I watched her until she was safely through the back door, hating that our evening must end.

I whistled as I walked back down the sandy lane, not caring if I should run into the Blackwood guards who were probably still stumbling around in the woods. The night was warm, so I took off my jacket. As I did, I heard a soft crinkling sound. I ran my hands over the fabric, finding the source in the outer lapel pocket. I withdrew a folded piece of paper.

My happiness dimmed when I beheld the note I'd stolen from Elias Sunbarrow's table, and I cursed my foolishness. Anyone could have stumbled across it, and I would have had to answer some very unpleasant questions. I balled it up, determined to burn it as soon as I got home.

The shock of my idiocy cleared my head a little. Enough so that not every thought was consumed by the desire to feel Sorsha's lips on mine again.

I looked skyward. The moon had begun its descent. I had several more hours until dawn. Plenty of time to complete my errands. Tomorrow, I would see what I could learn about this plot of insurrection and make my own plans for the masquerade ball.

Chapter Fifteen
Sorsha

It was easy to give in to the blooming attraction between us, to tease him a little. It was a simple task to tuck the paper back into his jacket as I ran my hand over his chest while we kissed, cloaked in shadow, his body pressed against mine. I had done my job well.

At least, that's what I kept telling myself. I pressed my fingers to my lips, still swollen and aching. Physical attraction was a pleasant additional benefit to my task, and nothing more.

As soon as I'd stepped back into the house last night, heart pounding from the fear and want, my hairpin had vibrated against my skull, making my teeth rattle. I removed it, clenched it in my hand, and made my way to Andromeda's office. I braced myself for an admonishment about leaving the grounds.

In her office, I gave my report. Which was really nothing, since I'd already told her about the contents of the note I'd stolen from Corvus. I did not mention our excursion into the forest. She listened, face a stony mask, then dismissed me without thanks or ceremony. If she was displeased, I certainly would have known. Or been locked in the basement.

Afterward, I tumbled into bed, exhausted. My arm and back were sore from throwing those knives, my body not used to the movement. Though I was tired, it took a long while for me to fall asleep. My body felt too hot, and I couldn't stop thinking of how good it felt to finally kiss Corvus.

When I woke, I slipped into a simple day dress and ran my hands over the gowns that hung in my wardrobe. Only a few of them were new, the rest were cast-offs from other courtesans. My face split into an involuntary grin as I contemplated what to wear tonight.

A commotion sounded in the hall, dragging me from heady memories of last night, of the way our bodies pressed together, our breath mingling, my pulse racing. I heard footsteps running down the corridor, doors banging open, and high-pitched shrieks.

I creaked open my door, unsure if the sounds were of delight or terror, and saw Ferdie barreling toward me through a gaggle of courtesans. "There's going to be a ball!" he cried.

"Really?" I asked, feigning ignorance.

"An invitation arrived this morning." Ferdie beamed.

"I bet Viviana is thrilled," I said, crossing my arms.

A hush fell, and we both looked to see Viviana striding through the hall as everyone parted before her. She kept her nose in the air and knocked on Andromeda's door.

After a pause, she swept inside, no doubt to make her demands and share her preferred guest list for the party of the year.

Tension settled as courtesans murmured in discontent. Everyone wanted to attend the ball, and everyone knew their chances of doing so were slim as long as Viviana held sway over Andromeda.

Lola's petulant wail rose above the rest. "It's not *fair*."

Ferdie rolled his eyes. "Oh, please. She'll definitely take her. Viviana likes to surround herself with her little minions so she can stand out as the crown jewel among bimbos." He sighed, his face crumpling a bit. "It was fun to dream for a minute."

"She can't seriously let Viviana dictate who gets to go. What did the invitation say exactly?"

"Something about a delegation from the House of Night being invited to attend."

I hummed low in my throat. "Delegation sounds rather formal, doesn't it? They did not invite us to entertain. Maybe Andromeda will pick courtesans who represent the house well," I offered, hoping to cheer him.

"You might be onto something there," he agreed, a small spark returning to his eyes.

A shriek rent the air, muffled a bit by the closed door, but Viviana's cry was unmistakable. She stormed out of the office, and we snapped our mouths shut as she stomped through the corridor, lips bloodless.

"Looks like there's a chance for us after all," whispered Ferdie.

The house became an explosion of tulle, satin, lace, and jewels as courtesans raided each other's closets for something to wear to the masquerade. Even if they weren't chosen to go, it was best to be prepared.

I stayed in the garden until twilight, gathering lavender and weeding. When I returned to the kitchen, Ivy accepted the basket of herbs with a raised eyebrow.

"And what about you, missy? Are you planning on going to that fancy ball?"

"I doubt Andromeda will choose me to go."

"Oh hush, you deserve to be there as much as they do. That Stormfall boy coming back again tonight?"

"Yes," I said, turning to the sink so she couldn't see the stupid smile that crept over my face.

"You better get going then," she warned. "Don't want to keep him waiting."

I nodded and scurried upstairs to get dressed.

Ferdie stopped me on the way there, his mouth set in a grim line. "Bad news," he said, leaning close. "She chose Viviana after all, and only five others." I could tell he was not one of them.

"I'm sorry, Ferdie."

"Ah well. Who would want to spend that much time with her, anyway? Have fun tonight, honey." He winked, then went to his own chambers down the hall.

I swapped my day wear for a black dress with sheer, gauzy sleeves. Instead of heading straight to the Emerald Parlor, I found myself knocking on Andromeda's door.

In a week, I had brought in more money than Viviana had in the past month. Shouldn't I also be rewarded? Viviana made demands all the time, and she got what she wanted.

"Enter."

Andromeda didn't bother looking up. Her focus was entirely on a piece of parchment, stamped with an official-looking seal.

"I want to go to the ball." My voice shook, despite my efforts to sound firm. I clenched my fists and did my best to channel Viviana.

She glanced at me above her spectacles, then shuffled the papers around her desk. I waited for her to say something. She simply folded her letters and ignored me.

"I've made you more money this month than anyone else. Even Viviana. I have not asked for a single thing in return. I am asking now. May I go to the palace, too?"

Andromeda placed a black feathered quill into a pot of ink and began to write. "You will not be going with us."

The small bubble of hope I had been carrying burst. Last night had ignited something in me, something that had been slumbering for a long time. The sound of the wind in the trees and the scent of soft earth had ignited a craving for being outside of the bounds of the house. A terrifying thought flashed through my mind.

I wanted out of this prison. I swallowed, bile making my mouth pool with saliva as I faced the hard, ugly truth. I was Andromeda's spy. Bound to her through my own blood, until she saw fit to release me.

"I don't understand." A single tear dripped down my cheek, as much from regret as the sting of rejection. I kept my hands still, fighting the urge to wipe my face.

Andromeda sighed impatiently. "I don't have time to justify my choices to every one of you. You are not going with us. That is final." She slipped the rest of her correspondence into a leather folio and snapped it shut with a *click*. "Go back downstairs. Your client will be here soon."

She slid the folio into her desk and rummaged around in the depths of the drawer, ignoring me once more.

Another tear escaped. I turned and fled before she could see me cry.

I sat in the window seat of the Emerald Parlor, furiously brushing away my leaking tears. Not even Corvus's impending visit brought me any comfort. The clock struck nine, and I tied my mask back into place. This one had ornate curls with points on each end, like the wings of a butterfly.

The glossy black clock in the corner ticked, echoing in the silence. A minute passed, then five. Corvus was late.

After ten minutes, the latch on the door clicked. I kept my gaze trained out of the window, looking out at the lemon trees in the garden. The warm, citrus-scented air dried my face of tears, but I could not bring myself to face him.

He sat at my feet. "What's wrong?"

I shook my head and looked at the space between us, unable to meet his gaze. He'd brought me another bouquet. Cranberry pink ranunculus and white roses. Something in my chest cracked at the gesture.

After a deep breath, I lifted my chin. His eyes were warm and full of concern as he leaned forward in his seat. The bruise on his cheek had faded completely.

"It's silly. Andromeda did not choose me to attend the masquerade."

"Of course she didn't," he said simply.

It felt like he'd punched me in the stomach. My face paled. "What's that supposed to mean?"

"You can't attend as a House of Night courtesan *and* be my guest of honor. Conflicting interests. Plus, no one outside of here knows about our little arrangement, and I am quite set on keeping you to myself. If you attend the ball as a courtesan, everyone will think they are entitled to you, and I will not be sharing. I'm terribly selfish, you know."

My mouth fell open in shock. I heard his words, but they made no sense.

He grinned roguishly, entirely too pleased with himself. "Will you accompany me to the ball, my lady?" He brought the flowers up with a flourish, offering them to me.

I leaned forward and swatted the arm that did not bear the bouquet. "You bastard."

He caught my wrist, and lightning passed between us, jumping from his skin to mine. I stilled as he leaned forward, stopping only when we were a mere breath apart. I could think of nothing else other than how badly I wanted to feel his lips on mine.

"Does that mean 'yes'?" he asked, his voice barely above a

whisper.

His warm breath caressed my mouth, and tingles of pleasure raced down my spine. My chest rose and fell rapidly as my heart thudded against my ribs.

"Yes."

"Good." He tucked in his wings and leaned back, eyes dark and dancing with mirth. He held the flowers toward me.

I swallowed hard, then took them gently in both hands. Little sprigs of bergamot nestled amidst the other flowers. I had never seen them used in a bouquet before. "Thank you." I inhaled the scent, sticking my nose into the soft, velvety petals. A lightness swelled in my chest, drowning out the sorrow.

Corvus propped one forearm on a bent knee, sticking his other leg straight out beside me.

I glanced up at him, noting the highly sensual pose. Gods, wasn't it my job to seduce *him*?

"You smell like that. Roses and bergamot." His voice was rough.

Heat pooled low in my core, and my toes curled. I stroked the petals with light fingertips and smiled.

"Do you want to know what you smell like to me?"

He nodded.

I set the flowers aside, careful not to crush them, and tucked my legs underneath me. Sitting on my knees in front of him, I watched his throat bob as he swallowed.

"Thunderstorms on a warm summer's night. You smell like rain and lightning itself."

His eyes darkened with desire. "That's oddly complimentary coming from someone who likes to call me arrogant or a prick every time she sees me. I must admit, I do like the sound of it. Very dramatic."

"Very fitting for you, then," I teased. "So, what's it like?

Going to the palace for a ball?"

"Pageantry and peacocking, rubbing elbows with all the folk who made it to the guest list, idiotic small talk, that sort of thing."

"What about food?"

"Oh, plenty of good food. The best Tenebris has to offer."

"And dancing?"

He flashed a lopsided grin. "Dancing, too."

"I'm looking forward to it. Though, I don't know how to dance. I'll have to practice."

"Would you like me to teach you?"

"I'd rather you teach me how to fight with those daggers." I looked pointedly at the hilt of his twin blades peeking out from under his jacket.

"I must admit, I'm relieved to hear it," he said.

"Why?"

He fidgeted, rubbing a hand over his knee. "Sorsha..." He paused, weighing his words. "There is some small amount of risk going to this masquerade. Are you okay with that?"

I frowned. "What do you mean?" His apprehension must have something to do with the note I'd found.

"There has been much unrest between fae and the king recently."

I immediately wanted to hound him with questions, but I bit my tongue. I couldn't seem too eager, despite my gnawing curiosity.

"It would be wrong of me to ask you to come with me, without you knowing the dangers," he said.

I slid my legs to the side, getting more comfortable. "Those dangers being?" My pulse quickened.

"What I tell you can't leave this room. I hesitate even to share my suspicions, but it would be wrong of me not to inform you of the risks."

"I see. Would it make you more comfortable if we spelled the room against eavesdropping?"

His brow pinched quizzically. "You can do that?"

I gave him a slow smile. "We can do many things here at the House of Night."

"It might be a good idea," he said, dropping his shoulders in relief.

"I'll be right back." I slid off the window seat and opened the secret panel in the wall, attaching a white cloth with a black star to the pulley. *Special request.* I sent it off to Ivy and Aster in the kitchens.

A few moments later, there were four quick knocks. I expected to find Aster, but when I opened the door, Andromeda herself stood in the dim hall, lips pursed.

I schooled my face and leaned toward her, whispering, "Silencing potion, please."

She cocked a delicately arched eyebrow at me.

"For good reasons," I said, brushing my hand against the pin in my hair.

She removed a little bottle from her pocket and placed it into my palm. "Don't waste it," she mumbled. She stepped back into the shadows and disappeared.

How had she known to come? The masquerade invitation must have her on edge. Which did not bode well for me. If Corvus did not share any worthwhile information… I wouldn't think about that now.

I closed the door. "Here we are," I said, showing the little bottle to Corvus. Holding it up to the light, I saw the same midnight-blue, viscous fluid Andromeda had used the night we made the blood pact, not the usual silencing potion that was given to courtesans.

I uncorked the bottle, spreading the thick potion on my finger; I swiped it around the door. I did the same to the large bay window. The air grew close with the lack of breeze. I could hear my breathing more clearly, and my mouth tasted metallic.

Corvus seemed to sense the shift in the air, too. He sat up and settled himself closer to me.

"So, why is going to a ball at the palace potentially dangerous?" I asked, wiping my hands of the potion's residue.

He dragged a hand through his hair. "There have been whispers of rebellion. The fae are angry that the king will not lift the ban on magic. Folk are suffering, and the leaders of the Fae Houses see him unfit to rule."

"They want the king to lift the ban and restore magic?"

"Yes."

"That doesn't sound so bad."

Magic is leaving Tenebris. The houses are plotting to do something about it. I want you to figure out what it is.

Andromeda already suspected they were going to take action. I needed to figure out what their plan might be.

Corvus's mouth twisted. "They want to depose him, if he will not step down."

I rubbed my thumb over my finger, thinking. "Have they tried talking to the king first?"

"More meetings are being held later this week. A delegation of the Fae will negotiate with him. But the king has a will of iron. Lucius Uriel has been named Primus. If he can't convince him, then it may lead to violence."

"Primus?" I'd never heard the term before.

"It's an old fae custom. When fae entered times of trouble or war, they would usually appoint a Primus, or leader. Normally, the Forum would make decisions jointly, by vote. A Primus is given more power, to move things like negotiations along more swiftly."

"And has the Primus been successful?"

He rocked back on the heels of his hands. "I'm not sure."

My stomach clenched, and I fidgeted, rubbing my thumb and fingers together. "What do you mean, times of war?"

"There are signs. The Blackwood armada is in the harbor, preparing for something. My father thinks the Blackwoods are readied to quell any whisper of fae uprising."

Seven hells. It sounded very ominous. My head spun with it all. I couldn't believe Corvus was so forthcoming with this information. Did Andromeda know of any of this? I forged ahead with my questions, driven by my own anxious curiosity as much as my desire for intel.

"How would the king remove the ban, anyway? How is magic *banned*? I've never thought about it."

Corvus frowned. "I have tried to find out. The mortals burned many old fae texts and records. Probably to cover up what they did."

"The more I think about it, the more it doesn't make sense. You can't ban something that is internal, that's a part of you. That would be like someone telling you to stop having wings."

Corvus shifted. His wings, which had been draped over the window seat, shrank toward him. "Oh, believe me, I tried wishing them away already."

"Why? They're beautiful."

He dipped his chin and straightened his jacket. "That is kind of you to say." He took a deep breath, and his wings relaxed once more. "But you're right. There must be something *external* blocking the magic."

"Perhaps your Primus knows," I suggested.

He shrugged. "Perhaps."

"What does this all have to do with the masquerade?"

He sat up and took my hand in his. A pleasant tingle raced up my arm all the way to my chest. He rubbed his thumb in smooth strokes, caressing the back of my hand as he spoke. "We love our pageantry. If there was a coup, it would be the perfect place. There will be lots of witnesses, and innocents. If there are guests in the palace, there's a possibility there will be less violence. Easier for the fae to take over that way. The king wouldn't want to risk killing any mortals."

A thought chilled me, making me stiffen. "How do you know of this coup? Are *you* planning to overthrow the king?"

"No," Corvus said, eyes wide. "No. Not me. I don't agree with the way the Blackwoods have handled things, but I am not part of a plot to kill the king."

Depose, remove, kill. Which one was it? How did he know all this?

"You're not, but you know someone who is."

"Yes." His face hardened, and he dropped his eyes to our clasped hands.

He would not tell me who. But I had more than enough to share with Andromeda. Perhaps, with time, I could uncover more.

"So, there's a chance a group of fae may try to get rid of King Blackwood at his own ball?"

"Yes. I understand if you no longer wish to attend."

I squeezed his hand. "I appreciate you telling me. But I still want to go. If you'll have me."

His eyes met mine. They were filled with happiness. "Of course I do."

I beamed. "Good." A thought flashed. "Hang on. What about the prince?"

"The prince?"

"Has anyone tried talking to him? Or is he as stubborn as

his father?"

"He might be, but I'm not sure," he said.

An idea ignited, sending a wave of excitement through me. "Corvus, what if, at the masquerade, *I* spoke to the prince? I can figure out where he stands on all this, if he can be reasoned with. I can try to find out what he knows about what's blocking the magic."

And I could report his opinions to Andromeda. Surely information from the prince himself would be enough to satisfy the terms of our agreement. This is exactly what she wanted me to do. A knot of guilt settled in my stomach, but there was no way I could tell Corvus the truth. He was my means to an end, after all. Nothing more.

Corvus rubbed his chin.

I tried a different approach. "If we can avoid any violence and restore magic, wouldn't that be better for everyone?"

"I don't like the idea of sharing you with some stuck-up mortal prince," Corvus finally said, voice rough.

"I'm a House of Night courtesan, remember?"

His mouth twisted, as if my words were sour.

"Please, Corvus. Let me try to help."

"You're determined to do this?" he asked.

I nodded, setting my jaw and squaring my shoulders. "Yes. I am."

He sighed dramatically. "Then I suppose we better get to work." He pushed himself off the window seat and turned, extending a hand to me.

I hesitated to take it. "On what?"

"If we're going to this ball, I want to make sure you know how to stab someone properly. And dance a waltz."

I let him pull me to my feet. "Daggers and dancing. How charming."

He flashed me a brilliant smile and tugged me into the center of the room.

My heart fluttered as I followed behind him, taking steps down a path I suspected I could never come back from.

Chapter Sixteen

Corvus

A sliver of golden glow seeped from Father's closed study door. He had been spending more time there than usual. Which was saying something because it's where he spent his time counting his gold. He was obsessed with it. It had only gotten worse since Max died, but in recent months his devotion to his business, and the amount of dinar we seized, had reached a fever pitch.

I paused in front of the closed door. Part of me yearned to knock and join him in his task, to be praised for taking interest in the matters of our house. But it was a foolish hope. Deep down, I knew he could not give me what I wanted. I shifted, about to leave for what promised to be an enchanting evening, when I heard Horatio's muffled voice make a sound of gloating triumph. I'd never heard him sound so happy in my life.

Instead of leaving, I pressed an ear to the door. I could only make out a few words, but what I heard cut my breath short.

Nearly ready. Trial. Weapon. Success.

The hairs on the back of my neck stood. A weapon?

I closed my eyes, feeling the cool wood press into my cheek. The low tenor of my father's voice reverberated through the door.

Subjects. Results. Promising.

My unease was buried under a wave of anger. My father was building a weapon. But for what purpose? What could he possibly have to gain from doing so? And what, or who, were they testing this weapon on?

Down the hall, a clock chimed the hour, interrupting my

train of thought.

I tore myself away from my eavesdropping, leaving my father and Horatio to their scheming and secrets. It was another piece of a greater puzzle, but I would think more on it later. Sorsha was waiting for me.

At the House of Night, Sorsha and I pushed the dark green velvet couches out of the way, clearing a wide space in the center of the parlor. Seeing her immediately wiped all thoughts of my father's plotting from my mind. Every thought, every sense, immediately attuned to her. We'd practiced dancing last night, and she'd thanked me with another earth-shattering kiss. Thoughts of tasting her made my blood run hot, but if I wanted to ensure her safety, I had to leave the kissing for later.

I slid off my jacket and unbuckled my bandolier, draping both over the back of a chair. I removed two sparring knives, dulled to prevent accidents, and handed them to Sorsha.

"Where's your weapon?" she asked, weighing the blunted blades in her hands.

"Most folk around here use swords. Even I prefer them, sometimes. It didn't seem appropriate to bring one here, even if it's just a training weapon."

She pouted. "How am I supposed to learn how to fight against someone if it's not going to be realistic?"

I wanted to laugh at her stubbornness and the ferocious glint in her eye but crushed the instinct. While I thought her ambition endearing, I didn't want her to take my amusement as derision. "We'll get there. Fighting isn't about who is strongest, or who has the better weapon. It's about using your strengths to your advantage.

"You're stronger than most would expect, and you throw

daggers like a natural. The element of surprise is going to serve you the best. But when that fails, there are a few things you can keep in mind."

I stepped in front of her and tapped her throat. Her pulse fluttered under my fingers. "Most armor does not protect the neck." I took her wrist, lifted her hand straight out, and tapped her underarm. "Here is also rarely protected. And" – my mouth twisted in a grimace – "if your opponent is a male, a blow to the groin will topple them easily."

"Throat, underarm, groin. Got it." She clenched the daggers in a white-knuckle grip.

"Relax your hands. The daggers are an extension of you. You wield them, they do not wield you."

I grasped her wrists, testing the tension. She relaxed under my fingers. "Good. Stand with your knees shoulder-width apart, slightly bent." She sank an inch. Her skirts concealed her legs. I raised an eyebrow, glancing pointedly at them.

"Oh, come off it," she said, rolling her eyes. "I can't wear those pants in here."

"Why not?"

"It's just not done."

"Huh," I said, stepping back.

"What?" she asked, straightening and dropping the daggers to her sides.

"I assumed it wouldn't matter to you. That's all."

"Andromeda has very strict rules about how she conducts her business," said Sorsha, her voice cold.

I'd touched a nerve. "My apologies. I didn't mean to offend."

She sighed heavily. "You know what? Fuck it." She set the daggers down on a little side table and strode for the door. "I'll be back in two minutes."

"Sorsha, wait." I ran and caught her elbow, spinning her to face me. "You don't have to change. I was only teasing." I touched the curve of her cheek.

Her eyes, hard and brimming with tears, softened.

"Please. Come back over here."

"Fine," she said, pacified by my plea. "But next time I'm wearing pants under the skirt."

"Ah yes, the infamous Sorsha Sventura of the House of Night. The only courtesan who becomes more attractive the more clothes she puts on."

"Shall I kick you in the groin now, or later?" she asked sweetly.

I held up my hands in surrender and backed toward the center of the room. She followed me, picking up the daggers, her gaze flinty.

Gods, she was utterly bewitching.

"Back in your fighting stance," I said.

She dipped, keeping her eyes fixed firmly on me.

"Elbows bent. Bring them closer to your body. Protect yourself." I brought her hands closer to her center. "Good."

I stepped back a few paces, adopting my ready stance. I spread my hands wide. My wings naturally followed, extending behind me with a whisper.

"Now, attack me."

She ran her gaze from my feet to the tips of my wings, flexing her fingers around the handles of her weapons. Then she lunged, swinging the dagger wide. As I went to deflect her attack, she feinted to the other side, arcing the dagger through the air where it brushed my arm.

"Very good. Again."

We sparred for half an hour in slow motion. When I told her to freeze, I would gently correct her form, moving her arms closer to her body or widening her feet, before returning to my original stance. We flowed through a few fighting forms, letting her body become comfortable with the movements. She carved her daggers through the air, gaining more confidence with the repetition.

When her arms were visibly shaking, we stopped.

"I don't understand. I carried trays full of tea and biscuits up and down stairs for years, and *this* is tiring?" she cried, exasperated. She wiped the sweat from her brow and shook out her hands.

"Don't be too hard on yourself. The movement is different from what you're used to. Sparring uses entirely different muscles."

"I think I prefer throwing them," she said, massaging her wrists.

"Almost forgot," I said, going back to my bandolier. I stowed the sparring daggers and withdrew two flat throwing knives. "These are for you. To practice with."

Her cheeks grew plump with her smile. "Thank you."

"You're welcome." My gaze reflexively flicked to her mouth. I cupped her cheek and leaned forward, inhaling the sweet scent of her. My body demanded that I kiss her here, now.

"Would you like to play cards?" she asked.

I couldn't tell if her breathlessness was from sparring, or from my proximity. It was with great effort that I agreed.

She clapped her hands together. "Excellent. Time for me to beat you."

"You're very sure of yourself." I laughed.

She moved to the door, a wicked grin on her face. "I know just how to wear down your defenses. I set aside an entire tray of shortbread for you."

My mouth watered at the thought of the lemony, buttered confection.

Two hours flew by without my realizing it. As we played cards, we spoke of our childhoods, our favorite memories, our pastimes. We didn't need coy games anymore. The conversation flowed effortlessly, like I was speaking to a friend.

She shared how she'd come to work at the House of Night, abandoned here as a child, and my heart ached to think of how scared and lonely she must have been. I spoke of training in the yard with our stern, but fatherly captain. I shared some of the misadventures Dio and I had gotten ourselves into in our younger years, including the time we threw melons at passing guards and raced along rooftops to get away. And all the while I found any excuse I could to touch her, to be close to her. I brushed her hair from her temple, trailed my fingers down her arm, smoothed my thumb just under her mask. It was its own kind of exquisite torture – one I could see she enjoyed as much as I did.

The clock on the mantel chimed the hour, and I groaned, lowering my hand of cards. "I'm afraid I have another engagement this evening."

Sorsha's brows knit together, and I thought I saw hurt flash across her face. "You do?"

"My friend Dio has been woefully abandoned this past week. I'm afraid he insisted on coming to see me."

He had threatened to follow me to the House of Night and watch while I spent time with Sorsha. Only after I promised to see him directly after my visit did he agree to meet me at home.

"I see. Thank you for still coming."

"Of course."

She reached behind me, brushing her chest along mine. The contact sent my blood rushing again. "May I?" she asked, holding my bandolier aloft.

I nodded.

She wrapped her arms around me, crossing the strap over my left shoulder. Her fingers were deft, sliding over the supple leather.

"These are beautiful," she murmured, staring at the twin blades over my heart. "Why did your brother give you his dagger?" She ran her fingertips lightly over the handles, then stopped abruptly, cheeks coloring. She sat back, breaking the contact between us. "Sorry. It's not my place to ask."

"It's alright," I said, finishing with the buckle. I unsheathed the two blades, holding them out so she could see them. The blue gem sparkled in the candlelight, inviting and warm. Mine sucked in all the surrounding light like a black, ominous void. Both had silver filigree that twisted around the pommels like vines.

"They're fae-made daggers. Very few of them exist anymore. My father gave them to my brother and I when we came of age. It's a tradition to pass them down to the males in my family."

My throat tightened. I swallowed, trying to force the lump away. It never got easier, talking about Max. Father and I rarely spoke of him. Dio had seen me through the worst of my grief. But now, speaking of him was like picking a scab off a wound.

"Max was my older brother. He was murdered three years ago. By the Dawnstones."

Sorsha pressed a hand to her stomach. "I'm so sorry, Corvus."

I sheathed the daggers, trying to dispel the memory of blood staining Max's white wings crimson. The words flowed from me like a wave breaking upon the shore. I couldn't stop them.

"We were coming home from a night at the pub. We always fought with the Dawnstones. The feud between our houses goes back long before me. No one remembers how it started. It wasn't unusual to get into bar fights with them, harmless brawls. But things got ugly that night. Max knocked Lord Dawnstone's nephew, Aurum, out cold. His friends knocked us around a bit in return, but that was typical."

My stomach turned to lead, the scene replaying in my mind.

"We took our usual shortcut home, through some of the back alleys. Someone was waiting for us. They jumped me, stabbed Max, and ran off."

Sorsha placed a hand on my arm. The warm weight of her touch was comforting, and chased away dark memories of blood, the cold of death, and my vow for vengeance.

"If there was magic, he would have healed. Fae used to heal quickly. But he died. He bled out before I could get help."

"I'm so sorry," she said again.

"Thank you."

A heavy silence descended. Thoughts of kissing her, while still present, were now dimmed, smothered by the weight of those memories.

If she sensed the shift in the air, she met it with grace. "I appreciate you telling me." She bit her lip, and her eyes clouded with shadows. "I hope you feel like you can talk to me about anything. I'm very good at listening."

"You are," I agreed, regretting that my own sorry history had made her sad.

"I'm afraid I've made you late."

"He'll understand," I said, threading my arms through the sleeves of my dark blue jacket.

"If he doesn't, I'll take full responsibility," she said, echoing my words from last night.

It made me smile.

"The masquerade is three days away. Are you ready?"

"As I'll ever be," Sorsha said. "I've been practicing."

"Good girl."

I did not miss the shiver she tried to suppress. The sight

warmed me, chasing away the cold nightmares of the past. "I'm afraid I won't be able to see you until then. I'll be here at seven o'clock to escort you."

"Thank you. I'm looking forward to it."

"Me, too. Goodbye, Sorsha, darling." I kissed her cheek, lips scraping the edge of her mask, and I heard her breath hitch. There was nothing stopping me from kissing her here and now. But I knew that if I gave in, I would not leave this room until dawn.

I left before I could convince myself to stay. I peeked through the crack in the door as I closed it. Sorsha gripped her throwing knives, moving through one of the forms again.

It made me feel a little better about taking her to the ball, knowing she wouldn't be completely helpless if violence ensued.

Chapter Seventeen

Sorsha

My heart hammered in time with the rattling of carriage wheels over cobblestone streets as we made our way to the royal palace. Built right into the seaside cliffs, its many spires and turrets glinted in the setting sun, shining like jewels. It was one of the most beautiful things I had ever seen. I pressed against the carriage window, trying to take it all in. Only when we had passed through an enormous stone wall and were submerged in the palace's shadow did I tear my eyes away. Corvus watched me with a bemused smile.

I hadn't seen him in three days. I had grown so used to his nightly visits that the time felt longer than it should have. During his last night with me, I found myself wanting to dispense with the dancing lessons and the games and let that simmering pool of desire take over. I wanted to kiss him again. I wanted to do *more* than kiss him. But I couldn't.

I hadn't told Andromeda about his terrible family history. She probably already knew, anyway. But I did tell her about the potential coup at the masquerade. It made me sick to my stomach, encouraging him to confide in me, then letting his secrets spill from me like a sieve.

Smiling self-consciously back at Corvus, I sank back into the plush carriage seat. We hadn't spoken in several minutes, not since we passed his house, which he pointed out to me as we drove by. It wasn't that far from the House of Night. The Stormfall manor sat surrounded by wrought iron and stone, a weathervane perched on the highest gable.

I stared with fascination as we rolled through cobbled streets, drawing closer to the palace. Corvus sat back, completely unfazed by the grandeur of the seaside castle. He must have been here hundreds of times.

"Do you come to the palace often?" I asked.

"When the occasion calls for it." He still looked highly amused. His gray eyes danced with mirth.

Was he laughing *at* me?

"What's so funny?" I crossed my arms.

He shook his head and leaned forward, bracing his forearms on his knees. "Nothing. You're enchanting, that's all."

"Don't make fun of me," I scowled. I hadn't been outside the House of Night in years, and never once had it crossed my mind that I might find myself at the royal palace. He couldn't fault me for gawking.

"I'm sorry," he said, his eyes still boring into mine. "I didn't mean to be condescending. The way you view the world with such awe... I enjoy seeing that look on your face."

Warmth spread through my chest, despite my best efforts to keep my mind off how close we were. "You're forgiven." I huffed. "For now."

"Thank the gods, because if we had to go the entire night without speaking to one another, I don't know how I would manage." He fiddled with the button on his sleeve, his fingers twitching over the fabric.

"I'm sure you'd be fine, *Lord* Stormfall."

Corvus shook his head, his lightheartedness slipping. "These folk are vultures. They're always circling around each other, waiting for some minor slip-up of decorum or reason to damage a reputation. It's incredibly boring."

I rubbed my gloved hands together, the white satin letting my palms slide easily. "That doesn't sound boring at all." I swallowed, my mouth suddenly dry, and I prayed I would not be the source of some scandal, no matter how small. I didn't know how to interact with these fae and royals.

It struck me how woefully unprepared I was to spend an evening among the lords and ladies of Tenebris. I'd spent all my time worrying about dancing and if I could stab someone if they got too close. Now, I wondered if I'd had my priorities wrong.

Ever since Corvus had asked me to attend with him, it felt like he had lit a candle in my heart that warmed my entire chest. Which, now, made my insides twist with guilt. Because I hadn't said yes to his invitation solely because I wanted to go with him to the ball. I had a job to do, a blood oath to fulfill.

So, what did that make me?

Corvus's hand slid between mine. "Hey. You'll be fine." He gave my hands a gentle squeeze of reassurance.

My stomach continued to twist, but I squeezed back. "Of course I will. I'm with you, aren't I?"

"With any luck, this will just be some boring party," he said. "And if the worst should happen, you know what to do."

"Leave and stab anyone who gets in my way."

"Right."

"What about you?" I resisted the urge to plaster my face back to the window as we passed under another archway of sandstone. The carriage began to climb.

"Don't worry about me."

I nodded. He could take care of himself. I shouldn't worry. But as the carriage slowed and the golden glow of sunset hit his face, my stomach flipped with unease.

A warm ocean breeze caressed my skin as we dismounted, stirring the skirts of my gown, a midnight-blue trimmed with gold. I'd planned to wear the usual House of Night black, but the dress came yesterday, in a giant box tied with satin ribbon, and a note from Corvus.

The bodice hugged my every curve and had off-the-shoulder, puffed sleeves. The skirt was so voluminous the dress could have stood upright by itself. Little gold details added delicate sparkle. It even came with a matching gold filigree mask. It was the most breathtaking gift I'd ever received.

Corvus tucked my hand into the crook of his elbow as the carriage pulled away. From here, I could see the ocean glittering in the setting sun. Large ships bearing purple-and-black flags were scattered throughout the harbor, spilling out of the crescent-shaped bay and into the sea beyond. The scent of salt water mixed with the heady perfume of beach roses.

"What are all those ships?" I asked.

"The Blackwood armada," said Corvus in a low voice.

We reached the front steps, and I bit back the urge to ask my questions. Awe swept over me, as we were let into the palace.

Even though I was used to the opulence and pageantry of the House of Night, the palace's magnificent archways, stained sea glass windows, and thousands of candles that cast their warm glow over the party stole my breath. Finely dressed fae and humans waltzed around the ballroom while a small orchestra played on a balcony that overlooked the blue-and-white marbled floor.

Everyone in attendance wore a mask. The sight made me feel a little more at ease. Even if I made a fool of myself tonight, it would be harder for anyone to know exactly who I was.

As I took in the ball's splendor, Corvus's warm breath caressed my ear. A shiver raced down my spine as the hair on the back of my neck stood up. "Stay close to me, alright?" he whispered.

"I don't need protecting," I said in a low voice. I knew where to stick a blade if I needed to defend myself. He'd seen to that.

"I know," he said, sending another shiver down my back. "But I told you, I don't enjoy sharing." He glanced pointedly at a group of men who stared brazenly as we passed by.

My cheeks flushed, and Corvus straightened as a broad-chested man with wavy golden hair stepped into our path. Corvus stared intently. His body tensed and his features turned to granite.

The golden-haired fae smirked at us, then joined a small group standing off to the side of the dance floor. All wore clothing or masks emblazoned with a sun rising over a mountain peak.

"Do you know him?" I asked, trying to keep my voice casual as I burned with curiosity.

Corvus unclenched his jaw. "Aurum Dawnstone, one of the most despicable fae in Tenebris."

I had never seen him so shaken. He looked lost, caught adrift in some terrible memory. This was the one responsible for his brother's death. My heart ached for him. I hated to see him this way.

So, I did what he would have done for me. As a group of twittering fae with flowers in their hair swept past us, I leaned into him a little more, sinking into the warmth of his body. Corvus loved distracting me with those little touches and carefully placed whispers that made my toes curl. The feeling of my body jerked him out of his preoccupation. His wings flexed, the feathers brushing together with a whisper of sound. He blinked a few times in rapid succession, then turned his attention fully to me.

"But enough about villains. Tonight is for us, my sultry Sorsha. So, we will dance, forget our troubles, and drink the fine wine of our host." He grabbed two glasses of sparkling wine from a platter carried by a man in dark purple and black livery.

He handed one of them to me, then clinked his glass against mine.

I took a sip. The bubbles danced pleasantly on my tongue. "Sultry, huh?"

"Have you seen yourself in that dress? It's a very good thing you're here as my special guest, and not as one of your madam's little pets. I think more than one envious bastard here would love to share a dance with you."

He gestured to a group of fae with dark, hungry eyes who were staring rather pointedly in our direction. I'd be lying if I said it wasn't flattering, if not a bit unsettling. It would have been downright alarming if I weren't certain no harm would come to me while Corvus stood by my side. I noticed the wide berth people granted him, making sure not to bump into him, or his wings, as they proceeded to the dance floor to enjoy the party.

"Well, are we going to stand here all night?" I teased, wanting to maintain the lightness between us. "Or are you going to ask me to dance?"

He flashed that devastating smile and drained his glass in one go. He set it down firmly on one of the many little tables scattered around the perimeter, draped in amethyst purple cloth, and extended a hand to me. His eyes grew dark. "Dance with me, Sorsha."

I knew I could not blame the drink for the sudden dizzying rush that made me feel lightheaded, but the sound of his voice buzzed through me as if I'd had an entire bottle of fae wine. I had felt desire, but never knew I'd wanted to hear my name spoken with such need. My chest warmed, turning my limbs into liquid, and a voice deep within purred with satisfaction, knowing that if I wanted the sun and all the stars, he would fetch them for me.

I tipped my own glass back, draining the contents, and set it on the table next to his. I gripped the inside of his arm with one hand and gathered my skirts in the other. "I'd love to."

I floated as he led us to the very center of the ballroom. I only vaguely noticed the heads that swiveled in our direction and the tittering of shared whispers that flitted like fireflies among the folk gathered here. I trained my attention solely on the handsome fae before me, who wore his mask like a crown. Tonight, we were king and queen, ruling over ourselves, not caring what anyone else thought or answering to those who held power over us. We could forget about all of it, at least for tonight.

As the music played, Corvus placed a gentle hand on the small of my back. I laid my own gloved hand on his shoulder. Tonight was for us, and us alone. We spun, two twin stars circling in orbit. I do not know if we danced for a minute or an hour. The blood rushed to my cheeks, my heart thumped against my chest, my pulse beat in my palms as I held his hand. Everything except for him, his thundercloud eyes, his hungry gaze, faded away. We danced until I grew breathless.

Eventually, our feet stilled, though the ballroom still spun around me.

We stood, hand in hand, pressed close to one another, neither of us willing to interrupt this perfect moment. I looked at his lips as want flushed through me. I tilted my chin up to his face and leaned even closer to him, ready to lose myself in the feeling of his lips on mine.

A loud *CRACK* of metal smacking against marble brought me back to my senses. I whipped my head around to see, without completely breaking the connection between our bodies. Corvus pressed his hand more firmly into mine, steadying me, drawing me close.

Every head in the room turned toward a pair of polished double doors. A footman with pale skin and ash brown hair stood at attention, a metal staff clutched firmly in his hand. He smacked the rod upon the floor again and bellowed, "Announcing their royal majesties, King Tyrin Blackwood, Queen Elora Blackwood, and their son, Prince Tristan Blackwood!"

The doors swung open, and the royal family strode into the ballroom, wearing simple silver masks. The crowd regarded them with held breath, and a fraction too late we remembered ourselves, dipping our heads in acknowledgment of their positions. Queen Elora scrutinized the assemblage, her face pinched. Her ink-black hair twisted around a circlet of silver, set with sparkling amethysts, and a matching necklace bearing a purple gem the size of an egg glittered at her throat. She carried herself with every grace a royal should, shoulders back, head held high, and a particular way of peering down her nose that set herself apart from the fae and mortals gathered here. She commanded the attention of the room, even as she made her disdain for us all quite clear.

Her son looked like he'd rather be anywhere else. He appeared to be about my age, in his early to mid-twenties. He had the same black hair as his mother, though it direly needed a trim. His black waistcoat was creased and crumpled. As he passed by, I noted the dark circles under his eyes. He blinked heavily a few times before giving himself a slight shake. It looked like they had roused him from sleep moments before entering the ballroom.

He kept behind his mother and father as the family moved through the throngs of people crowding the dance floor. A low hum of sound pulsed as whispers were exchanged. Everyone stood still, waiting to see where the royals would land. They continued to weave around their guests, as if they were visitors in a gallery of statues.

King Blackwood strolled through the crowd, jovially oblivious to his wife's disdain and his son's unkempt appearance. The silver buttons of his jacket strained against his broad, barrel chest. He wore no crown, but a purple and black sash bore several impressive looking medals in a variety of shapes. They clinked as he escorted his queen to an awaiting pair of thrones on the far side of the room, beneath the balcony of musicians. The king's clipped hair was mostly gray, though some streaks of black still shot through it. His pointed beard and generous mustache had the same coloring.

The queen lowered herself onto her gilded high-backed chair and Tristan took his position, flanking her. The king waved at the crowd. The movement sent his medals dancing, sending high peals like wind chimes to echo throughout the chamber. "Thank you all for being here tonight. We are thrilled so many of you are committed to this pact of harmony. Tonight, we honor the covenant made between mortal and fae, and hope for many centuries of peace and prosperity. We seek to honor the old traditions, while inspiring the new."

The crowd shifted then, like seaweed dancing in a current. The air sizzled with tension, and murmurs of dissent mixed with those of approval. But the king was either brilliant or incredibly ignorant of the sentiments of his subjects.

I knew little about politics, but I could tell we stood on the precipice of a knife's edge. One remark, one gesture, could tip the balance into chaos or contentment.

"Your Majesty," a voice rang, more clear and true than King Blackwood's. The ghost of some forgotten power danced in the spaces between syllables, as if the speaker had been used to commanding legions with his words. Every face in the room pulled toward the male who'd spoken, a fae with incredibly large golden wings and bronze skin.

Corvus gripped my elbow and pulled me even closer to him as the room waited with bated breath to see which way we would fall.

Chapter Eighteen

Corvus

I instinctively pulled Sorsha closer to me as the crowd parted. More than a few hands drifted down to waistlines, ready to pull weapons should they need them. There were few who did not recognize the potential danger we found ourselves in. The air crackled with tension as the room turned their attention to Lucius, who stood only a few dozen feet away from the Blackwoods.

I knew what was coming. Lucius, my father, Lord Sunbarrow, they'd been plotting for gods knew how long. The coup would not happen in the dark of night, cloaked in shadows. No, the usurpation of these mortals who claimed to rule, spewing false promises of peace, would happen now in front of a public audience.

With a sudden jolt, I realized I did not care to stop them. While Lucius was an insufferable narcissist, he would see magic restored, and that would do more good than a few bags of gold ever would for the poor of this city. If blood was to be spilled, it *should* be that of these foolish mortals who did nothing as their people suffered.

But I would do whatever necessary to protect Sorsha from harm. I pulled her tighter to my side, ready to shield her from whatever violence would unfold here tonight. She sank into me. The small part of my mind that was not on high alert hummed in satisfaction.

Lucius addressed the king proudly, stepping into his role as Primus as if he were born to it. His golden wings shone ostentatiously in the candlelight, more resplendent than any jewels the mortals wore.

"On behalf of the Great Fae Houses of Tenebris, we thank you for your continued commitment to peace." Lucius's voice rumbled over the crowd, demanding their attention.

A tense silence fell over the entire room. Lucius gave a small bow, wings fanning behind him with a soft *whoosh*. "We are delighted to be your honored guests this evening and look forward to building a bright future together."

The partygoers remained frozen, eyes darting between this commanding fae and the human king.

But no daggers were drawn, no declarations of war or cries of outrage followed. Instead, the king nodded and took a seat next to his queen. Lucius turned his attention back to the fae who stood close to him, a group of sycophants hoping to gain favor with him. The humans shifted closer to their monarchs; an undercurrent of unease clung to them.

I loosened my grip on Sorsha's arm as the breath returned to my body.

"That was... interesting," she said as the crowd moved around us, preparing for the next dance. She looked up at me expectantly.

It took me a few moments to recenter myself. I cleared my throat, not wanting to betray how close I thought we had come to violence. I had miscalculated. Lucius would not incite a coup tonight. Appearances mattered too much to him. Fae were drawn to him. They always had been. Now that he was Primus of the Forum and had just publicly declared himself the spokesman for the Fae Houses, everyone wanted to be close to him. The note did not mean a coup. The stage was set for *Lucius.*

He was cleverer than I gave him credit for. He had just gained the trust of each fae in attendance with his public statement that he was willing to work toward peace, earning him more power in a single night than the royals had been scrounging together for the past half a century. Lucius had declared he would do whatever he could to protect the fae of Tenebris, even if it meant negotiating with mortals. So, when it did come time to depose them, he would have the full support of the city behind him.

Which meant the streets would run with blood.

"Corvus?"

I looked down at Sorsha, still pressed close to me. Adrenaline leeched away, and in its place came the sudden rush of desire. I studied the streaks of gold in her eyes. She was utterly breathtaking. I brought my thumb to her chin and stroked her jaw. Gods, I would have torn this room apart to keep her safe. My chest felt tight with emotion. Her lips parted slightly. It took every ounce of self-control not to pick her up and whisk her to some private room where I could kiss her for hours.

"Yes, princess?"

Her face scrunched up with displeasure, shifting her mask. "Ew. I do not care for *that* particular nickname."

"My sultry Sorsha you shall remain, then." I couldn't stop my lips from curving into a soft smile as her cheeks went pink and she dropped her gaze.

She took a step back, sending a rush of cool air between us. I offered my arm to her, desperate to feel her close to me again. She took it, rolling her eyes, but her cheeks were still flushed, and she was smiling, too.

I led her to the perimeter of the ballroom where we stood, side by side, watching the city's elite fawn over one another, desperately trying to improve their stations and chances at wealth. Though the fae had lost their magic, its absence had not tempered their greed.

Sorsha leaned in conspiratorially. "So, tell me about all the Great Fae Houses, my lord."

"The man with the golden wings and pompous face is Lucius Uriel. Primus of the fae. They all worship the ground he walks on. Including my father."

"And where is he?"

I scanned the room, looking for him. He stood behind Lucius, and Malachite Dawnstone.

"To the left of Lucius. The one on his right is Lord Dawnstone. And Elias Sunbarrow is coming toward them now. All the esteemed heads of houses, getting cozy with one another." I could not conceal the bitterness in my voice. Sorsha noticed.

"You don't get along?"

"They only want one thing. Power. And money. So, two things."

"And you don't?" I shouldn't be hurt by the skepticism in her voice, but it stung. I wasn't perfect, and I never would claim to be. But it unsettled me, how much I wanted to show her who I really was.

Even the darker parts of me.

I placed my hand on the small of her back. "There is only one thing I want at the moment, darling."

She sucked in a breath of air but did not pull away. "As much as I'd like to find out what that might be," she said, pressing her hip into mine, "I think now might be a good time to make friends with the prince."

I darted a glance to the royals sitting on their thrones. The king spoke with some mortals, who touched their masks and laughed, enjoying the lark of a masked fae ball. The queen still had a sour look and steadfastly ignored her husband. Her son continued to stand, flanking her throne. He stifled a yawn with the back of his hand as the musicians played another waltz and folk crowded the dance floor.

"He looks miserable." A bitter taste coated my tongue. Her attention shouldn't be on another while I was pressed so close to her.

Despite the pretty speeches of peace, unrest still simmered beneath the surface. I needed to be ready. My father wasn't working on a weapon for nothing. Whatever Sorsha could glean from the prince might help me understand and plot a path forward.

"Perfect opportunity, then." She sounded like she was trying to convince herself that was true.

I remembered the way she'd rubbed her hands together in the carriage before we arrived.

"You can do this. Because not only are you incredibly beautiful and utterly bewitching, but you are very clever. And make a great first impression."

"The first time we met you had to help me off the floor," she said, grimacing.

"And look how well that's worked out for us."

She dug an elbow into my side. "You are insufferable."

"I know." Some of the fae were breaking off into smaller groups, their eyes turning toward the royals like seagulls circling a tide pool. "Looks like our window is closing. You ready?"

"As I'll ever be."

I guided her to the dais before she could change her mind. "I'll distract the queen while you talk to the prince." Her shoulders relaxed a bit as we walked.

I wasn't looking forward to the task myself, especially when it meant I wouldn't be able to hear every word of Sorsha's conversation, but it had to be done.

We stopped in front of the royals and bowed with our hands

clasped together. Queen Elora's eyes flashed with surprise and irritation. No one had dared approach her. Everyone was too busy speaking to her husband, who hadn't even noticed our approach. Her eyes lingered a little too long on my wings. I forged ahead, despite her frosty countenance. "Your Majesty. Corvus Stormfall, at your service. This is Miss Sorsha Sventura. We wanted to thank you personally for your gracious invitation."

"So, you *do* have manners," she said bitterly.

The prince scrunched up his face, almost in a mirror image of the woman sitting before me. "Mother," he chided.

She pouted, admonished.

"We are honored to have everyone here tonight," he said, glancing between us.

I squeezed Sorsha's hand, trying to bolster her.

She released her fingers from my grip. "Your Highness, this is my first time here. I wonder if you would like to dance? I have so many questions."

The prince's eyebrows shot up from behind his mask.

The queen scoffed. "So much for manners. My, you're very forward."

Sorsha blushed, but she kept her chin held high, her eyes on the prince.

I felt a swell of pride as she held her own against them.

"I would be delighted, Miss Sventura," the prince replied, ignoring his mother's commentary. He stepped around the throne and extended a hand to her.

Sorsha's face split into a wide grin, and something bitter twinged in my chest. I dipped my head as they passed.

"You mustn't think ill of her," I said, not liking the sneer the queen flashed in Sorsha's direction as she and the prince made their way to the ballroom floor. "She is curious to learn all she can while she is here."

Queen Elora turned her steely eyes to me. "And it had nothing to do with the fact that my son is of marrying age and the heir to the throne?"

A storm raged inside my chest, and a great thunderclap boomed within me at the idea of Sorsha being with anyone else. I vehemently opposed the idea of her with the pathetic mortal prince.

"I am afraid she is spoken for," I said coolly.

"You fae with your territorial mating. Insufferable." She picked an invisible piece of lint off her gown.

"I'm afraid fae mating has quite gone from the land, with no magic to sustain it."

No thanks to you or your husband.

I tried my best to rein in my temper. Sorsha needed more time with the prince. Gods, what would Max do? Probably stroke her ego. The thought made me faintly nauseous.

"Forgive me, but you are not from Tenebris, are you?"

"No," she sneered.

"I thought not. There is a certain quality you possess unlike any I have seen from the mortals in these lands."

She narrowed her eyes at me. "And what might that be?"

Intolerance. Pride.

"A certain regality to your nature, as if you were born to rule."

Her spine straightened another impossible inch. The gems in her tiara and at her throat sparkled in the candlelight. "My father is King Adamite of Emeraulde. I was betrothed to dear Tyrin at a young age and sailed here to become his queen and bride."

That explained much. There were no fae in the kingdom across the western sea. Those lands were wholly human.

"And how do you find Tenebris?"

"It is not as civilized as Emeraulde. Tyrin tells me indoor plumbing and hot water were only installed in most homes within the last half century. No indoor electricity, either."

"Magic used to power much of those commodities," I said. "We've had to come a long way in a short amount of time to compensate for its loss."

She sniffed, unsympathetic to our plight, and looked past my shoulder.

Time to end this conversation. Bowing, I bid my farewell, grateful to leave the company of this bitter woman.

I avoided the cluster of fae surrounding Lucius. My father stood among them, and had no doubt seen me chatting casually with the queen. My eyes scanned the room, searching for Sorsha. She and the prince were pressed into the wall, flushed from dancing.

I watched as she placed a hand on his shoulder and leaned in close, laughing at something he'd said. Fire raged in my chest, my stomach twisted in knots, and the edges of my vision went dark. It was more than I could stand.

Chapter Nineteen

Sorsha

As the prince and I took our place on the dance floor, I was keenly aware of everyone's eyes on me. Mortals and fae did not bother to hide their curiosity and gawked openly, whispering as we passed.

The only consolation was that no one knew who I was, save Viviana and the other courtesans, but I doubted she would tell anyone. She was hanging onto the arm of one of her frequent clients, the fae with blond hair and long, pointed ears. She stared daggers at me as I passed, but she could not touch me here.

Anxiety made my throat tight, and my heart pounded with new ferocity in my chest. Not in the strangely pleasant way it did when Corvus was acting particularly vexing, but in a horrible way that made me feel like my whole body pulsed with every pump of my heart. I tried to focus on the task before me, instead of my nausea.

Information. That's what I was here for. Maybe if I pretended he wasn't a prince, it would be easier.

It might not be too hard to imagine. He didn't carry himself in the haughty way his mother did. If I passed him in the street, I wouldn't know he was a member of the royal family. His ink-black hair fell nearly to his shoulders in a messy tumble, and he walked with a slight slouch.

We took our places as the music began, a gentle, slow tune that didn't require me to count the steps in my head. "Thanks for dancing with me," I said. "I'm actually not very good at it."

He smiled, flashing a dimple in his left cheek. "Truth be

told, I am wildly out of practice. My mother hasn't made me attend a dancing lesson in years." He moved stiffly, his body conveying the truth of his words.

"I think you're doing fine."

An awkward silence filled the space between us as we both tried to keep in time with the music. I tried to think of what to say. I'd said he was doing *fine*. Not great, or splendid. What if he took offense? It was hardly a flattering compliment.

The prince interrupted my spiraling thoughts. "So, you wanted to ask me something?"

"Right." I stepped under his outstretched arm and spun before returning to my place in front of him. "I am not a member of a Great Fae House, so I don't know anything about politics. But I was wondering what you could tell me about this alliance between mortals and fae. The one your father was talking about."

He tilted his head. "Hmm. I think it is important for fae and mortals to work together, to try to make Tenebris a prosperous nation. I think both sides are trying to make that happen, but there are, of course, skeptics who think unity and collaboration is a bad idea."

"I don't think it's a bad idea. For what that's worth."

"That is good to hear. My father only ever hears counsel from his advisors, or other titled humans. The fae only ever send members of their houses to speak with us. We do not hear directly from those who are living and working in the city."

I wasn't surprised. If the other heads of houses were anything like Andromeda, then of course their goal would be to manipulate the royals in their favor. It seemed very unlikely they could agree on what was best for Tenebris.

"And what does this prosperity look like to you?"

"Good trade with other nations, a mostly content populace,

little internal conflict. Those types of things."

Well, at least that was something.

After a beat, the prince continued. "I must admit, when you asked me to dance, I didn't know I would be giving a report on my philosophy of governance."

"Sorry." My face flushed.

"Don't be."

I had already made a fool of myself. Why not speak plainly? I doubted I would ever speak to the prince again or come back to the palace.

"It's just that the fae don't know you. At all. They have been ruled by their houses for centuries. You all come in two hundred years ago, take away magic, and then everyone is supposed to be friendly? Working toward a common goal?" I lost the beat. My feet stopped moving, and I gave up entirely on trying to dance.

The prince frowned, dropped my hands, and stared at me. Any amusement at my impertinent questions had vanished. I felt a shiver of fear race down my spine as I realized I had gone too far.

"If you spoke that way to my mother or father, they'd probably throw you in the dungeon."

Shit. My heart hammered in my chest again. I took a step back, ready to run at the exact moment he called for the palace guards.

"However, I find your candor refreshing, if not a little insulting."

I pressed a hand to my chest, trying to keep my heart from bursting out of my ribcage. My silk glove was damp with sweat. "Seven hells," I muttered.

He cocked a smile, flashing his dimple again. "Walk with me?"

"Sure," I wheezed, taking his arm.

We picked our way through the throng of people who were still dancing. It was only once we had made it safely out of the twirling couples did my heart slow.

"I didn't mean to insult you," I said sheepishly.

Prince Tristan leaned against the wall with his arms crossed, knocking his crown askew. He didn't straighten it. I pressed my back to the wall, letting my weight sink into it.

"I didn't have a say in my great-grandfather coming to Tenebris," he said, staring across the room at the king and queen. "And I can't control what my father does now. I just have to rule after them."

Admirers surrounded the king while Corvus engaged in conversation with the queen. From the pinched look on her face, it didn't look like it was going well. I had to make the most of my time with the prince while I had him.

"Why not restore magic?" I blurted, before I weighed if it was wise to ask such a thing. He continued to stare at his parents, avoiding my question. "Surely the Fae Houses would be much more receptive to your rule if you did so?"

"It is impossible," he said with such finality that I knew if I pushed him on the subject, I *would* be thrown in the dungeon. My heart sank a little. But, since I wanted to get back to Corvus as soon as possible, I dropped it.

"I understand. Thank you for answering my very rude questions, Your Highness." One side of his lips crooked upward, and I felt less panicked. I needed to leave this conversation on a positive note. I didn't want him to remember me for only being uncouth and abrasive. The music stopped and couples clapped.

In the hush that followed I heard a low-pitched humming noise coming from his direction. It felt like there were tiny tremors traveling from somewhere in the wall to reverberate in my ribcage. "What's that noise?" I asked, leaning away to determine where it was coming from. The strange buzzing hummed in my bones even after I pulled away from the wall.

Prince Tristan flashed his eyes toward mine. "What noise?" His crown slipped a little further.

"It's like a humming, or a buzzing sound." The music started up with the next tune, a lively reel, and the strange sound was lost. I must look absolutely mad. Not only did I have the gall to insult him, but now I was hearing things. "Never mind." I realized I had leaned in quite close to the prince in my efforts to find the source of the sound. "I promise I am a nice, sane person, despite all evidence to the contrary."

The prince laughed, which made me feel better. "Then tell me truthfully, Miss Sventura, why did you ask me to dance with you tonight? You aren't the typical sort my mother tries to throw at me. I don't think your interest is in marrying me."

My mouth fell open in shock. "You thought your mother was trying to set us up?"

"Well, not after your strange line of political questioning."

I gaped at him. "That is certainly not my goal, Your Highness. Like I said before, this is my first time here. I know very little of what goes on outside the walls of my home."

His face pinched a little, a shadow of his mother's countenance. "And why is that?"

"I am a courtesan. At the House of Night."

His face paled a little. "I see."

"So, no, Your Highness. I do not intend to trap you into matrimony."

The prince finally straightened his crown, and another awkward silence fell between us. I scanned the room. Corvus had left the queen, and he made his way around the dancing couples. Viviana had circled closer to where we stood, and I knew she was waiting for her opportunity to pounce on the prince.

I leaned in conspiratorially, wanting to end our conversation with some levity. "You see the girl with the purple gems in her hair? She's standing over by the tables in the corner."

He flashed his eyes toward the tall, circular tables. "What about her?"

"Her name is Viviana. She is the prime jewel of the House of Night, and I believe she means to make herself a princess by the end of the evening if you're not careful around her."

I laughed and touched his shoulder gently. The strange buzzing feeling came back, traveling up my fingers all the way into my ribs. The sound came from *him*. My smile faltered ever so slightly as I pulled away. Curiosity flashed behind the prince's silver mask, but Corvus's arrival saved me from any questioning.

Corvus placed a hand on my elbow as he addressed the prince. "Your Highness," he said tersely, inclining his head.

"Thank you for the dance," I said to the prince. "And for answering my impertinent questions."

"Any time, Miss Sventura. You know where to find me." His gaze flicked to Viviana, who was now only a few paces away. "If you'll both excuse me, I must see if my mother needs anything."

I sank into an awkward little curtsey as he left. When I rose, I spied Viviana staring daggers at me. She turned away in a swirl of skirts and stalked back over to her paramour.

I opened my mouth to ask Corvus if he wanted to dance with me again when he muttered, "Come with me."

He slipped his hand into mine and led me out of the ballroom. We walked at a brisk pace down a dimly lit hallway. Something was wrong. His shoulders were stiff, and he did not look at me or speak to me.

The incessant buzzing faded as we moved further from the party, and I wondered if the champagne was to blame for the way my insides had vibrated. We reached the end of the hall and stepped into a dim room, lit only by a few candles and a swathe of silver moonlight that filtered in from a set of arched windows.

Corvus closed the door, throwing the lock. He ripped his mask off and dragged a hand through his hair. He took deep, ragged breaths and refused to look at me.

"What's wrong?" I asked, unable to keep the worry out of my voice. "Did something happen with the queen?"

He laughed bitterly. "No, not with the queen. This is too dangerous. I never should have let you go off on your own."

"I was perfectly safe. We were in a crowd, not some darkened room of the palace." I gestured exasperatedly to where he had brought me. I could see a large four-poster bed set against the far wall, draped in sheer white curtains that fluttered in the sea breeze. A desk and chair, a bookshelf, and a vanity adorned the room. We had broken into someone's apartments.

"You don't understand. Maybe it wasn't tonight, but I know the fae are plotting to overthrow them, and I thought... what if it *had* happened tonight? What if you had been hurt?"

He had grabbed me so fiercely when the golden-winged fae addressed the king. He'd refused to let me go until the dancing began again. My mouth went dry. Seven hells, he *had* thought there was going to be a violent takeover. I had only trained with Corvus a handful of times. The dagger strapped to my thigh with a bit of cloth would have offered me some protection, but not much against the trained skill of fae and human guards.

I pushed my anxiety away, trying to convince myself, more than Corvus, that everything was alright. "Well, it didn't. I'm fine."

"Oh, yes, I'm sure you are after flirting with the prince."

"I was only doing what we agreed on," I said hotly, crossing my arms. "You may pay Andromeda for the privilege of seeing me, but I am not a thing to be owned, Corvus."

He balked, and the color drained from his face. "Sorsha. I would never presume to *own* you." He stepped back, shaken at the accusation. His wings flicked jerkily as he paced.

Suddenly, his ridiculous, petty behavior made sense. "You're *jealous*," I whispered.

Corvus stopped pacing and stared at me. He held his arms stiffly by his sides, hands balled into fists. "How much will it cost to free you from your contract with the House of Night?"

"What?"

"How much is the price for your freedom?"

It felt as if all the air had been sucked out of the room. I couldn't get enough breath into my lungs to answer him. Surely, he didn't mean to pay for my freedom himself? Even if he gave Andromeda the gold, it would not free me from my blood pact with her. But something in my chest cracked as I beheld him standing before me.

"Don't be absurd," I said, and the rest came pouring out in a torrent. "What has gotten into you? You don't go around buying up people's contracts. What is your *problem*?"

"My *problem*," Corvus growled, "is that you are all I think about. Day and night, waking and dreaming. You occupy my every thought, Sorsha. And the very idea that you think I only want to be around you because I pay for the privilege, that I would dare claim any ownership over you, is abhorrent to me."

He closed the space between us in three swift strides, but he kept his hands firmly at his sides. "I claimed your contract because, from the first moment I saw you, you captivated me. I couldn't stand the thought of another's hands on you, of your fire being slowly smothered by servitude to someone who would not care if you lived or died. So, yes, I laid claim to your contract, but never to *you*."

My eyes grew wide, and my heart thumped so hard in my chest I thought it might burst. "When I saw you with him, I couldn't stand it. I told you, I'm incredibly selfish." He laughed bitterly. "I want you to be mine, and mine alone. But *not* because of a godsdamned contract." His breathing was fast and shallow, his eyes dark.

I, too, found it hard to breathe. I couldn't tear my eyes away from his lips as the maddening scent of lightning crackled between us. "You are the most utterly vexing person I have ever met."

His face fell.

"But despite your arrogance, I can't stop thinking about you, either," I admitted.

He brought a hand to cup my cheek, and the warmth of his touch sent a tremor through my entire body. His fingers trailed the edges of my mask, caressing my skin.

"I want to kiss you senseless."

"Then why don't you?" I whispered, tilting my chin up. I took a tiny step closer to him, pressing myself along his body. The cool metal hilts of his twin daggers pressed against my exposed flesh, sending a strange hum through me.

I remembered our first night together in the Emerald Parlor, how he'd withheld his kiss because he thought me indifferent. He wanted to know that I craved his touch as much as he craved mine. "I need you to."

My words triggered something within him. With a low growl and a soft gust of wind, he claimed my mouth with his and I saw stars.

Chapter Twenty

Sorsha

Lights danced behind my eyes, dazzling and bright, as our kiss moved from a soft, tentative brush to a heated exploration. His tongue darted between my lips, and I opened for him, letting him in. I sank fully into the kiss, resting my hands on his chest. He cupped the back of my neck while sliding his other hand around my waist, pulling me closer.

His lips were soft and warm. Heat thrummed through my core, chest, and legs. I'd never felt desire like this. I let out a soft moan of satisfaction and every fiber of my body ignited with smoldering heat. I met him with equal intensity, running my hands over his shoulders and chest as he cupped the back of my neck and jaw. My mask pressed uncomfortably into my face, barring me from getting as close to him as I wanted to.

We weren't in the House of Night. No one needed to know if I removed my mask tonight. I was already on the path to wickedness, with my lying and stealing and dishonesty. A little more wickedness wouldn't harm me now.

I broke the kiss for a moment and reached for the ribbon at the back of my head.

"Are you sure?" asked Corvus, breathless.

"Yes," I whispered.

"Then let me."

I dropped my hands and allowed him to tug at the ribbons of my golden mask.

For a moment, the world felt too wide. The darkness rushed into my periphery, making me feel exposed. I couldn't remember the last time I'd been unmasked at night. My mask dropped to the floor. Corvus cupped my face delicately with both hands, tilting my head to meet his gaze, steadying me.

"Beautiful," he breathed.

My mouth twitched into a nervous smile. His hair fell softly across his forehead, and his eyes had turned nearly liquid with desire. "You are, too."

He ran his fingertips delicately over the apples of my cheeks, down my neck, and over my collarbones, making my skin prickle. I raised on my tiptoes and threw my arms around him, needing to drown myself in the sensation of his touch. I kissed him fiercely, and heat pooled low in my belly as our tongues clashed against each other.

Gods, I'd wanted this.

My heart pounded as we kissed and blood rushed in my ears, drowning out everything but the sounds of our breath. Corvus slid his hands down my arms, tugging at the voluminous sleeves of my gown, freeing me from them. He reached around my back and deftly loosened the ribbons of my bodice.

It was clear he had practice with undoing a woman's dress, but I found I didn't care. He was here, with me. Tonight was for us. I would not think about whatever lay beyond the walls of this room. I would not think about Corvus's past lovers, the threats of war, or my pact with Madam Andromeda.

I pushed everything away, slamming it behind a mental door of stone as my fingers found the buttons of his jacket, then the buckle of his bandolier. I let them both slide to the floor to join my discarded mask.

The top of my dress came loose. "Wait."

He froze instantly. "Do you want me to stop?" he asked, voice tinged with concern.

"No," I said. I absolutely did *not* want him to stop. But I had never let anyone see my scars before. I struggled to find coherent words as desire continued to make my head spin. "I have some scars. On my back," I said finally.

Corvus remained as still as stone. "I have seen some of them," he admitted.

The less severe of them peeked above my clothes, no matter what style of dress I wore. Courtesan dresses were revealing by design. But he hadn't seen the worst of them. "They are... bad." I peered into his face, still searching for the words I wanted.

His eyes narrowed slightly, and his mouth thinned.

"I haven't looked at them in years, and I don't think I'm prepared to let anyone else see them, either." The tight knot in my stomach loosened as I said the words. It wasn't that I didn't want to have sex with Corvus, but I felt too self-conscious to let him see the terrible marks on my flesh. I wasn't ready for that level of intimacy yet.

"I don't want to do anything you're not comfortable with," he said, caressing my face again.

Gods, it felt so nice to feel his touch where only cold metal or stiff fabric usually pressed against my skin. My core clenched with renewed desire.

"This is rather cumbersome," I said as I fluffed my skirts. "I would like to take it off. But please, don't look at my scars."

"I promise I won't."

I bit my lip and nodded.

He grabbed both of my hands. "Do you trust me?" he asked, searching my face.

I looked closely at him, my eyes scanning for the slightest trace of deceit, even though I knew I would not find any. Something twisted in my chest as I realized I *did* trust him. He'd never given me a reason not to.

Guilt, cloying and thick, threatened to stamp out my desire.

No, I thought, reasoning the gloom away. There was a difference. I only stole the note and reported on him because I was forced to. Andromeda had bound me to her service. There were consequences, deadly ones, if I did not comply with her demands and provide her information about the fae and their plans. I only did those things because I had to, not because I wanted to.

Realization dawned on me as I took in the set of Corvus's jaw, the plane of his cheekbones, the light in his eyes. What I wanted was *him*. And if that meant finding another way to get information to Andromeda, then I would stop using him for my own ends.

My spying on Corvus ended tonight. I would find another way.

I left my past transgressions behind me, stepping into my acceptance of the passion between us. My heart filled as I replied, "Yes. I trust you."

He dropped my hands and shed his shirt. I drank in the sight of his broad shoulders and muscled frame. Seven hells, he was stunning.

He placed one hand at my waist, the other at my chin. He gently lifted my mouth toward his, and sparks ignited between us once more. I let myself sink wholly into the sensation of his touch. Our breathing grew heavy, and I couldn't stop the soft moans of satisfaction coiled in the back of my throat.

The backs of my legs bumped the bed. I hadn't even realized we'd moved across the room.

Corvus tugged the last of the tension from the ribbons at my bodice. It fell to my waist, leaving me exposed before him. He trailed kisses across my shoulders, my breasts, my stomach, until he knelt before me. He gently tugged the skirts down my hips. I stepped out of the voluminous pool of fabric, placing a hand on his shoulder to steady myself.

"Sit," he said, his voice rough.

I obeyed as my head spun. I sank into the downy mattress as if it were a cloud. Corvus took off my dancing slippers, tossing them over his shoulder. He trailed his fingers up my thigh, grabbed the top of my stockings and removed them one by one with a whisper. Gooseflesh raced up my body.

The only thing left was the cloth wound around my thigh, my makeshift sheath for my throwing knife.

"Remind me to get you a proper weapon sheath," he growled, untying the knot of fabric. He unwound it, slowly, torturously. Every inch of me ached for his touch. But he was still clothed from the waist down.

"You have some catching up to do," I said, once he had placed the knife on the small bedside table.

He kept his gaze fixed on mine as he undid his belt with one hand. A thrill went through me at the confidence in the gesture. He kicked off his pants and stood bare before me.

I swallowed, my pulse racing as I took in the thick length of him.

Corvus approached the bed. "Lie down."

I did, sinking further into the bed. The blankets were cool, and I felt better knowing my back was covered. My heart squeezed, knowing he had orchestrated the position for me so I would feel more at ease.

"Tell me what you like, darling."

"I know this may seem surprising," I said, as he propped himself up on an elbow next to me and trailed his fingers through my hair. "But I've never enjoyed sex. Or, at least, I have never had sex that was pleasurable for me."

He placed a gentle kiss on my brow. "I would very much like to remedy that, but we don't have to do anything that you don't like."

"I want to," I pleaded, reaching for him. Gods, I needed him to touch me. My body burned with want.

"I mean, I have taken care of myself before. That's always nice," I muttered when he still didn't move. I had figured that out easily. One could only be surrounded by so much sex before they needed to satisfy themselves.

Corvus's lips crooked into a smile. "My sultry Sorsha." He trailed a thumb over my bottom lip. "Show me," he commanded.

And I did.

He trailed kisses all over my body as I swirled my fingers over my throbbing center. He teased me with the lightest touches. As I was about to find my release, he pulled my hand away.

I writhed against the sheets, first in desperation, then in pleasure as he kissed me between my legs.

My whole body spiraled inwards before exploding in a sea of stars. He gripped my thighs, sending me over the edge with his tongue.

My fists released the sheets as I settled back into my body.

"Seven hells," I panted.

"Oh, the things I can show you, Sorsha. This is only the beginning."

He placed both forearms on either side of my head, caging me with his body. The slight weight of him felt so good. He kissed me, his own breathing growing as ragged as mine.

He dipped a finger inside me, then another, sending me writhing once again. His fingers pumped frantically inside me, the palm of his hand hitting the exact spot where I needed him. A sound like something between a mewl and a sob wrenched through me as I crested over the peak, my inner walls clenching against his fingers.

"Fuck, Sorsha," he groaned, sending a wave of pleasure

through me.

I found him in the dark and stroked him lightly. His breathing grew ragged. I placed my mouth on the head of him, and swirled my tongue around, catching the bead of moisture at his tip.

I had never wanted to pleasure someone in this way before. It had always been a chore, something to endure. But the sounds Corvus made as I teased him with my tongue ignited a dark satisfaction. I took in as much of him as I could, and worked him with my tongue and light caresses from my fingertips.

Corvus swore and came inside my mouth.

I trailed my tongue over him through his release, lying back down only after I had wrought every last drop of pleasure from him.

He crashed down next to me and ran his fingers along my jaw in lazy, soothing strokes.

As the sweat cooled and my breathing returned to normal, I turned on my side to face him. My eyes were heavy; my whole body felt limp with pleasure. I wondered what time it was. We had to go, had to get dressed before…

"Sleep for a little while," said Corvus, brushing my hair away from my face. "I'll have you home at dawn."

It was all the encouragement I needed. With a contented sigh, I sank fully into the softness of the bed and fell asleep within minutes.

Chapter Twenty-One

Corvus

I looked. Damn me to seven hells, *I looked.*

I couldn't stop myself. I wanted to know, had to know, who had done this monstrous thing to the woman who consumed my every thought.

She'd rolled over in her sleep with a soft little sound that made me hard again. Moonlight bathed her in bright white light. The blanket slipped, exposing her back to me, and I looked.

Her scars were brutal. Large, jagged lines snaked around her shoulder blades, splaying out from a concentrated nexus of raised tissue at the center of her back. White and red marks crawled up her shoulders like cruel vines. There was no skill or magic involved in what had been done. It looked like someone had taken a serrated knife to her flesh and carved what they wanted from her. I felt my entire body go rigid with blinding hate for the one who had done this to her.

I would kill them. I would find whoever did this to her, even if it took me the rest of my godsdamned life. I would stab my dagger through their heart and watch as the light left their eyes. But not before slowly carving up their flesh, mark for mark, mirroring what they had done to Sorsha.

My heart pounded in my chest as my blood boiled, demanding vengeance and retribution. I inhaled through my nose, willing myself back to calm. I grabbed the edge of the blanket and dragged it back up her shoulder. Her mask lay discarded on the floor of this stolen bedchamber, alongside mine and the rest of our clothes.

As I pressed my lips to her temple, I stroked a long strand of hair away from her face. Yes, she was utterly, devastatingly perfect. It had been better than I had ever imagined. As I tugged the blanket upward, something I had missed in my initial glimpse of her ravaged skin made me freeze. Emblazoned into her flesh with thin white lines and hidden amidst the other scars was the crest of House Dawnstone.

In one earth-shattering moment, everything snapped into place with bone-cracking clarity. She was abandoned as a child. The golden shade of her hair was unique. It all made horrible sense. Even as my mind tried to deny it, to look at the lines seared into her flesh as nothing more than a coincidence, I knew what this meant. I swallowed, fighting to breathe past the sudden tightness in my chest.

My heart shattered into a thousand pieces of jagged glass. I felt hollow, unable to accept this truth that lay before me. The worst part was that I had broken her trust. I had looked at her scars when she asked me not to, and now I could not unsee the Dawnstone mark upon her.

Max had borne the mark of House Stormfall, a symbol of his destiny to rule. Long ago, when magic had flourished, the marks manifested on the flesh of powerful fae. Those with the strength to carry on their bloodline bore the symbols of their houses. Now, they were rare. I, of course, did not have one.

A sickening thought broke through the fog of my turmoil. Did Sorsha know? Is that why she had asked me not to look, so I wouldn't see the proof of her lineage preserved on her flesh?

No. I knew she would not keep such a thing from me. There had been no deceit in her eyes as she made her plea.

I lay on my back with my stomach churning, my throat impossibly dry. I stared at the ceiling, trying to collect thoughts that scattered in every direction. For hours, unable to sleep, I lay there as shadows crawled across the room. There were several facts I could not ignore.

The first was Sorsha did not know of this brand upon her skin, which led me to the second conclusion. She was the lost Dawnstone daughter. A child who had been snatched away from her home, never heard from again and presumed dead.

A memory flashed suddenly, interrupting my thoughts. As a child, my brother and I had visited the Dawnstone estate, a manor nestled into the base of the mountains. We had ambled over paths of granite shale, wound our way through thickets of pine trees, trying to shake off the annoying presence of Lord Dawnstone's daughter, determined to trail us and join in our fun. Her long white-gold hair and wings had been as bright as a beacon amidst the evergreens, so we easily avoided her. When Father's business was done, we were called back to the manor to say our goodbyes. The girl watched us as we left, face splotchy with tears, clinging to her mother's skirt.

When I first met Sorsha, she had smelled so familiar. I couldn't place where I'd experienced that scent before, but now it all came back as I lay next to the little girl from the mountain manor, all grown up. My heart twisted, aching for her. She'd had a family, a home. She had lived in comfort. What had happened to her? Who had brutalized her? What had become of her wings?

I knew with certainty she couldn't be anyone else.

And I was perilously close to being in love with her.

The first pale glow of early morning began to fade the black from the sky. The party was over, and I needed to get Sorsha home. But I couldn't gather the strength or will to move, to wake her, to face the dawn.

Because the third fact, the one that made my palms slick with sweat and my heart race frantically in my chest, was that her kin had murdered my brother – and I did not know how to reconcile my feelings for her with the hate I bore for her family.

In the pre-dawn gray of morning, I roused Sorsha from her sleep. She flashed me a dazzling smile when she woke, rolling over as languid as a cat.

It broke my heart anew.

I was numb, but I forced myself to return her grin, pushing through the sickening guilt and remorse that choked me. We collected our scattered clothing, and I turned around as she dressed to give her privacy. I did my best to ignore the tight set of her lips, the way her smile did not quite reach her eyes, as we departed. We walked in silence down the still corridor, a pale ghost of the merry place it had been last night.

The carriage ride was excruciating. She kept glancing at me, and I knew she could tell something was amiss. I did not know how to tell her of the brand upon her back, of her ties to the most terrible folk in Tenebris. I couldn't tell her that I could never see her again.

My emotions swirled within my heart like a turbulent sea. I felt submerged underwater, unable to think, to breathe, to hear.

"Corvus?"

I whipped toward Sorsha, yanked from the feeling of drowning.

She leaned forward, brows knitted with concern. "Are you alright?" she asked.

If I could play the cad around my father, I could certainly pretend like nothing was wrong with Sorsha. At least until I figured out what to do. I donned my mask of confident ease.

"Yes, sorry," I said, smoothing the lapels of my jacket. "I'm still reeling from last night."

"Oh?" Her face pinched.

Shit. I was such a bastard.

"Not that," I said. "That was…" My chest threatened to

burst. I longed to confess everything to her, to tell her of her heritage. But I had betrayed her trust. "Amazing." I gave her a lazy smile. "I was thinking of what the Forum plans to do next about the royals."

Sorsha relaxed, though her eyes remained slightly narrowed. "Right. Lord Uriel and the king seem committed to coming to some sort of peaceful agreement."

I rubbed my chin, unsure of how to share my doubts about Lucius's public statement.

"Would it help if I saw the prince again? He seemed quite amiable. Last night he said it was impossible to remove the ban on magic, but I have a feeling there's more to it. Perhaps he knows more than he's letting on," she mused. "Maybe he knows what is blocking the magic in the first place. Then we can go from there."

The mere thought of her spending any more time with that insufferable prick made me feel nauseated. But maybe it was for the best. I opened my mouth, ready to encourage her plan, but it was impossible to turn off my feelings for her completely. "I don't think that's a good idea. It could be dangerous."

She shrugged. "We'll see."

The carriage clacked over stone and slowed as we reached the House of Night. I opened the door and helped Sorsha down into the courtyard, brightly lit with the first rays of sun. I let my hand linger in hers for a moment longer than necessary, knowing it would be the last time I held it. The lightning still simmered between us, crackling with heat. But the terrible sadness in my chest dampened it.

"Thank you, Corvus," she said, fidgeting with her skirts. "I had a marvelous time."

And I ruined everything. I banished the thought and dropped her hand. "As did I. Thank you for accompanying me."

"When should I expect you?"

"Perhaps in the next day or so." I glanced at the pale gray stone at my feet. "I have a few things to see to."

"You know where to find me," she said, and I could hear the hurt in her voice. It added another wound to my already bleeding heart.

"Until next time."

She started to walk away, but I grabbed her wrist. I needed to kiss her. One last time.

I brought my mouth to hers, pouring all the things I could not say into the kiss. She grew soft in my arms. I kissed her hungrily, with an intense ache, knowing everything between us had to change.

"Goodbye," I whispered, breaking the kiss. Then I let her go.

She let herself in the side garden gate, glancing once over her shoulder before disappearing into the grove.

I glanced up at the house, wondering what to tell her. What to tell her madam.

My thoughts snagged. Shit. If I stopped coming to see her, what would that bitch do to her?

If I could never see Sorsha again, at least I could free her. I could make peace then, knowing I had not abandoned her to whatever cruelty her mistress would inflict on her. My sorrow quickly shifted, morphing into anger-fueled purpose.

I didn't bother knocking. I threw the door to her office open, the edges of my vision white.

Andromeda's eyebrows flew up.

I placed my palms on her desk, leaning close. "How much for her freedom?"

The madam returned her quill to its ink pot and calmly closed the ledger she'd been updating. She stood silently, face blank, and closed the door. "So, you know." She folded her arms expectantly.

I balked, unease rocking through me. I did not suspect Andromeda knew of Sorsha's lineage. But she was a dragon who guarded secrets like treasures, collecting them like priceless gems to use to her advantage. This was, perhaps, one of her most valuable secrets.

"Of course I know," I said through gritted teeth. "How long have *you* known? Did you think no one would ever find out?"

She breezed past me as she returned to her desk, unbothered by my fury. "It was only a matter of time."

Realization dawned as I put the pieces together. "You were paid off. To keep her identity a secret."

"Naturally."

My thoughts flew to Sorsha. A stabbing pain in my heart came with the renewed realization that her family had abandoned her.

"But *why?*"

"I never asked. Her mother left her here when she was a child and offered to pay me a large sum of money to keep her as a serving girl. When the payments stopped coming in, Sorsha became my courtesan. Luckily for me, *you* are the one who wanted exclusive access. You will keep her secret and continue to pay me."

A muscle twitched in my jaw. "It would have come out eventually who she was. Her mark is not hard to find."

A corner of her mouth twitched upward. "No. Took you long enough to see it, though."

"What would you have done if someone else, someone other than me, had seen her mark?" I asked through gritted teeth.

"Burned it off. Or at least concealed it beneath more scar tissue. It is a magical brand, after all. Goes past the skin. It would have been painful, I expect. Thankfully, it didn't come to that."

I had never wanted to strangle someone so badly. She spoke

so casually of further mutilating Sorsha for profit. I was sick to death of greedy fallen fae. They could all burn in the deepest pit of the seven hells. I might send them there myself.

"How much for her freedom?" My voice was icy.

"Her contract is not for sale. She belongs to me. And you'll pay me for the privilege of her company."

I leaned over her desk, resting my fists on the polished wood, and glared down at her. "I will tell her. I will tell her she's the Dawnstone daughter."

"No, you won't." Her face was a mask of calm.

I towered above her, demanding an explanation. I longed to wrap my hands around her neck.

"What do you think will happen when the truth gets out? When *she* finds out? You know she will want to seek out her father," said Andromeda.

And with sinking dread, I knew she was right. My vision grew fuzzy as a torrent of emotions washed over me. There was no telling what her father would do.

I never meant for things to go this far. I never meant to grow so attached to Sorsha. But I did. And my heart could not take it.

Her cousin had *murdered* my brother.

Andromeda had thought through all possible scenarios and had come out on top.

I knew what I had to do, and I knew I may never recover from the pain of it. I whirled from her office, slamming the door behind me, never to set foot in the House of Night again.

Chapter Twenty-Two

Sorsha

I was slow to rise the afternoon after the masquerade, dragging myself from pleasant dreams in which Corvus and I were a tangle of limbs and breath. I dressed hurriedly, eager to see him again and ask him what was wrong. He'd said nothing had changed, but I knew something was bothering him.

At first, I thought it was something I'd done. I wondered if I'd been dissatisfactory in bed. I hadn't prioritized his pleasure over mine. It was the first time I'd opened my entire self to someone, and it had felt incredible. From the look on his face, as we finished together and lay afterward, draped in each other's arms, I knew that wasn't it.

But something between us had grown the tiniest thorns that pricked at our contentment and bliss. Before we parted, he had kissed me deeply, desperately. What was he not telling me? My stomach grumbled as I twisted my hair into a loose knot. I would pry the answer out of him the next time I saw him.

In my haste to get to breakfast, I nearly missed the small envelope that lay on the floor, pushed under the threshold. I stepped directly on it, crinkling the paper. My name was scrawled across the front in Corvus's neat hand. I hoped he felt more comfortable telling me what was on his mind in writing. I smiled as I ripped open the envelope and read the greeting.

My darling, sultry, Sorsha,
 I meant every word I said last night. I am forever changed, having known you. Which is why I would rather

cut out my heart than tell you this but I must: I can no longer see you.

The blood drained from my face. My knees hit the floor. My breath caught in my chest. I forced myself to keep reading.

This is not your fault. I understand if you hate me, but I see no other way to protect you. To protect us. There are things in motion now that cannot be stopped.

Do not worry about your madam. I have made arrangements and will continue to pay your fee. But I cannot see you. No matter how desperately I want to.

I am sorry.

Yours evermore,
Corvus

Hot, angry tears spilled down my face. I clutched the letter between both hands and read the words over and over until the ink blurred together and I could not see past my tears. No one had prepared me for heartbreak. Those who lived in the House of Night knew better than to grow too attached. It was too messy, too complicated. I didn't account for these feelings to grab me while I was unaware and twist themselves around me like moonflower vines.

I don't know how long I stayed there. Long shadows crawled across the walls and floor. The sounds of courtesans and guests seeped in through the floorboards and through the open window, carried in on the warm summer air. Night wrapped itself around me like a cloak, and I let my swollen eyes close as the thousand shards of my broken heart buried themselves deep into my soul.

I woke several hours later, my neck stiff and back screaming in discomfort. Birds chirped outside among the lemon trees. I got gingerly to my feet, rolling my shoulders and neck, and shoved the now crumpled letter into my dress pocket. I pushed open the door and walked absentmindedly down the hall, not caring where I was going. My feet walked the familiar path to the garden.

I sat on the stone lip of one of the raised herb beds, fingers trailing through the dirt and plucking errant weeds. There were more invasive shoots than I liked to see. Lately, I'd spent all my time with Corvus, or thinking about him when I was not with him. I was such a stupid fool.

My thoughts churned, but as I worked amidst the plants, I settled into myself. The pain of rejection faded to a dull, throbbing ache. My fingers hummed pleasantly as I tended to the herbs. I picked dead leaves and buds, placing the debris in my skirt.

I was, and had always been, a commodity he was paying for. The pain he had taken to ensure my fees were taken care of was a cruel reminder. Andromeda had been very certain he would not tire of me. I didn't know her reasoning, but clearly, she had miscalculated. Unless...

What if he, in that arrogant and egotistical head of his, truly believed being apart was the best solution to a problem he had discovered? What if he believed we were in danger? I knew enough now to understand the relations between fae and mortals were at a breaking point. Something terrible might happen if the royals did not restore magic, or if they could not reach a compromise with the fae.

Horror pulsed through me as I realized one last fact: I

was still beholden to Andromeda to relay information to her through our blood pact.

I did a quick scan of my body, looking for fissures or signs that my ending was imminent, as my heart raced wildly. I examined my hands and the faint scar where Andromeda had sliced my finger open. It looked the same. I didn't feel any different, other than being utterly, foolishly heartbroken. I was honestly surprised I hadn't dropped dead immediately after reading Corvus's letter, seeing as my ability to hold up my end of the pact had vanished. But here I was, and I felt fine.

My heart began to slow, though my palms were clammy. I was okay. Which meant I could still fulfill my bargain. There must still be a way. There had to be.

I scooped the dead plant matter and weeds into my hands and deposited them into a pile next to me, making room for the echinacea and fairy slippers I wanted to harvest. Despite the mugginess in the early morning air, I knew fall would come swiftly, bringing with it a new slew of minor sicknesses and ailments. Every year, it seemed like more courtesans grew ill with the change of seasons. We would need plenty of tinctures and remedies on hand.

The work helped me think. With my hands busy, I could put aside my heartache and concentrate on my current predicament. Until I knew Corvus's reason for his idiotic letter, I couldn't blame him. I could make assumptions all night long, but I wouldn't be truly satisfied, or able to let this go, until I got more answers from him.

For now, it was easier not to think of him at all. It was going to save me a lot of pain and sleepless nights if I could lock thoughts of him away. I would place my memories of him right next to the place in my ribcage where I kept the memories of my mother. They would stay there until I was ready to hold them again.

A bitter, angry tear slipped down my cheek. I wiped it away, smearing dirt onto my face. Birds chirped loudly as they flew over the courtyard's high stone wall. A soft breeze blew the sweet, tangy scent of the trees toward me, and I inhaled it deeply. My heart was heavier with the added weight of this new sorrow, but I could manage. I had to if I ever wanted out of here.

I brought the herbs inside, where I bound their stems with twine and hung them to dry from a wooden rack Ivy had let me build for this purpose. As I twisted the rope around the plants, my thoughts drifted to last night.

It had been breathtaking. Now that I'd had a taste of what life could be like outside these walls, I desperately wanted to find a way back out. But I couldn't rely on Corvus to spirit me away like a princess again. No, only an actual prince could convince Andromeda to let me leave the House of Night.

My fingers stilled on the rough twine. A desperate idea came to me in a sudden rush. I *did* know a prince. My heart twisted, and another errant tear slipped down my cheek. Seven hells, I had to pull myself together. I dropped my supplies and made for the upstairs parlor, taking the stairs two at a time.

The house was still sleeping. I could write my letter undisturbed, without having to answer the incessant questions I knew would be flung at me once everyone had sufficiently recovered from last night's revelry. Viviana was sure to have some choice words for me. I wrote my note before I could talk myself out of my foolish idea.

Your Highness,
I have some information that may help you with the matter we discussed last night. Please come see me at The House of Night at your earliest convenience.

Yours,
Sorsha Sventura

P.S. Thank you for the dance.

I studied my work, pleased with it. It was short and urgent, but not alarming. When it was intercepted, as it certainly would be, there was nothing there to invite the king's soldiers to storm our gates and demand answers. The prince was at an age where contact with women would not be unusual. He didn't strike me as a man who frequented the pleasure house, but this was a personal invitation to the House of Night. Andromeda did not go around handing those out.

It was a carefully crafted piece of bait to get him in the door. And once I had him here, I'd sink the hook in. I didn't need Corvus to rescue me. I was going to get out of here; end my blood pact and my servitude. Even if I had to claw my way out. I folded the note and sealed it with a drop of black wax. Now I had to ask Andromeda to get it to the palace for me.

I reached up to touch my hairpin, but it wasn't there.

Godsdammit. I forgot to put it in before I left my bedroom. I didn't want to think about what would happen should I miss her summons.

My heart sank when I saw the pin was glowing silver and vibrating softly on the bed. Andromeda was already expecting me. I picked up the ornament, tucking it into my messy hair, and heard it emit a low note, as deep as the lowest string on a cello, right next to my ear. I prayed she hadn't been waiting long and ran full tilt out of the bedroom.

Panting, I knocked. *One, two-three, four-five.*

"Enter."

I steadied myself with one deep breath before obeying.

Andromeda raked her gaze over me, a tiny frown creasing her

face. She tossed a small bottle toward me, filled with silencing potion. I caught it clumsily against my chest, one hand still clutching the letter to Prince Tristan. "Take care of that, then sit."

I uncorked the bottle, letting the viscous liquid form a seal at the bottom of her office door. I sat across from her, placing the empty bottle on her desk, which was clean once more. No trace of pen, papers, ledgers, or masks. Funny how she sought to compartmentalize her dealings. It made me wonder if the information she needed had anything to do with her house specifically, or if it was her own curiosity she wanted to satisfy.

"Report."

I had to be very careful here. I did not want to say anything that wasn't true, but I didn't want Andromeda to know how much Corvus told me yesterday. Yes, he had hurt me, but I refused to spy on him anymore. "There is a fae-led plot to overthrow the Blackwoods. Lord Stormfall is aware of it. In fact, he seemed to think a coup was going to happen last night."

Andromeda's frown deepened. "This is not new information."

I swallowed, my mouth suddenly dry. She knew the royals could have been killed last night, and she still went to the palace? Not only that, but she brought her most valuable courtesans with her. What was she playing at? Perhaps I could figure that out, too, if I could get the prince to speak with me. "Prince Tristan is genuinely committed to an alliance between mortals and fae. He believes that peace is attainable, even though he knows fae don't like his family."

Andromeda made a sound in her throat that was caught between an exasperated sigh and a laugh. "He is a foolish boy."

"I need you to deliver this." I held up my letter.

"He will no doubt see you this evening. It can wait." She placed her hands on the desk.

"It's not for Lord Stormfall. It's for Prince Tristan."

Andromeda stared at me hard, and I reminded myself to keep my shoulders back and chin held high.

"You're not serious."

"Everyone saw us dancing last night. Why shouldn't I send him a note? Invite him here? It is entirely plausible he would want to see me again."

She stuck out her hand for the note as she rummaged in one of her desk drawers. I reluctantly handed her the letter. I couldn't tell if she was pleased or extremely irritated with me. She withdrew a small circle of glass framed in bronze. It looked like a monocle missing its chain. She held it up between her eye and the paper. The glass magnified her eye to four times its normal size. She scanned the note briefly, looking through the glass, her engorged eyeball whizzing across the paper.

"The matter you discussed last night?" she probed.

"The alliance between mortals and fae. Like I said, he's very determined to make it work."

"And what information do you have to relay to him? Why do you need to speak to him, and not Lord Stormfall?"

I rubbed my hands together. "I think he needs to know his family is in danger."

Andromeda dropped the magnifying glass and tossed the letter onto the desk. "Absolutely not."

"You want information? Cor— Lord Stormfall didn't have any you didn't already know yourself. But if the prince knows his family is in danger, and I can convince him to keep that knowledge a secret, he might be able to approach the situation from another angle. There might be spies in the palace we don't know about. He could do some digging on his end."

Andromeda rubbed a spot over her left eye. "This is either very clever or incredibly foolish. I'm inclined to believe the latter."

I waited, palms still pressed stickily together. The sweat on my hands released the faint scent of echinacea and earth. I hadn't even had the time to wash after tending to the garden.

After a few moments, Andromeda's fingers stilled. "Fine," she said, palming the letter.

"When he arrives, I'll give you three days to provide me with new information."

I tried not to show the panic that threatened to choke me. It was nowhere near enough time. Prince Tristan was a complete stranger to me.

Corvus had been different. Yes, I had to pry him for a little information, but he had sought *me* out. I felt tears pick my eyes and blinked hard to clear them. I couldn't fall apart again. Not now. "Two weeks," I countered.

"One, and that is my final word."

I nodded, not trusting myself to speak. I'd never challenged Andromeda on anything. Adrenaline rushed through my veins, making me feel lightheaded.

"It will be delivered tonight."

I rose from my chair, tears still threatening to spill at any moment at the sudden sharp reminder that Corvus would not be coming this evening.

"If this plan of yours fails, I trust you will return to the previous one. A little jealousy is good for a male, but too much can sour everything."

Chapter Twenty-Three

Sorsha

Two days passed before I heard any word from the prince. I tried to keep myself busy by tending the garden and adding to our stores of salves and tinctures. Ivy and I had an unspoken agreement. I helped her with a few minor tasks in the kitchen, and she continued to let me use what I needed to make the remedies, so long as I didn't use the stove when she needed it.

We didn't speak much. Ivy had never been the sort to pry, and I didn't feel like talking about what had happened during, and after, the masquerade. I was fine so long as my hands were occupied. I couldn't even bring myself to tell Ferdie about what happened and had to endure his relentless teasing about my involvement with "the delicious Stormfall boy."

It was only in the quiet moments between waking and sleep that I allowed myself to think about him. The stars felt cold and far away as I stared out the window at night with an ache in my chest. When I couldn't stand indulging in self-pity for a moment longer, I turned my thoughts to the prince and my plan.

The fine hairs that escaped my bun clung to the back of my sweaty neck as I stirred over a modest flame, melting beeswax to be molded into candles. I fanned my face, trying to cool myself. The air was sticky despite the open windows. Suddenly, Ferdie barged into the kitchen, letting the swinging door bang into the wall.

"Sorsha Sventura, you absolute strumpet. The *prince*?" He brandished a purple envelope with a silver seal before him.

If the loud bang of his entrance wasn't enough to give me a minor heart attack, then his loud proclamation nearly did. I dropped my wooden spoon and wiped my hands furiously on my apron. "*Shh!* You idiot, keep your voice down," I hissed. I marched toward him, extending my hand for the letter.

Ferdie pouted but handed over the envelope without hesitation. My name was scrawled in silver ink across the front. "You didn't even tell me you were writing to him! You're not juggling two guys at once, are you?" The gleam in his eyes showed me he very much *hoped* I was seeing two guys at the same time. While it was customary for House of Night courtesans to entertain multiple clients, he knew my circumstances were different.

"It's nothing as scandalous as that." I broke open the seal and skimmed the note before folding it into a small square.

"Well, what did he say?"

I checked the door had fully closed, then shut the kitchen window for good measure. "You can't tell anyone. He's coming here. Tonight," I said quietly, trying to keep my voice from carrying.

"The *prince* is coming to see you? What about Stormfall?" Ferdie whispered, eyes popping.

"Lord Stormfall is occupied for a few days." The lie came easily. I almost believed it to be true, like that was the real reason he wouldn't be the one to visit me tonight. "Listen, you can't tell anyone. If Viviana hears about this…" I didn't have to finish the thought.

Ferdie's brow wrinkled. He had no love for Viviana, either. "I can try to keep her distracted. But there is no way this is going to stay secret after this evening. Won't he come with guards or something? She's going to find out if the royal carriage pulls up to the front gates."

"I'll deal with it then. But you can't tell anyone, alright? Promise me."

"Seven hells. A lord and a prince in less than two months!"

"*Ferdie.*"

"Alright, alright, I promise." His delight faded slightly as he said, "Be careful, okay? I know he's a prince, but he's the *Blackwood* prince."

"I know," I mumbled. I knew what Ferdie was trying to say. That I shouldn't involve myself with the family who banished magic from Tenebris and made everyone's lives miserable. That he was not like us. "Trust me."

"Come to my room after dinner. I'll help you get ready."

My stomach clenched. "I can manage on my own." I didn't have it in me to pretend to be excited about the prince's visit. Not when my stomach churned with anxiety. I hadn't even thought of what I would say to him yet.

"He's a *prince*," Ferdie whined. "You can't wear your usual. Besides, when Viviana *does* find out, I want to see her combust. Which will only happen if you are looking ten times more fabulous than she is."

I didn't like admitting it, but it would be satisfying to humble Viviana. I could imagine her look of bloodless fury when she saw Prince Tristan had come for *me,* not her. "Okay."

"I have just the thing. See you after dinner. I have so much to do!" He scampered out of the kitchen without a backward glance, leaving me to ponder the wisdom of trusting him with my secret.

Ferdie proved good to his word. After dinner, he let me into his room where he had been hard at work on his latest creation, a stunning dress with sheer black tulle laid over a gold, shimmering fabric. He'd decorated the waistline with black lace flowers and pearls that crept up the bodice and included straps that tied into bows at the shoulder. His talents were truly wasted here. He could make a fortune dressing the elite of the city. Even though I still felt sick to my stomach at the prospect of meeting the prince again, I couldn't help but gasp when I saw the dress.

Behind a dressing screen, I shimmied quickly out of my plain daywear and slipped into the soft gown. The fabric was light and airy, and the corset held me in all the right places. The warning bell chimed, five minutes until doors. But instead of dressing himself, Ferdie dusted my skin and hair with glittering golden powder and tied a black mask set with the same floral and pearl appliqués to match my dress. He stood back, admiring his handiwork.

"Thank you. You didn't have to do this for me," I said, my voice thick. Despite his thirst for gossip, he was a true, dear friend.

"Please, I haven't had an occasion to make something spectacular in a while."

I brushed the fabric of my mask with my fingertips, making sure it was secure. He shrugged out of his own day clothes, stepping around strips of fabric, pins, and shears that had exploded all over his room during his frenzied creation. I looked down at the dress again as he expertly swiped eyeliner and powder around his face. I couldn't believe he'd made this in a single afternoon, but not even the absence of magic could entirely squash the innate abilities of his tailor bloodline, fae known for the magical creations they could make with fabric.

A clatter of carriage wheels on stone had us lunging for the window. Ferdie's room overlooked the courtyard, and he could monitor all the comings and goings of the folk who visited.

Another wave of nausea overtook me as I saw the amethyst purple carriage pull up to the wrought iron gates.

Two guards with silver swords at their hips flanked the carriage door as it opened, and Prince Tristan Blackwood stepped out wearing a modest white shirt, black vest, and black pants. He also carried a sword.

"Looks like it's time for you to go," said Ferdie as he yanked me away from the window. "Good luck, have fun, don't do anything I wouldn't do." He had the audacity to wink at me as he shoved me out his door.

We marched quickly down the empty hall. Most courtesans had already taken their places downstairs. "I'll try to keep Viviana distracted for as long as possible, but I don't think you'll have a lot of time before she finds out."

I opened my mouth to thank him again but stopped short when Viviana's saccharine voice cut through the hush of the house as we reached the landing. "Your *Highness*. How good it is to see you again."

I swallowed hard and forced myself to take the stairs at a leisurely pace as my heart pounded. So much for secrecy.

"Come with me, Your Highness, I would be happy to entertain you this evening," Viviana crooned. She held her hand out, inviting him to take it.

The prince rested his hand on the hilt of his sword as his guards flanked him. He stood stiffly, straight-backed and chin held high. My movement on the stairs caught his attention, and his eyes met mine.

"Actually, I am here to see Miss Sventura. My apologies. Perhaps another time." He deftly stepped around her and met me at the foot of the stairs. He took my hand and pressed a chaste kiss to my fingers. I wanted to crawl under my covers and hide. My neck grew hot and flushed as every eye in the main parlor turned toward us. Instead of running back up the stairs, I smiled at the prince.

"It's nice to see you again," I said as calmly as I could. "If you'll follow me? I have a room prepared for us."

Prince Tristan offered his arm to me. "Lead the way."

I rested my hand in the crook of his elbow and steered him to the Emerald Parlor. Our footsteps echoed along the polished floors as soft chatter floated around us. The guards followed us down the hall. I didn't know what I was going to do about them. Before I could come up with anything, we reached the dark green doors. "Here we are." I swung the door wide and gestured for him to enter.

"Your Highness," interrupted one of his guards. He had a scruffy red beard and broad shoulders. "We'll check the room beforehand."

"Sorry," the prince said with a rueful smile. "Is that alright?"

"Please, go ahead." I stepped out of the way as the guards did a quick sweep of the room. The other one, a shorter man with long brown hair tied at the base of his neck, even took a small sip of the wine, sprinkled a powder into the glasses, and wiped them clean again with a cloth he produced from his pocket.

The prince watched their movements with a rather bored expression. I swept my foot across the threshold nervously.

"All clear," the red-bearded guard pronounced, coming back out into the hall. They stationed themselves on either side of the door, closing it behind us.

We settled ourselves into two chairs by the wide window. I couldn't bring myself to invite him to the low settee where Corvus and I had sat only a few days ago. I poured two glasses of wine, steeling myself for the conversation about to take place.

"So, Miss Sventura. I admit your note quite intrigued me." He took the wine, but didn't drink.

"Thank you for coming," I said. "I couldn't send the information I have in writing."

He tapped a finger on the table and leaned forward. "My parents do not know I am here this evening. However, I am sure I will get an earful from them in the morning once they find out where I have been."

I twisted my hands in my lap. There was an unspoken, subtle threat there. *This had better be worth my time and effort.* I swallowed hard and steeled myself to take the plunge before I could change my mind. My entire future, my entire life, depended on tonight. "There is a plot to overthrow your family," I whispered unceremoniously. There was no point in drawing out any sort of charade.

The tapping stopped, and a tense silence grew between us. "I know we just met," I went on, desperate to fill the void and convince him I was telling the truth. "And you have no reason to trust me or believe what I am telling you. But I thought you should know."

"Why are you telling me this?" The prince kept his face an impassive mask.

"The fae want their magic back. Desperately. I thought if you knew how badly they want it, you might change your mind about it. It would help you and your family. And" – I swallowed, preparing to embellish the truth – "I like you. You humored me with a dance at the masquerade. I don't think you're a bad person, and I don't think anyone deserves to have their family taken away from them. Or be taken away from their family."

"They mean to separate us?"

I shook my head and whispered, "I think they're going to kill you."

Tristan slumped back into his chair. "Oh. Well, I knew *that* already."

"You did?" Panic made my hands go numb. If I didn't have any new information for him, then my plan was going to fail.

"Yes. Madam Andromeda is a good friend of my mother's. It was the whole reason the House of Night was invited to the masquerade, after all. She may not like the fae, but she's not stupid. She knows we need allies. The masque proved to be the ideal setting for displaying the alliance."

"Is that the only reason you agreed to come here, then? Because Andromeda supports your family?"

He gave a wry smile. "It certainly helped. I knew the chances of my murder were significantly less, at least. And I also enjoyed speaking with you the other night."

Heat bloomed in my cheeks at the compliment, more from embarrassment than flattery. But he didn't know that.

"I am curious how *you* gained such information."

I bit my lip. He'd never need to know about Corvus's involvement. But I had to gain his trust. To do that, I had to extend trust to him. I had to give him something believable and play to his emotions. "I have my ways. Folk tell me things," I said with as much nonchalance as I could muster.

I scanned the room, searching for something to write with. Pen, ink, and scrap paper sat over by the little bookshelf near the window nook. I tapped my ear and shot the prince a look, hoping he'd catch my meaning. I went to retrieve them, keeping my footsteps light and quiet. It wasn't just the guards I was worried about. I didn't know how Andromeda would react to what I was about to share with the prince, and I didn't dare call for the silencing potion again. Then she'd know what I was up to. I doubted his guards would allow it, either.

His eyes narrowed, but he gave me a curt nod and played along with the ruse. "Of course. You seem like a very trustworthy person. I suppose it's your eyes."

I laughed, even as my stomach clenched. "My eyes?" I returned to the seat across from him and set pen to paper.

"Yes. They are very… expressive."

"Thank you." I slid the quick note I had written to him, along with the pen.

I am Andromeda's spy. I can help.

His eyebrows shot up as he read.

"I would say the same about you. Except I think it's your smile that is so captivating," I continued, trying to fill the silence and mask our covert, written conversation.

"Is that why you asked me to dance with you at the ball? I don't recall that I was in a particularly merry mood that evening."

I wrung my hands together. His note was taking longer than mine had. "No, but I could tell you were miserable. I thought I might save you."

He finally slid his reply to me.

You must not be very good if you go around telling someone you just met that you're a spy.

"I thought princes were supposed to save ladies from distress," he said. "Not the other way around."

I scowled at both the note and the comment, and quickly scribbled.

Do you want my help or not?

"You must read too many stories, Your Highness. Nowadays, it is very clearly the lady who does all the saving. Especially when the prince is in a very difficult position."

"Indeed." He read the note but did not pick up the pen. "Well, Miss Sventura, perhaps you wouldn't mind saving me again."

Was this an acceptance of my offer to help? "I am happy to serve in whatever manner you require."

"Is that so? In that case, you may call me Tristan."

"Then you must call me Sorsha."

"Sorsha. I gladly accept your offer. Perhaps you would provide your help at the palace tomorrow afternoon? There's to be a meeting between the Fae Houses and my father to determine next steps to strengthen the alliance. It would make me feel more at ease if you were there. And we can spend some more time alone together. It will appease my guards, too, if you came to the castle instead of me coming here."

My hands trembled. I had gotten exactly what I wanted: an invitation to the palace. The chance to get closer to the prince and find something that would release me from my oath. Hope swelled in my chest, almost big enough to cover the ache that still throbbed there.

"Thank you, Tristan. I shall be there." I grinned, letting all my hope shine through, and slid my hands across the table to scoop up our notes.

Tristan placed his hand on mine, stopping me. His skin felt cool against mine. "Perhaps we can move to the sofa? We'd be more comfortable there." He pointed to the fireplace across the room. He released me, and I nodded to show I caught his intentions.

I balled up the notes in my fist, ready to throw them into the fire once we crossed the room. Tristan was cleverer than I initially gave him credit for. He was skilled at masking our conversation and movements with flirtation.

"Certainly."

My foot caught on the ornately carved leg of the table as I stood, and I pitched forward. I collided with Tristan's chest and a painful jolt went through me, like a shock of lightning. A little cry wrenched itself from my lips at the contact.

Prince Tristan caught me, one hand wrapping around my

waist and the other at my elbow. He stepped back but kept one hand on my arm as he peered at my face. "Are you alright?"

"Yes, I'm sorry, I…" I panted, trying to regain my breath after the sudden shock of pain. I rubbed my chest. "I'm fine."

We both looked to the door, expecting the guards to rush in, but the door remained shut.

He let go but continued to study me warily. "What happened?" he whispered.

I searched for the right way to describe it. "A… A shock. Like something pricked me with a thousand needles all at once," I replied in a hushed voice.

Tristan frowned slightly. He looked concerned, but beneath his pinched brow lay… suspicion.

When I was sure the moment had passed, I went to the mantel, thrust our notes into the fireplace, and struck a match. I watched until they curled into nothing more than ashes before settling onto the settee.

Tristan joined me, startling me when he brushed a stray lock of hair away from my ear and leaned in close. He whispered, "We're going to have to make this look convincing. Are you comfortable with that?"

His breath made the hair on the back of my neck stand up. I did not want Tristan. Not in the way I had wanted Corvus. My throat tightened with the pain of missing him. I buried the emotions, steeling myself. I would do whatever was necessary. So, I nodded and breathed, "Yes."

Tristan leaned in, but as his chest brushed my arm, the painful jolt whipped through me again. Instinctively, I shoved him off. He let out a small grunt of surprise. I clapped a hand over my mouth to contain my gasp and my horror. I had *shoved* the prince.

"What is it?" he asked, bewildered.

"I'm sorry," I whispered once the needle-stabbing sensation had subsided. "It's every time you touch me. That feeling."

He cocked his head and placed a hand over his chest as a flicker of realization crossed his face.

"What? What is it?"

"Not here," he murmured. "Tomorrow. At the palace. We'll talk then." He dropped his hand but continued to stare at me.

I shifted uneasily. I could practically see the wheels turning in his mind. Something was happening, but I did not know what. "I'm sorry. It startled me."

"The fault is mine. I'm sorry if it— if I hurt you."

Apparently, I was not the only one keeping secrets. "It's alright."

Tristan stood and gave a perfunctory bow. "You have given me much to think about. I look forward to seeing you tomorrow. I'll send a carriage for you."

He was halfway to the door before I had a chance to stand. "Thank you again for coming tonight," I called after him.

"It was my pleasure." He opened the door and swept out of the room. I stood motionless, listening to the sound of the prince and his guards' footsteps echo down the hall.

My head spun. I'd gotten an invitation to the palace. The prince put his tentative trust in me. Everything had gone according to plan, yet I felt empty. Hollow.

I left the parlor only when I was certain everyone had gone to sleep. I stole quietly down the halls in the hush of early dawn and shut my bedroom door softly behind me. A flood of astringent smells made my eyes water. As my vision adjusted to the gloom, I saw the wreckage.

The bed was soaked through with wine, the bottles left carelessly behind. One of them had been shattered, leaving glass shards scattered across the floor. The door to my wardrobe hung open, revealing the few clothes I had. They were ripped and slashed, tossed carelessly around. The jars of salves and tinctures I kept here were smashed; the smells of herbs and medicines mixed with the sharp smell of alcohol made my eyes sting.

I regarded the devastation with detachment. A strange numbness settled over me as I saw my masks crumpled, bent, and cracked. My one bottle of perfume was overturned over the small vanity in the corner. The vase, which had been holding the drooping flowers Corvus brought me a week ago, lay on its side. Petals were scattered everywhere, ripped and shredded.

The dress I wore to the masquerade hung over the chair next to the vanity. It looked suspiciously untouched. My heart caught in my throat as I stepped around the glass on the floor and drew back the curtain, letting more light into the room. I didn't want to care about the dress. But it was the nicest thing I owned, made even more dear because of who had given it to me. A single tear dripped down my cheek as I saw the word "whore" written in red lip paint across the midnight-blue fabric, ruining it.

I stood in the middle of my trashed room and wrapped my arms around myself. I started shaking. Another tear slipped down my face as I took in the shredded clothes, broken jars, and stained sheets. The longer I looked, the angrier I became, until my sorrow turned to white-hot rage. I knew exactly who did this.

Viviana had bullied me for years, and I had let her. It was easier to let her tear me down than to fight back, to let her make herself feel better by insulting me or tripping me. But this time she had gone too far. My fists clenched at my sides, and my

breath came in short, shallow gasps.
I would make her pay.

Chapter Twenty-Four

Corvus

I didn't leave my room for an entire day, claiming illness, so I wouldn't have to speak to anyone. It was hardly a lie. I didn't feel like myself at all. Sleep eluded me, even though all I wanted to do was close my eyes and forget about the terrible thing I had done. I lay on my bed for hours, caught in a waking nightmare, my body numb.

At some point, someone deposited food outside my door. Even though my stomach had been growling for hours, I only half-heartedly picked at the bread, cured meat, and cheese. It all tasted like ash.

The weight of knowing Sorsha's lineage sat on my chest like a boulder. Her kin had murdered Max. Killed him in cold blood, in the most despicable, dishonorable way imaginable. If I continued to see Sorsha, it would be an unforgivable betrayal of his memory. Our houses had always been at odds, vying for power and favor, trying to best one another in the pettiest ways. If the Dawnstones suspected their lost daughter had returned and was dallying with a Stormfall, our biggest concern would no longer be a coup of the mortal royals. Civil war between our houses would be certain, even against Lucius's wishes.

If it were anything else, I would have rather plunged my dagger into my heart than stay away from Sorsha. She must have gotten my note by now.

I deserved the worst sort of punishment. Memories of our night together tortured me as I tossed and turned. Her lips had been so soft, her breathy moans made my blood run hot. The way she had stroked my wings with tentative fingertips...

A pounding on the door jolted me awake.

Dio opened the door, letting himself in.

I groaned and rolled over, shoving my pillow over my head. He yanked it off a second later.

"What's wrong with you?" Dio asked, not unkindly.

"I had to break it off with the girl I was seeing," I replied. My voice was hoarse with disuse.

"The Night House one?"

I shoved myself into a sitting position. "Yeah."

"But you were mad about her. What happened?"

"Nothing. It's just... it won't work out."

Dio crossed his arms. "Hmm. That's a shame. Good thing Mira is asking after you. She misses you. Maybe you should go pay her a visit? I'm sure she'd welcome you back with open legs."

"*Dio.*"

"Sorry, I meant arms."

I sighed and scrubbed my hands over my face. I was suddenly very thirsty. When was the last time I'd had something to drink? I reached for a pitcher as Dio continued to run his mouth.

"She said she would come find you herself if that's what it took to win you back. Poor girl. She's smitten with you. Hard as I tried, she couldn't be persuaded to warm my bed. She longs only for you. It's sickening, actually."

"Says the one who tried to sleep with my ex," I replied flatly after downing the entire glass of water. His behavior did not bother me. I had made it very clear I wasn't seeing her anymore. And Dio was, well, Dio. He didn't get attached to his partners in the same way I did. Sex didn't mean as much to him. To be fair, it hadn't meant all that much to me, either. Until recently.

I poured myself another glass of water as an ache pulsed through me.

"Corv." Dio's voice was uncharacteristically solemn.

"Yeah?"

"Seriously, what happened?"

"You're so nosy."

"I know. What I mean is, are you okay?"

"No. But I will be." I had to believe it was true.

Dio clapped me on the shoulder, making me slosh water all over myself and onto the floor. "Good," he said, ignoring the mess. "Because I actually came to talk to you about something other than romantic conquests."

"What?" I shook my hands, drying them.

"It's getting worse."

"What is?"

"Everything. There's a strange sickness spreading through the western Shale. There's no medicine, little food. Folk are getting desperate."

I hadn't gone down to the Shale since the night before the masquerade, and my visits hadn't been as regular ever since I met Sorsha. But things couldn't deteriorate that quickly – could they? I yanked my shirt over my head, replacing it with a clean one. I needed something to focus on, something to *do* other than sit in my room and feel sorry for myself. It made me selfish, but turning my attention to the ruination and destitution of other folk would be a welcome distraction from the wrenching pain in my chest. I needed to see for myself how dire things had become.

But not before I told Dio about my father's murderous invention. "There's something else we have to talk about, too."

Dio waited with folded arms.

"I overheard my father talking with Horatio." I paused, glancing over my shoulder to make sure the door was closed. "It can't leave this room."

Some might call it foolish, divulging sensitive information to a Frostgrove, but Dio was my best friend. He'd seen me through everything. Though he could be an ass, he was loyal to his core.

The frenetic energy that seemed to constantly vibrate off his skin quieted. His eyes became wholly clear. "I'm listening."

I told him what I'd overheard in my father's study. "They definitely were talking about some sort of test."

Dio frowned. "What kind of weapon?"

"I'm not sure. But why else would they need one, if not to overthrow a king?"

"Dawnstones haven't been giving you much trouble lately?"

I shook my head. "Haven't seen them since you got your nose broken."

"And your father has no plan for revenge of his own?"

"It's not outside the realm of possibility, but he's so caught up in winning Lucius's approval. He wouldn't risk it. Lucius keeps going on about unity and loyalty. I don't think assassinating a Dawnstone would win him favor with our new illustrious Primus."

There was a beat of silence. Then, I asked the question I'd only dared think. "Would it be so bad if they were gone? The royals."

"I think we both know it would be better for everyone if they disappeared."

A moment of silence passed between us.

"Let's go to the Shale," I said, my attention once again on the plight in the streets.

We walked at a fast clip down the hall and were almost to the stables when Horatio's slimy voice rang through the hall. "Corvus."

I gritted my teeth at his informal address. He never would have dared to call Max by his given name, nor would he have risked the slight in front of my father. But I had more pressing things to worry about than his insults.

"Yes?"

He thrust a small stack of papers into my hand. "Overdue accounts. See to them immediately. Your father expects a report in the morning."

I thumbed through the stack. Two brothels, one apothecary that catered only to the upper class, and a tavern. I could handle four stops and still get to the west side, as long as everyone coughed up the right amount of coin without too much protest.

"Fine."

Horatio slinked back into the shadows, no doubt happy to be done with an errand he thought was beneath him.

I shoved the papers into my pocket and turned to Dio, whose eyes had gone as hard as ice chips. "Leave it," I said under my breath, and he showed remarkable restraint by turning heel and striding out the door with me.

It was a long night, one I threw myself into, trying to bury my heartache. My own troubles seemed much less in the face of so much suffering. I was needlessly violent with the thug who ran a boxing ring in the upper Shale. My daggers were dripping blood by the time he handed over the full amount he owed, and he was left with one less ear.

After all the coin on my list was collected, Dio and I set to our task on the western side of the city. The horrors we saw burned in my mind long after we reemerged into the soft, glowing lights of the wealthier districts. No amount of ale could dull the sting of what we'd witnessed, but three tankards certainly helped.

Father was waiting for me at the head of the table when I returned home, surrounded by correspondence. "Well?" He kept his eyes trained on the papers in front of him.

I wanted him to look at me.

The bruise on my face had faded thanks to Sorsha's healing ointment, but the memory of it was still raw. He'd never struck me in the face before – never let his temper overshadow his ability to reason. Perhaps he was ashamed of what he'd done.

I placed the sack of gold on the table and tried not to feel too anxious about how much it had lightened over the course of the evening. "How goes the Blackwood plot? I was rather shocked Lucius didn't seize his chance at the ball," I drawled, keeping my voice light despite wanting to grab my father by the shoulders and shake him.

Look at me.

"It is not our place to question Lucius's machinations. Things are progressing." He moved one sheaf to a stack, placing the next in front of him.

A hot wave of anger crested in my chest. I bit my tongue hard enough to draw blood.

Look at me!

"Of course."

Father heaved a sigh and grabbed the bag of gold, weighing it in his hand before pocketing it. "We're to return to the palace tomorrow. The Fae Forum has been summoned to speak with the king."

I crossed my arms as anger continued to simmer in my stomach. I wouldn't mind giving the king a piece of my mind. Or helping Lucius depose him. They were selfish, arrogant bastards who were slowly strangling their people, all because they wanted to control the one thing they couldn't have.

"What time do we leave?"

"So interested in politics lately, Corvus. Seems like I finally knocked some sense into you."

I bit my tongue again. The tender spot sent a jolt of pain that kept me from unleashing.

"We depart at noon. Do not embarrass me this time."

"I won't." I marched out the door, not bothering to say goodbye.

Chapter Twenty-Five

Sorsha

As the carriage wheels rolled over the cobblestones, I focused my thoughts on my lingering rage instead of the roiling anxiety in my stomach. I hadn't yet decided how I would extract my revenge for Viviana's cruelty, but it was soothing to let my mind wander over scenarios of smashing her room to bits or cutting her hair while she slept.

The smell of salt grew stronger as I neared the castle. I swallowed, trying to clear the lump in my throat. There was a very good chance Corvus would be here today. The thought sent my heart racing even as a bottomless pit opened within me. Not even my fury could smother the yawning ache.

Before I had completely sorted out what I would say to Corvus if he was here, the carriage pulled to a stop at the steps of the palace. Andromeda had given me a note bearing her seal, declaring I was to represent her at this meeting. She'd been invited, but after I told her that I had secured an invitation from Prince Tristan, she ordered me to go in her stead. Her ready agreement made me more than a little wary. A disinterested guard broke the seal, then waved me through the wide double doors.

In the absence of partygoers and revelers, the palace was disconcertingly quiet. The rooms seemed larger, the ceilings higher, and I felt very small as I followed behind a servant dressed in palace livery. We wound our way through twisting corridors and passed under windows of rainbow sea glass until we reached a dark paneled door.

The servant announced me. "Miss Sventura has arrived, Your Highness."

Tristan opened the door, wearing a very formal jacket with polished silver buttons. In the daylight, it was easy to see the circles under his eyes, nearly the same dark purple hue as his attire. "Thank you." He gestured me into the room.

A large map of Tenebris, as tall as I was, hung on one wall. A table bearing several opened books and rolls of parchment sat in the center of the room. High arched windows let in plenty of sunlight, and the cry of gulls filtered in, mixing with the crashing sounds of surf.

"Where is everyone else?"

"The meeting will be in one of the receiving chambers on the first floor. This is my private study. I thought we should talk strategy beforehand. It would be very poor form to throw you to the wolves without fair warning."

I wasn't sure whether to be grateful or insulted. But he was right. I had no idea what to expect or how to act. I'd spent my entire life blending into the shadows. Now, I was to represent not only Madam Andromeda, but the entire House of Night. The weight of it settled on me all at once, nearly buckling my knees. "Thanks," I managed weakly.

The prince studied me for a moment, tapping a finger to his lips. "Do you know the other Fae Houses?"

"I can name them." My face grew hot. I had been studying hard. I'd found an old book in one of the parlors, *The Great Houses of Tenebris,* but it was clearly a long-forgotten relic. The pages were damp and smelled of mildew. It must have been more than half a century old. Each house had a chapter devoted to them and listed lineages, marriages, and deaths of all the family members of the fae families.

Tristan stared at me, like a tutor waiting for their pupil to recite their lessons.

I ticked each house off my fingers, rattling them off. "There's Day and Night. Frostgrove, Sunbarrow, Thornspring, Stormfall, and Dawnstone."

"And Uriel," said Tristan darkly.

House Uriel hadn't been in the book. "Right."

Tristan let out a tired, brittle sigh. "It's probably best if you sit next to me. I can point out who is who. The real work will be after the meeting."

"But if I sit further away from you, I'll be able to see and hear things you might not." I wanted to be useful. The prince was treating me like a delicate dignitary, not someone who had spent most of her life eavesdropping on illicit conversations. "I can handle it," I said, with much more conviction than I felt.

"Of course, forgive me. I fear another sleepless night is catching up with me." His gaze flicked to the enormous map on the wall, its edges frayed.

"You don't sleep?"

He turned back to me with a rueful smile. "Not lately. There is much for me to think about. Anyway. Lucius Uriel will sit closest to my father. He's speaking for all the Fae Houses now, it seems."

He cleared his throat. "You know, this could be dangerous, especially if the conversation goes poorly. There will be guards, and you know many in this meeting would like to see my family dead."

"I know how to defend myself," I said.

"I should at least give you a weapon." He looked about the room.

"Who's to say I don't have one already?"

"No, I mean a dagger or something…"

I reached under my skirts, ignoring the prince's scandalized face, and withdrew my dagger from where I'd strapped it to my thigh. "Happy now?"

Tristan cleared his throat. "Yes. I suppose that will do."

He blinked hard, scrutinizing my dress. "What are you wearing?"

I touched my hands to the skirt of my dress. After the ornate gowns I had been wearing the past few weeks, an old serving dress was distressingly plain. But Viviana had shredded my other suitable clothing. I'd found this one, unscathed, hiding at the bottom of my wardrobe. A reminder of what I would always be to her. "It's all I had."

"I think we can do better. One moment."

He rang for another servant and spoke in a low voice to her. Within minutes, she returned bearing a new dress. She escorted me to a private bathing chamber where I slipped into the gown. The color was a deep purple, almost black. It was quite snug, made for someone thinner than I. I couldn't lift my arms above my shoulders, but it would do.

Once I had changed, Tristan led us back to the main floor, down an ornate staircase carved to look like coral.

We walked into the meeting room, passing under a silver arch inlaid with purple gems. The king sat at the head of the long table, surrounded by fae. Lord Uriel, the one with the golden wings, was directly to his left. A stocky male with rich, brown skin was stationed next to Lucius, and another with a shock of white hair and ice-blue eyes sat across from them. A broad-shouldered fae with skin like Tilly's, tree bark and lichen-mottled, was also present. Two males who wore white cloaks strapped to their shoulders with ornate golden clasps stood like guard dogs.

A female I'd never seen before was also there, dressed in pale gold. She sat with her back ramrod straight, hands clasped in front of her on the table, and did not speak to those around her. She, along with everyone else, ran their eyes questioningly over me as I gave a quick curtsy to the king and approached the empty seat next to the woman draped in shimmering fabric. Tristan drew the high-backed chair for me, making sure I was settled before taking the empty seat next to his father.

"I take it Andromeda will not be joining us?" she asked tersely.

I parroted the phrase Andromeda had given me should anyone question my presence. "She sends her regrets."

She made an indistinct sound in the back of her throat. "You'd think she'd at least have the decency to tell me she was sending a proxy." She scanned the open windows that lined the back wall, overlooking the cliffs.

I shifted my weight onto my left thigh, feeling the press of the dagger's handle, and let the pressure ground me.

We sat, waiting for the rest of the remaining attendants. There were still two empty chairs. Soft murmurs of conversation hummed, masking the underlying tension that lay over the assembled party.

The male in the white cloak stared hard at me, a curious expression on his face. His wide brow was furrowed, his bushy bronze eyebrows drawn together in concentration. I could feel his eyes on me as I continued to scan the faces of those assembled, trying to match them to their houses.

Footsteps sounded down the hall. A faint rustling sound preceded the last guests, and my heart plummeted into my stomach. Corvus and his father entered the chamber. My lips tingled and my pulse thudded in my ears at the sight of him. I pressed my weight harder into the dagger, letting the bite of it pull me out of whatever melancholy fantasy was about to spring forth.

Corvus took one of the remaining seats at the table across from me, but I kept my gaze on the king. I could feel the air pulse between us, but I would not give him the satisfaction of staring at him.

"Now that we are all assembled," said the king, "we may begin."

Lucius began his address in a honeyed tone. "Your Majesty. We come to you hoping an arrangement can be made that will be mutually beneficial to all gathered here today."

"And what arrangement would that be?" the king asked, a frown pulling at the corners of his mouth.

"The restoration of magic to Tenebris."

There was a tense beat of silence. The woman next to me clenched her hands together so tightly I could see the whites of her knuckles.

"Impossible," said the king brusquely.

The male who had been staring at me spoke. "Your Majesty, with all due respect, I believe it *is* possible, but for whatever reason, you will not *allow* it. There is a difference between the two."

"We've managed these last two centuries without it. We will continue to do so."

The stocky fae spoke next. "The Sunbarrow lands are not producing as they should. The soil craves magic. We're losing profits. It's been hard enough to feed our own, let alone trade with Grauradur or Emeraulde."

"Profits are indeed falling," said Corvus's father. "I am sure you are also feeling the strain on your coffers."

Now I had an excuse to look in their direction, I let myself glance at Corvus as his father spoke. He slouched in his chair, with one foot crossed over his knee. His hair fell untidily into his face. He looked like he would rather be anywhere else.

I clenched my hands, letting my nails bite into my palms. The fate of our land, of the people, was being discussed. He could at least have the decency to look halfway interested.

Then I saw the hard look in his eyes.

Before I could puzzle out what that look meant, the king offered his rebuttal. "A few slow economic years do not call for an upheaval of our entire way of life."

"We have already suffered an upheaval," said Lucius. The pleasantness had gone from his voice. Now he spoke with the sharp authority he had used at the masquerade ball, cutting through to the heart of the matter with razor efficiency.

"Before the Great War, fae and mortals lived in harmony with each other, while magic flowed freely through the land. Once your family took power, they banished magic to keep control over the rebels. There *are* no more rebels. None of us suffer dissenters on our lands. The Great Fae Houses are mere shadows of what they were, their power interred in tombs of silence, lost to us. When magic is restored, there is no guarantee that the fae will regain the strength they have lost. Our blood has been without it for so long, it is entirely unknown how we will react."

Tristan sat beside his father, thin-lipped, as Lucius spoke. He leaned forward, as if he wanted to interject.

"Then why risk it?" asked the delegate on my right. "If we don't know what will happen when magic is restored, why chance it?"

The king extended his hand toward her, emphasizing her point. "Precisely. Lady Reya speaks sense. It could do much more harm than good."

"Soon it won't only be Sunbarrow crops that fail," said the one with tree-bark skin. His voice was willowy, like the whisper of wind through the trees. "The lakes and streams on our land are receding, the trees grow brittle. The woods and waters crave the magic, too."

The king's face grew red. "We *will not* restore magic."

"Our defenses are too weak to withstand an attack without it, Your Majesty," said the man in the white cape with deadly calm.

"Who said anything about an attack? That's fearmongering, I say! Warmongering!"

Lucius got to his feet, sending his chair scraping against the sandstone floor. He leaned his palms on the table as his wings flared and stretched behind him. "Then explain the troops at the northern border."

The king said nothing. A vein pulsed in his forehead.

My palms grew clammy. A military force was at the border? Corvus had failed to mention that. I thought our worries lay within, that the only threat to Tenebris was ourselves.

"What troops?" asked the man with white hair and incredibly snow-pale skin. He flashed a worried glance around the table. Lady Reya stiffened.

"They are on a military training exercise," interjected Tristan, breaking his silence. "Same as the ships in the harbor."

Lucius straightened to his full height. He seemed to grow twice his size, towering over the table and all those assembled around it. There was a sound of steel as the guards who stood around the room drew their swords and stepped forward.

I tightened my fists further to keep from shaking.

"It seems you are unwilling to cooperate with us, Your Majesty," said Lucius, ignoring the approaching guards.

The king leaned back in his throne, one hand placed on the table in front of him. "You think I don't know what is really going on here, Uriel? I know just how much *profit* you all see with your smuggled, pathetic magics." He shook his head.

"How far you all have fallen to rely on your little black market. I have half a mind to raid the entire city – your house included."

He pointed a finger accusingly at me. My cheeks flushed as he called out the House of Night. But he wasn't wrong. Andromeda had built her success on the exclusivity and illicit magics she could offer. Her paltry parlor tricks made her a fortune, and everyone knew it.

The king jabbed his finger back at Lucius, and my chest eased as the attention shifted away from me. "*That* is the peace I offer you. I allow you to run your little black-market schemes with little resistance. In exchange, you let me rule my country how I see fit." He pushed himself back from the table and marched toward another door set into the back wall of the chamber, ignoring Lucius's imposing figure and the murderous glares from those still seated. "You're all dismissed. Now, *get out.*"

Tristan followed behind his father. Two guards closed the door behind him and barred the way should anyone seek to follow them.

Lucius turned to address the fae still seated. "My friends. Times grow dark indeed. We assemble at the Forum tomorrow. At dawn." He swept from the room without another word.

Several fae got up to follow him. The guards stood menacingly close to us with their blades still drawn. I rose from my chair, knees shaking. I knew I should follow behind everyone and exit through the front. I had instructed the carriage to wait for me. But the talk of military forces at our border had awoken a deep unease. Did Andromeda know about this? My heart sank. This information alone wouldn't be enough to satisfy the blood pact. I needed something more.

I walked calmly past the guards flanking the silver arch, ignoring the aggravating pull toward Corvus. I let the fae who had left before me get a good way down the hall. I risked a quick glance over my shoulder to be sure no one would see me, then dipped into a side hallway.

It took me a long time to find Tristan's study again. All the doors looked the same, and I passed the same portrait of an imposing mountain wreathed in flame twice. Eventually, I found my way to the second-floor study and knocked. When there was no answer, I let myself in.

The room was empty. I collapsed into a nearby chair and placed my forehead on my knees. Taking a deep, shuddering breath, I tried to fight my idiotic instinct to run back downstairs and demand answers from Corvus. But he hadn't even tried to speak to me. So, what was the point?

He was an arrogant prick. Not worth a moment more of my time.

A strange sensation flooded my nose. I pressed the back of my hand to my face, tasting copper. A smear of blood stained my skin. Shit. My stomach clenched. I touched my other hand to my hairpin, wondering if I had missed a summons from Andromeda, but the metal lay cool and still under my fingers. What was happening?

The door banged open, startling me. I shot to my feet, whirling to see Prince Tristan, looking pale and drawn.

"Sorsha. You're still here."

"Yes, I'm... I wanted to ask you..." I fumbled for the right words but lost them as I watched him sway unsteadily on his feet. "Are you alright?"

He barked a humorless laugh. "Fine, I suppose. Now that I know I won't be murdered this hour." He collapsed into an adjacent chair.

"I'm sorry. It must be taxing." I wiped my hand discreetly on my skirt, cleaning the blood away.

"You could say that." The color returned to his face, but he still looked ill. "Your fae kin are quite determined to do me in, by scaring me to death, if not by killing me outright."

I grimaced. "Not entirely my kin. I'm half-mortal, half-fae."

"Oh, sorry. I assumed…" I swore a look of confusion flickered across his face as he shook his head. "Well. You do work at the House of Night."

I shrugged. "Being a fae is not a requirement for employment. Anyway, I wanted to ask you about something. What military exercise are your troops doing at the border?" If I could get more information on what they were doing, something that no one else knew, then maybe Andromeda would be satisfied.

Tristan rubbed a hand across his face but didn't have time to answer before the door banged open and the scent of thunderstorms crashed through the room.

Chapter Twenty-Six

Corvus

I could barely draw breath at the sight of Sorsha sitting next to the prince, wearing that fucking Blackwood-purple dress. The knife of regret twisted brutally in my heart, knowing I was the one who had driven her to him.

Of course, I'd followed her. She was headstrong and foolish for wandering around the palace after their guards had drawn their swords on us. What if they had caught her? She had no regard for her own safety.

All throughout the meeting, I was keenly aware of her presence. The very air between us seemed to vibrate. I'd followed the sensation as we left, giving my father some trifling excuse about staying in the district for some amusement. He'd been happy to let me go, diverting his full attention to breaking into Lucius and Elias Dawnstone's heated conversation.

In the main corridor, the hum beneath my skin pulled me toward the hall she'd slipped into. I had a hunch she was off to meet the very man I wanted to speak to.

When I opened the door, I wasn't sure what I would find. A hideous mental picture of her wrapped in his arms had me gritting my teeth, but they were only talking.

She stared at me, her mouth set in a hard, thin line. As my eyes met hers for the briefest moment, I could see the hurt that swam there. It hit me like a punch to the stomach. I wanted to kneel before her and beg her forgiveness, but then I remembered she was a Dawnstone, I was a Stormfall, and star-crossed we must be.

I focused my attention on the sniveling prince beside her, the one who had dared lie to our faces about the military's movements. I let the force of my anger propel me forward.

"Pardon the intrusion, Your Highness," I said, though I didn't want his forgiveness at all.

"Stormfall." His fingers flexed to the weapon at his waist. "How did you get past the guards?"

"I have my ways." I'd simply followed Sorsha, but I liked that he thought me capable of sneaking around unseen. If he feared me, perhaps he'd take me more seriously.

Sorsha shifted in her chair, but I kept my eyes trained on the prince, ignoring the ache in my chest. "I found that meeting dissatisfying and insulting."

The prince adopted a mask of steel. "My father has decreed that magic will not return. His word is final."

There was a tense beat while I collected myself. "Have you seen the poor of this city, Your Highness?"

"We get reports regularly," he said, dismissively.

"I didn't ask you what your reports have told you." I crossed my arms. "Have you *seen* them?"

"Corvus—" began Sorsha.

But the prince interrupted her. "No, Lord Stormfall. I have not seen them."

"Your people are not simply poor. They are starving, and not for lack of trying to take care of themselves. More will continue to die. A sickness is spreading through the Shale. It won't be long before it reaches the inner city. You do not know how your people suffer." I fought to keep the sneer out of my voice as my wings twitched, stirring the air.

"You need to come with me. You need to see with your own eyes what has befallen your people."

The prince regarded me coolly as I breathed heavily through

my nose. I didn't know how else to convince him that the city was desperate. They needed help. They needed their magic back.

"Fine."

I had to keep my eyebrows from arching in surprise. Was he so easily convinced?

He rose to his feet. "Despite what you may think of my family, I want to help. I want to do what is best for Tenebris."

He squared his shoulders, having come to some decision. "I will accompany you on one condition. Sorsha comes with us."

I clenched a fist as unease rippled through me. "Why?"

He shrugged, nonchalant. "I feel safer when she's with me."

Sorsha's brows knit in confusion, which made my unease about his interest in her grow.

"No." If he was going to be tight-lipped about his intentions, then there was no way she would be going with us.

Sorsha shot to her feet. "Of course I'll come."

"It's too dangerous," I shot back.

"What, and it's not too dangerous for the prince to go by himself out into the city?"

"He can wear a disguise. And he can defend himself, if necessary," I said tersely.

With a ferocious glare, Sorsha reached up under her skirt and whirled. There was a brief flash of silver, then a *thunk* as her knife sank into a large map on the wall, striking the heart of the city.

She turned back to me triumphantly. "I've been practicing."

The prince raised an eyebrow.

I didn't have any reason to keep her from coming along, other than my reservations about the prince's motives. I still had a deep urge to protect her. But if I wanted any answers about why the prince was interested in keeping her close, perhaps I shouldn't get in the way. "Alright. You can come."

Sorsha strode over to the wall, removed her dagger, and re-sheathed her weapon. I studied the rug, focusing on the ridiculous floral pattern instead of Sorsha's fingers skimming up her thigh.

"So," she said, drawing my attention back to eye-level. "When do we leave?"

I noted the prince's slightly flushed face with a flicker of annoyance, but forced myself to swallow it so we could make our plans.

We left the palace at eleven o'clock, after darkness had well and truly fallen. The moon shone brightly, glinting off the sea as we walked around the back of the sprawling castle to our carriage.

Sorsha and the prince had both changed into plain, dark pants and shirts. There had been much arguing about whether Sorsha should wear her mask, but she'd been adamant about keeping it on. When I'd suggested that it would draw too much attention to her, she glared at me with such fire that I knew she was thinking about plunging her dagger into me. We'd settled on her wearing a hooded cloak, despite the warm night, and my blood was spared from being spilled in the prince's study.

Sorsha's carriage took us to the edge of the royal sector. It was a mile walk to the westside neighborhoods from there, but neither of them objected. Smells and sounds morphed and changed as we traversed through the city, sticking to shadows and avoiding the brightly lit gas lamps that lined clean, cobbled streets.

I led the way. Sorsha and the prince only murmured to each other occasionally, keeping a suitable distance away from me. I was conspicuous as it was. There was no cloak that could cover my wings, and I'd traversed these paths enough times that people recognized them. Whenever I cast a glance over my shoulder to make sure they weren't too far behind, I caught Sorsha looking around wide-eyed, taking in all she saw. In my urgency to get the prince here, I'd almost forgotten she'd never walked these streets in her adult life. Soon she'd see it all, just as the prince would. I tried not to feel guilty about it.

Smells of cooking wafted from brightly lit windows and awnings as we walked. The chatter of mortals enjoying themselves floated down the streets. I stopped by a few stalls selling fresh bread and dried meat, filling a small bag with as much as I could.

Slowly, the laughter faded into silence as we approached the river. Only the occasional infant wail or shout broke the stillness. The streetlamps grew dim, then dirty, until eventually there weren't any lights at all.

Then we heard the moans of the sick and dying.

I stopped on a street corner near the top of the sloping neighborhood, waiting for Sorsha and the prince to catch up. The fae homes here were cramped and dirty. Rags hung in the windows in the absence of glass, and puddles of stagnant water mixed with piss created a foul odor. The streets were empty, save for the occasional drunken fae who stumbled from an alley only to slip into another one.

Sorsha came up behind me, stopping near my elbow. "This is horrible," she whispered.

"Come on," I said.

We walked down the empty street, which grew narrower. The buildings closed in tight on either side of us. The putrid stench of the river made my eyes water. Suddenly, the street spit us out into a wide lane that ran parallel with the river where the most destitute fae in Tenebris lived. Here, the fae had made their homes from what they could scavenge. Wooden poles and boards draped with fabric, broken shipping boxes stacked together, or old sails. Many fae slept right in the street. There were so many.

I led Sorsha and the prince down the street. There were a few fae lying in the road who were not sleeping, but dead. Their bodies were in varying stages of decay, some bloated and swarming with flies and maggots. We walked until we reached an old warehouse, gutted and turned into a makeshift shelter for those who were sick and had strength enough to make it here.

A small voice croaked from a shadowed doorstep, "Look, Mama. The bird man is here."

I stepped toward the voice and saw a young fae with treebark skin, leeched of all color, crouching next to an even paler older female. The child looked at me with large, luminous eyes.

"Hello." My chest squeezed painfully.

The mother did not stir, despite the feeble nudging from her child. She was dead.

"Mama," croaked the child again, before a fit of coughing left him gasping for air. "Mama, please. The bird man is here."

I reached into the bag of food and withdrew a soft roll and a few pieces of jerky. As much as I wanted to give him the whole bag, I knew it would make him a target for other hungry folk.

"Here. Eat this. It will help you feel better."

The child took the food from me with shaky fingers and a whispered thanks. He tore a tiny piece from the roll and put it in his mouth.

I straightened, knowing there was nothing I could do for his mother. No amount of food or gold could bring her back.

We turned the corner and made our way back up the sloping street. I handed out as much food as I could to those we passed, but it wasn't enough. It was never enough.

It started off as a way for me to wash away the sins of my father. As I resorted to increasingly violent means of extracting the black-market fees from the folk on father's list, I would come and redistribute some of the gold. Penance for my own transgressions. But over the past year, things had gone from bad to worse. No matter how much food or gold I gave, they still suffered.

I focused on my breath, trying to calm my fury. While things had steadily decayed, the Blackwoods did nothing. I only hoped that now, after seeing the desperate need of his citizens, the prince would restore our magic without his father's consent.

When we came to the top of the hill, I felt calm enough to hold a conversation. I stopped and turned to face Sorsha and the prince.

Sorsha removed her hood. The moonlight caught the tear tracks on her face. The prince was pale, his lips bloodless.

"Now do you understand?" I asked, my voice low and lethal.

"Yes," he said hoarsely.

I waited for him to say something. But his eyes had a faraway look, like he wasn't seeing me.

"Then you'll restore our magic?" I pressed.

"It's not that simple," he whispered.

The acrid rage that had been eating away at me all evening surged before I could draw breath. I grabbed the prince by the front of his shirt and slammed him into a stone wall. Sorsha let out a cry. "What the fuck? You saw them. They might be fae, but they are still your people. They are sick and dying. *Help them!*"

The prince wrapped his hands around my wrists and jutted his chin out. "I will help them. But it is not as easy as convincing my father to un-banish magic," he said mournfully.

"Tristan." Sorsha's voice shook. "Please."

"You don't know what it is you are asking for."

I shoved the prince into the wall again before dropping my hands. My chest heaved with frustration. "What about this is so hard to understand? Do you want to go tell that child the reason his mother is dead is that it's not *convenient* for you?" I shook my head. "Maybe you deserve to die after all."

"Killing me will not bring your magic back." Now the prince was growing angry, his careful diplomatic facade cracking. A vein throbbed in his temple, and he clenched his fists at his sides.

"With you out of the way, there's nothing to stop us from restoring it."

"Many more will die, if we are gone."

"What the fuck does that mean?"

"I can't tell you."

My fingers crept to the daggers strapped to my chest. It would be so easy to kill him here. There were no palace guards to defend him, and no one would come running if he screamed. I let myself imagine what my father would say if I told him I'd murdered the Blackwood prince.

The prince threw up his hands, interrupting my murderous thoughts. "I can't tell you, but I can show you."

"Fine," I spat, leaving my daggers in their sheaths. "Show me. Then I'll decide if you get to see the sunrise."

The prince frowned, but nodded, accepting my terms. "We need to return to the palace."

"Looks like we better get moving, then. Lead the way. If you try to run, I'll kill you."

The prince turned on his heel and began the trek back to the palace. This time, I left no distance between us but kept right behind him, ready to cut him down if he tried anything.

"Corvus, don't do this," pleaded Sorsha. "You can't kill him."

She grabbed my arm, but I yanked it away.

"Watch me," I hissed.

"I know you, Corvus. I know you wouldn't do this."

"What if he's making it worse? What if he can help, but is choosing not to? Why does he get to decide who will live and who will die?"

I saw the prince's shoulders tense, but I did not care about his feelings.

Sorsha pulled away, leaving an ocean of space between us. If there was any chance of repairing the damage I'd done, I was sure I'd destroyed it.

Chapter Twenty-Seven

Sorsha

My feet were leaden as I walked next to Corvus. The horrors I had seen tonight kept playing over and over in my mind as we made our way back up the sloping street. My breath came in short little bursts that had nothing to do with the slight incline of our trek. Bile threatened to make me spill the contents of my stomach, but I swallowed it down.

Between the cries of the dying, Corvus's threat to kill Tristan, and my own overwhelming feeling of helplessness, I was sick and numb all at once. My pleas for Corvus to see reason, my attempts to convince him he was better than the threats he made, were pointless. I could feel the anger rolling off him in waves as we walked, and I knew he wouldn't listen to me. No matter how much I wanted him to.

I quickened my pace to walk next to the prince, leaving Corvus behind. I felt his hard stare boring into my back as we made our way back to the brightly lit streets of the upper sector, but the golden glow of lamplight could not push out the darkness in my thoughts.

What did Tristan have to show us that was so horrible? What could possibly be worse than what we had seen tonight? A chill rolled through my stomach.

"Is your driver discreet?" asked Tristan. "Or will he tell Lady Andromeda we've been gallivanting through the city all night?"

"You don't have to worry about Andromeda," I replied as my shoes clacked on the clean cobblestones. Porter, the burly fae who drove the carriage or who stood guard outside the gates, was a quiet sort. He spoke in short, gruff sentences. I doubted he'd go blabbing to Andromeda that he'd driven us all over the city. Not when I was beholden to share that information with her already.

"It's not her I'm worried about."

I waited for him to elaborate, but he didn't offer any explanation, leaving me to ponder what he was trying to ask.

We clambered back into the black carriage despite Tristan's hesitations. He murmured something to the driver. Corvus sat brooding in the corner, hunched in as far as he could despite the wide berth of his wings.

I rested my forehead on the window. My eyes itched; my limbs were heavy. It had been a very long day. I tried to let the rocking of the carriage lull me into a light sleep, but I couldn't get the sight of that starving child's hollow face, the blood, the vomit, the death, out of my mind. I snapped my eyes open as the carriage came to a halt.

The sharp sound of crashing waves told me we hadn't returned to the palace as Tristan said we would. Corvus placed one hand on the hilt of a dagger.

"We'll be going back through the caves," said the prince wearily, completely unfazed by Corvus's hostility. "What I have to show you lies far beneath the palace." He opened the door and hopped down onto a rocky lane.

I dragged myself out of the carriage, stumbling on tired legs. Tristan extended a hand to me. His palm was warm as he wrapped his fingers around mine. He quickly let go once I had both feet safely on the ground. I looked around, gathering my bearings.

We'd stopped at the top of a narrow dirt path that sloped down into the rocky cliffs. The sand on the beach below glittered like scattered stars in the moonlight. The soft glow of the city lay far behind us. It was quiet, save for the crashing surf, as there were no buildings or people nearby.

"You can tell your driver to wait for us back at the palace," said Tristan.

I relayed the prince's instructions, and the carriage rattled away, leaving us stranded.

The cool sea air whipped escaped tendrils of hair across my face. I looked up and down the path, making sure we were indeed alone, before lowering my hood and letting the breeze brush softly against my cheeks. I stood there for a moment, letting the salt-air and moonlight wash over me.

Feeling a bit more awake, I turned back to Corvus and Tristan. Corvus stared with an odd, pinched look on his face. Tristan walked down the path toward the cliffs, leaving us to follow.

"Remember, prince. Try anything and I will gut you," Corvus warned with a growl as he unsheathed his onyx dagger.

Gods, he was insufferable. The small spark of tenderness that had awakened in my chest vanished. I didn't have the mental clarity to come up with a snappy retort to his rudeness. I was too focused on minding my footing. Even though the moon cast enough light for us to see by, the path was still rocky and uneven.

We hiked down the cliff side in silence until we reached the sands below. The sea spray tickled my face as it crashed against the rocks. We sidled alongside a narrow strip of rock until we came to a slit in the cliff face, just wide enough for Corvus to slip through. He hissed as his wings scraped the sides of the rock.

Inside was dark and smelled of seaweed. I placed a hand on the narrow passage and my fingers came away wet and slimy. A low humming noise thrummed in my ears and in my bones. The passage grew wider as we walked deeper into it. My skin tingled, and another bout of nausea rolled through me. I swallowed hard at the bitter taste in the back of my throat as we found ourselves in an enormous cavern.

Tristan lit a gas lantern, which cast long shadows over the walls and shale floor. The darkness seemed to reach back at us, trying to swallow up the feeble glow of the lantern. I shivered and averted my gaze from the dark.

"Down here," Tristan said tiredly, as he brought the light further into the cavern. There was a slight slope to the rock that led to a long swath of sand. A large pool, as still and smooth as glass, extended past the reach of the lantern's light.

Tristan set the lantern down and crossed his arms. "Don't touch any of it."

My feet sank into the cool, soft sand, and a gasp escaped my lips as I beheld the strange sight.

Pieces of the night sky lay scattered on the sand, their edges jagged. I moved around the perimeter of where they lay. They were darker than night. Darker, even, than the deepest shadows of the caverns. They swallowed the lamplight, devouring it. I bent close to one piece, but quickly stepped back as another wave of nausea caused bile to rise in the back of my throat. The low hum grew stronger the closer I got to them. I felt the vibrations in my teeth and in my chest.

I pressed a hand to my stomach. The shards, some as tall and broad as me, lay arranged in a loose oval shape. If you pushed them all together, they would form a massive hole.

"What in the seven hells is this?" breathed Corvus.

"How much do you know about sources of magic?"

Corvus shifted on his feet, his wings straining away from the shards on the sand, as if they knew danger lay in the broken pieces. "Not much."

"This is a focus portal for magic. It distributes magic to lands and territories within a certain radius."

"How?" Corvus rubbed his thumb over the inlaid stone in his dagger in thought.

"I don't know exactly how it works, but from what I understand, it's like a mirror, refracting magic from a greater source through it. I've spent the last few years studying it, magic, and where it originates from. There's an old fae library that had some books on it, but I'm not exactly welcome there anymore. And it doesn't seem like anyone, mortal or fae, was ever invested in the science behind where their magic came from to begin with."

"That's because it's magic. There is no science behind it."

Tristan shrugged. "Maybe. Maybe not."

"But it's broken," I whispered as I finally understood the horror of it all. I couldn't tear my eyes away from the jagged edges of the large shards at my feet. They were magnetic, yet equally repulsive. I pressed a hand to my stomach.

"This is why there is no magic in Tenebris," confirmed Tristan.

There was a heavy beat of silence. A thousand questions flew through my mind, but one sang above the others. "How did it break?"

"My great-grandfather was a severe man," said Tristan. His shoulders sagged. "He was concerned with keeping a hold on the power he'd won for himself, though he claimed the victory was for all mortals. They wouldn't have to live under the thumb of the powerful fae who had abused them for centuries. The fae did not appreciate being tricked by a mortal man and were going to depose him."

"Sounds familiar," Corvus said icily.

Tristan ignored the jab. "My great-grandfather found the

mirror, brought it here, and smashed it, cutting off the supply of magic."

"So, how do we fix it?" Corvus asked, his voice tight.

"It's not just broken. It's *corrupted*. The magic has been trapped in there, unable to refract. Something is happening to it."

The air felt very close, as if it was actively trying to smother us. I felt a deep sense of dread take root in my blood as my whole body continued to thrum with strange vibrations. A wave crashed on the rocks at the mouth of the cavern, echoing into the silence around us.

"If any shards of this mirror get into the wrong hands, it's over. The pieces still have terrible power on their own." Tristan kept his eyes fixed on me as my stomach continued to flip.

"The ships in the harbor, the military on the northern border. We're not getting ready to attack, we're on the defensive. My father received intelligence a few weeks ago. Grauradur is planning to take the shards for themselves. We must be ready. We need the fae on our side, but my father has let everyone think we're *choosing* to smother magic."

"So why don't you tell them the mirror is broken?" I asked.

"My father is too proud. I've tried to make him see reason, but we can't trust all the fae. They're actively planning a coup or our murder, remember? I need your help." Tristan turned to me.

His eyes were filled with quiet desperation. "We must fix the mirror before something terrible happens. I think if we repair it, we'll be more prepared to hold off against invasion. The land needs its magic back. So do the fae. If we're going to stop an attack, we need all the help we can get."

I blinked. "Why are you looking at me? I don't know how to fix this."

"I think you do."

Corvus tightened his grip on his dagger. The rustling of his wings echoed in the cavern.

"You react strongly to the shards," said Tristan. "The night I first met you, you said you heard humming. The ballroom is directly above this cavern, about a mile up. You touched a shard through my clothes the other night and said it felt like you were being shocked."

"So," I said uneasily. "Maybe it's because I have some fae blood. I bet Corvus can hear it, too."

Corvus's lips were thin, his eyes steely and thunderous. "No. I can't." He peered at the shard at his feet. "But it doesn't mean we can't test your other theory."

He put a finger on one of the broken pieces as Tristan lunged for him. "Don't!"

The surface of the mirror rippled like water beneath Corvus's touch, and my mouth gaped in horror as thin spider veins of black shot up his finger. His eyes rolled back into his head. His mouth opened in a silent scream.

"Corvus!"

The black veins raced up his neck, turning the whites of his eyes as dark as midnight. His wings flared, growing to twice their size. Corvus shuddered as the veins continued to spread over him. His wings trembled violently before exploding in a tornado of black feathers.

My feet were already moving, carrying me toward him. I didn't stop to think. Tristan and I both reached Corvus at the same time, colliding into him. We knocked him off his feet, breaking his contact with the shard as we slammed into the sand.

I pushed myself up, scrabbling for purchase. Corvus lay flat on his back, eyes closed. His wings had vanished. Tendrils of corruption spread across his skin like a vicious poison.

I called his name and shook his shoulders. My chest was tight. I couldn't get enough air. "Tristan. Help him."

Tristan shook his head. "I've never seen this. I don't know what to do."

Time slowed as I registered the gravity of the situation. Corvus's skin was quickly losing color. The corruption continued to spread slowly over his skin, like moss overtaking a fallen tree. The veins spread outwards from somewhere around his chest, but I couldn't see their origin. I felt my arms reaching for the daggers he wore, not conscious of what I was doing. As soon as I touched the hilt of the blue sea-stone dagger, a wave of warmth rushed through me, sizzling and almost too hot.

I unsheathed the blade and sliced open his shirt. The venom stemmed from above his heart. The stone within the dagger's hilt glowed at the proximity, casting silver-blue light across the cavern. I pressed my left palm on Corvus's chest and squeezed my thumb into the sea stone with my right hand, channeling the light toward the corruption. It simply felt like the right thing to do.

Light flared beneath my palm. The black tendrils shrunk, racing back to the center of Corvus's chest as the air around me crackled and grew hot. Sweat dripped down my brow. My arms shook as the burning light raced through my veins, but I did not let go. The pool of black was shrinking, the light burning away the spot of blooming night.

Another moment, and the poison had shrunk enough so that my palm covered all of it. I felt its sticky pulse beneath my hand. I closed my first around it and pulled it away from Corvus's chest. It came away reluctantly, trying to cling to his body. I tugged, gritting my teeth until it detached.

Corvus gasped as air rushed back into his lungs, but I couldn't tear my attention away from the pulsing contagion in my fist.

A shiver raced down my spine. The thing in my hand squirmed, trying to break free. Disgust at the utter *wrongness* of it made me gag. I fought the urge to fling it away from me, but I didn't want it to come back and attach to any of us. I couldn't be sure it would simply slink back into the mirror.

I gagged again. The sea-stone dagger flared, guiding me. I slammed my fist onto the sand, then brought the dagger down, moving my hand away at the last possible second, plunging the shining blade into the center of the writhing corruption. It sank wetly into the sand like blood and did not stir again.

"Oh, my gods," breathed Tristan.

I pushed myself away from the spot, desperate to get away from it. My head was pounding. A last wave of nausea made me turn my head and retch into the sand until my stomach was empty. The light from the dagger faded until only a silvery sheen remained.

"What the fuck was that?" Corvus rasped.

I wiped my mouth with the back of my hand, then lurched back to him. I felt myself settling back into my body, as if I had been floating above everything, merely watching the scene play out instead of living it. "Are you okay?"

Corvus pressed his hand to his chest, then examined his fingers. "Yeah. Yeah, I am."

I sank onto my knees and burst into tears. I dropped the dagger and buried my face in my hands, still feeling sick as a wave of relief crashed over me.

A warm hand rested on my shoulder. The soothing scent of petrichor rolled over me.

"Hey. I'm alright."

I brushed the tears away. Corvus moved awkwardly. Something about him was wrong, off-balance.

"Corvus. Your wings."

He craned his neck around, trying to look at his back. "Well. Won't Father be pleased." His tone was light, but his face was pale.

"What the fuck happened?" I asked, turning to Tristan.

He knelt on the sand, unmoving, eyes fixed on the dark wet spot where I'd stabbed the corruption.

"I think you cleansed corrupted magic." His eyes met mine. "I knew it. You have artificer blood."

I felt Corvus stiffen. "How can you be sure?"

"She reacts strongly to the mirror's presence. From what I could gather from the books I found, the mirror was constructed by ancient fae who could create magical items and weapons. They were called artificers. And if Sorsha can feel the magic within the mirror, it must mean you have the same abilities, or at least something very similar."

"My mother was mortal. I don't even know who my father is."

"But you are half-fae." Tristan shrugged. "And that part of you is stronger than the mortal part. The point is you can cleanse the corruption in the mirror. You might even be able to put it back together. Whatever magic is in your blood responds to the mirror."

There was an unsettling, manic gleam in his eyes.

My limbs still shook from the effort of extracting the twisted magic from Corvus. Sweat cooled on my face and down my back, making me shiver. There was no way I could do that again. "I think we got lucky."

Tristan pointed to the shards. "The magic is bottlenecked inside there, twisting in on itself. *Things* keep slithering out. I tried killing them. It didn't work." He lifted his shirt. A terrible black scar slashed along the right side of his rib cage.

"Where are the ones that escaped?" I asked. My lips felt numb.

Corvus braced his palms into the sand. "And how come they didn't suck on to you like it did to me?"

"They're slow and will go back into the mirror if prompted. They just need some encouragement," said Tristan.

"Like what?"

"Blood. And I don't think they like mortals as much, or it would have attached to me, as they did to you."

I pressed my fingers to my puffy, swollen eyes. This was all too much.

"Sorsha."

I dropped my hands. Tristan knelt before me. Corvus leaned forward, body tense and ready to spring. The prince didn't seem to notice. "I need your help. If we don't find a way to fix this, then everyone's lives are at risk. What happened to Corvus will happen to us all, if the Grauradurian faction doesn't get to the mirror first and use it against us. If we cleanse the mirror and mend it, magic will come back."

My heart sank into my stomach. If there was something I could do, shouldn't I at least try to help, even though it might seem impossible? What difference was there between making healing salves and tinctures and this?

A big fucking difference.

I squashed the thought. I wanted to heal, to mend, to help others. This was a broken thing that needed fixing, and my heart pulled toward the task, even as my body shivered at the memory of holding the corrupted magic in my palm.

But something else nagged at me, kept me from agreeing immediately to help the prince, who seemed all too happy to fix the item that kept his family in power.

"And you don't mind if magic comes back? What if the fae

rebel against you with their powers restored?"

"A good ruler puts the needs of his people first. What happens to me is secondary."

Corvus huffed through his nose.

I studied Tristan, who met my stare. The gleam in his eyes wasn't mania. It was desperation, yes, but more than that. It was hope.

Something inside me cracked. "Okay. I'll try to help."

"Sorsha," began Corvus.

"No. I want to help. We need the magic back. What you showed us tonight… it can't go on like this. I don't want anyone else to die or suffer. If there's a chance I can help, then I want to."

His face grew grave. "Whatever help I can offer, it's yours. Both of you."

"Thank you." Tristan glanced at the entrance of the cave. "It's getting late. Do you think you can come back here tomorrow night to try cleansing another shard? We need to assess what you can do."

"I think so." I'd have to give a convincing reason, create some sort of cover story, but if I could make it seem like it was related to gather intel on the fae coup, then I could get away with it.

"Good. Don't breathe a word of this to anyone. This location and the existence of the mirror are of utmost secrecy."

"Of course."

"Sure," agreed Corvus. "There's only one problem."

The prince knit his brows together. "What's that?"

Corvus jabbed a thumb at his back. "How do we explain this?"

The prince rubbed his chin. "Good point. Let me think." He got up and paced around the shards, studying them.

The sea-stone dagger still lay in the sand next to me. I picked it up, brushed off the sand, and held it out toward Corvus. "Sorry. I had to borrow it."

He didn't take it. "I'm tempted to let you keep it. It's much more useful to you than it is to me. Especially if you're coming back tomorrow night."

"You're not coming?"

"I have some other business to attend to."

An awkward silence filled the space between us.

"Keep it safe for me. For now."

"Alright." I clenched my hand around the hilt, letting it fall to my side.

"I have an idea," Tristan said as he came back toward us. "Your wings vanished when you touched the mirror. Your wings are inherently magical. Fae used to summon their wings at will, concealing them when they were not needed. The mirror contains a vast amount of magic within it. I wonder if, in this instance, like calls to like. If the magic in you responded to the magic in the mirror—"

"So, what's the idea?" I interrupted. I had a feeling he could have gone on a good while about his theory.

"Sorry. I think you have to touch the mirror again."

Corvus shook his head. "No fucking way."

"Absolutely not," I said. "I don't have it in me to do that again."

"No, sorry. Not directly, but through a barrier. You want a small amount of exposure to it, not direct contact."

Corvus met him with stony silence.

"It's perfectly safe." He sighed. He unbuttoned his shirt and withdrew a long, thin velvet pouch. He opened it, careful not to touch what lay inside. "I keep a shard in here, on my person at all times."

"Why?"

"So the mirror can't be made whole again without me being there. A safety precaution, in case someone finds the other pieces and tries to weaponize them."

It was a clever move. "I've touched it," I said, turning to Corvus. "It feels like a little zap of lightning. If anything happens, I'll be right here."

"Are you sure? I thought you said you didn't have it in you to do it again."

"If I need to, I can."

My chest squeezed. *For you, I will.*

"It's worth a shot, I suppose."

I gripped the sea-stone dagger, praying I would not need to use it again.

Corvus pinched the velvet pouch. There was a great gust of wind, followed by a boom of rolling thunder. The dagger flared brightly, reacting to the presence of magic as a tornado of darkness swirled around us, the nexus at Corvus's spine. The scent of summer rains grew stronger as another boom of thunder pealed within the cave. From the darkness, soft black feathers formed, taking the shape of wings. They grew as Corvus gripped the shard of glass, his face screwed in concentration.

"It's working," I shouted over the rushing wind and thunder of the rainless summer storm that had erupted inside the cave. "Get ready to let go!"

"I can feel it," replied Corvus, eyes still squeezed shut. His wings continued to grow, the black feathers catching the glinting silver-blue light of the dagger with brilliant iridescence.

After another breath, Corvus released the mirror shard. The thunder and wind ceased abruptly. The darkness receded and the dagger dimmed.

My chest eased. He was unharmed.

Corvus flared his wings, rustling the feathers softly. "Glad that worked."

"Time to go. Someone will have heard that," said Tristan, rising to his feet and stowing the velvet pouch back inside his shirt. "The guards won't be able to find their way in here, but we don't want to run into them in the halls." He extended a hand down for me.

I accepted it and pulled myself up. He moved to collect the lantern, leaving me with Corvus, who I couldn't bring myself to look at.

Instead, I focused on the beautiful blade in my hands. I placed the dagger into the sheath strapped to my leg, withdrawing the mundane training knife Corvus had given me. I held it for a moment, wondering what to do with it, before sliding it down the front of my dress, nestling it between my breasts. As long as I didn't trip, it should be fine.

Corvus swallowed audibly. "Seven hells, no. You want to impale yourself? Here." He withdrew a sheathed dagger from his boot and handed me the sheath with a wink. "I think you're ready to move on from training knives. Keep this one in your shoe."

"We *really* should go," said Tristan. He shifted from foot to foot.

"Right. Lead the way, Your Highness." Corvus moved to follow Tristan further into the cave.

I tucked the sheath into my boot with a faint smile, then plucked the knife from my bodice. I wasn't ready to part with it. Not yet. I slid the training knife next to the dagger strapped to my thigh, wedging it firmly in place before I hurried after them, tying my mask back around my face.

We sneaked back into the palace through cavern passages slick with damp. We emerged into a small cellar, the groomsmen's house at the edge of the stable yard, and entered the palace through the back without attracting any attention from the guards. Tristan had their schedules all memorized. We navigated back to his study without being seen.

I cleaned up as best as I could, washing my mouth out and smoothing my hair into a loose bun. Tristan and I made plans to meet tomorrow evening, then made our way to the courtyard where the House of Night carriage stood waiting for me.

Corvus insisted on seeing me home. We sat in silence as the carriage pulled away from the palace. Dawn was breaking, and the gulls began their forlorn cries as the sky turned a faint shade of pink.

My eyes were raw, my mouth dry, and I had sand everywhere. I was too tired to be afraid of what lay ahead. My heart was heavy with the sorrow of what I had seen. The suffering, the death, all because of the cruelty of one man who wanted to rule.

"Are you okay?" asked Corvus, his voice rough with exhaustion and something more.

I gave him a weak smile. "I'm fine. You?"

"Yes. Thanks to you."

His hands were clenched into fists, resting on his knees. He tucked his wings in tight, but they seemed too big for the cramped carriage. They brushed the ceiling and stretched a little wider than I remembered.

"You made your wings a little bigger, didn't you?" I asked, unable to keep the stupid grin off my face.

He flashed a crooked smile back at me. "After what I went through, I think I earned it."

I rolled my eyes. "You're so vain."

"But you like it, though." His eyes were dark, hungry and

searching.

He was right. I *did* like it. I liked all of him. "Corvus, I—"

His lips were on mine before I could finish. The carriage swayed as he dragged me onto his lap. I sank into him, feeling the evidence of his arousal between my legs as I straddled him. I gasped, and he covered my mouth with his, slipping his tongue inside.

My limbs turned to liquid. After everything that had happened tonight, this is what I wanted, what I *needed*. I needed to feel him, to press my hands against his chest, to feel his beating heart.

I felt his fingers slip under the edge of my mask. I nodded slightly, giving him permission to take it off.

Without the mask, our kiss deepened. He fisted my hair, pulling me closer to him. I surrendered myself wholly to the kiss, to Corvus, to the feeling of our bodies pressed together. Our breath melded as we captured each other's sighs and moans with our kisses. A single thought thundered through me, breaking through the haze of my want. He was here. Alive.

A single tear slipped free. Corvus brushed it away with his thumb.

"What's this for?" he asked huskily.

"I almost lost you," I whispered.

He gently lifted my chin and looked at me with a deep sort of sorrow, body stiffening. "Sorsha, I can't—" His voice broke a little. He cleared his throat and released his grip on my waist and hair. "I'm sorry. We can't do this. Not anymore."

I bit the inside of my lip and pushed myself off him, dropping into the plush seat.

"Right. Forgive me," I said flatly. "I forgot myself."

"You don't have to apologize. I am the one who... I shouldn't have kissed you."

I continued to stare out the window. I couldn't look at him. "No harm done."

We rode in silence the rest of the way. The chill that crept over my arms had nothing to do with the temperature.

My hair pin vibrated the second we crossed through the iron gates into the House of Night's courtyard. Gods, I was tired. I wanted to sleep. But I was sure Andromeda was looking down on us, watching my arrival, making sure I came to offer my report.

Corvus helped me out of the carriage, squeezing my fingers as I descended. "Be careful," he whispered as he bent his lips close to my ear. I forced a girlish smile and dipped my chin, hoping anyone still up and watching would see nothing more than flirtation, even though my heart had cracked open, pricking me with jagged points.

I whispered, "You don't have to worry about me anymore." I withdrew my hand from his and headed for the grove of lemon trees, not wanting to use the front door. It wasn't until I rounded the corner that I let my shoulders sag. The hair pin vibrated fiercely, making my head throb.

I slowed my pace, giving myself time to get my story straight. There was no way I could tell Andromeda all I had seen tonight. My fingers had just brushed the latch of the back gate to the kitchen garden when I heard footsteps behind me.

Chapter Twenty-Eight

Sorsha

I froze with one hand on the gate, holding my breath. The quick, light patter of feet on the stone path sounded behind me. I let my hand fall from the gate as the tiny, horrible bubble of hope in my chest popped. The steps weren't his. I turned toward the sound, wondering who else could be outside the house at this hour.

Looking back down the path, I saw a flash of a skirt vanish behind a cluster of lemon trees and clipped hedges. My hairpin pulsed, tugging me inside. I ripped it out of my hair and held it in my hand as I crept toward the place I had seen the girl vanish. If it was Viviana, I could get her in trouble and start paying her back for destroying my things. I could lock her out. Andromeda would give her a tongue lashing for being outside without permission. I smiled with satisfaction at the thought.

As I drew closer, I caught the murmur of voices. Tiptoeing around the trees, I saw a man dressed in simple clothes. His boots were caked in dirt. His back was to me, and a girl's arms snaked around his neck. He didn't look like a patron of the house. His disheveled clothing and lack of finery gave him away. I crouched low and dared another few feet, keeping to the trees for cover. From here, I could see the girl's tree-bark skin clearly.

My eyebrows shot up in surprise. I backed away slowly, not wanting to disturb Tilly's tryst. I made it safely back to the gate without being discovered. Maybe he was a lover from her previous house of employment. Whoever he was, her secret was safe with me.

Curiosity satisfied, another wave of exhaustion washed over me. I let myself in through the back door and made my way upstairs to Andromeda's office.

After spreading the silencing potion over the threshold, I sat across from my madam, using every ounce of strength I had left to keep my eyes open. If I wanted to, I could lay my head down on her desk and fall asleep right there. But I couldn't get to bed until I had answered her questions.

"No, the queen was not in attendance."

Andromeda frowned. "And Lady Reya?"

I blinked heavily. "She was upset you sent me as your proxy."

Madam Andromeda let out a snort. "Typical of her. What of our Primus?"

Seven hells. How long was this going to go on? I let out a heavy sigh, then described Lucius Uriel's arguments, the king's retorts, losing his temper, and the poor end to the meeting.

After I finished, she was silent for a moment. She tapped a long fingernail on her desk. "I am having regrets about appointing you to this position, and I do not like to be disappointed."

Usually, the threat would send me into a panic. But I was too tired to care. "I went to the meeting, and I've told you everything that happened. I entertained the prince for the evening but wasn't able to get anything useful out of him."

Andromeda frowned. "Need I remind you that you made a blood pact? You swore you would report, to my satisfaction, any information you had?"

There was a hot rush between my eyes. Pain radiated in my head. Shit. My chest tightened. I brushed my nose with the back of my hand. It came away sticky with blood. Much more than there had been in the prince's study.

"Would you rather I make up some more interesting information to give you?" I snapped. I should never have agreed to this. Not when her terms had been so ambiguous. But I had wanted my mother's letter and jumped at the opportunity Andromeda had presented to me, disregarding what my freedom might cost me. Now, I wasn't sure what I wanted at all. Everything was so complicated.

"I would prefer if you would tell me the truth about what you were doing last night. You stink, your makeup is smudged with perspiration, and you have tracked sand into my office. If you were entertaining the prince last night in the comfort of his royal palace, you would not look like you were rolling around in the dirt."

I should have known Andromeda would see right through my lie. She was observant, clever, and ruthless. So be it. I would tell her the truth, but not all of it. A lie of omission was different from outright deception. I crossed my arms, letting the blood drip from my nose. I hope it stained her carpet.

"Fine. I went to the prince's rooms after the meeting. I intended to seduce him for information. Lord Stormfall interrupted us and insisted the prince persuade his father to restore magic. The prince refused, but Corvus convinced him to accompany him to the river district so he could bear witness to the suffering of his people."

Andromeda opened her mouth to interrupt me, but I kept going, letting my helplessness and rage pour out in a torrent. "The prince insisted I come along, too. So, I'm sorry if the smell of me offends you. I saw some of the most horrible things imaginable last night. Death and sickness and suffering. It was terrible." My voice cracked with emotion that wasn't feigned.

I wiped my nose again, clearing away the blood. It stopped

bleeding at the confession of where I had truly been. Andromeda leaned back in her chair. "Interesting. Now, that wasn't so hard, was it?"

I gritted my teeth and clenched my fists in my lap.

"And what did the prince say in response to this tour of suffering?"

"He said it's not as simple as it seems. He did not elaborate."

"Hmm. And then?"

I sighed. My whole body ached. My mind was fuzzy; my tongue felt thick and heavy in my mouth. "We went back to the palace, snuck in through a side entrance. The prince did not want to be seen coming back. Lord Stormfall accompanied me back here."

Andromeda nodded, satisfied for the moment. "You're dismissed. I hope next time we meet you will make your report honestly the first time I ask for it. Is that clear?"

"Yes, ma'am."

"Go."

I left her office in a haze. I barely remember splashing water on my face before falling into my unmade bed. It was dry, though still wine-stained from Viviana's vengeful destruction. I fell asleep instantly and dreamed of shadows reaching in the dark.

The royal carriage came for me at nightfall. I wore the purple dress Tristan had given me, since it was now one of the few items of clothing I had. It loudly declared he favored me, and even though it made me feel like an imposter, it provided an excellent cover for why I was spending so much time at the palace.

A pair of guards escorted me to Tristan's suite, where a candlelit dinner awaited us. I'd assumed we would go to the cavern straightaway. My stomach tightened at the prospect of making polite conversation with the prince for an hour. We still didn't know each other very well. What would we even talk about in front of the guards?

"It's nice to see you again," he said, pulling one of the high-backed chairs out for me.

"Thank you for inviting me, Your Highness." The food smelled divine. Fresh bread, a small roast chicken, and some greens in dressing were laid out on the table. My mouth watered despite my nerves.

Tristan poured me a goblet of wine, then turned to the guards. "That will be all, gentlemen. Please leave us undisturbed for the evening. If Miss Sventura has not returned to her carriage by... two o'clock?" He looked at me.

I played along. "Let's make it three," I said in a flirtatious tone that I did not recognize. I took a sip of my wine and kept my eyes fixed on the prince.

"As you wish, my lady. If she has not returned by three, then you may come fetch her."

The guards nodded, accepting their orders, and left us.

Once the door was safely shut, I dropped my flirtatious countenance and leaned back into the chair.

The prince laughed. "Is it so tiresome to flirt with me?"

I sat up straight again, mortified that I had offended him. "I'm sorry, I didn't mean it like that." I straightened the silver cutlery next to my plate, desperate to be doing something. "I'm just tired. It's been a lot to take in."

Tristan took a piece of bread from the bowl on the table, then handed it to me. "I don't disagree with you there. The nights have been long ever since I learned of it." He did not speak directly of the mirror. Even within his private rooms, he was careful to guard his secret.

"And when was that?" I bit into the bread, savoring the taste as butter melted on my tongue. It was heavenly.

"Three years ago. Though, back then, I lost little sleep over it. It wasn't an urgent problem." He carved the chicken, then extended his hand for my plate.

"Thank you." I chewed my bread in silence as he served me. I was unsure of what else to say. I took my plate back and speared some chicken onto my fork. Our silverware clinked softly, echoing in the quiet.

"So. How long have you worked at the House of Night?"

I swallowed. "Since I was a child."

The prince's face darkened.

"As a serving girl," I added quickly, which eased the prince's look of dismay. "Andromeda does not believe in making courtesans out of children. I have only been a courtesan for the past five years."

"I see."

"I don't think I'm very good at it. Some seem born to play their part. I've never felt like I quite fit in." I was rambling. He didn't need to know all of this. My throat tightened as I reached for the goblet of water before me and took a hearty swallow.

"Even with all the tutors and lessons on how to be my best princely self, I still feel like I don't know what I am doing most days," he confessed.

"From what I've seen, I think you're a very competent prince."

"A prince who is hated by his people, who can't figure out a way to save them." There was no bitterness in his words. Only defeat.

He had been shouldering this burden alone for the past three years. His pallor and the dark circles under his eyes made a lot more sense. It wasn't just that he was staying up late, reading his books on magic theory and making sure no magical corruption escaped the broken mirror. The isolation weighed on him, too.

I leaned forward, bracing my hand on the table. I didn't know what it was like to be a member of the royal family, but I knew what it was like to be alone. "We'll figure it out. You don't have to do it by yourself anymore. I'm here to help you."

He offered me a small smile. "And for that, I am grateful."

A fresh wave of determination bolstered my spirits. "So. When do we get to work?"

After we finished our meal and changed our clothes, we waited for another half hour before sneaking to the sea cavern.

The nausea hit me as we entered the cave, but I had come prepared. I slipped a little bottle from my pocket and placed a few drops of ginger and mint tincture under my tongue to settle my roiling stomach.

"What is that?" asked Tristan, as I pocketed the bottle.

"The shards make me feel sick. This helps."

"Is it magic?"

"No, just herbs."

We walked toward the cave pool, my borrowed boots sinking into the soft sand. Though I had steeled myself for the nausea, the dark, jagged pieces of glass were still disarming. The way they swallowed all light, radiating a terrible power, made me want to stay as far away from them as possible. I tried not to think of the way the corruption had pulsed sickeningly in my hand the night before.

"So, where do we start?" My voice was small, echoing in the

cave's vastness.

Tristan handed me the lantern, then opened the book he had brought with him.

I held the light aloft, casting a warm glow across the pages. The book was old. The parchment was yellowed, the ink faded in some spots. A scrawling script in a language I couldn't read danced across the pages, disorderly and scattered. There were drawings, symbols, and lines that looked like the notes of a madman. Doubt curled in my stomach.

"You can read this?"

"Most of it. It's in old fae. Notoriously tricky to learn, but I've been practicing. The drawings help."

I squinted at the words, completely lost. "That's very impressive."

He flashed me a genuine smile, the first I'd seen all evening.

"Does it tell you how to mend the mirror?"

"The theory is here. This is an old artificer text. The principles apply to weapon forging, but it's a place to start. If I have translated it correctly, it suggests tapping into your own source of magic and binding it to the metal, or in this case the mirror, imbuing it with your power."

Any hope I had in making progress tonight vanished. I gripped the lantern tightly. "Any instructions on how to tap into a person's magic source?"

"Not in this book, I'm afraid."

"Right."

Tristan snapped the book shut. "Let's find the two smallest shards that go together, and have you hold them. We'll see what happens."

My hands grew clammy. "And if something slithers out of them?"

"I have a feeling the corruption won't want to tangle with

you again, but we'll be ready. You brought that dagger of Stormfall's?"

"Yes." Since I had changed into pants, I'd slung it around my waist. My fingers found the hilt. The metal was warm and sent a soft, pleasant tingle through my arm.

"Good. The smallest pieces are over here."

We strode toward the shards that lay closest to the cave pool. There were two broken pieces no bigger than my palm. Each one had a smoothed edge to them, clearly belonging to the outer rim of the mirror. I knelt before them, Tristan right beside me. We set the lantern next to us, where its light shone feebly across the black glass. I unsheathed my dagger and placed it on the sand within easy reach, then tried to still my shaking hands.

"You can do this." His words were meant to comfort, but I could hear the desperate hope within them. I was the first real chance he had found at reforging the mirror and saving his people. I tried not to think how much was riding on this – on *me*.

Before I lost my nerve, I grabbed the two pieces, careful not to cut myself on their sharp edges. I closed my eyes, fighting against the bile that rose in the back of my throat. I focused solely on the mirror in my upturned palms.

Beneath my initial instinct to drop the pieces and run, there was a quiet simmering. Sound grew muffled, my breathing slowed. I reached for the feeling, tentative and curious. The magic within the mirror bubbled sluggishly, reaching back for me.

Something deep inside my chest stirred, moving even more slowly than whatever lay within the mirror. I tunneled toward the feeling. Was this the source of my magic? Brought to life by the magic within the mirror? Whatever it was, it began to stir, stretching awake like a cat after a long nap.

A warmth, like the golden rays of afternoon sun, spread through my chest. I could almost feel the sunbeam and the dust motes that swirled within it like glitter. A smell – pines, and crisp, clean air – broke through the dank salt of the cave.

Tears welled beneath my closed eyes. I knew, somehow, that this smell, this *feeling*, was home.

The mirror shards hummed. They pulled toward one another, asking to draw together. It would be so easy to nest them where they wanted to be. They were broken and heartsick, having spent so much time apart.

Please, help us, they whispered. *Make us whole again.*

I obliged and brought my hands together.

Tristan gasped, and I opened my eyes. The surface of the mirror had become liquid, like when Corvus had touched it last night. Only this time, there was a bright golden seam between the two pieces. My chest swelled. It was working.

The pieces vibrated; the surface of the glass trembled fervently as the light welding the shards together faded completely. The surface began to harden, melding into one piece.

Before the surface set completely, a sudden surge of wrongness welled from the depths of the glass.

A sickening tendril of corruption slithered from the joined pieces. It was smaller than the one I'd stabbed last night, but the potency of its ichor made my stomach roil. The corruption sprang forth from the mirror as the glass hardened into one solid piece. The monster tried to wrap itself around my wrist. I dropped the mirror shard, letting the corruption fall with it. They hit the sand with a soft thud.

"Ready your dagger," Tristan said in a low voice.

I snatched the sea-stone blade. It flared brightly in my palm, sending a shock of warmth through my arm to my chest, reaching for the place where my magic still frothed.

The corruption lunged for Tristan. He leaped backward, knocking over the lantern. The light dimmed but did not go out. I could still see the black ooze as it slithered toward the prince.

Steeling myself, I plunged the dagger into the heart of it, falling to my knees. My head pounded, the corners of my vision blackened, but I channeled every ounce of my strength and will into the blade in my hand. The corruption writhed and screamed as the dagger pierced its shadowy center, before finally melting into the sand.

I sat back, panting, as sweat dripped into my eyes. The newly forged piece of glass lay where I had dropped it, now quiet and still.

"Are you alright?"

"Fine," I gasped. "You?"

"I'm unhurt."

It had been easier this time to kill the poison that had attempted to flee the mirror, but only because I knew what to expect. I wiped the sweat from my brow, trying my best not to rub sand all over myself. My heart was heavy. I had fixed a part of the mirror, but the pride of my accomplishment was extinguished as my gaze swept across the cavern floor, taking in the amount of broken glass that remained.

"If we have to kill a corruption every time we put two pieces back together, this is going to take forever." My eyes burned with unshed tears. The thought of having to do this again and again made my heart race. Blood roared in my ears; my breath was tight in my chest. I couldn't do this.

I couldn't do this.

"Sorsha." Tristan grabbed my hand. "It's okay. Breathe."

I wanted to jerk my hand away, to bite back that air would not fix this unsurmountable problem. Instead, I focused on breathing down into the soles of my feet. The panic lessened its grip, but anxiety still bubbled beneath my skin.

"There has to be another way," I managed, fighting to speak past the tightness in my chest.

Tristan did not let go of my hand. I let the warmth of his fingers, the soft grit of sand between our skin, ground me.

"I've looked, Sorsha," he said quietly. "I spent a year trying to do it myself. You're the only one who can."

My breath hitched again, despite my best efforts to remain calm. He squeezed my fingers.

"That's not to say I won't keep looking," he said firmly. "But this is the way forward for now. If we find something better, we will change course. We will do what we can, when we can."

A weight pressed down on me as I thought of the horrible suffering I'd seen last night. "But folk are dying without magic." At this rate, hundreds would die before we could restore the magic that had been lost.

"We cannot solve this problem overnight. You are helping them by shouldering this burden." He paused, glancing at the shards of night around us. "By trying."

It struck me again just how long he had been toiling alone under the weight of this secret.

I let my fingers fall from his and lifted my chin. "You're right."

He stooped and plucked the newly forged piece of the mirror from the sand. "Here," he said, offering it to me. "You should hang on to this. Perhaps if you carry it, you will become more accustomed to the feeling of magic, and it won't make you feel so sick."

"Good idea." I took the shard, still black as night, but no longer filled with light-devouring hunger. It was no bigger than the length of my hand. I slipped it into the pocket of my pants, and could feel it humming through the fabric, though its whine was not the sickly tenor of the broken shards. It was not a comfortable feeling, but it wasn't unpleasant, either.

"I think that's enough for tonight," said Tristan, scooping up the lantern.

"No," I said, gripping the sea-stone dagger. "One more."

"Are you sure?" asked Tristan. He squinted at me, trying to gauge how depleted I was.

I was tired. I wanted nothing more than to leave this godsdamned cave and never come back. But I still had some strength left, and the night was far from over.

"Yes," I said, with more confidence than I felt. And so, we set to work.

Chapter Twenty-Nine

Corvus

It took a significant amount of willpower to keep myself from storming into the House of Night and demanding that Sorsha never step foot in that cave again. Every part of me screamed to remove her from the danger of that cursed mirror, but I knew doing so would only further drive us apart.

Which shouldn't be a bad thing. After all, I was the one who had vowed I could not see her again. But I was still pulled to her in a way I couldn't explain. Just being close to her ate away at my resolve. I hadn't been able to stop myself from pulling her onto me in the carriage, from claiming her with my mouth and touch.

The incident in the cave had shaken me. The feeling of her body pressed against mine soothed my lingering shock; her gasps and scent affirmed that I was still here, alive. After the horrible, crushing darkness had swallowed me, leaving me cold and aching, her warmth was a balm to my very soul.

Then I remembered she was Dawnstone, and my blood had chilled once more. It was dizzying, how badly I wanted her and how guilty I felt for it.

A week passed. I hounded my father's footsteps, bearing the weight of Horatio's sneers and snide comments as I tried to find out more about the weapon he was so fascinated with, or when the Blackwoods would be unseated from their thrones. They were waiting for something, a signal or sign, but I couldn't figure out what it was.

Toward the end of the week, I found myself outside the gates of the House of Night, wondering if Sorsha was inside. I caught sight of her stepping into a carriage emblazoned with the royal crest. I fought every instinct that told me to follow her.

We were done. I owed her nothing, and she didn't need my permission to see the prince.

The drug den in the upper Shale peddled much stronger stuff than Madam Andromeda's passionate elixirs. It was one of the few places I did not mind shaking down for extra dinar. The owner, a wiry man with black facial hair who was perpetually surrounded by a cloud of gray smoke, could rot in the Tenebris river. The potions he sold caused such a deep sense of euphoria that clients lay draped over pieces of furniture with vacant expressions and blown pupils. The lighting was dim in the den, but I made for Strickmyre's back office without hesitation.

A guard, a barrel-chested man with arms as thick as tree trunks, blocked my path.

"You 'ave an appointment with Mister Strickmyre?" he said while squinting at my face and wings.

"We have a standing arrangement. He's expecting me."

"He never said nothin' about any arrangement to me."

A muscled feathered in my jaw. Gods, why did this always have to be harder than it needed to be? "I doubt Strickmyre shares his appointment book with you. Now, if you'll excuse me." I stepped forward to brush past him, but one of those timber-thick arms lashed out across my chest, blocking me.

"I highly suggest you reconsider your actions," I warned.

"Wouldn't be doin' my job."

I let out a hot rush of breath though my nose. A few quick movements, and the guard was howling on the ground, gushing blood from the soft flesh of his armpit.

No one in the den behind us even stirred at the noise, sucked into listlessness by the potions they imbibed.

"You sonuvabitch," growled the guard as he struggled to rise from his knees.

I didn't bother looking behind me as I cleaned his blood from my dagger and stepped further into the hall. "You'll want to get that looked at, sooner rather than later. Hope I didn't slice an artery."

Strickmyre was in his office with a merchant, going over a piece of paper. They froze when I entered, and I didn't miss the look of annoyance that flashed across Strickmyre's face. "Evening," I said, and leaned against the door, my wings splaying widely across the wall. "I'm in no rush tonight, Strickmyre. Take your time."

I cleaned my nails with my dagger, appearing totally at ease, even as my stomach clenched. A low-hung iron chandelier bathed the room in light, illuminating the fine furniture and plush rugs.

The two murmured in hushed voices. The merchant quickly rolled up the paper and cleared his throat when he reached the door.

I moved out of the way, approaching Strickmyre, but I didn't bother to sheath my dagger. He responded well to its sinister shine. The door closed, leaving us alone.

"Been making my staff bleed on my floors? Those rugs are imported, you know," he sneered.

"Four thousand this month," I said. Father only requested three, but a thousand dinar would go a long way in the Shale. What I had been spending before was no longer enough. The sickness was spreading, and fae were dying at a rapid rate. With a thousand dinar, I could get food and medicine.

"No. What a terrible liar you are."

I placed the tip of my dagger into his desk, splintering the wood. Strickmyre's lip curled, and gray smoke billowed from him like an undulating current.

"Let's not draw this out. Four, and I'll be on my way."

"It'll be three, as usual," he said, reaching for a small chest he kept at his desk. It wasn't even locked. He flipped open the lid and withdrew a satchel of coin.

He placed the bag on the desk, but I didn't take it. Instead, I steeled myself for what came next.

"Fine. I'll be keeping this then." Strickmyre reached for the bag, making his second mistake of the evening.

Before he could blink, my dagger pierced between the fine bones of his hand, pinning his palm to the desk, fingertips just out of reach of the bag of gold. Blood began to pool, filling the air with its tang. Strickmyre's eyes widened in shock, but, to his credit, he did not cry out.

"Four thousand." I repeated.

"You and your father can fuck right off," he hissed. "You fucking Great House fae won't be in charge for much longer, anyway."

"Is that a threat?" I reached for my chest but found the sheath where my sea-stone dagger should have been was empty. Right. Sorsha had it.

I swallowed and flipped my mental switch, the one that tethered me to emotion, to reason, to feeling. There was nothing before me now but my objective, and the obstacle keeping me from it. The air shifted as my wings fanned delicately.

The mundane dagger at my hip would suffice. I placed the tip under Strickmyre's fingernail and began to carve.

He was remarkably stubborn. He only had four fingernails left by the time gold made it into my pockets.

I left the den with two small bags tainted with Strickmyre's blood and felt no remorse about smashing a few vials of his sinister poisons on my way out.

The streets were quiet. Slowly, I settled back into myself with each step that carried me away from the den of malice. I clenched my jaw – the feeling of prying the man's fingernails away with my knife still echoed in my hands. I told myself that he deserved it. But the words rang hollow.

As I rounded the bend toward the lower Shale, I had a horrible thought. One that sent a cold chill through me and stopped me in my tracks.

Sorsha was risking her very life to try and fix the mess the Blackwoods had wrought upon our land. And what was I doing? I looked down and caught sight of my dagger, glinting in the faint glow of the streetlamp, still marred with ruby drops. My stomach clenched in knots. No amount of money could fix the plight in the Shale. I could remove a thousand fingernails from the privileged, greedy elite of this city and it wouldn't cure the sick or feed the hungry. And as much as I thought deposing the Blackwoods would do some good, what we needed was *magic*.

I rubbed a hand over my eyes, letting a wave of exhaustion roll through me. This isn't who I wanted to be. This isn't what I wanted to do. In Max's absence, who had I become?

There was still a small glimmer of hope. I'd promised the prince I would help if I could. There was another way to try and make things right. Clenching my fists, I resigned myself to the fact that I owed him a visit.

The following evening, I found myself back in the cave.

The prince hadn't hesitated to take me up on my offer to

help repair the mirror, though he had looked wary when I barged into his study without the accompaniment of any palace guards. I'd simply lied my way past the front gate. I took no small amount of satisfaction from seeing him thrown off by my ability to waltz around the palace without detection.

We took an unmarked carriage to the outskirts of the city, then walked for a half mile to the cliffs in silence. Part of me still debated whether to kill him. I think he could sense my dilemma and kept a good distance away as we descended the cliff's rocky face.

When we entered the cavern, Sorsha stood and brushed sand from her pants.

She crossed her arms. "Nice of you to show up."

I fought the urge to smile at her annoyance. "I'm here now." I was sobered by the dark circles under her eyes and the pallor in her face. Had she been sleeping at all?

"Good thing, too," said the prince, butting in. "The corruptions are getting bigger."

My wings stirred the damp cave air around us. "Why?" He hadn't mentioned that little detail when we'd spoken earlier.

Sorsha pointed to the pieces of glass by her feet. Each was about two hand-spans wide. "I forged these together this week from smaller shards. But every time I make them larger by adding more, the monsters get bigger, too."

The hair on the back of my neck prickled, and the coppery tang of self-loathing coated the back of my throat. I'd left her to do this dangerous task on her own. Not that she couldn't defend herself. But magic could be unpredictable. Especially the corrupted sort.

"Since the dagger you lent me works to kill them, we think you should be able to kill them with yours, too."

We. A pang of jealousy cut through my anxiety, burning like a white-hot knife. I inhaled through my nose, trying to dispel it.

"Just don't let it touch you," said Tristan.

"I won't." There was no way in all seven hells I'd let one of those things get close to me again. Not after last time.

"Good," Sorsha said. She took her position next to the midnight glass. Tristan stepped a few feet away, clutching a book to his chest.

I unsheathed my dagger and tried not to revel in the satisfaction that I was the one who would stand beside her, not the prince. "Ready when you are."

Last night I cut away a man's fingernails without much trepidation. So why did I feel this crushing sense of dread now?

Sorsha picked up a small piece of glass and knelt by the larger fragments. A tense moment passed. As the surface of the mirror pieces moved languidly like pools of spilled ink. A bright, soft light appeared between the two pieces, causing the surface of the glass to bubble rapidly before stilling and hardening. Sorsha shook as the light began to fade, and something sinister, all spindle-sinew and horrid angles, pushed itself against the surface of the glass.

"Get ready," she said, her voice trembling with effort.

I gripped my dagger and focused on the shape that emerged from the midnight-black mirror.

A dark, oil-slick of a creature broke through the surface, wrenching free of its prison as the last light from the seam faded. It hit the sand with a soft *thud* and scrabbled toward me with desperate, jerky movements. When it was a foot from me, I lunged, aiming straight for its center. Instead of meeting cold, crushing darkness, my dagger plunged into the sand. My breath caught, and the hair on the back of my neck stood once more.

As I spun, trying to find the slippery thing, Sorsha cried, "Look out!" My heart hammered painfully against my ribs, but

I did not let my fear cloud my thoughts.

"Behind you." Sorsha lunged past me, toward the creature, knife drawn.

It avoided the tip of her blade by a hair's breadth and scrabbled further down the sand on limbs that bent hideously and dripped poisonous ichor.

"Don't let it get away," barked Tristan. The corruption made for the water, unnervingly fast.

I sprinted after it, my wings flexing and beating of their own accord. I could have sworn they helped propel me forward. My feet felt lighter as they skimmed across the sand, and gusts of wind lifted my hair from my sweaty brow. I was gaining on the corruption, surging past Sorsha. All my focus was set on stopping the twisted magic.

The cave pool was only a few feet away. I made a last desperate lunge, my wings gusting behind me. I slammed onto one knee and thrust my dagger downward. The creature shrieked as the tip of my blade nicked its sickly flesh. It slipped into the water and out of sight, down into the murky depths of the cave pool.

Shit.

I rose slowly, cursing myself. The three of us stood at the pool's edge, as ocean water lapped mockingly at our feet.

"If that comes back…" started the prince.

My throat tightened. Would it attack civilians? There was no telling the havoc a thing like that could wreak. I wouldn't wish the feeling of choking in its cold abyss on anyone.

Sorsha cut him off. "It won't. It was afraid. I could feel it."

The prince rubbed his eyes with the heels of his hands, a childlike gesture that revealed how exhausted he was. I almost felt sorry for him.

Sorsha laid a hand on his shoulder, and jealousy reared its ugly head once more.

"Come on," she said. "Let's try another one."

I tightened the grip on my dagger, determined not to allow the next one to slip away.

"No," said the prince, dropping his hands. "We're done for tonight."

"But—"

"There's something I haven't told you."

The sound of waves crashing against the stone echoed in the mouth of the cave. I braced myself for treachery and tightened my grip on my weapon.

"We're being followed. Someone is starting to suspect. I think it's best if we don't come here for a few days."

I flicked my gaze toward the mouth of the cave, half expecting to see someone in the shadows, watching us. But there was nothing but rock and sand.

"How do you know you're being followed?" I asked. Every sense was on high alert as adrenaline continued to course through my veins.

"I'm very careful," he said. "I set traps. Little things that let me know if someone's tried to get into my chambers or follow me down the hall when I'm coming back from here. A few of them have tripped in the last day. Enough so I know it's no mere coincidence."

Well, thank the gods he wasn't stupid. But he should have told us before we'd come here tonight.

"Any idea who's trailing you?" It would be telling if it were fae or mortal.

"No. I'll send a note once I feel like it's safe. Three days, no more. I'll invite you to a little party I'm having. Guest list of two." The prince gave a sad half smile.

I looked across the gently undulating water as the surf crashed at the cave's mouth. We'd all suffered this long without magic. Surely a few more days would not make that big of a difference. And Sorsha was exhausted. She needed rest. I didn't relish the idea of waiting that long, but perhaps this was the most sensible approach. Especially if someone was trailing the prince.

Sorsha relented. "Fine. We should all leave separately, then."

The prince tucked his book under his arm. "Agreed."

I wanted to escort Sorsha home, to make sure she made it safely. Besides, it wouldn't look odd for us to return to the House of Night together. We'd done so before. But I didn't want to be an overly protective asshole, either.

"I'll leave first."

"Good idea," said the prince. "No one would dare tangle with you, Stormfall."

At least he still thought me intimidating. Good.

I bid them good night, holding Sorsha's gaze a little longer before turning to the mouth of the cave, fighting every instinct to stay by her side.

Chapter Thirty

Sorsha

My heart hammered as I slipped into the side garden gate. After what Tristan had said in the cave, I couldn't shake the fear I had been followed. Who was trailing him? Did they suspect anything about the mirror? My blood chilled at the thought of it getting into the wrong hands. Terrible scenarios ran through my mind.

Ichorous creatures slinking through the streets. Fae dying of sickness and disease. Corvus consumed by the fatal corruption.

I banished the last image from my thoughts as I approached the House of Night.

A stifled cry from the cluster of lemon trees at my back made my blood run cold. I froze, straining to hear. There was another muffled grunt of pain, a rustle of leaves, then stillness. My blood rushed in my ears, and my palms grew slick with sweat. The sounds were coming from the exact spot I'd seen Tilly meeting her lover. And it sounded like she was in trouble.

My heart plummeted. So much for getting inside unseen.

I dashed back to the grove, leaving the gate open behind me so we could run into the house together if need be. I unsheathed my dagger, letting the weight of it anchor me.

The purple livery of the Blackwood guard was unmistakable, even in the darkness. He loomed over Tilly menacingly, a burly man with a barrel chest and scruff at his jaw. I heard more footsteps running in between the trees, toward the house. I tightened my grip on my weapon and cleared my throat.

"Is there a problem here?" I asked.

The guard whispered something to Tilly, then hastily backed off into the tall hedges that kissed the iron gates, shrouding them in greenery.

Tilly stepped into a patch of moonlight, her features rigid, her shoulders thrust back in defiance.

"Oh, Sorsha." Her voice was as hard and brittle as ice. "Always sticking your nose in where it doesn't belong."

I took a step back, shocked by her tone. This was not the Tilly I knew. This was someone else.

"Sorry," I stammered, taken aback by how angry she was. "I thought you might be in trouble."

There was more rustling behind me. Quick footsteps crunched in the gritty path. Something was very, very wrong here. I took another step away from Tilly. My vision tunneled in on her as my heart beat quickened. My hands went numb with fear.

"And you thought you'd rush in and save the day?" she sneered. "I don't need your help. In fact, you'll be the one begging on your knees by the time I'm through with you."

She twirled a silver key around her finger. The iron gate creaked. I heard more footsteps, more low whispers. Who had she let in?

The trees were pressed in too close. My lungs could not expand to give me adequate breath. "What are you talking about?"

"I'm talking," she spat, "about how your fun and games are over. For all you whores in your big fancy house, sitting on all that magic like dragons hoarding treasure."

"Tilly, I—"

"Shut up."

There was a bright silver flash as the moon glinted off the wickedly curved blade Tilly thrust at me. There was a jerky, erratic quality to her movements. I jumped back, widening the distance between us.

"I looked out for you. Tried to help you," I said, trying to calm her.

She shook her head. "Unbelievable."

She swung her blade toward me again. Shadows enveloped me as my back hit the trunk of a tree, sending the crisp, bitter tang of lemons into the air.

"But what would you know? You've lived a nice, cozy life in there for years. The only place you go when you leave is a literal *palace*. Well, allow me to educate you."

There was a distant shout from somewhere in the house and a scream that made my blood run cold.

"Do you even know where all the magic comes from?"

I shook my head, not trusting myself to speak. I clenched the sea-stone dagger tightly, hiding it in the folds of my skirt. My hairpin dug painfully into my scalp, but I pressed my head harder against the tree, trying to dislodge it. I had to keep her talking.

"We trade for it?"

"The watered-down swill that bitch gets doesn't just appear here. It's imported from the north, on the backs of *my* people. They're little more than slaves. Well, we're done with that now." She huffed a breath through her nose.

The hairpin was almost loose. I shook my head again, playing up my naivete even as my heart pounded in my chest. There was another scream from the house. "We?"

"The rebellion is coming for you all. For everyone who makes a profit from our magic, who lines their pockets and doesn't think twice about the suffering of others."

"But, Tilly, I'm indentured. Same as you."

"Don't make me laugh. You dine with a prince or a lord

every night. You have no idea what real suffering is. That bitch Viviana doesn't hold a candle to the suffering I've seen. That I've experienced personally."

The pin slid out of my hair. I caught it between my back and the tree. I couldn't remember how to send messages to Andromeda with it. She'd only ever summoned me. But I had to try.

"Stop this. Please."

"No. The only way to get you people to listen is to take away your nice things. The House of Night will fall. A fitting signal to everyone in Tenebris. The rebellion is coming. And we have much more in store."

I leaned forward enough to let the pin slide down my back. I caught it with my free hand and squeezed, trying to send any amount of magic into it. Flame. That's what she'd told me, the first day she'd given it to me. I thought of the mirror shard concealed in my bodice. I'd wrapped it in a leather cord and wore it as a necklace. The mirror shard sat between my breasts, concealed by my clothes. It stirred, as if waking to my call.

"I've seen it," I whispered, hoping she'd mistake the strain in my voice for terror. My heart was in my throat as I tried to send my warning through the hairpin. I thought of fire and heat as I squeezed, the tiny pool of my magic frothing at my call. *Under attack. Run.* "I've seen the suffering in this city."

Tilly glared at me and took a step closer, coming under the shadows of the tree, her knife still held out before her. She stood, leering up at me, little more than an arm's reach away. "Oh?"

"Down by the river. I saw how the fae are dying without magic. A sickness is spreading. I want to help. That's why I've been spending time with the prince, to try to—"

"Shut up," said Tilly again through gritted teeth.

I wasn't sure if Andromeda had received my message. I had

to get into the house to warn everyone.

Tilly tightened her grip on her knife. "There's only one way this gets solved."

"How? What are you going to do?"

Tilly smiled, but it did not reach her cold eyes. "Burn it down."

I pushed off the tree, using the momentum to swing around toward the garden gate. I ran for the house. A bitter, acrid stench in the air made my eyes sting.

With a snarl, Tilly crashed into me, sending us both sprawling. I dropped the hairpin but held on to the dagger. I scrambled to my knees. Tilly grabbed the back of my head and pulled my hair. I gasped in pain as tears blurred my vision. My mask pulled loose from my face as she threw me backward into the dirt. She was stronger than she looked.

I twisted onto my side as she brought her blade, as long as my forearm, downward. It plunged into the dirt as I rolled and sprang to my feet.

"Tilly. *Please*." I should have thrown my dagger instead of pleading with her. But she wanted the same thing I did – to help people.

My plea cost me my opening, and she lunged for me again. Her knife caught my pants, tearing the fabric.

One minute she was behind me. The next she was at my flank. Shock, cold at first, then hot and burning, wrenched through me, stealing my breath.

With every ounce of strength, I tried to fight off the excruciating pain that coursed through my body as her blade sank into my side. I gasped. My breath came out in a soft moan.

I felt the blade slide back out of me, and I screamed as burning fire consumed me. It was more painful than being touched by the obsidian mirror, more excruciating than using my magic to dispel corruption. It was the worst pain I'd ever known.

My knees bit into sand and stones. I pressed my hand to my side beneath my ribs. A strange, sticky warmth oozed between my fingers.

My hearing grew fuzzy.

Tilly ran off into the night, dashing behind the trees.

I had to get up, had to move. I thought I heard screaming. Ferdie was inside. I had to help him.

I clenched my jaw and shoved my forearm against my side. My sleeve grew saturated with blood. Tears of agony streamed down my face. I dug deep inside myself to find my last remaining bit of strength and stumbled to my feet. It was hard to breathe. I braced myself against a nearby tree, propping my body upright. I still had the sea-stone dagger clenched in my hand. I couldn't let it go. It was Corvus's brother's. He'd given it to me to keep it safe.

Corvus.

He would help me. He could help the others.

I took three steps before I had to stop. My breath came in short little gasps. It hurt so much.

Suddenly, everything grew silent. Then, there was a deafening *BOOM* that tore the night asunder.

An invisible force threw me to the ground. I screamed as pain lashed up my side, burning me from the inside out. My vision swam. Hot air gusted over me. I turned my head to take in the horror. Incredible heat washed over me as the House of Night went up in flames, engulfed in a massive explosion. Glass shattered. Screams were quickly silenced. The only thing I could hear was the crackling of fire as it devoured, reaching up the tallest spires of the house.

The heat grew unbearable. I could no longer hear anything,

but I forced myself to move. Away from the House of Night. I don't remember reaching the front gates or making it down the long drive.

Then, it was cold. My arms and face grew numb. I focused on taking one more step. And another, and another, until I found myself in a circular courtyard of stone.

I beat on the front door, distantly noticing I'd left a bloody handprint on the wood. The door swung open, bathing me in a golden glow. I squinted against the harshness of the light.

I forced my numb lips to form words. "Corvus. Please."

Then I tumbled into darkness as the world slid out from under me.

Chapter Thirty-One

Corvus

I rubbed my eyes with the heels of my hands, trying to chase away the pull to sleep. The candles in the study burned low, and the tall mahogany clock showed just past one o'clock.

Dio had just left after I'd turned down his invitation for revelry. I wasn't in a very merry mood. I offered him a room for the night, but he insisted on making a stop at the pub, even after I refused to go with him.

I looked back down at the book open on the table. Several others were stacked next to it, all of them useless. None had any answers about the mirror, but the book before me was promising. It was a scathing history of the Dawnstone House, penned by someone who had undoubtedly been wronged by them, but there was mention of their artificers buried beneath the slander. If I wasn't able to help Sorsha kill the corrupted magic for a few nights, then I could make myself useful by gathering information.

The words on the page blurred together, but I didn't think I could sleep. My mind repeated the same thought again and again: Sorsha was a Dawnstone artificer. I'd seen her cleanse corrupted magic and mend what was once broken, with nothing but her own innate abilities.

But even with her gifts, our progress was slow. There had to be a way we could speed up the process of repairing the mirror. If not for Tenebris, then for Sorsha.

It was why I was here, in the library, instead of in bed. The prince had found his information in books, and he was a mortal with paltry access to our histories and chronicles. I'd hoped we would have some information about magical weapons, containment, anything that could help me fix this whole godsdamned mess.

I picked up my dagger, the familiarity of the cool metal handle offering some comfort. My guess was that it was a Dawnstone dagger, as was its twin. An artificer probably crafted it. It certainly held magical properties. Sorsha had stabbed that slithering nightmare of corrupted magic, and the dagger had responded to her, awakened by her touch.

Worry tangled my thoughts. If she was a Dawnstone artificer, she may be the last of her kind. If folk ever discovered who she was, she would be in danger. Her skill and lineage made her more than valuable. They made her a threat. One my father wouldn't hesitate to use to his advantage.

I closed the book and slumped into my chair, wondering again if I should tell her what I had seen branded onto her back. She was going to find out, eventually. But would she know the significance of her family line or recognize the dangers on her own? Probably not.

Shoving myself back from my seat, I crossed to the window. I opened it, trying to rouse myself from my sleepy stupor. I inhaled deeply, smelling smoke in the wind. There must be a fire in the city.

My thoughts drifted back to my worries. It was like a loose tooth that demanded pulling. I should warn Sorsha about her family, her lineage, her abilities.

But it wasn't my place. It also meant I'd have to confess to seeing her scars. I'd broken her trust. I couldn't bring myself to tell her.

A pounding on the door dragged me from my mental volley.

"Corv, it's me." Dio's voice was tight. Something was wrong.

I crossed the room quickly and wrenched open the door. His pale face stared up at me, pinched with worry.

"What is it?"

"There's a girl here to see you. She's in rough shape…"

The edges of my vision went white. My heart was seized in an ice-cold fist. "Who is it?"

Dio stepped back, shaking his head. "She didn't say, she passed out. I ran into her when I was leaving. There's a lot of blood."

I didn't hear anything Dio said after that. I sprinted down the hall, my heart pounding in rhythm with my steps.

"Where?" I growled over my shoulder.

"Front door."

I barreled around a corner, then another. I focused on increasing my speed, trying to outrun the terrible thoughts that flashed in my mind.

Sorsha was slumped in the entryway. Blood pooled around her in crimson lakes. Her beautiful golden hair was stained dark with it, her face pale.

I knelt beside her. Blood seeped through the knees of my pants. There was so much of it. I couldn't tell where it was coming from. "Sorsha."

Her breath was too shallow, her color too pale.

Something inside me snapped.

I flipped her over as gently as I could and ran my hands over her, trying to assess where the blood was coming from. There was a stab wound, lower left abdomen. I ripped my shirt off over my head, pressing the fabric to her.

We couldn't stay here. I had to move her. If my father found us… if he found out who she was…

"Dio. Go get a medic. Tell them I can pay whatever they want. Go *now*."

He rushed past me, skirting around the pool of blood.

I scooped Sorsha into my arms, doing my best to keep pressure on her wound, and carried her to my bedchamber.

"Corvus?" she mumbled, barely coherent.

"You're going to be alright. I've got you."

She faded, drifting back into unconsciousness, taking pieces of my heart with her.

Two hours later, the medic departed with three sacks of gold after stitching Sorsha back together. The first was for his services and discretion. The other two were for the little glass bottle of magic salve that would speed her healing process.

Ferdie had seen to the mess in the hall. I didn't need a trail of blood leading my father to my chambers.

Sorsha lay against my pillows, hair splayed around her face. She was still too pale. Her sturdy frame looked small in one of my shirts, which was large enough to fall to her thighs. I'd taken great care to hide her scars from the physician.

A fire burned in the grate, casting dark shadows across her face. I'd carefully tucked blankets around her to keep her warm. Her chest rose and fell in a steady, quick rhythm. She had lost a lot of blood.

Blood that was all over my own hands and clothes.

Dio saw me staring at the rusty crimson. "So, this is the one, huh?"

A lump formed in my throat. What she should be was nothing. A flirtation ended, a courtship cut short. But I could not rid her from my life or extricate her from my thoughts. I answered simply. "Yes. She is."

"Go get cleaned up," he said. "You'll only scare her to death if the first thing she sees when she wakes is a gory, brooding monster instead of the handsome devil you usually are."

I should bathe. Or at least put on a shirt. But I couldn't leave her side.

Dio placed a hand on my shoulder. "I'll keep watch. No one comes through that door."

I nodded. "Thanks."

It took me a full ten minutes to scrub all traces of blood from my skin. My clothes were ruined, as were hers. They'd need to be burned. I grabbed a fresh pair of pants and a clean shirt, threading my wings through the slits in the back.

The gravity of the situation hit me as my adrenaline wore off. Someone had tried to *kill* her.

A terrible, burning anger swelled through me. I would find whoever did this to her and inflict on them the worst pain they could imagine. Only when I heard them beg for death would I grant them the mercy of killing them.

A soft knock on the door kept me from snapping entirely.

"Corv. She's waking up."

I was at her side in a moment. She needed to keep still for the healing salve to work. Knowing her, she'd wake thrashing and fighting. I slipped my hand into hers and called her name.

She opened her eyes and immediately tried to sit up, gasping when the pain hit her.

"Easy. You have to lie still."

Her fingers tightened around mine. "Corvus."

"Welcome back."

Dio waved lazily from his post, back pressed against the bedroom door. "Hello, lovely."

"That's Dio. He's my good friend," I assured her.

He gave her a nod. "Wish we were meeting under better circumstances. Corvus has told me almost nothing about you.

Which means he is determined to keep you all to himself. I can't tell you how many times I've almost gone to visit you in your manor of mystery."

Sorsha paled further. "The House of Night. It's gone," she said in a panicked, hoarse voice.

"What?" I tightened my grip on her hand.

"Tilly, she blew it up. Ferdie, Madam Andromeda... I don't know if anyone survived." Tears pricked her eyes. She tried to sit upright again and hissed.

"The smoke," I said, remembering the scent from earlier. "Did *Tilly* hurt you?" I felt hot all over as my blood boiled.

"Yes," she whispered, brow furrowing with the painful memory.

I turned to Dio, my expression dark.

"I'll find out what I can." He reached for the door handle, but Sorsha stopped him.

"No, you can't go. They might still be there."

"They?" he asked.

"She wasn't alone. There were others, a group of rebels. From the north."

My mind flashed to the map in my father's study, of the prince's talk of training exercises in the north. Was this the threat they were preparing for? If so, they'd done a poor job defending the border. It appeared they were already here.

"I'll be careful," reassured Dio, eyes glinting with a hint of mischief.

"Dio," I cautioned. This wasn't some bar fight. They had stabbed Sorsha, tried to kill her. I didn't want him getting hurt, too.

He threw up his hands in surrender. "I swear. Intelligence only. No talking to the rebels. Even if they're pretty." He saw himself out, leaving Sorsha and me alone with our hands still clasped.

The silence between us was as thick as overgrown weeds and as sharp as bramble thorns. Sorsha disentangled her fingers from mine. I mourned the loss of her touch.

She reached for her chest, shoulders tense, but relaxed as her fingers found a cord of leather at her neck. "I'm sorry. I hope I didn't trouble you, barging in like this."

"Trouble me?" What in seven hells was she talking about?

Her hand clenched the sheets, twisting the fabric nervously. "I only remembered you weren't far from the house, and I wasn't thinking clearly."

I placed my own hand over hers, stilling her fidgeting. "You're welcome here. It's no trouble at all. You needed help."

"But I know you don't want to see me," she whispered, unable to meet my gaze.

My chest tightened under the weight of all I wanted to say to her. I longed to confess how I craved her, how the separation I had forced upon us was slowly driving me mad. But to confess my feelings meant I must also confess my transgressions. And I was afraid of what she would think of me if I did.

I stood, hating myself for it. "You should get some rest. Your wound will heal quickly. Put this on it if it starts to pain you again." I handed her the jar of salve from the nightstand.

She took it, careful not to let her fingers brush mine.

Dio's chair was still situated near the door. I moved to it, propping my feet up on a footstool and letting my wings drape to the floor. "Sleep, Sorsha. I'll keep watch."

She blinked heavily, exhaustion and something heavier settling over her. She was asleep within minutes.

I crossed my arms and watched her slow, even breaths as my mind warred between two options: tell her the truth about her lineage or lie to her. Bile churned in my stomach. Whatever decision I made, I knew that there would be no turning back from it. Not after tonight. There was too much at stake now, and another rebuke of her attempts to bridge the gap between us would snap whatever tender threads connected us. Forever.

My brother's dagger lay on the bedside table next to Sorsha's sleeping form, still coated with stray drops of her blood. I stood quietly and retrieved it, bringing it back to my post. The weight of it was comforting. I set to cleaning the blade, removing the dark, clotted crimson stains. I hadn't given it a second thought when I'd lent it to her. But now that it was back in my hand, I realized how much I'd missed it, this last connection to my brother.

I'd promised Max vengeance as he faded from me, his blood pooling into the cracks between cobblestones. I remembered the burn of the vow on my lips, how my words had singed my mouth at their utterance.

I swear the Dawnstones will pay for this.

My tears mixed with the blood on his cheeks as the light faded from his eyes. My tongue burned with my promise. I wasn't sure if there was a touch of magic in it, or simply the agony of loss, consuming my very soul.

Sorsha stirred, moaning softly as she tried to curl on her side. She didn't wake, but she found stillness on her back.

It was fitting that I should never have the stunning, tenacious woman who slept before me. It was my punishment for letting Max die. Because there must have been something I could have done differently. There must have been.

As I cleaned the dagger in slow, soothing circles, my thoughts continued to dwell on dark if-onlys and eternal guilt.

Chapter Thirty-Two

Sorsha

A throbbing pain in my side woke me. My mind was fuzzy as I surfaced from dreams of smoke, darkness, and pine trees. It took me a moment to remember where I was, what had happened. My eyes shot open as my heart hammered in my chest, certain I was still in danger.

Corvus was slumped in his chair, mouth open and snoring softly. I knew he'd only fall asleep if he knew we were safe. By the looks of the dark circles under his eyes, which were starting to rival the color of Tristan's, I'd say he was just as exhausted as I was.

I untwisted the cap on the jar as another wave of pain made me clench my teeth. But I couldn't apply the medicine with dirty hands, or else I'd infect the wound. I scanned the chamber again, realizing I was in Corvus's bedroom. It certainly wasn't how I'd imagined spending a night here.

The room was adorned simply. Quality furniture of dark, polished wood decorated the space. The bed was simple, though the headboard was intricately carved, bearing a relief of waves crashing on cliffs in a terrible storm as lightning streaked the sky. A small sofa, desk, armoire, and tables were scattered about, each surface covered with either a discarded item of clothing or a weapon. He was messy. A corner of my mouth quirked up at the homey sight.

My smile quickly fell as another wave of pain slammed into me. I saw the door at the other end of the bedroom. Gingerly, I sat up, but the pain made me gasp.

Corvus roused at the sound, straightening in his chair. "What is it?" he asked, voice gritty with sleep.

"Nothing, I'm alright. Is your bathing chamber through there?"

He rubbed his face, rousing himself. "Yes."

I clenched my teeth and tried to swing my legs over the bed. Corvus rose, stepping forward to help.

"I can manage," I said. A wave of pain made me see stars and the edges of my vision went blurry.

"Don't be ridiculous."

Before I could protest, he swept me up into his arms and carried me across the room. Instead of arguing, I let him. The feeling of him, his warmth, was comforting. I know I shouldn't lean into him or read into the gesture as anything more than a practical way to get me where I needed to go, but I still felt cold, and I wasn't sure if it was from my wound or from lingering fear.

He set me down gingerly on a bench near the sink. "Do you need me to stay?"

"No, thank you."

"I'll be outside. Call me when you're done."

I nodded. Once the door was shut, I began the slow process of relieving myself, washing, and applying more salve. A task that would have taken me two minutes took a quarter of an hour. Tears pricked my eyes, as much in frustration as in pain. I let them fall silently down my cheeks for four breaths, then pulled myself together. The salve was quick to work, numbing my aching gut within a minute. I was able to pull the door open on my own.

Corvus, seeing that I was steadier on my feet, merely offered his arm to me. I took it partly out of necessity, partly because I craved his touch.

I only let go when I was seated on the bed again, my mind

and heart churning. His actions did not align with his supposed wish for us to be apart. Why couldn't he tell me his reason for wanting to be apart? If it was some attempt to protect me, then he was woefully misguided. Tilly had tried to kill me, there were monsters in the caves, and war was on our doorstep. He couldn't protect me from all of it.

After everything tonight, I refused to believe he did not care for me. I was tired of pretending like it didn't matter to me. It might have been the pain, breaking down those walls I'd built around my ribs, shielding my heart, or it might have been his touch that cracked them like a battering ram. Either way, I wanted answers.

He stood at the edge of the bed, looking down at me with beautiful gray eyes, and I couldn't take it anymore.

"Corvus," I said, voice trembling with anger and something like longing. "We can't keep doing this."

His eyebrows shot up and his wings rustled. "I don't know what you mean."

"I can't keep pretending."

He stiffened, clenching his hands at his sides.

"Sorsha, we can't—"

"Tell me why. Give me a reason."

He took a step back, and my throat tightened at the added space between us. "It's complicated."

I shook my head. "Don't do that."

Corvus ran a hand through his hair. His wings flicked in irritation. "You don't need me. You seem very satisfied with the prince's company as of late."

"What are you talking about?"

His features grew sullen; a muscle tensed in his jaw. "You're spending every night with *him*."

"I did it for *us*!" I couldn't take it anymore. I couldn't pretend like his feelings didn't matter to me. I couldn't deny he was all I thought about every godsdamned moment of every day.

"You're so stupid, Corvus!" I said as unshed tears choked me. "You pushed me away first. You pushed *me* away. How else was I supposed to see you?"

The color drained from his face, and he went as still as stone. I wanted to fall into his chest and sob until I couldn't breathe.

"You wanted to see me again?"

"Yes." I let the tears fall, unable to contain them any longer.

He stared at me, stricken. "Fuck, Sorsha."

"Tell me what I did," I sobbed, as the feelings I so desperately tried to bury came crashing to the surface in a terrible tidal wave. "What did I do wrong?"

It was a question that had plagued me for years. There must have been some reason my mother abandoned me. Maybe it was something I did. Or perhaps I was a bad child who deserved to be tossed away, locked behind gates of iron and forgotten. I twisted my fist into the sheets, unable to bear the weight of my grief. I pressed my other hand to my chest, trying to keep it all contained, but it spilled out like sand through cupped fingers. I couldn't breathe; I hurt so much.

I felt his arms around me, shushing me, rocking me as I cried.

"Sorsha, I'm sorry. I'm so fucking sorry," he said, and his voice rumbled through my chest like thunder. I focused on his warmth, on how good it felt to be wrapped in his arms and my breath started to slow.

"Darling, look at me."

He gently cupped my face between his palms, wiping away the falling tears with his thumbs. I looked up at him as he tilted my chin, my whole chest throbbing. "It's not your fault. It's nothing you did. I would take it all back if I could, I swear

I would. But I had to keep you safe. I *had* to. I should have realized… gods, you're right. I am stupid."

He kissed my cheeks, trying to soothe the ache. I clutched his shirt in both my fists, never wanting to let him go.

"I'm safe when I'm with you," I whispered hoarsely. "You saved my life."

He dropped one hand to my shoulder, keeping the other cupped against my cheek. "Only because you saved me first."

A bubble of hope swelled within me, but his expression was still dark and serious. "Why did you push me away?"

"I broke your trust, Sorsha. I'm sorry."

The bubble shrank to almost nothing. My stomach turned to lead. "What do you mean?"

"I saw the scars on your back. The night of the masquerade. You fell asleep, and I saw them."

I scanned his face. That was it? Seven hells, *that* was why he pushed me away? My own sins were much more damning. My palms went clammy, and my heart stuttered. How would he react when I confessed my own transgressions to him?

His brow was furrowed, mouth downturned, eyes swimming with guilt. He truly felt horrible about breaking my trust. I saw my own guilt reflected in his face.

I waited for heartbreak, or at least disappointment, to dampen my desperate longing for him, but it didn't come. I had asked him not to look. But after everything we'd been through, it seemed so trivial. It didn't bother me that he had seen them.

"I don't care about that." I would have gladly shown them to him now. I would happily give my whole being to him if he'd let me.

"Sorsha," he said softly, barely above a whisper. "Do you know who your father is?"

I blinked. "My father? No, I never knew him. It was always

just my mother and me, as far back as I can remember."

"And how long ago was that? What is your earliest memory?"

I drew back from him a little as confusion took hold. My stomach twinged as pain began to set in again. "Why are you asking me this? " I still didn't understand. "You're fae. You have a better memory than half-fae or mortals. I don't see what that has to do with me."

"But you *should* be able to remember, Sorsha. You're fae, too."

My mother had never spoken about her own family. I'd assumed she was mortal. "So? What does that have to do with who my father is?" The fire crackled in the grate. I suddenly felt too hot.

"You have a scar above your left shoulder blade that does not match the rest." He spoke each word in a deliberate, measured manner, as if trying to hold back his own torrent of emotion.

The blood drained from my face. I felt my fists go slack, releasing Corvus's shirt. "What?"

"You need to see it."

"Corvus, just tell me. What is it? What are you talking about?" Panic made my voice come out higher than usual. Something carved into my back had scared Corvus so badly he felt like he couldn't see me? I knew there was something wrong, something he wasn't telling me.

He hesitated, brow scrunching with uncertainty.

"*Please.*"

He looked around the room, scanning for something. "Come here." He helped me to my feet, and I swayed as a wave of pain crashed over me.

Corvus held my hand as he led me to a full-length mirror. He returned to his bathing chamber, emerging with a small, hand-sized one. He extended it to me, and I took it in my trembling hands.

"I can tell you if you want me to, but I think seeing it for yourself will help."

I clutched the mirror and fought the wave of fear that twisted in my stomach.

"It's your choice, Sorsha. I won't force you." The light was nearly gone from his eyes, his mouth set in a hard, determined line.

I would believe him, whatever he told me was carved into my flesh. But he respected me enough to give me the choice between trusting him and seeing with my own eyes the harm that was done to me. I took a shaky breath. "Okay." I turned around, slipping my arms free of the sleeves of the borrowed shirt.

Goosebumps rose on my neck and arms as the cool air hit my back, clammy with sweat. I held up the shirt with one hand, covering my front, and clutched the mirror with the other.

"Ready?" he asked, voice low.

I nodded. My throat felt impossibly tight.

Corvus stepped back, leaving nothing between me and my reflection. I angled the little mirror so I could see the scars that ravaged my back.

A low moan escaped my lips as I took in the mass of scar tissue that exploded from the center of my spine and crawled up toward my neck and shoulders. The pink and white gouges were uneven. Whatever cuts had been made into my skin had been sealed with inexperienced hands. Some of the scars puckered from where stitches had been hastily placed. It was brutal, and terrifying.

My throat closed, and metal bands wrapped around my chest, making it impossible to breathe. I should remember getting these scars. I should know why I had these wounds.

Why didn't I? Who had done this to me?

I changed the angle of the mirror so I could see the mark Corvus wanted me to look at, fighting through a torrent of rising grief and sorrow. Hidden among the twisting ropes of scars were a collection of lines as big as a coin, small compared to the size and scope of the rest of the scars that cleaved my flesh. I had seen this mark before. A mountain with a rising sun cresting over the peak.

My eyes flicked upward, searching for Corvus's face in the reflection. He wasn't looking at my back. His eyes were fixed on my face, watching for my reaction. He looked... devastated.

I squeezed my eyes shut and slipped the shirt on again. "What is it? I've seen it, but I can't remember where." My entire body trembled. Pain flashed again in my stomach, white hot and angry. The salve was wearing off. I turned to face Corvus.

His eyes were full of sorrow. "It's the mark of House Dawnstone."

My knees grew weak. I clutched the mirror in my hand and focused my entire will on staying upright. A thousand questions raced through my mind. Dawnstone? Why would I bear their mark?

"Why?" My lips were numb. I was hardly conscious of forming the words. My ears rang, muffling all sound.

Corvus said something, but I couldn't make it out. All I could hear was the rush of blood in my ears. I tried to take a step toward the bed. I needed to sit down. The mirror slipped from my hand, and the world went black.

I woke again on the bed, head swimming and mouth dry.

Corvus leaned forward and grabbed my hand. "Hey. Are

you alright?"

My mouth was too dry to speak. I nodded and pushed myself up on my elbows. My stomach didn't hurt too much. He must have reapplied the salve for me. A pitcher of water on the nightstand caught my eye.

Wordlessly, Corvus poured me a glass, bringing the cup to my lips.

I drank deeply, trying to sort the tangle of my thoughts.

"I'm sorry," said Corvus, setting the cup back down. "That was too much. Your injuries, I didn't think—"

"Why do I have their mark on me?" I asked. My words rang hollowly in my ears.

"You're the lost Dawnstone daughter."

"The what?" I'd never heard of her.

"About fifteen years ago, Malachite Dawnstone's daughter and wife were kidnapped. Everyone thought his daughter would be found quickly, because she bore the mark of their house and had white wings."

My stomach churned. The world threatened to tilt again, but I gripped the sheets, trying to anchor myself. "That doesn't mean it's me. Anyone could have put that mark there, especially when they were carving up the rest of my back."

"The mark is different," said Corvus solemnly. "It's not a scar. It's a symbol of your lineage." He rubbed a thumb over his bottom lip. "Max had one. He bore the Stormfall mark."

It was true, the lines were different. Not the garish pink and white ropes like the rest of my scars, but something more delicate.

"Do you have one?" I hadn't seen one when we'd shared the night together, but I had been... preoccupied.

"No," he said. A sad smile tugged at his lips. "Not worthy of it, I suppose."

"What does worth have to do with it? You're the most worthy person I know. You care about the wellbeing of others. That is an uncommon trait among the fae." I slipped a hand over his and gripped his fingers. Gods, did he really think that of himself?

He squeezed back. "The marks are just a myth now, anyway. Who knows what they truly mean? But, long ago, those who bore the marks of their houses were fit to rule them."

My throat tightened and my eyes pricked with unshed tears. "My scars..." I placed a hand over my mouth. I swallowed painfully, then let my hand fall to my lap. "You said the Dawnstone daughter had wings."

Corvus nodded solemnly. His lips were thin. He tightened his grip on my hand.

"Someone cut them away," I whispered.

"It makes sense," said Corvus.

I closed my eyes. Revulsion rolled through me in thick waves.

Oh, gods.

If it was true, then why couldn't I remember such a thing?

Thoughts churned in my mind, so quick and fast it was hard to grab onto one before the next came crashing in its place. But one thought snagged, begging to be examined.

"The Dawnstones murdered your brother. Is that why you couldn't see me? Some feud between your houses?" It came out more callously than I intended.

Corvus drew his hand away from mine, crossing his arms at his chest.

The gesture felt like a punch to the stomach.

"You have to understand—" he started.

"No, look, I get it." I cut him off, as hurt and anger bubbled to the surface. "You don't want to be associated with me. Over something I have no control over. Something I didn't even know was there until a few minutes ago."

"That's not it," he said. He ran a hand through his hair and sighed.

"That's what it sure as hells seems like."

Corvus stood, the legs of his chair skittering across the floor. A gust of wind whipped through the chamber as he began to pace, wings twitching behind him. "You don't understand. If my father ever found out who you were, what you meant to me, he'd use you as a bargaining chip. He would use you to get back at the Dawnstones. And I *cannot* let that happen."

The breath raced from my lungs. "Corvus."

He scrubbed his hands over his face before he whirled to face me. "What I'm trying to say, Sorsha, is—" He froze. His eyes went wide.

The hair on the back of my neck stood up as adrenaline shot through me. "What?"

Footsteps sounded down the hall, growing closer.

Corvus set his mouth in a hard, grim line. "Someone's coming."

Chapter Thirty-Three

Corvus

The echo of my father's baritone commands and the sound of footsteps cut my words short. Terror wrapped an icy fist around my heart. I could protect Sorsha from most things, even monsters made of magic. But I could not protect her from my own father.

There was no time to tell her to hide, to run. Not that she'd get very far. Her wound was still fresh, her face pale with pain.

The footsteps were heavy, accompanied by the clank of steel. Father was not alone. I feared the reason he would bring his personal guard to knock on my door in the early hours of the morning.

BANG. BANG.

"Open up, Corvus," barked my father.

My mouth grew dry as I forced myself to don my mask, the rakish son who'd spent another night gallivanting in the city with pleasurable company.

I opened the door a crack and pressed a forearm to the frame, blocking the view into my room. "Father," I drawled. "I'm a bit preoccupied at the moment."

He raked his gaze across me, lip curling with disdain. His eyes glittered with fierce determination. "Where is she?"

"I'm afraid you just missed my nighttime companion." I prayed my voice did not betray the fear in my heart. A party of six guards, dressed for battle, stood behind him.

"Step aside, Corvus."

In the span of a heartbeat, I weighed my options. I could

resist, refuse to let my father in. I would have maybe half a minute to find a way to get Sorsha out before the guards broke down the door. My opposition would only raise or confirm my father's suspicions. If I acquiesced, then I had a better chance at downplaying Sorsha's importance.

I swung the door wide, and stalked back over to the bed, arms crossed. I flicked my gaze to Sorsha, trying to convey my thoughts. *Keep calm. I'll handle this.*

Her lips thinned, and she drew the blankets up to her chin as my father entered, flanked by two of his men.

"Your name, girl." He barked.

"Sventura, your grace," she replied. She cast her eyes to the floor demurely. "Sorsha Sventura."

"Andromeda's pet. Stand."

Her voice took on a sharp edge. "My lord, I am not decent."

"What is the point of this? Since when do you care who warms my bed?"

"I *care* when she may be our enemy," he spat.

My wings flared and my fingers itched to grab the hilt of my dagger, but my weapons lay on the table in the corner. "I don't know what you're talking about." How the fuck did he know who she was? Had the medic seen her scar after all? Who had betrayed her?

Father motioned for the guards to take her.

I stepped forward, spreading my wings to shield her, dropping all pretense of nonchalance. "Stand down."

They hesitated for a moment.

"You obey *my* orders," Father snarled at them. "Step aside, Corvus, or I will have you removed."

I remained as still as stone.

"Get the girl."

I bent my knees, readying myself for their attack. My mind

whirled, calculating, trying to come up with a plan to keep her safe.

"It's fine, Corvus. I don't have anything to hide."

Bile rose in the back of my throat as Sorsha struggled to rise from the bed, her forearm tucked defensively against her wound. She gripped the jar of salve in her other hand, holding it close. I held out my hand for her, which she took with trembling fingers. I squeezed, trying to reassure her. I felt as if I'd been tossed overboard and was struggling to stay afloat.

She did her best to stand to her full height. Even in her bare feet and swimming in my shirt, far too large for her, she still bore herself with defiance. My heart swelled.

Father studied her, eyes blazing with hellfire. I wanted nothing more than to knock him out cold. He did nothing to hide the contempt on his face.

"Where has your madam hidden herself away?"

Sorsha's eyes widened. "She's alive?"

"Answer the question. No doubt your profession requires you to be an adept liar, so let us dispense with any deception. Where did she go?"

Her pulse fluttered in her neck. She swallowed hard. I expected her to be relieved. Instead, her shoulders tensed. "I don't know. Truly."

Father's face fell, disappointment creasing his features. He turned toward the captain of his guard. "Keep her in the dungeon. We can use her later, if needed. Andromeda seems to favor her."

"No." I thrust my arm out in front of Sorsha, even as relief threatened to buckle my knees. He didn't know she was Dawnstone. He only wanted to know where Andromeda was. I didn't have time to wonder why. Right now, protecting Sorsha was my only concern.

"I will personally gut you and the girl if you defy me again," said my father, a vein pulsing in his temple.

A light hand rested on my outstretched arm. I turned to Sorsha, who looked at me with fire in her eyes.

"I won't let them hurt you," I said in a low voice.

"I know," she whispered, and squeezed my arm before stepping around me. "I trust you will do what's best for yourself, Corvus. As always." She flicked her golden hair over her shoulder. Father's eyes narrowed at the gesture.

"If Andromeda is alive, then I am still under her employ. She'll want me back in one piece," she said to my father. "Or I expect you'll be the one who will be paying the bill."

Father did not deign to reply, only motioned for the guards to take her. As she passed by him, he squinted. "Wait."

Icy dread flooded my limbs.

"Hold her."

"No," Sorsha protested as she was seized roughly. The sound of swords being drawn sent a chill skittering down my spine.

"Get your hands off her," I growled, lunging toward them. The cold bite of steel at my throat made me freeze. One of the guards pressed his sword to my neck, hard enough to draw a small trickle of blood.

I could only watch as Father pinched her chin between his fingers, tilting her face upward.

Sorsha clenched her jaw and stared defiantly back at him. Her face was bare. She hadn't been wearing a mask when she arrived last night.

"Your eyes. A most peculiar shade. I have seen them before. Hold her." Father withdrew the small dagger he kept as his hip and slashed her shirt at the back as she struggled against her captors. He opened the shredded fabric, exposing her scars and the telltale Dawnstone crest seared into her flesh. His face grew pale.

"Dungeons. Now," he spat.

Sorsha struggled against the guards, but her wound had left her weakened. She was completely defenseless.

"Sorsha!" I shouted, as she was dragged from the room. I'd never hated myself more than in that moment. Who was I, to let them take her away from me? I was weak. Worthless. My gut twisted as shame flooded through me.

My father interrupted my self-loathing. "Leave. Send for Horatio."

My pulse thudded hollowly in my ears as the guards left.

Father tore into me as soon as the door closed. "How could you? The daughter of your enemy, of the swine who murdered your brother?"

"I'm not sleeping with her," I said dully. "She was hurt in the attack. She came here for aid."

"And instead of finishing the job, you *healed* her?"

"Yes," I snapped. A muscle twitched over my right eye.

"Luckily for you, we now have the perfect leverage. Malachite will do whatever we say to get his daughter back."

"No." A hot, bubbling sensation spread from my chest, radiating toward my head, my arms, my stomach.

Father ignored me, talking faster as his excitement grew; he paced the floor. "The Blackwoods die tonight. Lucius has finally decided to move, and we will be rewarded for our loyalty. Lucius will recognize the sacrifices I have made. And Malachite will finally bow to *me*."

"*No.*" Boiling magma flowed through me, pushing out every thought of fealty, of duty, of self-preservation. My shame burned me from the inside, turning into a terrible hatred, hardening into steely resolve. "You're not using her as a ploy for power, Father. Release her. Now."

"Watch your tongue. If Mercelles were here, he would understand. Instead, I am forced to put up with you and your ineptitude. Come. Get dressed. I have need of your services tonight."

A storm raged in my chest. I realized I wasn't just angry at myself, but at my father for what he had done. How he had used me for his own selfish ends. How he continued to abuse the memory of my brother to belittle me.

"This is not what Max would have wanted," I said. I could barely speak past the constriction in my chest.

My father finally stopped his pacing. He shoved a finger in my face. "Don't you dare speak to me of what Mercelles would have wanted. What he would have done. You took him away from me and now dally with the kin who killed him. Your treachery will not go unpunished. Think about where your loyalties lie, Corvus."

His threats, which usually cowed me into submission, could not pierce the armor of my anger. My breath was hot as I exhaled through my nose, ready to barge past him and forsake my family honor. I had to get Sorsha out of here.

But then I blinked. I saw before me not the terrible tyrant of a father who used violence to achieve his ends. Before me stood a broken male, who grasped for threads of power to fill the hole that ate away at him every hour.

Anger had made my father what he was. I would be damned if I let that anger corrupt me, too.

I took another breath, exhaling through my mouth. I looked at my father, seeing the fear behind his eyes for the first time. "You are blind if you think they will ever respect you. This will not sway them."

Father recoiled, disarmed by my sudden calm.

"They're going to kill the royals, and whoever else stands in their path. Who is to say you won't be next?"

His mouth hung open like a bloated fish.

"There is another way to do this. I know how to restore our magic. But I need her help to do it."

My father narrowed his eyes at me. "Impossible. If Lucius has not yet figured out a way, it cannot be done."

"Your loyalty is misplaced, Father. Release Sorsha, and I will see it done." I hated how much I hoped he would see reason and abandon his supplications and thirst for power to help me instead.

"You conspire against me," he said coldly.

My heart sank.

There was a faint knock on the door. Father did not hear it.

"You conspire against the fae with your mad schemes. Enough, I say."

"Father—"

"*Enough*. The girl will go to Lucius. If it is as you claim, then he might have use for her. You, I have no use for. You will rot here until we have seized control, then I will let the Primus decide what is to be done with you. From this day forward, you are no son of mine."

Numbness spread through me. I should have been more surprised at my father's declaration. Somehow, I wasn't.

"My lord?" Horatio's reedy voice drifted through the closed door.

My father kept his gaze fixed steadily on me. "Enter."

"Sir," said Horatio, sweeping into the room. "I have brought it, as requested." In his hands he cradled a cylinder, cast in silver. It was no bigger than a loaf of bread. Unease stirred in my stomach as my skin prickled.

"Good. Corvus will test it before we depart." He finally tore his gaze from mine, moving toward the door.

Horatio paused, twitching with barely concealed glee. "My lord?"

Father stepped into the hall. "Do it."

Horatio's beady eyes darted around the room, landing somewhere behind me. He tossed the cylinder onto the bed, and rushed from the chamber, slamming the door behind him.

I lunged for the handle, but the door would not open. I yanked with all my strength, desperate to get to Sorsha, as a high-pitched whine began to sound. It grew louder and louder, increasing in pitch until all I could hear was the shrill whine in my head, behind my eyes.

I kicked the door and rammed my shoulder into it, but my strength faded as the noise grew in intensity. A searing white light flooded the room.

I pressed my palms to my ears, trying to block out the noise. The light was too bright. The noise sent waves of pain crashing around inside of my head. I think I screamed, but I could not hear myself over the noise. I turned to the bed, squinting as tears ran down my face. There was a sudden *pop* that I felt deep within my chest and head before darkness crashed around me, leaving me to drown in the terrible high-pitched wail.

Chapter Thirty-Four

Sorsha

My body was stiff, and my gut ached, though it could have been worse. I should have been bleeding all over the place. I hadn't gone down here without a fight, and any other wound would have reopened with my kicking and bucking. I blacked out from pain before I'd made it to this cell.

The guards hadn't taken the bottle of salve away. I lifted my shirt and gingerly spread more medicine on the wound, gritting my teeth through the pain. Tears ran down my cheeks, but after a few minutes the pain faded to a dull throb, and I could breathe normally.

Once I could move again, I slowly pushed myself up to stand, leaning against the damp stone wall for support. It was musty and dank down here. Weak light filtered in from high slits in the stone, barely wide enough for my hand to pass through. There were two other cells connected to mine, one on either side, separated by a lattice of reinforced metal.

I tugged on the bars, but they held strong. There was no way out of this on my own. I hoped Corvus would come get me out. My mouth was dry, and my stomach groaned. I couldn't remember the last time I'd eaten. Yesterday afternoon?

A band sounded upstairs, making me jump. My heart pounded in my chest. I leaned against the cool metal as images from last night came unbidden. The hard glint in Tilly's eyes, the smoke drifting through the trees, the flicker of orange light, the phantom sting of pain as the knife slid into me.

Andromeda was missing. What about Ferdie and the others?

Had they made it out in time? My throat grew tight, and my entire body trembled. The house was gone, and I had nowhere to go. No home to return to.

The sounds grew louder, closer. I pressed myself into the back corner of the cell, as far away from the door as possible. There was another loud bang, and two guards passed in front of my cell door, carrying Corvus between them. I bit back the instinct to shout his name and pressed deeper into the shadows.

They threw him into the cell next to me, locked the door, and left.

Once I was sure they had gone, I knelt next to the bars that separated us. "Corvus. Wake up."

His wings were splayed at awkward angles, concealing his face. I squinted in the dim light, trying to assess him for damage, but whatever they had done to him, I could not see. I tried calling his name again, but he did not wake. Any hope I'd had of being set free vanished.

I lost track of how long he lay there. My heart pounded and my blood boiled. What had they done to him?

I paced my cell, applying more salve whenever I felt pain begin to resurface. After several more applications, I found the wound had closed entirely, though my abdomen still felt sore. When my mind started to drift toward despair, I smelled the ointment and rubbed it between my fingers, trying to parse out the ingredients. There were some I was familiar with. Calendula. Comfrey. Echinacea. But there were others I could not place. They seemed oddly familiar somehow, though.

When thoughts of last night's horror, and the phantom pain of being stabbed made me grit my teeth, I tried to focus on getting out. I ran my hands over every inch of my cell, every bar and stone, but I found no weakness to exploit.

After what felt like hours, Corvus finally stirred with a groan.

"Corvus. Are you okay?"

He pushed himself up, moaning again. He cradled his head in his hands, his wings curled reflexively around him. His movements were jerky, pained.

"Are you hurt?" I whispered.

"My head," he said through clenched teeth. "I can't see."

My heart stilled. I had to remain calm. I inhaled through my nose, shoving away my panic. "I have the salve, Corvus. Can you come closer? Maybe it will help."

He managed to get to all fours and vomited.

"Deep breaths," I said with as much calm as I could muster once he had finished. "It's going to be alright."

"I still can't see." His voice was strained, fighting against hysteria.

"Come here. It's going to be okay. Take as long as you need."

He shuffled forward, breathing heavily.

"You're almost here. Reach out your hand."

He continued to inch forward until his fingers closed around the damp metal. His knuckles were pale with the force of his grip. I placed my fingers atop his, trying to reassure him. "Okay, good. Hold on a minute more."

I spread the medicine across my fingertips and stuck my arm through the bars, but he was still too far away. "Lean your head against the bars so I can reach."

He did, and a pale beam of light illuminated his face. He was ashen, his brows knit together with pain. He blinked rapidly, trying to clear whatever blocked his vision, then screwed his eyes shut.

I slowly dragged my fingers across his brow, massaging the ointment into his clammy skin. He raised his head slightly, letting me work the ointment across his forehead, over each eye, at each temple. His color began to return, though he still looked pale, and he refused to open his eyes.

He began to sag, and I could tell the pain was leaving him. Exhaustion was taking its place. "Sleep, Corvus."

He lay down, facing the bars, and pushed his fingers through a gap. I lay next to him, taking his hand in mine, and his breathing grew slow and rhythmic.

I dozed in and out, resisting the pull to sleep, and watched the pale light track across the floor.

After some time, he blinked his eyes open. "Sorsha."

I tightened my grip around his hand. "Can you see?"

"Yes," he said. He barked a shaky laugh, the relief plain on his face. "My head doesn't ache so much anymore, either."

"Good."

"And you, are you hurt?"

"Nearly healed, I think."

We stared at one another through the iron bars, fingers clasped together. I swear I could feel his pulse in my own fingertips. "What did they do to you?"

He let go of my hand and sat up.

I missed the warmth of his fingers, the reassurance of his touch. I sat up, too, and faced him through the lattice.

"Are we alone?"

I nodded. No guards had come or stood watch in the corridor.

"There was some kind of device, made of silver. It made the most horrible noise and shone with bright light. It must have been the weapon my father has been working on."

"For what? Why would they need such a thing?"

His lips thinned. "To overthrow the king."

"Why would they test it on you? Why now?" The questions spilled out of me faster than I could control.

"Because it's tonight. They're going to kill the Blackwoods

tonight, and Lucius will take control."

My heart pounded in my ears, and I felt the blood drain from my face. "We have to get out of here. We have to warn Tristan." I looked at the slits in the stone wall at the top of our cells. I could make out the pale pink and orange of sunset. Time was running out.

"Even if we escape, I don't know how we can stop my father and the other fae."

"We can worry about it later."

"I am not keen on being blinded and feeling like my head is being split open again."

"Then we fix the mirror. They won't kill me, not if they know what I can do. You said that all they want is their magic back. What if we give it to them?"

Corvus shook his head, which made him wince. He stopped and rubbed his chin. "I'm not sure anymore that they'll stop once they have it. There's too much at stake for them now."

"What do you mean?"

Corvus's tone grew bitter. "They want power. My own father would rather disown me than stop this madness."

I clenched my fists, wishing I could take his pain away. "I'm sorry."

He grew quiet for a moment. A strange tension, as thick as sea fog, settled between us. He paused, searching for what he wanted to say. "I'm afraid of you getting hurt again."

A fissure opened in my chest, but there were more important matters at hand. Our feelings, as much as they begged to be untangled, needed to be put aside. "I feel the same way, but I have to do this, Corvus. I have to help if I can."

I balled my hands into fists, steeling my resolve. "Folk are counting on us to see this done, even if they don't know it. If we don't help, then who will? I know folk are angry and getting desperate. They will rip each other apart if we don't do something, and they will continue to die unless we fix the magic."

Corvus crossed his arms. "Even though you are incredibly stubborn, to your own detriment and to my eternal chagrin, I am proud to know you." He flashed a soft smile.

I pressed a hand to my chest, trying to hold in the swell of emotion those words elicited. I wanted nothing more than for the bars between us to vanish, so I could throw myself in his arms. I wanted to touch him, to claim him, to let him know how much he meant to me, and how scared I was. But it would have to wait.

"I am proud to know you, too."

Warmth spread through my limbs as he held my gaze. Then, he cleared his throat and looked around the cell. "Well. First thing is to get out of here." He got to his feet and tugged on the bars. His wings flexed with his movements, the feathers reflecting the soft golden glow of sunset that filtered into the cell. The way they caught the light was breathtaking. They were flecked with streaks of darkest blue and midnight purple. Only at night did they appear as dark as a mirror shard.

"While I am flattered you can't keep your eyes off me," he said as he examined the hinges on the cell door, "I might need some help figuring out how to get out of here." He stepped back and crossed his arms. "Max and I used to play down here when we were younger. I wish we'd hidden a spare key *in* the cell instead of outside of it."

"That's it!" I pushed myself to my knees and plunged a hand down the front of the enormous shirt. I withdrew the leather cord slung around my neck and removed the mirror shard I kept there in a little pouch.

"I thought that was going in an entirely different direction,"

Corvus said, coming closer to the bars.

I chose to ignore him.

"I'm not sure that edge is sharp enough to cut through these bars," he continued as I freed the obsidian glass.

"What does the key look like? To the cells."

"It's a big, clunky key. Made of iron, of course."

"But what does it *look* like? Describe it." I pressed the shard between my palms, feeling the slow stir of dormant magic within.

Corvus knit his brows together. "It's about the length of your hand, with two bits sticking out. They have notches in them." He rubbed his brow, straining to remember.

I could do with that for now, I focused on trying to get the general shape of the key in my mind, picturing it as solidly as I could. Imagining I felt the cool touch of iron, the smoothness of the handle, the heft of it.

Please, work.

I tapped into the well of sleeping power, deep inside my core, letting everything around me fade away. The air around me grew quiet and still. I had done this before. I had wielded this magic, forged it anew. I could wield it again. Because there was no other choice.

The obsidian between my hands pulsed in time with my heartbeat, the magic stretching up to meet me, slow as sunrise. I reached for it in turn, holding the image of the key firmly in my mind.

A pulse shot through my hands, up my arms, and through my chest. The glass shifted into something smooth and round. I opened my palms and within my cupped hands lay a key, black as night. I grinned up at Corvus, triumphant.

"I didn't know you could do that," he said, eyebrows raised.

"Me neither. Can you remember where the notches are

supposed to be?"

"I think so."

"Show me." I held up the key between us, so he could point to where the notches needed to go.

Though he was careful not to touch the glass, he reached through the bars and wrapped his fingers delicately around my wrist, caressing the soft skin there. Heat flooded through my core, and I bit my lip. He made it so hard to focus.

It took a few tries, and I tried not to panic as the light began to grow weaker and sunset fell. Eventually, I got the notches to line up where they needed to go. It was awkward trying to get the key into the lock from the other side of the door. I had to crouch, and shove my arm through the bars, feeling blindly for the keyhole. Corvus directed me as much as he could with his own face pressed against the bars, just able to see if I was headed in the right direction.

After a minute of fumbling blindly around, my palms grew slick. I placed all my focus on keeping a firm grip on the key, terrified I would drop it and lose our chance at escape.

When the key finally slid into place, I turned it with trembling fingers. The tumblers withdrew with a solid *thunk*, and the door creaked open. My heart hammered in my chest as I poked my head out the door, making sure we were truly alone. The corridor was short, only the length of the three cells. On the far end were stone steps and a wooden door.

I hurried to Corvus's cell and popped open the lock with ease.

For a moment, everything stilled. There were no bars between us, nothing to keep me from throwing myself into his arms. But guilt clawed its way into my pleasant thoughts, chilling them.

"There's something I have to tell you."

Tristan and his family were in danger. The other fae could already be at the palace. My blood rushed in my ears, and every part of me wanted to run away from this conversation. But Corvus had told me the truth, and I owed him the same.

Corvus's brows knit together as he took a step forward, reaching for me. Warm, strong hands wrapped around my elbow, my shoulder. "What is it?"

My throat grew tight, knowing he might never forgive me for what I'd done. But there was no way forward without trust. "I spied on you. For Andromeda." The rest came tumbling out of me in a torrent. "I am bound to her." My ears rang in the silence after my confession. I searched his face, desperate to know what he was thinking.

"Bound to her?" he whispered, flinching.

"I concealed from her as much as I could," I said vehemently. "I told her about the note in your jacket, the one about the masquerade. But that's all, Corvus. I swear. She wanted information about the coup and thought you would know something."

My voice cracked, tears making it hard to speak. "I shouldn't have done it. I'm sorry. She left me little choice. I'm sorry, Corvus. I'm so sorry."

The tears streamed fully now, coursing down my cheeks. I made no move to stop them. I thought I would feel better, telling him everything, but I only felt disappointed in myself. For not telling him sooner. For having made the godsdamned blood pact in the first place.

Corvus brushed my tears away with his thumb, which only made me cry harder. I didn't deserve such tenderness.

A horrible, aching thought punched through my guilt, stopping the tears. I made myself look into his eyes, which swirled with a torment that matched my own. "I wasn't pretending to like you, or be attracted to you," I said quietly. He had to know, had to understand that, despite all of it, I hadn't lied about that.

"Oh, I know, darling." He brushed his fingertips across my temple, smoothing my hair.

"You do?"

The corner of his mouth lifted as he brought his thumb and finger to my chin, tilting it upward. Even through the pain of my admission and guilt, want stirred in my stomach at his touch.

"There's only so much of that you can fake," he said, as he pressed his body flush against mine.

I inhaled sharply as the heat of him sank through the thin fabric of my shirt.

"And you aren't faking." He rested his forehead against mine. My breath quickened as he trailed his fingers down my neck and collarbone.

"You're not mad at me?" I asked.

"No. I'm not." He lifted his brow from mine. "We both did things that we regret. I broke your trust. Something I still haven't forgiven myself for, and probably never will. You were put in a difficult situation and did what you needed to survive. I can't fault you for that. I forgive you." He brushed his thumb against my lips.

My knees grew weak. Even after revealing the ugly truth to him, presenting myself to him in the worst light, he forgave me. "I forgive you, too, you know."

He placed a kiss to my forehead.

"I will be honest with you from now on," he vowed.

"Me, too."

"Then allow me to start by saying how pissed I am that we have to go stop a coup right now." He grabbed my waist with one hand and cradled the back of my head with the other.

My mouth parted as he pressed his arousal between my legs. My core ached with need, my chest rising and falling as I fought to catch my breath. The air between us crackled. I darted my tongue across my lips, anticipating the warmth of his kiss.

"I have something else to tell you," I murmured. "Something important."

He had to know how much he meant to me. How I would do anything for him.

"Corvus!" A voice in the house called for him, desperate. "Corvus!"

"Shit. It's Dio."

We broke apart, the urgency of the task ahead of us chasing away thoughts of losing myself in Corvus's touch.

"Down here!" called Corvus, taking my hand. We headed toward the door.

In the hall upstairs, a flurry of steps pattered down the hall. Dio came screeching into view. He placed his hands on his knees, trying to catch his breath. "We've got problems."

Chapter Thirty-Five
Sorsha

We ran to Corvus's room to retrieve our weapons and find me some clothes. Dio trailed close behind us, relaying the news.

"They're all at the palace," he said. "I waited until your father left so I could come get you. I heard him say they threw you down here. And may I say that I showed *remarkable* restraint in not gutting him right then and there."

At his bedchamber, Corvus whipped open his wardrobe and threw some garments around. He marched to a chest of drawers, and found what he was looking for, leaving the mess in his wake. He strapped on a leather vest, and smirked. "How noble of you."

"But the honor of hitting the bastard really belongs to you," finished Dio.

I really liked Corvus's friend. "You showed more restraint than I would have." I dug through the discarded clothes on the floor, looking for something that might fit.

Dio barked a laugh. His eyes danced with mirth. "No wonder you like her, Corv."

Corvus buckled his daggers around his chest and slung a sword at his side. He turned to us with a furrowed brow. "Grab what you need from the yard. Meet us outside. We have to hurry if we're going to stop them in time."

Dio paused, eyes flitting between us. "You mean to stop them? Why?"

"Because I can bring our magic back without killing anyone," I said.

Dio's mouth dropped. He spluttered, looking for words and finding none.

Corvus placed a hand on his friend's shoulder. "It's true. We'll fill you in on the way."

We raced out of the front door, my heart hammering in my chest. I didn't know what we would find at the palace, but I knew it wouldn't be good. Corvus led the way to the stables and quickly prepared his horse.

He hoisted himself up onto a beautiful dappled stallion, its legs long and lean. I never realized how big horses were until now when I stood right beside one. My palms grew damp.

He reached down a hand for me. I shifted on my heels.

"Vego is a good horse. You'll be safe."

I reluctantly extended my hand. Corvus pulled me up to sit in front of him. I gritted my teeth at the ache that pulsed through my stomach as I settled into the saddle. As soon as I felt secure, Corvus snapped the reins and kicked the horse's flanks. I lurched forward, but Corvus wrapped his arm around my waist and pulled me tight to his chest, steadying me. The clack of hooves thundered in my bones as we sprinted toward the palace, racing against time.

The gloom grew thick as dusk settled. Tiny pinpricks of starlight shone against the blue and purple of early twilight before being obscured in a swirling fog.

We reached the palace in minutes. Sea breeze whipped my hair back from my face as Corvus dismounted the horse. Dark storm clouds brewed on the horizon, ominous and brooding. There were no guards barring the door or patrolling the walls. I fought to still my trembling legs and prayed we weren't too late.

"Dio, go around the back. Through the servant's entrance," commanded Corvus.

Dio pouted, ready to argue.

Corvus held up a hand. "If we run into trouble, we're going to need rescuing. Think you can handle that?"

Dio placed a hand on the pommel of the sword he wore at his hip. "I'm always up for rescuing you, sunshine." He winked, before becoming serious once more. "You can count on me. Don't get killed. Either of you!" He tossed the reins of his horse to Corvus and sprinted for the back of the palace.

Corvus shook his head. "Dio's always been an insufferable flirt. It worked very well on me once before, but no longer."

"Now you just prefer to be insulted?"

Corvus balked. "I thought we were well past that, darling."

I rolled my eyes. Thunder boomed on the horizon, chasing the levity of the moment away. My chest squeezed. Tristan was in trouble. "We're wasting time. We need to go. Now."

Corvus turned to his horse. "Vego. I'll see you at home."

Vego dipped his head, nudged his companion, and the two horses set off back through the gate. Corvus grabbed my hand and pulled me through the main doors. My heart pounded as we entered the cool dark of the palace.

Our footsteps echoed in the crushing silence, bouncing off the high ceilings and sea glass windows. No lamps had been lit, and the gloom of twilight pressed in all around us. We paused at the base of the grand staircase, ears straining for any sound. "Where could they be?" I asked, my voice barely above a whisper.

Corvus frowned. "Let's check upstairs."

Corvus took the lead. We moved as swiftly and silently as we could. I kept one hand on my dagger. The blue stone pulsed beneath my palm. I wasn't sure whether it was trying to reassure me or warn me of the danger ahead.

We finally heard voices once we reached the upper landing. Low, gruff tones punctuated by the queen's sobs drifted down the long hallway. Strange shapes lay on the floor of the corridor, hard to make out in the dim light. The air was tinged with the scent of the storm to come, cold and unyielding.

As we crept down the hall and grew closer to the dark shapes, my stomach plummeted. They were palace guards, dressed in the vestments of the Blackwood house, sprawled across the floor as if felled by some great force.

Corvus bent to the nearest one and pressed his fingers to his neck. Blood seeped from his ears and eyes in sticky burgundy rivers. Corvus shook his head, letting his fingers drop from the corpse. We stepped lightly around the dead men littering the hall until we reached the ornate double doors of the great room.

I leaned in close to the crack of light spilling between the closed doors, straining to hear what was going on inside over the pounding of my own pulse. Corvus locked eyes with me and pressed a finger to his lips as the queen wailed once more.

"Your time is running out, and I grow impatient," said a voice. "Tell me where the Aetheris is."

Tristan's reply was gruff. "I told you, I don't know what you're talking about."

I pressed a fist into my stomach. He was still alive. We'd made it in time. My relief did not last long. There was a brief silence, then a thud. The queen howled. I widened my eyes, looking to Corvus, ready to bust through the doors on his signal.

He only shook his head and mouthed silently, *"Not yet."*

They were hurting him, and Corvus wanted to wait? For what?

"Once again, it is not hard to miss," said the voice. I finally recognized it, though it dripped with sarcasm instead of honey.

Lucius. "It's about as tall as I am, or would be if it were still intact. A very large circular mirror, made of black glass."

I gripped my dagger firmly in my hand, stifling a gasp. Corvus's frown deepened as Lucius continued.

"My spies do not lie. You have a fascination with fae artifacts, spend much time requesting old books from various houses. You think no one sees your late-night returns to your rooms, your skulking in the night. All evidence indicates you know very well where it is, so I'll ask you one last time. Where is the Aetheris Mirror?"

There was a beat of silence.

A shout from the queen: "No!"

I didn't stop to think. I lunged forward and pushed open the doors. Corvus made a noise in his throat but followed me.

"Stop," I said. Everyone in the chamber froze for a heartbeat, turning to see who had intruded upon them. I was not prepared for the scene that greeted us.

The king was slumped in his ostentatious chair at the far end of the long table, pinned there by a sword that stuck out of his chest. His purple doublet had turned black with blood. A small trickle of it leaked from the corner of his mouth. His eyes stared blankly out, unseeing. The queen sat beside him, her crown askew and face tear-streaked, flanked by Corvus's father and Lord Sunbarrow. A silver cylinder sat on the table in front of the royals.

Lucius stood at the other end of the table with his wings spread wide. He was the only one in the room who did not wear armor. He aimed his sword at Tristan's chest, who was on his knees on the sandstone floor, beaten and bloodied. His face was a mess, one of his eyes already swelling shut. Behind him stood Lord Dawnstone and his nephew, both dressed in shining gold chest plates and greaves.

I locked eyes with Tristan, trying to convey a sense of calm and control. He looked like a hollow shell of the man I knew. His eyes were dull, shoulders slumped. His hair, usually roguishly tousled, hung limply against his cheeks.

"Stop," I said again, with as much mettle as I could. My knees shook, and I prayed no one could see.

Slowly, Lucius turned to face me. He lowered his sword a few inches, but kept it trained on the prince. "Andromeda's presence is not necessary," he said in a scathing tone. "Therefore, neither is yours."

We stood, silent and unmoving as a roll of thunder sounded in the distance. When we did not leave the chamber, Lucius's jaw ticked. "What is the meaning of this, Magnus?" He didn't even bother addressing Corvus. My hatred for him grew.

I flicked my eyes to where Lord Stormfall stood with the queen. His face was pale, and he clenched and unclenched his fist. "Unfortunate timing, my lord," he said, gathering himself. "My son has brought a gift for you."

"It will wait until we are finished here," he said, turning his attention back to Tristan.

"Go outside with the girl," commanded Corvus's father, not daring to leave his post.

I felt the anger rolling off Corvus, who'd come to stand close behind me. His whole body was tense. He trembled with rage, mirroring my own teeth-clenching anger. They did not even deign to speak to me or see me as a threat. I breathed heavily through my nose, trying to slow my pounding heart.

"I know how to fix your mirror," I said, lifting my chin and looking squarely at Lucius.

He swiveled the point of his sword toward me. "You know the location of the Aetheris?"

I did my best to ignore Tristan's pleading face as Lucius took a few steps toward me. I stood my ground. "I know how to *fix* it," I repeated.

"Doubtful," said Lucius, prowling ever closer. His sword gleamed menacingly in the candlelight.

I swallowed the terror that swept through me and steeled myself for what I was about to do. "I am the lost Dawnstone daughter, and I am an artificer."

Lucius cocked his head curiously at me, studying me with renewed interest.

Lord Dawnstone and his nephew exchanged a glance, and Tristan's mouth fell open in shock.

"You claim to be Malachite's lost daughter?" asked Lucius. "Interesting. Malachite." He beckoned for Lord Dawnstone to approach. He took his place beside him, one hand resting on the hilt of his sword. I looked up into my father's eyes. I don't know what I expected. A sudden recognition, an embrace, to know I had found my family and they wanted me back. All I found in his eyes was cool calculation.

He squinted at me. "She bears not the wings of my daughter, nor her scent. It cannot be her."

"Kill her, then," commanded Lucius. "I've no use for her."

"Wait," I cried, as Lord Dawnstone began to draw his sword. Corvus moved to stand beside me. "I have the mark. The Dawnstone mark."

"Show me."

I turned toward Corvus, whose jaw was clenched, eyes wide with fear. "Help me?" I asked quietly.

He nodded. He clenched the hilt of his sword so tightly that his knuckles were pale.

I unbelted the three straps that crossed the front of my leather vest with trembling fingers and let it fall to the ground. The tension was thick, and another boom of thunder sounded, closer this time. I turned around, and Corvus lifted the hem of my shirt to expose the scars on my back.

"Seven hells," someone whispered.

"Well, Malachite?" prodded Lucius. "If she did have wings, it appears they have been removed."

Someone took a step. Corvus dropped my shirt and growled. "No closer."

I turned my head to see who had approached. Lord Dawnstone stood with a hand outreached. "A true mark will respond to the touch of its bloodline. It could still be faked. There are many who claimed to be my daughter. None were legitimate." He withdrew a dagger from his side and pricked his own finger, letting the blood swell there. He did not sheath his weapon once he was done. My mouth grew dry.

I placed a hand on Corvus's arm. "It's alright," I said, with much more assurance than I felt.

"You make one wrong move and you're dead," he said, before shifting aside to allow Lord Dawnstone – my father – to approach.

My knees still trembled, and my stomach flipped. I knew it was foolish to trust the fae who had butchered a king. I was entirely at their mercy. But I had to convince them I could help, that further bloodshed could be avoided. This was the only way I knew how.

Another footstep, then I felt the warm touch of blood against the raised flesh of my back. Something burned, tearing through me, and my mouth opened in a wordless scream as agony tore through me. My flesh caught fire and burned with such intensity that my vision went black. The pain did not feel like the cold bite of steel, but something bitter and corrosive. It was so sudden, so quick, I was powerless to stop it. I fell to my knees as images flooded through my mind, too fast for me to process.

I felt Corvus's arms around me, holding me up. There was a boom of thunder, a crash of lightning, and everything faded into darkness.

Chapter Thirty-Six

Sorsha

The mountain mist was cold that day, sticking to the tips of my wings and eyelashes. My heart pounded in my chest as I raced up the path, passing wildflowers and piles of gray stones. Tears blurred my vision, and I slipped on a loose rock, landing hard on my hands and knees. I focused on the pain, the bite of shale into my skin, instead of the fear that made my head feel fuzzy.

I didn't mean to make Mama and Papa angry. I showed them what I'd made, and they had started screaming at one another. I cried, but they ignored me. I didn't think what I did was wrong.

"We will use her talent!" shouted Papa.

"You would curry favor by selling our daughter to the highest bidder. Have you no love for her?"

"It is because I love her, and you, that we must do this. Grauradurians would pay mountains of gold for an artificer's talents. We train her up, then send her off when she is ready."

"No, Malachite."

"She will do her duty to this house, as will you."

"I will not accept this!"

"I am your husband. You will do whatever I say."

Mama started crying, too. I covered my ears and ran outside. I didn't want to hear them fight anymore.

I threw the flower I'd made on the ground. Its glassy petals shattered into pieces, scattering into the rock.

It was dark when I finally came home, cold and hungry. Mama was waiting for me. She took me into the stables before I could go inside and get warm and have my dinner.

"We're going on a little trip," she said, her eyes red from crying. She wore a black cloak and carried a small leather bag. "Put these on, my dove." She gave me a plain black dress. It was made of rough, scratchy fabric, and was not very pretty. But I wanted to make Mama happy, so I put it on. At least it was warm.

"Where are we going?"

"It's a surprise," she replied with a tight smile.

"Is Papa coming with us?"

She pulled a cloak over me, draping it clumsily over my wings. "No, he is staying here. Get in, my dove."

We got in the carriage and rode fast into the night. Mama kept looking out the window. I tried my best to stay awake as we entered the fields at the bottom of the mountain, but the smoother road rocked the carriage, pulling me into sleep.

Mama held my hand as we walked down alleyways and dirty streets. We walked for a long time, and my legs grew tired, and my wings hurt from being cramped under the cloak, but I kept my promise and did not make a sound.

After a long while, we came to a shabby wooden door. Mama knocked in a little pattern. A man with white wiry hair and large round spectacles opened the door.

"Bring her in."

A strange smell made my nose wrinkle. We walked though his little house to a room in the back. There was a big wooden table, stained rusty brown. There were strange silver instruments, and lots of bottles in all different shapes and sizes in cabinets along the wall. Something inside one of the bottles moved.

I didn't like it. I gripped Mama's hand tightly.

She crouched down beside me and pulled me close to her. "You *must be my very brave girl," she whispered. She kissed my forehead, then straightened.*

"Payment?" asked the old man.

Mama gave the man a sack of gold coins. They clinked as he weighed it in his hand. "Get her on the table."

"Come here. Lie down, my dove." She lifted the cloak from my shoulders, freeing me.

"No, Mama. I don't want to." It was wrong here. I could tell something bad was going to happen.

"The doctor needs to look at you. Be a good girl for me."

My heart lodged in my throat, but I climbed on the table. My hands and knees shook as I lay down on my belly like Mama told me to.

The old man grabbed my wrist and locked it in a leather cuff. It was too tight. I started to kick and scream, terror taking over.

"Hold her down."

I felt the weight of Mama pressing down on me as I pleaded to be let out. She was crying, too.

There was a sting on my arm, then my head grew fuzzy, and I fell into a deep dark pit of nothing.

I couldn't move for the pain. Everything hurt so much. I vomited into the sheets. Mama placed a cool cloth on my forehead. I screamed when she rubbed a paste on my back, which dulled the pain but did not remove it completely. I stayed awake all night, whimpering.

There were happy memories, too. Memories of eating supper, huddled together by the light of a lone candle. Walks through

gardens where she pointed out the names of plants and shared their properties. The smell of freshly baked bread at the bakery where she worked. But the happy memories were scattered between those of fear and pain, worry and flight.

Afternoon sunlight streamed through the windows of the boarding house kitchen. Mama handed me a bag and began to shove food taken from the shared pantry, sending a flurry of motes to dance in the afternoon sun. Her lips were tight, face pale, as she moved through the cupboards.

"Mama, won't we get in trouble?"

The woman we were staying with did not put up with thievery in her kitchen.

"I'll pay her back, but we have to go. Now."

"But why?" I trailed behind her as she raced up the stairs to our little room. It was small, and we had to share one bed, but it was clean and better than the shack by the river we'd been in a few months ago.

"I'll tell you when you're older. Put your cloak on. Hood up."

I did as she asked, despite the warmth of the day. We left without saying goodbye.

We'd never had much, but we had each other, and that was enough. I'd stopped asking about Papa years ago, because every time I asked, a shadow passed across Mama's face, and she went quiet for the rest of the day.

We walked through the city streets, past the busy market square, and through the outskirts of the city. We passed houses with sprawling lawns, tall trees, and flowering shrubs. Sweat trickled down my back, the cloak suffocatingly hot, but Mama kept her hood up, so I did, too.

Eventually we reached the top of a long hill and came to a set of iron gates. There was a courtyard of stone with a large fountain in the center of it, and the air smelled sweet and tangy, like lemons.

Someone let us through the gates and into the mansion. We stood in the entryway, waiting. The black floors were polished so well that I could see myself reflected in them. A woman came down the stairs, wearing a silver mask and dress so fine it made my mouth drop open.

"Lady Andromeda," said Mama, bobbing a little curtsey.

"This is the girl?" said the woman as she came close to me and peered at my face under my hood. She grabbed it, and let it fall back. The cool air felt good on my flushed cheeks. "Pretty." Her eyes gleamed with dark stars, and I tried to make myself as small as possible.

"She's a hard worker. She can cook and clean."

The woman tapped a finger to her chin. "I may have other uses for her."

"That is not what we agreed on," said Mama sternly.

Lady Andromeda sighed and turned away from me. "Well, if you change your mind…"

"I won't."

"Pity." She turned her attention back to me. "Alright, girl. Get down to the kitchens. Ivy needs help preparing for tonight." She pointed her long finger down the hall.

I turned and waited for Mama to follow. She stood, still as a statue. "Aren't you coming, Mama?" I asked. My voice shook.

My question broke the spell of her stillness. She folded me in an embrace. "Not this time, my dove. I love you. I'll come back for you. I promise."

Before I could say anything, to ask her why, to beg her to stay, she turned on her heel and rushed out the door, leaving me in the dark, glittering mansion. Alone.

I gasped, coming back to the present, feeling like I had fallen back into my body from a great height. I sat up too quickly, and stars danced in my vision. I blinked, trying to clear them as a crushing wave of grief and the phantom pains of the terrifying back-alley surgery tore through me. My chest heaved for breath, and I pressed my hands into the cool sandstone floor, trying to loosen the grip of memory.

Lord Dawnstone and Lord Uriel still towered above me, peering down with scrutiny. Corvus had been right beside me before I'd lost consciousness, but he wasn't here. I got unsteadily to my feet, and saw him standing next to Tristan, who was still on his knees. Shock and horror left me breathless once more when I saw that Corvus pressed the tip of his blade into Tristan's back, standing guard over him along with Lord Dawnstone's nephew.

Curtains billowed as a gust of wind blew through the chamber, and thunder boomed.

"Altheia, my daughter," said Lord Dawnstone, jerking my attention away from Corvus. He kept one hand on the hilt of his sword. "Forgive me for not recognizing you. The magic in your scars veiled your true identity from me."

I felt as if I'd been scraped raw, exposed for all to see. *Altheia.* The name was foreign, though I knew at one point it had been mine.

My mind reeled, still processing the flood of regained memories. I asked the only question I could. "Why?" It was as much a question for him as it was for Corvus, who stared at me with an intensity I could not understand, his blade still trained on Tristan's back.

Lord Dawnstone's face darkened. "Your mother mutilated you to keep you hidden, then sold you off to a lesser house. I tried for years to find you. And now, here you are, returned to me."

"Where is Mama? Did you ever find her?" Something deep within me already knew the answer. My memories had shown me what kind of male my father was. But I had to hear it from his own lips.

"I did, eventually, locate your mother. When she did not tell me where she'd hidden you, I did what had to be done. Traitors have no place in House Dawnstone."

Lucius looked pleased at this utterance. "And I hope you have learned your lesson about marrying humans, Malachite."

My father's face remained as still as marble. My gut wrenched.

The queen whimpered from her throne, tearing me from fresh waves of grief. I remembered the reason why we had come here. To stop him from murdering Tristan and his family. To restore magic.

"Will you let me help you now?" I asked, lifting my chin to the winged fae.

"You may be a Dawnstone, but there is no proof you can aid me," he said dismissively.

"I am an artificer," I said desperately. "I can prove it." I reached for the shard of obsidian glass that hung around my neck, still in the form of a key, and I took a step back, removing myself from their reach should they decide to take it for themselves.

I searched for the humming of the mirror in the caverns deep below us. It did not take long to find. I let the vibration flow through me, traveling through the soles of my feet to rumble through every part of me. I closed my eyes and let the magic bubble up from where it slept within. Changing the key back into its original form was much easier when I could feel the presence of its larger whole. I opened my eyes and held up the shard before me.

Lucius was unimpressed. My heart sank. "Unfortunately," he said, waving a dismissive hand. "I am already in possession of an artificer with your talents. Shifting materials is small magic. Hard to accomplish in our current predicament, but it can be done." He turned to where Tristan knelt, eyes still hollow, no longer interested in what I had to offer. "The question remains, how did you come to possess a piece of the Aetheris?"

I held my tongue, not wanting to betray its location. If I did, they might kill the prince.

"Seize her," sighed Lucius.

Lord Dawnstone moved to take my arm, but I scrambled back, clutching the shard.

"Wait. Even if you do find the mirror, you need someone who can kill the corruptions."

Lucius paused, then stalked slowly back toward me, golden eyes burning. "What corruption do you speak of?"

Before I lost my nerve, I dropped the shard to the floor, then stomped hard on it with the heel of my boot. It cracked into two pieces. The fissure had upset the balance of magic held inside of it. The two pieces burbled, the surface of them turning oily and slick.

I bent down and quickly scooped them up. They pulled toward one another, seeking to be rejoined. I brought them together, hanging on to the thread of magic within me. The scent of warm sunlight and pine, a smell I now recognized as the Dawnstone mountains, my childhood home, flooded through me.

I swallowed back the pain of those memories, and golden light shimmered between the two pieces at the seam of their breaking. As it faded, the wrongness that lay within reared its ugly head, springing to the surface of the unified shard. I let the corruption ooze from the mirror and drop to the floor with a sticky thud. It scrambled forward, though it was slow, smaller than those I had previously killed. I placed the shard in my pocket and clenched my dagger as Lord Dawnstone readied his weapon.

Everyone in the chamber shifted uneasily. The queen, whose wailings had been incessant, grew silent. I flipped the dagger in my hand, and cocked it back at my shoulder, but Lucius stopped me before I could strike.

"Halt," he commanded, extending a hand. He watched as the creature oozed forward, leaving behind a stained, rotted mess on the floor. "I didn't think it was possible," he breathed with triumph. The corruption slithered toward him, moving like oil on water.

He mumbled something under his breath I could not understand, and the corruption halted in its tracks. It inclined its head toward Lucius, waiting.

My hands went numb as Lucius pointed to where Tristan knelt. The creature obeyed and crawled forward.

I had to do something. Quickly. I threw my dagger, hoping to kill it before it reached him. My father lunged for me, knocking my arm as the dagger left my fingers. It spun wide, clattering harmlessly onto the floor only a few feet away. He grabbed my arm. "No!" I screamed and bucked away from him, trying to retrieve it, but he was much stronger than me.

He grabbed the back of my head, pulling my hair, while the other arm held me firm against his chest. I kicked and struggled as the corruption continued to lurch toward the prince. I looked to Corvus, pleading wordlessly with him to help, to stop this. His face was set in a mask of stone, unreadable, unreachable, and my heart began to break. I couldn't understand why he did nothing. Was the confirmation of my parentage too much for him? Was he finally washing his hands of me, because my kin had murdered his brother?

Lucius prowled toward his prisoner. "Tell me where the Aetheris is, or we shall see what happens when the maledictus feasts upon your flesh."

The name rang through my head. How did he know so much about the corruption? I fought for breath against the panic squeezing my chest. "You have to stop," I pleaded. "Let him go, *please*." I hated how pathetic I sounded, but I was out of options.

"Time is running out," said Lucius as he stepped alongside the slithering maledictus. They were an arm's reach away. Tristan grew even more pale, but he did not yield.

I wished I could be as strong. But I wasn't. I was too afraid of losing someone I cared about. "I'll tell you where the mirror is!" I screamed.

Lucius whispered in that slithering tongue to the creature, stopping its death march.

"No, Sorsha," whispered Tristan, staring at me through hollow eyes.

"I'm sorry." Tears streamed down my face, not just from the pain of having my hair pulled so tight I thought my scalp might bleed, but from the breaking of my heart.

"Tell me quickly," demanded Lucius. "I grow tired of these games."

"I need to know you won't hurt him."

"You have my word."

"That means nothing to me."

Lord Dawnstone yanked my head back, exposing my neck to the ceiling. "Impudent brat. Do not question the Primus's honor. You shame your lineage."

Lucius ignored him. "I shall not cause any physical harm to him. Now, *tell me where the mirror is.*"

"It's in the basement," I said. Tristan sagged, disappointment flooding his features as if I had mortally wounded him. Guilt twisted in my gut, sharp as a knife, but I had to do this if we wanted some chance of survival.

I swallowed. My mouth was so dry. My knees shook and I was glad that my father held me upright. "At the House of Night."

Lucius eyed the prince carefully, scanning for his reaction. His dismay was enough to convince him I spoke truly. "Malachite, if you would be so kind."

My father released me, and I sank to my hands and knees. "Well, Thea. Lead the way," he commanded.

I kept my head down as Lucius continued to give orders. "The house suffered some damage from the blasts, but the foundation should remain unscathed. Gods know that witch had it warded tightly. Malachite, with me. Magnus, Elias, stay here to guard the queen and the boy."

I barely heard him. All my focus was on my dagger, just out of reach. I peered up at Tristan through the curtain of my hair, locking eyes with him. He gave an imperceptible nod, and I lunged.

My father shouted, and I could hear his thunderous footsteps behind me, but I was faster. My hand found the hilt of the dagger, closing tightly around the cool metal. I shifted my weight, bringing myself to one knee. I spun, the fabric of my pants tearing against the grains in the floor, and released.

The dagger hurtled toward the corruption, the bright blue stone glinting as it sailed through the air. It struck true, catching its center, pinning it to the floor where it let out a terrible screech.

Tristan launched himself forward, hitting Lucius behind the knees, clearing the way for me as I scrambled to my feet. The Primus stumbled, caught off guard. It was enough.

I reached for my magic as I lunged for the corruption, letting it pool into my palm. I dove, throwing myself onto the ground. The air knocked from my lungs as I hit the floor, but I closed my hand around the dagger once more.

Wincing from the pain and trying not to panic at the sudden lack of oxygen, I drove my magic through the metal to sink into the twisted creature it pierced. The dagger flared with light, and the corruption melted into the sandstone with a screech, leaving behind an acrid stain that stung my eyes.

Lucius's annoyance shifted into fury. His golden eyes flared with outrage, wings sending a strong gust of wind through the room. He whirled and kicked Tristan to the side.

Tristan fell, clutching his ribs. He did not get up.

Corvus and Aurum lazily approached, standing over him as Lucius wrenched me from the ground.

"Enough," he said. He thrust me into the awaiting clutches of my father. "Hold her."

Lord Dawnstone squeezed my arm so tight I thought my bones might crack.

"We make for the House of Night. If you try anything that foolish again, I will end your miserable life. I do not care who you are. Malachite has said there is no place for traitors in his house. Since you have proven yourself to be treacherous, I think he would enjoy disposing of you himself."

I struggled against Lord Dawnstone's titan grip but killing the corruption had sapped me of what little strength I had left. Between being stabbed the night before and having to use so much magic tonight, my body couldn't take it.

The tip of my father's sword rested against my neck, cold and sharp.

"He's right. You're as troublesome as your mother," said Lord Dawnstone, shaking me. "It won't take us long to dig through the rubble, Primus. I doubt we need her now."

"Kill her then, if you wish."

As I felt the edge of my father's sword begin to slice my bare throat, Corvus exploded.

Chapter Thirty-Seven

Corvus

I couldn't pretend any longer.

When Lord Dawnstone brought his blood to Sorsha's fae mark, something deep within me had snapped into place. An empty space I didn't know I carried was now filled by *her*. I grew hyper-aware of her presence. I could smell the fear on her, taste her resolve, feel her heartbeat like a phantom drum on the wind.

It was the most exhilarating feeling. When she fainted and I held her in my arms, every instinct demanded I grab her and run. A slumbering beast had woken in my chest, ready to maim and murder anyone who came close to her. It was like my feelings had been amplified a thousandfold, blotting out everything but the desire to keep her safe. To protect her.

Some part of me, the tactical side now buried under this primal instinct, urged caution. If I ran now, we could make it out unharmed. But I don't think she'd ever forgive me for leaving the prince and giving up our chance for peace. So, even though every fiber of my being begged to flee, I made myself rest her head gently on the stone floor, and stand. My hands shook with the effort of leaving her.

"Well, your gift has been delivered," I said. I leaned into all those years of playing the part of indifference to shield my emotions. I dared a glance in my father's direction, unsure if he'd be livid that I'd escaped, or suspicious of my willingness to hand Sorsha to the Primus. I found a cold gleam of satisfaction in his eyes. He dipped his chin, acknowledging what I'd done.

A week ago, the small nod might have filled me with pride.

All I'd wanted was to earn my father's approval, to know some corner of his heart still loved me. Now that I had it, I felt nothing but disappointment. In myself, for having cared so much when he clearly cared for me so little, and in him, for not being the father I needed him to be.

Lucius and Malachite spoke in hushed voices. Lord Dawnstone kept his eyes fixed firmly on Sorsha, who did not stir.

"I'll help Aurum watch over the prince, shall I?" I marched to stand sentry alongside him. Only, I took it a step farther and placed the tip of my sword against the prince's back.

The prince turned and glared at me over his shoulder. I raised an eyebrow in warning. "I'd behave if I were you."

He turned forward once more, and we both stared intently as Sorsha jolted awake, gasping for breath.

I watched in horror as she called for the corruption within the mirror, desperate to make Lucius see reason. It took complete concentration to not bolt to her side, but I held firm, fighting against the mesmeric connection between us.

My chest tightened with terror as Lucius spoke in a language I'd never heard before, commanding the corruption to approach the prince. When the corruption, the maledictus, lurched toward us, I gripped my sword tight, ready to strike should it get too close. As Sorsha's dagger was knocked harmlessly from her grasp and she looked at me, pleading, I kept my face stoic. I knew Aurum was watching like a hawk, ready to strike at the slightest provocation. If I was busy fighting him off, I couldn't protect her. So, I waited, even though it broke me.

I was fraying, coming apart at the seams. Thunder boomed overhead and lightning flashed against the sky; it felt like the storm was trapped inside me. It thrashed around, almost to the point of pain, begging for release.

As Lord Dawnstone placed his blade against Sorsha's neck and I saw the hope leave her eyes, I finally snapped.

Lucius was right. This had gone on long enough.

I whirled on Aurum as a crash of thunder boomed, shaking the sea glass windows in their frames. Aurum was unprepared. He'd been staring with tightly wound frenzy, waiting for Malachite to spill Sorsha's blood across the floor.

He brought his blade up to parry mine just in time. But the force of my blow was strong, and a white-hot heat coursed through my veins, making my heart pump wildly in my chest. Years of training, of envisioning this exact moment, made the force of my blow too strong for him. He staggered. I dropped my shoulder and shoved into him, sending him sprawling.

Before he could right himself, I was there, pressing my own blade into his throat.

"Release her, or he dies," I hissed, my wings flaring wide, sending a gust of air through the chamber.

Aurum spat on my boots, amber eyes burning with hatred. "Your brother never had the gall," he said. "I doubt you do, either."

I pressed the blade deeper, drawing a rivulet of crimson to stain his flesh. I did not dare take my eyes from him. He was a seasoned fighter and would exploit any weakness. "Now, Lord Dawnstone."

I heard a thud as Sorsha hit the ground, gasping. "Release my nephew," Malachite demanded.

"Come here, darling." I said, ignoring him.

Sorsha was there in a moment, placing a hand on my shoulder. The raging storm within me faded to rumbling, soothed by her touch.

"Corvus," she said. Worry tinged her voice.

I knew there was no easy escape for us now. There was

nothing for it. Violence was to be our end.

"Get the prince," I whispered. I withdrew my blade from Aurum's neck, plunging it into his upper thigh. It would do enough damage to slow him down, but not kill him. Though I'd dreamed of spilling his blood for years, to avenge Max's death, I knew this was not how justice was to be done.

My only concern now was getting Sorsha and the prince out alive, and leaving before Lucius found the true location of the mirror. I couldn't begin to guess what he wanted with it, but from the way he coaxed that horrid creature forward, he knew more of it than we did, and that scared me.

Sorsha grabbed the prince by the arm and hauled him to his feet. The door was on the other side of the room. I needed to clear a path for them.

"You're a real piece of shit, Aurum. You know that?" I taunted him, drawing the attention of the fae in the room. Let them think me the hotheaded brawler, the belligerent second-born, a disgrace to his house. "Hiding behind your family name when everyone knows you murdered Max."

"You've got no proof." He was on his feet now, dripping blood onto the sandstone.

I pivoted to place myself between him and Sorsha, keeping my blade trained on him.

"Enough," Lucius commanded. His voice boomed across the chamber. "Get control of your son, Magnus."

"He is no son of mine. I disown him as my son and heir. He is no longer affiliated with my house."

Aurum grinned wickedly. "Finally." He lunged for me with blind hatred.

I parried the blow, driving him back toward Lord Dawnstone and Lucius, their swords trained on me.

"Then he is a traitor," barked Lucius. "Kill him." He snapped his fingers as Aurum continued to advance. "Malachite, get the girl."

"Run!" I shouted to Sorsha. Then I unleashed my fury.

I drove forward, the clash of my blade against Aurum's rang in the chamber. The queen screamed at the outburst of violence.

Tristan dashed for his mother with Sorsha closely on his heels, but Lucius stalked over to the queen. His wings flared as thunder boomed. "I've had enough of your screaming."

The prince roared as Lucius plunged his sword into her chest, piercing her heart. Her scream died in her throat as blood burbled from her mouth. Her head lolled onto her chest, silenced.

Sorsha tugged on the prince's arm, trying to drag him away from the slaughter.

Aurum whirled, reaching for a curved knife at his side. He aimed for Sorsha and the prince.

My wing extended without conscious effort. I clenched my jaw so hard I thought my teeth might crack as the blade buried itself into the delicate membrane. A grunt escaped my lips, despite my efforts to remain silent. Blood dripped from my feathers onto the floor, sinking into the rough stone.

I leaped at Aurum anew, channeling my rage and pain into every stroke. His eyes grew wide, face pale, as he beheld my fury. He screamed, outraged, even as I forced him back. We had almost reached the front of the room.

A scuffle sounded behind me, and Sorsha screamed. Terror went through me. The split second of hesitation cost me, and Aurum lunged. I dodged his blade but felt the tip of it scrape against my forehead, hot and blinding. Blood dripped into my eyes, and I tuned into every sense, grounding myself, waiting for the opportune moment to strike.

Aurum was tiring. His breath came in ragged bursts, and

sweat dripped into his face, slicking his blond hair. The gold half plate armor he wore was more for show than battle. Wearing it tonight would cost him his life.

In one fell swoop I plunged my sword into the soft flesh at his jugular, cleaving his head from his shoulders.

Blood spurted from the wound. His body fell to the floor with a sickening clang. His head rolled silently away, his mouth still open in a cry of rage.

Aurum Dawnstone was dead.

There was no time to dwell on it. I whipped toward Sorsha. Lucius cornered them as she and the prince crouched behind the pair of thrones.

"Lord Uriel," I shouted. I pointed at him with my blade, wet with blood. "You're next."

He sneered at me. "We're leaving," he said to the fae who flanked him. "We make for the House of Night. The Aetheris is the only thing that matters now."

Malachite Dawnstone gave a guttural cry as he beheld the ruined body of his nephew and heir. "I will kill you!" he screamed, and broke away from Lucius, headed straight for me.

He crossed the distance between us with greater speed than I anticipated. His sword sank into my other wing as I whirled. I miscalculated. He was faster than I gave him credit. A cry wrenched itself from my lips as he dragged the blade through my wing, sending black feathers to the floor, shredding it. Blood spurted from the wound, splattering his golden chest plate.

Through the haze of pain, I heard a crash behind me.

"Corvus!" Dio shouted. He raced into the room with a blade in each hand.

"Get Sorsha out of here!" I commanded. I did not dare to take my gaze away from Lord Dawnstone. His face was bloodless with fury; spittle flew out of his mouth as he gave a war cry, slashing his sword downward.

The force of it jarred through my arm, rattling my bones.

Dio didn't argue. He leaped over the long table, placing himself between Lucius, my father, and Elias Sunbarrow. "Go, I'll hold them off!" he cried.

"I'm not leaving without Corvus!" Sorsha said.

"We'll be right behind you, *go*!"

Relief crashed through me as Sorsha and the prince ran behind me, through the double doors and down the corridor. She would be safe. And I would join her soon.

Dio was at my side in a moment, ready to spill blood.

Malachite brought his arms wide, an invitation. "Go ahead! It will take more than you two to take me! Justice will be done!"

"Help Sorsha," I said with steel in my voice.

"Corv—"

"*Now!*"

He set his mouth in a hard line, nodded once, and ran after them. Dio did not need this blood on his hands. He would be banished from his house for slaughtering a noble fae. I was already disavowed.

Malachite set upon me with the force of three trained warriors. Again and again he struck, the force of his blows unrelenting.

Suddenly, he dove out of the way, wide eyes trained on a point behind me.

I whirled, tucking in my useless wings close, ready to meet the new threat. I saw one of the ichorous corruptions stalking into the room on limbs that bent at wrong angles, with teeth as sharp as needles. It headed straight for Lucius.

Sorsha.

She must have created another one. She needed to run, to get to safety. I had to trust that Dio would see it done.

Satisfied that the maledictus was not set on feasting on his flesh, Malachite turned his attention to me again.

I grew weak as our blades crashed together over and over. I was losing blood. My sword arm trembled; my parries barely saved me, until Malachite knocked the blade from my hand completely.

He shoved with the hilt of his sword straight into my chest, knocking the wind from me. I landed hard on my back. I tried furiously to rise, but my limbs would not obey me.

Malachite stood above me as I lay in a pool of my own blood. My wing was shredded, the cut in my forehead dripped crimson into my eyes. The thunderstorm inside my chest still raged, but I'd lost too much blood.

I reached for my blade, which lay a few inches out of reach. Lord Dawnstone stomped on my outstretched fingers, breaking two of them. I clenched my jaw as pain shot through me, not wanting to give him the satisfaction of making a sound. My head swam, and I could feel my heartbeat slowing as blood continued to spill.

At least Sorsha and the prince had escaped. Whatever fate now befell me, I could accept it knowing she'd made it out alive.

Malachite drove his sword through my right shoulder, and I could not stop the sound in my throat, betraying the agony of it. As he withdrew the blade, my blood coating it ruby red, there was a commotion in the hall, but it was hard to hear what was going on. It felt like I'd been plunged underwater. Sound was distant, and my thoughts lost clarity. I felt like I was caught in a swelling tide. I blinked again, trying to focus, but the lights had taken on a hazy quality, coronas of light making halos of the torches.

Malachite looked over his shoulder.

Lightning flared again outside, and as I felt a cold darkness wrap itself around my heart, I saw her.

Sorsha drove the shard of the mirror, honed to a jagged point, across her father's neck.

Malachite made a terrible gurgling sound as his hand scrambled toward his throat. He dropped his sword to the floor with a clatter. His blood seeped through his fingers, gushing in time with his heartbeat. But his blood was not red, as it should have been. It was black, as dark as a starless night, and oily.

Sorsha screamed, dropping the shard, and clutched her hand to her chest.

I lifted my head, trying to reach her, but I didn't have the strength.

Lord Dawnstone took his final, ragged breaths, and fell still. There was a distant commotion behind us, near the head of the table.

Sorsha fell to her knees and dragged herself to my side, tucking the hand that had dealt the death blow close to her chest. Through the haze of blood loss, I knew something was wrong.

"Corvus," she said, tears dripping from her cheeks. "Don't you dare leave me. I have to tell you something important, remember?"

I blinked. Her presence was a buoy in this fog-plagued sea. I brought my fingertips to her face. Warmth buzzed through my fingers as my flesh made contact with hers. I saw the black ichor that crept up her hand, staining the tips of her fingers ink-black, spreading up her wrist with necrotic tendrils.

"Sorsha." Her name left my lips with a whisper. I let my fingers fall away, but not before they brushed the back of her hand, as light as a feather. She shuddered.

"I'm here, Corvus. I'll always be here."

"Sorsha, I..." She laid a hand on my chest.

"Shh, don't try to talk. It's going to be okay."

The fog began to creep in again, clouding her face. I needed to tell her that I loved her. No, not loved her, it was more than that. Seven hells, I needed to tell her I was *bound* to her, body and soul, and would be for all eternity. Not even the gods of the underworld could keep me from her. I would find my way back to her, even if they sought to take me from her. I tried to tell her, but my lips were numb, my breath grown short.

Another presence knelt beside her.

"You can heal him," it said, breathless and exhausted. I felt a pressure on my shredded wing and would have cried out from the pain of it if I'd had any breath left.

"I don't know how," she said, voice breaking.

"Yes, you do. It's the same way you renew the mirror shards. It's the same theory, Sorsha. Start here."

She pressed her trembling hands to my wing, soft as a kiss. There was a beat. "I can't, Tristan."

"Yes, you can. All the research says they're related, forging and healing. Forge his flesh. Make it whole."

Another beat, then a warmth like a late summer sunset began to trickle into me, spreading from the gashes in my wing, to my chest, my head, my abdomen. Golden light flared, and the pain began to leave me. I felt the delicate bones beneath the feathers snap back into place. I jolted, but hands held me down firmly.

I drifted, held within golden light, and knew that the underworld would have to wait to claim my soul.

Chapter Thirty-Eight

Sorsha

The carnage was devastating.

I stabilized Corvus, who now looked as if he was merely sleeping on the blood-soaked floor, but death clotted the air around us. Every part of me felt numb.

My father lay dead at my feet. His black blood had finally stopped oozing from his neck. Aurum, my cousin, lay where Corvus had slaughtered him. The king and queen sat in their thrones, drenched in blood, a macabre tableau in death.

Tristan sat ashen-faced beside me, staring blankly at them. He'd come with me when I told him my plan. I couldn't leave Corvus to face them alone. And without any weapons, the only thing we had was the mirror shard. I'd forged our two pieces together in the hall, releasing a maledictus from their joining, and sent Dio to get help.

Lucius, Lord Stormfall, and Lord Sunbarrow had fled. The corruption we'd set upon Lucius, desperate for a diversion, had stained the floor with its ichor, leaving a trail through the room. The Primus had been so intent upon commanding it, uttering those awful sounds, he hadn't noticed Tristan come up behind him. The prince stabbed him in the back, but his mortal strength was no match for Lucius. He'd been wounded but was very much alive. After that, they ran, and the maledictus was nowhere to be found.

I glanced down at Corvus. His eyes were still closed, his face peaceful. It was only now, in this moment of stillness and shock, that I noticed the strange hum that pulled me toward him. It was like every part of me yearned to be close to him. Something had snapped when I saw Lord Dawnstone standing over him, plunging his sword into his shoulder.

Instinct had set my hands moving without my being wholly conscious of what I was doing. The shard molded into a deadly weapon so quickly, without any effort. Time slowed as I contemplated my next move. Corvus lay on the ground at his feet, his blood soaking into the floor. Terror seized my breath. I couldn't lose him. Not now.

My father, the lord of a noble house, was poised to murder him. The one person who had shown me kindness and affection. My memories, now returned, had shown me my father's character. He was a cruel, heartless fae who would sell his own daughter, who would hunt down and kill his own wife.

Fury burned through me, hot as fire. My knuckles turned white as I gripped the handle of the glass knife. He was no father of mine.

I reached for the weak spot above his armor and dragged the blade across his flesh as vengeful fury burned through me.

My hand still tingled but had returned to its normal fleshy pink color. I opened and closed my fingers, searching for any further damage. The horrible, aching cold had eased as the corruption fled my body. The warmth of my magic had driven it out as it mended Corvus's broken body.

Was this the consequence of using the magic, when it was wielded with violence? I shuddered to think of what might happen should Lucius get his hands on the remaining pieces. He would have to be stopped.

Corvus coughed, jolting me from my thoughts. I threw my arms around him, not caring if I should show restraint. He wrapped his arms around me, holding me to him.

"Are you okay?" I asked, breaking myself away to examine

him, but I did not let go. My chest was tight. A small sob escaped my lips.

"Yes. Thanks to you." He pushed himself into a sitting position, taking in the devastation around us.

"Tristan helped," I said, suddenly embarrassed.

"Then thanks to you both."

Tristan nodded, but he kept his gaze fixed firmly on his family, eyes blank and far away.

"What now?" I asked, letting my hands fall into my lap. The adrenaline was leaving me. My limbs were heavy and aching.

I looked to Corvus, hoping he would have some idea of what our next steps should be. Our eyes locked, and it felt like a raging fire had kindled in my chest. Though my body felt as if it was filled with sand, it also felt *alive,* as if a charge of lightning were thrumming in my bones. Corvus took my hand in his, and the feeling intensified, tingling in the places where our fingers touched.

"We need to leave, before Lucius comes back. Your Majesty..." He looked toward Tristan.

"Yes. I suppose I am king now," he said flatly. Then, as if he didn't mean to say it aloud, he murmured, "Is it worth it? All this death... just for a taste of freedom."

I wasn't sure how to answer him. I'd spent so long clinging to the familiarity of the House of Night, even at the expense of my liberty. Instead of leaving, I chose to stay. I'd *chosen* to live at Andromeda's mercy. It wasn't out of loyalty, but fear. Maybe it was my dormant memories, cautioning me against the hardships my mother and I had faced when we were on our own, or the stories I'd heard from patrons at the House of Night, but I hadn't wanted to leave the life I knew, afraid that what I would find would be worse.

In some ways, it was. I had seen things more terrible than

I ever could have imagined. The imbalances of power, the pain and suffering, the horror of magic corrupted.

But then I realized, kneeling amidst the bloodshed of the coup we had only partially stopped, that there were people willing to fight for something better. Corvus. Tristan. Dio, and even Tilly, as misguided as she was, only wanted something better than this.

We could try and make this land less cruel. We could restore magic, and fight for those who could not fight for themselves.

I latched onto the thought, clinging to it like a life raft. I rested a hand on my grieving friend's shoulder, trying my best to comfort him.

"I'm sorry we weren't able to save your parents," I said quietly. "But I won't stop fighting. Otherwise, they would have died for nothing. I have to believe that we; you, and me, and Corvus, can try to make things better."

"We will help you carry this burden," agreed Corvus. "I know I doubted you at first. But your compassion will make you an excellent king."

Tristan swallowed thickly, then nodded.

Corvus turned back to me. "And you, Sorsha – I mean, *Altheia* Dawnstone, are the ruler of your house. Aurum was Malachite's only heir. You are his daughter, his direct descendent."

A weight settled on me, heavy as a block of stone. I was Lady Dawnstone and had begot my title through blood. Did it make me any better than the fae who killed the Blackwoods, or who were implicit in their murder? I felt the color drain from my face. "My name is Sorsha." I don't think I could ever answer to the name my father gave me. My stomach clenched. "What does it mean? I don't know anything about... about *ruling*."

"You thwarted a coup, saved my life, and sent the Primus running with his tail between his legs. I am confident that you will manage."

"They don't even know I exist," I said. Whatever family was left in the mountains had no idea I was alive. It was all too much. I pressed a hand to my stomach.

"We'll figure it out." Corvus grabbed my hand and squeezed, reassuring me. "But for now, the king needs us."

I nodded, my mouth dry with the thought of stepping into all of the responsibilities that came with my name. I wasn't a serving girl or a courtesan any longer. I was a godsdamned *lady*. I would rather kill a whole horde of corruptions than face that fact.

Corvus got to his feet and extended a hand down for me. My throat felt tight with all the things I needed to say to him. I'd nearly lost him. It took considerable effort not to throw my arms around him and kiss him as a desperate yearning swelled in my chest.

But no, he was right. Tristan needed us. There would be time for talk, and maybe more, later.

I took his hand and joined his side. He continued to hold fast to me as we began the work of putting things right.

Chapter Thirty-Nine

Sorsha

I returned to the House of Night the next day. Corvus had demanded he accompany me, but Tristan needed him at the palace. Besides, this was something I had to do myself.

I'd expected to find nothing but the bare remains of the manor, given the heat of the blast and fires that night. As I walked up the long drive, I steeled myself for what I might find.

The damage was minimal, but the east wing, where Andromeda's office and the courtesan's sleeping quarters were, was utterly destroyed. Blackened beams stuck up in jagged points toward the sky. But Andromeda's wards must have been strong, for the rest of the house remained intact.

Ferdie grabbed me into a strong embrace as I entered the foyer. "Holy fuck, I thought you were *dead*."

I wrapped my arms around him, squeezing tightly. I'd been so worried, but the casualties were minimal. Two had been trapped in their bedrooms, unable to escape. But Ferdie, Ivy, Viviana, and the rest of the courtesans were unharmed. They'd smelled the smoke and run before the blast ignited.

Andromeda, however, was nowhere to be found. Viviana took command of the house, boarding up the doors until it could be decided what should be done next. Ferdie told me she'd gone through Andromeda's office several times, looking for valuables or money, but there was nothing left but charred remains. Even her desk, as large and imposing as it had been, had disintegrated into ash.

Viviana tried to stop me from looking in the office. She

screeched at me as I climbed the stairs. "Sorsha, I am in charge now and I *expressly forbid it!*"

There was a time where she'd made me furious, and I did everything I could to avoid her. She was petty, mean, and cruel, but she did not hold sway over me any longer. I was determined to ignore her, but she yanked me back by the shoulder as I crested the landing.

I stopped and turned to face her. Her eyes were wild; her usually lustrous hair was now dull and limp. "You may call yourself the mistress of the House of Night, and you are, undoubtedly, a worthy successor to Andromeda. But I am no longer a courtesan. I do not work for you, and you are not mistress over me. Now, let me pass. I have business here."

She stalked back down the stairs with her head held high, and muttered, "Good riddance." Her flock was waiting for her at the foot of the stairs, ready to follow her command.

It wasn't the desire for jewels or gold that drove me to the remains of Andromeda's quarters, but hope that my mother's letter somehow survived. I also wondered what had become of the vial of my blood, the one that bound me to Andromeda. My heart sank as I beheld the destruction.

Nothing remained but piles of soot. It did not sit well with me that Andromeda's safe, which she was so keen to protect, had not withstood the fiery blasts. Perhaps she had put too much stock in her outer wards, leaving her innermost treasures less fortified. I pressed a hand to my stomach, mourning the loss of the letter, of never knowing my mother's final words to me.

Back at the palace, it was getting dark. Summer was ending and the nights fell faster, staining the sky with indigo and violet hues. Tomorrow, Tristan would be crowned king.

Supper was a short affair. Tristan retired to his room early, exhausted and jittery at the prospect of his coronation. Corvus and I talked as the flames in the fireplace turned to glowing embers. It was nearly midnight when we left for our rooms down the hall. Corvus escorted me to my chambers, stopping at the door. Stars winked beyond the open sea glass windows, and the smell of beach roses floated through the vaulted corridor.

I leaned my back against the polished wood door to my new quarters. The air was thick with tension and things still unsaid. Instead of bidding me goodnight, he hesitated.

"Stay with me tonight." I let the yearning I'd been stamping down for the entire day bubble slowly to the surface. My heart pounded in my chest, desperately hoping he would say yes, terrified he would refuse.

Corvus's thundercloud eyes were dark and full of want. I could feel the tensions between us crackling like lightning about to strike. I leaned into the storm, wanting to be swept away by it, by him.

"Stay with me," I repeated, more boldly than before.

He took a small step toward me, his body tense. "Seven hells. I thought you'd never ask."

He leaned one arm against the door and cupped my waist with his other hand. Desire pooled low in my belly. I parted my lips. My need for him made my breathing quick and shallow.

"I still haven't forgiven myself for making you think I didn't want you," he said.

I could feel his breath against my lips.

"I'm sorry for thinking that loyalty to my father, my family name, was somehow more important than you are." His brows drew together.

I placed a hand on his chest. "I forgive you."

His forehead smoothed, but his body remained rigid, every muscle tense. "Tell me you want me."

The corner of my mouth curved, remembering how he'd teased me that first night in the parlor. It felt like a lifetime ago. But I was done with teasing. I wouldn't contain my desire any longer. "I want you, Corvus."

Before I could draw my next breath, his mouth claimed mine. I ran my hands over his chest, through his hair, scrambling to feel him beneath my touch. His hips ground into me, making me gasp as I felt the proof of his desire.

A low moan escaped his lips, and I fumbled for the door handle. We tipped into the room on unsteady feet. He kicked the door closed behind him, hands never leaving my body. He tangled them in my hair, trailed his fingers lightly over the top of my dress, before cupping me firmly in his grip. He stroked me there, through the fabric, and my breasts grew heavy, aching for more.

I grabbed the edge of his shirt, pulling it up over his head. His wings flared wide behind him, casting shadows around the chamber as moonlight danced across his bare chest. He was breathtaking. I moved for his belt, but he placed his hands over mine. "Are you sure?" he asked.

"Yes," I gasped. "Please, Corvus. I need you."

He unleashed himself, tearing my bodice down from my shoulders, claiming me with his tongue. He teased the sensitive peak of my breast with deliberate strokes, making me dizzy with want. I writhed against him, barely able to stand it.

I reached for him, stroking him. A low, guttural sound escaped him as I worked him through his clothes.

He deftly pulled my dress from my body, leaving me stripped bare before him. His eyes trailed over the generous curve of my thighs and hips with reverence. "You're so beautiful."

I dropped to my knees before him and unbuckled his pants. I took him in my mouth, teasing him with my tongue as he cursed. He gathered my hair in his hands, holding it away from my face as I slowly stroked him with my tongue. He swelled, growing even harder.

"Your turn," he growled. And before I could blink, he scooped me into his arms. I wrapped my legs around him, pressing the pulsing center of my core to him as he carried me into the bedchamber.

He placed me gently down upon the bed, resting both arms around my face. He kissed me, claiming me with a wild passion. He pressed against my entrance. My body was tight and hot from the feel of him. I needed him. Now. With a whine, I ground my hips into him, seeking my own pleasure.

"Not so fast, darling. I plan to take my time with you." He lowered himself between my thighs and worked me with his tongue. My fists gripped the sheets. My breathing grew ragged as I neared release. Just when I thought I would die from pleasure, I came, gasping his name.

My legs trembled as he kissed his way up my stomach and chest before licking the column of my throat. I stroked his hair away from his face as he brought his gaze to mine.

He looked at me so tenderly, as if I were the only thing in the world that mattered. It gave me the strength to say what was in my heart. "Corvus, I..." A lump formed in my throat. I swallowed, trying to loosen it.

He cupped my face. "I love you, Sorsha. I should have told you the moment I realized it, and every day afterward."

"I love you, too." My heart felt so full. I traced the tips of my fingers over his face, memorizing the contours of his flesh.

He kissed me deeply, and my breath caught in my chest once more. "I don't wish to be parted from you ever again." I clutched his shoulders.

"I will stay by your side, always. If you'll have me," he promised, whispering in my ear. The soft touch of his breath sent shivers down my spine, renewing my ache for him.

"I wouldn't want it any other way," I said.

"Then say you are mine, Sorsha."

"I'm yours."

At my proclamation, he thrust into me, making me gasp. Stars of pleasure burst behind my eyelids.

"And I am yours," he said, thrusting into me again, sending waves of pleasure through me.

"Yes."

Something snapped into place between us. I felt as if my whole body were filled with cosmic light, as dark and mysterious as a distant star. It made my blood boil with desire, my need for Corvus overwhelming. I moaned with reckless abandon, crying out his name.

He must have felt it, too. He increased his tempo, slamming into me as our bodies grew damp and hot. I rolled my hips in time with his, our bodies perfectly in rhythm. We chased our pleasure together, lingering on the knife's edge of completion as long as we could, before finally finishing together, Corvus moaning my name.

The celestial feeling subsided as the tremors faded from my body, but it did not vanish completely. Once our breathing slowed and our bodies cooled, we fell asleep tangled in each other's arms. My limbs felt liquid with sated desire. My head rested on his chest, rising and falling in time to his breath. I drifted peacefully, the happiest I'd ever been.

A week later there was still no word of where Lucius had gone.

Tristan had been kept busy picking up the pieces of the Blackwood monarchy. There was a quiet funeral for his parents and the guards who had lost their lives defending the palace. The terrible device that Corvus's father had invented was locked away in the depths of the cellars. Corvus had wanted to drop it into the ocean, but Tristan had suggested we keep it to study. If we knew how it worked, then we could learn how to disable it and prevent any future harm.

The new king put on a stoic mask during the day, seeing to matters of business with his father's advisors and other palace officials. In the days that followed, the circles under his eyes showed no improvement. Grief lay thick upon him, for even though he did not agree with their politics and posturing, Tristan had lost his entire family.

We tried to help him as best we could. Corvus acted as fae emissary when needed. The days were spent hard at work, planning what we would do next, what I would do as the heir apparent to House Dawnstone. Corvus and Tristan wanted me to go to the Dawnstone territory and make myself know. I knew the longer I delayed, the harder it would be, but fear made me freeze when any talk of my lineage came up.

My nights were spent with Corvus, tangled in his arms, his scent. We had carved out our own bliss from the horrors of the past few weeks, seeking solace in each other.

Until one night, I dreamed I was drowning in ink-black blood.

I felt the slide of my mirror shard against flesh, and the wave of blood that spurted from my foe rose up to choke me, pushing through my nose and mouth. I clawed at my face, trying to free myself from it, but I was suffocating. My head was on fire, starved of air, as the corruption overtook me.

I woke with a start, terrified that my dream had manifested into life. I brought a hand to my face and felt something hot and sticky. Blood ran from my nose, soaking through the sheets I'd clutched around me. The moon had slipped behind the clouds, making it too dark to see.

Corvus stirred awake as I pushed myself out of bed, my veins icy with terror. I rushed to the bathing chamber and lit a candle with trembling fingers. I held my fingers before the flame, and breathed a sigh of relief when I saw my blood remained red.

I heard the padding of Corvus's footsteps as he entered the bathing chamber. "Sorsha? What's wrong?" He took in the sight of me, drenched in blood, and the color drained from his face. "Are you hurt?" His whole body tensed as he reached for me.

"I'm alright. Just a nosebleed."

The light indeed made it look like I'd suffered a mortal wound. It was a lot of blood. My hands trembled as I wiped my face.

He helped me clean up, running a cloth dipped in warm water over me. When the bleeding had stopped and the last traces of it had been scrubbed from my skin, we made our way back to bed. Corvus carried a taper candle, lighting the way with one hand, while gently pressing the other to the small of my back.

There was a soft whisper as an envelope was thrust beneath the door. I stripped the blood-soaked sheet from the bed as Corvus went to retrieve it. He brought it back, squinting at the fine script I would recognize anywhere.

My heart sank. As I broke the nondescript seal, something silver and sharp fell from the envelope. Dread coiled in my stomach as I beheld the ornament. I brought the letter close to the candle so I could read. Corvus placed a hand on my shoulder, leaning in to read with me.

Dearest Sorsha,

Thank you so much for sending the hounds to raid what's left of my home. Lord Uriel was more than displeased when he did not find what he was looking for. I have added the costs of the excess damage he caused to your remaining debt.

Please return to the house at your earliest convenience. I expect a full report when I see you.

Your Madam,
Lady Andromeda Nyxara, House of Night

P.S. You dropped your hairpin. You really should take better care of your things.

Corvus glanced at me, brows knit.

My hands trembled as I folded the note once more. The House of Night was not done with me yet.

Acknowledgements

Thank you to Adam, my supportive husband, life partner, and best friend. This book is dedicated to you. I am forever grateful for the love we share. Thanks to my family and friends who have celebrated every small success along the way. Thank you to my Romantasy Book Club (the wings are for you). Your enthusiasm and support mean so much. Let's go to happy hour and the bookstore real soon. Thank you to my BookTok community; our shared love of reading always brightens my day.

Many thanks to the team at Cranthorpe Millner for bringing this story to life. Victoria Richards and Kirsty Jackson for your editorial eye, Hazel Andrews-Oxlade and Lauren Barnes for marketing, and Becca Stevenson for the most gorgeous cover.

A big shoutout to booksellers, librarians, and reviewers who help make author dreams come true. Finally, thank you, reader, for picking up this story.